Alone to Live

A Time to Love

A TIME TO LOVE

Beryl Kingston

C

CENTURY • LONDON

Reprinted by Century in 2003

3 5 7 9 10 8 6 4 2

First published in the United Kingdom by Macdonald & Co (Publishers) Ltd
First published by Century in 1997

Century
The Random House Group Limited
20 Vauxhall Bridge Road, London, SW1V 2SA

Random House Australia (Pty) Limited
20 Alfred Street, Milsons Point, Sydney, New South Wales 2061, Australia

Random House New Zealand Limited
18 Poland Road, Glenfield
Auckland 10, New Zealand

Random House (Pty) Limited
Endulini, 5a Jubilee Road, Parktown 2193, South Africa

The Random House Group Limited Reg. No. 954009

www.randomhouse.co.uk

A CIP catalogue record for this book is available from the British Library

Papers used by Random House are natural, recyclable products made from wood grown
in sustainable forests. The manufacturing processes conform to the environmental
regulations of the country of origin

Printed and bound in Great Britain by Biddles Ltd,
Guildford and King's Lynn

ISBN   0 7126 7842 5

To R.D. and our family

To everything there is a season and
A time to every purpose under heaven

A time to love and a time to hate;
A time of war and a time of peace.
                                    Ecclesiastes

Chapter One

It was 1886 and the coldest February in London for thirty years. Snow fell remorselessly, day after shivering day, so that roofs were perpetually white with it, although the streets below were soon smeared and discoloured and ridged with frozen slush. In the dark alleys of the East End the usual mounds of horse dung, rotten fruit, decomposing vegetables and discarded ash had been embedded in ice for such a very long time that they had acquired the familiarity of permanence, and in the West End it was impossible to keep the pavements clear before the fashionable frontages of Bond Street and Piccadilly even with a willing army of underpaid unemployed to do the work. On many days a narrow pathway was all they could manage and even that was furred with snow again as soon as the ragged shovellers had moved on into the next street.

Above the dazzle of that white roofscape the sky was a dirty grey like unwashed underwear and the air it pressed down upon the inhabitants was so cold it bit their lungs. All outdoor work had been frozen to a halt at the start of the year, and now the unemployed were in a desperate state. Nobody who could avoid it stayed out of doors for long. The poor huddled beside their inadequate stoves and the rich built fires in every room. Between the blue-white of the snow and the grey-white of the sky, plumes of smoke rose from a million chimneys, thick and suffocating and in every shade of grey and brown and yellow, from slate to sulphur.

The river coiling between north and south of the powdered city was sluggish and sullen and looked curiously exposed, the few boats struggling in its chill waters black in the feeble light of a colourless sun. In the quieter reaches above London

Bridge ice floes drifted on the surface of the water and knocked against each other with an eerily hollow reverberation. It was an eldritch city, a city bewitched, a city under a curse.

To Emmanuel Cheifitz, tailor and master cutter, in his one bleak room in Wilson Place down in the unfed tenements of Whitechapel, the intense cold was just the most recent in a long series of miseries and misfortunes, so frequent and persistent that, had it not been for the fact that his new wife Rachel was expecting their first child, he really felt he was almost immune to them. Despite his poverty, or perhaps because of it, he was an excessively proud man, and took a perverse satisfaction from the fact that whatever vicissitudes God might have in mind for him, he could endure without complaint. For was He not an inscrutable God, of infinite wisdom, and was it not His high purpose to test His chosen ones in the fires of pain and persecution?

So he ignored the ache of hunger in his contracted belly and the stabbing fire of chilblains on his fingers and toes, and when he could find work he worked, and when he couldn't he did his best to cheer his neighbours. And from time to time when he needed comfort for himself he would play cards and gamble a little, Pontoon or Solo usually, and only for farthings, or ha'pennies, when the tailoring was paying better. But it was enough. It gave him excitement and a taste of hope and a sense that life could be enjoyable.

He was a gentle man and had a scholarly air about him, being tall and gangly with long thin hands and narrow feet. He wore the long black coat of the orthodox Jew, and the flat-brimmed black hat that he'd brought with him from Warsaw when he was fourteen, because it belonged to his father and his father was dead. His hair was limp and thin and mouse brown, and his beard was straggly and inadequate, but between them his face had character, with a long straight nose and high cheekbones and blue eyes capable of many expressions, tolerance, patience, a gamut of passions, and even an occasional flash of sardonic humour. It was a strong face, a face that knew how to endure.

But then, as if extreme cold were not punishment enough to test even the most devout, his inscrutable God sent him two

8

further hardships. First his job disappeared altogether, then he received notice that he had three weeks in which to find other accommodation, because all the houses in the immediate area of Flower and Dean Street were going to be demolished as part of a slum clearance scheme. Now, just when he needed money for his new child, and money for food, and money for coal, and key money for another room, he was down to his last shilling.

The tailoring trade always went into decline after Christmas, when there was less money around and less demand for new clothes, but this year the decline had become a stoppage. Little work became less, and less, until finally in the first cold week of February there was no work at all, no cutting for Emmanuel and no basting or button-holing for Rachel. No work, no money, no food, and a baby due to make its appearance at any time.

'Today, tomorrow, next day maybe,' Mrs Finkleheim said, sighing with the wearily satisfied resignation of her race. 'Who knows? They come ven they good an' ready. They ain't buses, these chickens. Sense a time they ain't got, yet.' She lived in the rooms below Emmanuel and Rachel, and having agreed to act as midwife was already in charge of them.

Emmanuel's serious face was creased with the worry of it all. He knew that birth was difficult even at the best of times and that a labouring mother needed to be sustained by good food and warmth, and shouldn't be worried. And, besides, this child was already dear to him, his first child, his first most wanted, most welcome child. He'd even given up gambling to save money for this child, and now it was all gone except for the shilling.

'I will go to Goulston Street again,' he promised Rachel earnestly, speaking the Polish of their native land. It was the third morning of his hungry unemployment. 'I will stay there all day. Whatever work offers, I take. Tonight we eat, I promise. We still have a shilling. We are not destitute. I will earn money for food tomorrow, and money for another room I promise.'

'We try the Board of Guardians, maybe?' Rachel offered timidly. The weight of her unborn child was dragging her down, so that her shoulders drooped and her face was gaunt and her brown eyes looked enormous. She was on her knees cleaning the stove, the battered brush trailing from her chapped fingers, her sacking apron taut across her belly, her skin grey with dirt and fatigue. The sight of her, meek and pregnant and unwarmed and uncomplaining, made Emmanuel feel more guilty than ever. He ought to go to the Guardians. She was right to suggest it. But going to the Guardians was begging, and he would do almost anything rather then end up a *schnorrer*.

'I will try everything,' he assured her. 'All day. Everything.' She continued to gaze at him, trustingly and hopefully, and the weight of her dependence drew a final painful promise. 'If I still have no work by evening,' he sighed, 'I will see the Guardians.'

But no matter how eagerly he promenaded, nor how hopefully he caught the eye of the few sweaters who appeared in Goulston Street that morning, there was no work. He haunted every sweatshop the length and breadth of the area, in Wentworth Street and Goulston Street and Petticoat Lane. Then he tried Flower and Dean Street and Thrawl Street and all the dark forbidding alleys between them. But the tailors there, like him, had received notice to quit, and in the struggle to survive they had no work left to offer. He crossed the main road to try in Berners Street and trudged, rather hopelessly now, through frozen slush and over piles of rotting vegetables to the new market in Spitalfields. And there, in the late afternoon, when his back ached with the tension of walking and waiting, and his spirits were lower than they had ever been, he heard the whisper of the possibility of work.

It came from Abe Grodzinsky, who sold cucumbers for pickling and was a Polack too and went to the same synagogue.

'Try Covent Garden. Portering. Bay 3. I didn't send you, you understand?'

Emmanuel walked there at once as darkness intensified the cold and naptha flares were grudgingly lit, to drop their yellow light on all the stalls as he passed. And he made himself remember the words of the Proverbs, and tried to draw

10

comfort from them, 'For a just man falleth seven times and riseth up again.' But he was hungry and weary and demoralized, and when he saw Covent Garden rising so prosperously before him in arcades of glass and wrought iron he feared it would be no place to welcome a Jew. Nevertheless he picked his way over the black cobbles, past carts and steaming donkeys, and porters balancing incredible piles of baskets on their heads, until he found Bay 3.

The foreman was a formidable individual. He wore a good quality suit, as Emmanuel noticed at once, and a new bowler hat, very spruce, and although his shirt was sweat stained it was white linen, no less. He stood a full head and shoulders taller than the tailor and was more than twice his weight. But he admitted a need of porters. 'Tem'pry. Unloadin'. Taters. Cabbige. Carrots. 'Ard work,' he said, hooking a blunt thumb into the warm cloth of his fob pocket.

'Yes,' Emmanuel said humbly. 'Alvays I vork hard.'

'Tailor, intcher?' the foreman said, looking at Emmanuel's narrow shoulders, and noting his stoop and the thin wrists protruding from the shabbiness of that long foreign coat.

'A cutter,' Emmanuel said proudly, because he was a skilled cutter and he knew it.

The foreman wasn't impressed. 'Not your line a' country, this,' he said. 'Not be a long chalk, I'd say. Ain't fit fer tailors. Not be rights.'

'Alvays I vork hard,' Emmanuel promised and now he sounded anxious.

'Tell yer what I'll do,' the foreman said, rocking back on his heels as he gave the matter thought. 'Take you on spec. See 'ow yer do. Start now. Work two, three hours. We got a lot ter shift. Then I'll see. Carn't say fairer'n that, can I?'

'Thank you,' Emmanuel said.

But the man wasn't listening. He'd already turned and was walking away. 'Horrie!' he yelled as he went. 'Number 3 bay. Taters.'

So for the next three hours Emmanuel struggled with round baskets full of potatoes and heavy as lead. After a while he learned the knack of balancing two of them on his head, but their weight made him unsteady on his feet, so that he was jostled and thumped and kicked wherever he went. But he worked quietly and fearfully, trying to keep out of the way of the busy feet around him, and to ignore the ache of hunger in his belly. And at last the potatoes were shifted and the carts loaded, and the foreman returned to give his verdict.

'Four o'clock termorrer mornin',' he said. 'Three bob, two shifts, an' that's 'andsome.'

Hunger and need drove Emmanuel to ask for an advance. 'I have no money,' he confessed. 'Could ... '

'Work two shifts termorrer, then I'll pay yer. Carn't 'ave nothink yer don' earn, can yer?'

'No,' Emmanuel had to agree. But how would they manage with only a shilling?

Miraculously, when he got home the stove was alight and a stew cooking most succulently in the saucepan. 'Rachel, bubeleh,' he said, speaking Yiddish, 'how did you manage this?' She must have spent more than sixpence.

'Good neighbours we have,' she said, taking a sixpence and three pennies from her apron and showing them to him. 'You will eat now?'

'We will repay,' he said, as she spooned the stew into his bowl. The warmth of the steam made his chilled face prickle, but the smell of it was unalloyed pleasure. Good neighbours, lending from the kindness of their hearts. Not charity from the Guardians. 'We will repay.'

'Yes,' she said, breaking the remains of a half-quartern loaf into three pieces and taking the smallest portion for herself. 'Eat, Emmanuel, my dear. You have earned it.'

He took the bread, smiling at her, and watched as she wrapped the remaining third in a piece of cloth and set it on the shelf beside the stove. 'For the morning.'

'Tomorrow you will take the sixpence and buy coal and food,' he said. They would just about manage now.

'I should cook a meal for you midday?' she asked, anxious and timid and affectionate. 'You will come home?'

'I will come home, maybe,' he said. 'Buy bread and herring. Things that will keep till evening. Feed yourself and the child. That is important, Rachel. If it is possible I will come home.'

12

'You don't come home, you have money for a meal midday?' she persisted. 'You should eat midday, Emmanuel, or how will you have strength to work?'

'I have money,' he lied, and bent his head to eat his first spoonful of stew, and to hide his shamed expression. Because even such a necessary lie troubled him deeply. Once this child was born, he must be certain to avoid all lies, of whatever kind. For children learned by precept, and his must learn to be upright and honest in all their dealings.

That night they piled their clothes over their one remaining blanket, as usual, and went to bed early while the stove was still giving out some heat. For the first time in weeks they slept warmly. 'Tomorrow the foreman he promised to pay me,' Emmanuel said. 'You must redeem the blankets so soon as I return. It would not be seemly for the child to be cold.'

'A piece of chicken for Shabbas, maybe,' she murmured. The warmth was drifting her into sleep.

'The Lord is a buckler to them that walk uprightly,' he said, and the words were a prayer of gratitude. He could feel warmth on his face even at this distance. What a difference a fire makes, he thought. 'We will buy more coal tomorrow, Rachel,' he said. Then sleep sucked him away, just as he was training his mind to be sure to wake before three o'clock.

And his mind was obedient. It woke him every hour, on the hour, to the clanging reminder of the church clock at St Jude's. At three he got up, lit the stub of the candle, and used the chamber pot as quietly as he could, so as not to wake his wife. Then he put on all the clothes he possessed, even his long overcoat, for the room was freezing. The water in the washing jug was covered by a layer of ice which he broke quickly with his knuckles because that struck less of a chill. He washed his hands quickly too, but three times in the ritual way, and when he was cleansed he said the first prayer of his day: 'Thanks be to thee, Lord, for thou hast returned me to my soul, which was in Thy keeping.'

His breath plumed before him, ghostly white in the darkness, and as he sat in his cane chair before the dead stove, patiently packing his boots with newspaper to keep out the worst of the cold and the damp, he could see that the

13

windowpanes were almost entirely covered with the delicate, fern-leaf tracery of ice. Tonight, he comforted himself, they would have coal and food. The child would be welcomed with warmth and its mother fed with the best food he could buy. He ate the last portion of bread, chewing slowly, so that he could make the most of every mouthful, and washed it down with a little icy water from the tin jug.

Then he rearranged the piles of clothes on the bed, tucked their blanket firmly around his sleeping wife, took the candle stub in his hand and stepped quietly out onto the landing. The air there tasted of soot, and struck cold and very very damp, but it wasn't until he'd eased open the front door and let himself out into the street that he realized why. He was engulfed in oppressive darkness, and after a while he saw that it was being made worse by the gathering mists of a fog.

For a second his heart contracted with misery at the thought that it would take him too long to find his way to Covent Garden in such darkness, and that he might be refused the job if he arrived late. Then he scolded himself for being so faint-hearted, plunged his hands into the pocket of his greatcoat and set off, following the damp black walls of Wilson Place until he had groped his way into the empty chasm of Flower and Dean Street.

He was completely alone there, without a glimmer of light and with only the sound of his own snow-muffled footsteps for company, and he was afraid. For the Flowery was a byword for violence, and a hiding place for every kind of criminal. Why, only last week a Russian Jew had been robbed and beaten on this very corner. And now, in this fog, how easy such an attack would be!

But no attack came and in Commercial Street two carts loomed out of the fog on their slow way to Spitalfields Market, and the sight of them cheered him a little. The drivers were leading their horses and they both carried lanterns, but the light they cast was dimmed to a diffuse yellow glow, haloed in eerie blue, and was lost as soon as they'd passed. He had no idea what time it was, but at least by following the walls he hadn't lost his way.

The damp soon penetrated the thin cloth of his sleeves so

14

that goose pimples shivered onto his forearms and his toes numbed and his shins felt as though they were chapped with ice. What with the cold and the poor visibility, he was soon shuffling and stumbling, his forehead bowed against the evil-smelling vapour that hung and clung about him. He trudged through the deserted City, past the Bank of England, and found himself in a terrible emptiness with no walls to follow. And stumbled on, chilled and anxious, but doggedly trying several directions until he found Mansion House, a high white ghost looming out of the black pool where the seven roads met, and knew where he was again. Somewhere ahead of him church clocks were striking the three-quarters, and that made his heartbeats quicken with a terrible mixture of hope and panic. Only fifteen minutes to get there. Oh, if only it wasn't so totally dark. He found the corner of Watling Street, crept round the edges of the great wet ship that was St Paul's, and came at last to Fleet Street and the Strand where there were cabs creaking through the murk behind their glow-worm lights, and the vague shapes of other workers, bent and shuffling and on their way to the market.

Horrie was waiting for him, but the foreman hadn't arrived. The relief of it made Emmanuel's legs feel quite weak.

It was a long, cold, back-breaking shift, but it was a job and it would mean pay. He worked mechanically, straining under the weight of the baskets, his sweat as cold as he was, stopping now and then to cough the fog out of his lungs. A grudging daylight revealed that it was a real pea-souper, thick and greeny yellow, in which human forms were distorted into vague threatening shapes, hump-shouldered and faceless, glimpsed and gone, like creatures in a nightmare. Even their voices were changed, distanced and muffled by the pervasive murk, while the rattle of carts and trolleys and the scrape of boots and hooves were muffled too, as though the cobbles had been carpeted overnight. It is easy to be afraid, Emmanuel thought, when you are chilled to the bone and nothing is familiar. And he forced his mind to contemplate better and happier things.

At around eight o'clock there was a lull in the work and Horrie told his team that they could 'cut off and get a bit a' breakfast' if they wanted, but Emmanuel had nothing to get a bit of breakfast with, so he stayed where he was, sitting on the edge of a discarded trolley and occupying himself with his thoughts.

He remembered the day the letter arrived from his uncle in Warsaw, and how happy he'd been to think that a marriage had been arranged for him, and that after sixteen years working in this foreign land and living in crowded boarding houses alone among so many lonely men he was to have a partner. He was thirty years old and at last he was to have a partner. And he relived the day she had arrived at Gravesend, looking so small and frail and shy and Polish, with her head and shoulders wrapped in a red shawl, and her spine bent in anxious self-effacement. He'd loved her at once, for her gentleness and meekness and because she was drooping like a flower in the heat, and because when she finally raised her head to look at him her eyes were brown and afraid. 'I will care for you from now on, Rachel Rabinovits,' he had promised. 'I will be a good husband to you.' And she had smiled at him shyly and held his arm as he led her away across the sticky cobbles. And finally he thought of the child that was coming, the family he was founding, life resuming in its old comforting pattern. Both his parents had been killed in the pogrom, before he and his two sisters fled to England, but life went on. It was a warming thought even in the thick of the fog.

But when the first rush of work was over and the porters sloped off through the murk to the nearest pubs and the eel and pie shops, and the donkeys were rewarded with nosebags and were soon chomping contentedly and much too audibly, he was so hungry and so fatigued that memories were no longer any sustenance at all. Horrie had told them to be back within the hour, so there was no possibility of walking home for bread and herrings, because he would never get back in time. There was nothing for it but to stay where he was and endure.

When the bay was empty and there was nobody left to see his shame, he picked over a pile of rotting carrots and found four that were almost good enough to eat, at least in parts. But they made a poor meal and after he'd chewed what he could of them his stomach was still yearning for more. He would have liked to return to the pile and find something else to assuage his awful hunger, but the scavengers had arrived in force and were turning over the debris like crows, and he simply couldn't bear to be part of such degraded company. He might be poor and hungry, but he still had his pride.

He drifted away from the muddle of carts and baskets and discarded vegetables, glad that the fog had thinned a little and that now he could see to the other side of the road, and walked towards the Strand where the bustle of a busy thoroughfare would give him something to occupy his mind. He felt slightly sick and his stomach was strained with hunger.

He was rewarded by more activity than he expected. Something was going on, and in Trafalgar Square too, by the sound of things, for he could hear shouts and growls and hoarse cheers coming from that direction. Crowds of workmen were gathering outside Charing Cross Station and heading in small determined groups towards the square. He had nothing better to do, and he had to take his mind off his hunger somehow or other, so he followed them. He was curious to see what was happening. It might be a political meeting, it was true, and a gathering of that kind could be dangerous, but he decided to risk it.

It was a political meeting, and a very big one, complete with banners and men with loudspeakers standing on the fog-shrouded plinth of Nelson's hidden column and booming incomprehensibly towards the ranks of white faces, damp caps and ragged coats below them. The fog was patchy here and Emmanuel could see that the crowd filled the entire space of the square, in dark shifting masses. Thousands and thousands of men, and more arriving by the minute.

Politics alarmed Emmanuel Cheifitz because they roused ugly emotions rather too quickly. But as the men nearest to him seemed to be in quite an amiable mood, at least for the present, and it would certainly be warmer inside such a crowd, he edged himself in and pretended to be listening. Even after seventeen years in the country he still found English an impossibly difficult language, especially when it was spoken quickly, or boomed through a loud-hailer, or argued

17

passionately. But he did his best to concentrate and tried to ignore the fact that his belly was growling with hunger, and presently the word 'hunger' broke through both fogs and made sense to him.

'No government 'as the right,' the speaker said, 'to sentence 'onest workin' men to 'unger an' want an' destitution. We ain't criminals. We ain't committed crimes. If there was work, wouldn't we work?'

Agreement roared from every side. 'Tha's it! Work! Tha's what we want!' Determined roars, but not ugly yet, not dangerous.

But then a young man took the megaphone. A young man with a clear, strong, persuasive voice. And as he spoke, the atmosphere in the listening crowd changed and became sharper. 'Our rulers don't know how we feel, comrades. There they sit, all well fed and snug and smug in their gentlemen's clubs, and they haven't the faintest idea what it is to be hungry and desperate. They don't know and they don't care. There they sit, in their gentlemen's clubs. In Pall Mall. A few yards away.' He waved an arm towards Pall Mall. 'And they don't care. I will tell you what I think, comrades. I think we should leave this place. Nobody is listening to us here. We should leave this place now and march to Pall Mall and show them just how we feel. We should break their windows and beat down their doors and make them face us, man to man.'

Under the passion of his oratory the crowd seethed and shifted. Many were roaring approval, swaying towards him, faces lifted. Others were shouting him down and booing. Soon violent arguments were erupting on every side. The banner dipped forward and folded in upon itself and became a red arrow pointing the way, and a ragged column formed ready to follow it.

Time to move away from trouble, Emmanuel thought, for he knew from very early experience that men in a temper were just a little too quick to turn their wrath against the nearest Jew. Fortunately, his father had taught him how to handle this sort of situation, long ago, in Warsaw. He began to melt out of the crowd, quietly and unobtrusively, side-stepping and edging backwards so that he seemed to be facing the same way as

18

everybody else, moving when others moved and careful never to look anyone in the eye. Becoming invisible. Staying safe. Soon there was a yard of sulphurous smoke and trodden snow between him and the nearest workman, and his heel had reached the kerb. He crossed the road quickly, head down, and went back to Covent Garden at once.

Rumours spread all through the afternoon. Thousands were said to be on the march. The West End was besieged. The police had been driven back and were powerless. Troops had been called out. 'Great days, eh?' Horrie said as he and Emmanuel loaded yet another stack of baskets. 'We been downtrod jest a bit too long. Now we've turned. An' 'igh time too!'

He talks as though he'd been part of it, the tailor thought, instead of working here all day, but he was too weary to do more than grunt in answer. There was so much anger and excitement in the market all around him that he felt quite drained by it, even though he knew it was nothing to do with him. By the end of his second shift he was stupid with fatigue. The whole of London could have gone up in flames and he wouldn't have noticed or cared. Let other people have a revolution if that was what they wanted. He would be happy to settle for a fire and a meal and the quiet company of his wife.

At last work was over and he trailed wearily back towards the City, clutching his three precious shillings in the palm of his battered hand, aching for home. His pockets were heavy with potatoes and carrots and apples and nuts which Horrie had urged upon him as soon as work was over. 'Go on, mate!' he'd said. 'Take yer pick. We all do it. Part a' the job, pickin's is. If they don't want us ter take pickin's, they should pay us proper.' And although his conscience was troubled Emmanuel took what was offered, too tired and too polite to refuse. And in any case, there was a feeling of recklessness about this extraordinary day which communicated itself even to his sober rectitude. Perhaps this sort of behaviour was acceptable when you worked as a porter. He would ask the Rabbi on Friday.

The fog was still mercifully patchy. On his return journey he could see well enough to recognize the landmarks as he passed, but he travelled slowly and by the time he reached Ludgate

19

Hill he was ready to drop. When the demonstrators came marching up behind him, filling the road with their cheerful mass and singing 'Rule Britannia' at the tops of their voices, he hadn't the strength to get out of their way. Their energy washed him like a tide, and caught him up and swept him along. He found himself in the middle of the crowd, in the middle of the road, marching despite his fatigue and smiling at their infectious exuberance. They traversed the City, buoyant with excitement and the satisfaction of anger used.

When they reached the East End, people came out on the pavements to cheer them on, and Emmanuel was alarmed in case someone should recognize him and think he'd been part of it. But he was embedded in the march and couldn't side-step when they were all moving forward together.

'How'd it go then, Jack?' a woman called.

And several voices answered her triumphantly. 'We give 'em what for, missus. Put the wind up 'em good an' proper.'

'Good fer you!' the answer came back, and the crowd on the pavement clapped and cheered. They were like an army returning from a victorious war.

When they got to Commercial Street their ranks thinned as men stepped out of the march to left and right on their way back to their homes. They cast Emmanuel off at Flower and Dean Street like a small sprat tumbled from the edge of a great trawl net, and he scurried home through the foggy waters of Whitechapel with their song ringing in his ears, 'Britons never never never shall be slaves!'

He was still uplifted as he climbed the stairs to his room, and cheered too by the smell of fried onions that filled the well of the stairs. As he opened the door to his room, his mouth was watering.

But the smell inside the room was strange and alerting, a heavy warm smell, musty but with a peculiar and familiar fleshiness about it. It was the smell of a woman's blood, and as he received it and recognized it, he knew that it was the smell of birth too. The child, he thought, my child. Here at last. And this was a new excitement, welling up from profound depths, washing away all his other thoughts and reducing all the other experiences of his day to insignificance.

20

Rachel was still in the bed where he'd left her that morning, her body curled in a protective crescent round a fat bundle of shawls, and fast asleep, her eyelashes fringing her closed eyes with two patches of smudged darkness against the pallor of her skin. He was overwhelmed with tenderness at the sight of her, and torn with conflicting needs, wanting to wake her to be shown his child, and wanting to do the right thing and let her sleep, because sleep was natural after birth.

She solved the problem by waking of her own accord. 'You have a son, Emmanuel,' she told him dreamily, and her smile was beatific. 'See!'

He was on his knees at the bedside at once, even before she'd pulled back the edge of her red shawl to reveal a little rounded head covered with soft dark hair. 'A beautiful baby,' she said, taking the child's tiny hand between her finger and thumb and placing it delicately on Emmanuel's forefinger. And beautiful he was, with huge dark eyes and the merest button of a nose, and a little red mouth, perfectly formed, the top lip shaped like the letter M.

'A dolly,' Emmanuel said affectionately, using his mother's favourite endearment almost before he was aware that he'd remembered it. 'Great is our God and greatly to be praised for His loving kindness.' And the child grasped his finger and held it strongly.

'Such fine fat limbs,' Rachel said, lifting the shawl with her fingertips so that he could see the smooth flesh rounding their baby's arms. 'So soft.' She was languid with love for the child.

'David,' Emmanuel said. 'We will call him David. David the Beautiful.' And he looked down at the perfect features below him with greater pride than he'd ever felt in his life. From hardship and poverty, from persecution and exile, in the ugly squalor of this cold room, in the coldest winter in human memory, on a day of fog and violence and terrible despair, this child had been born. David the Beautiful. 'Such a son we have!' he said to Rachel.

And David looked up at his father with his huge dark eyes. And scowled.

Chapter Two

On his very first day at school David Cheifitz bit the teacher.

'Ai-yi-yi! Five years old and he bites already! For why you do this thing?' his father wailed, rocking in distress and incomprehension.

'I don't know, Father,' the child said unhappily. Which was true enough, for really it had all happened so quickly, one thing following another in such a smooth inevitable flow that he remembered the events now as one action.

The day had begun so well, with bagels for breakfast, which was a great treat. Then he and Mama had folded up his truckle bed and left the dark enclosure of their familiar living room and set off for the great adventure called education. It wasn't the Jews' Free School, which was where his father really wanted him to go, as he knew because he had heard him speaking about it so many times and so earnestly, and it wasn't the school where all his cousins had gone, because that was too far away, but it was 'education', and it was very very important. He knew that because of the solemn way his parents spoke about it, urging him to 'obey the teacher' and 'behave good', and although he only had the vaguest idea what these serious words actually meant, he promised to obey them, and felt, equally vaguely, that it would be possible to keep such promises.

Down and down they went, from the two attic rooms they'd lived in since they moved from Wilson Place, down the narrow staircase, blakeys clanging, past the second floor, smelling of stale herring, and the first floor, smelling of coal dust and burnt bones, and the landlady's parlour beside the front door, smelling of polish and almonds, down and down as though they were going down a well, like Jack Bruin in the fairy story.

Then they came out, pop, into the icy air of Fashion Street, and his mother turned up his coat collar and tucked her shawl about her face, and off they went, along the black chasm between the buildings, surrounded by hordes of other pupils in their flat caps and reach-me-downs, their shawls and holland aprons and brute black boots. He found them rather daunting, because they didn't greet him and because they all knew where they were going and what they were going to do when they got there, for even the youngest of them had had a fortnight's schooling already while he was wheezing with bronchitis at home. But he didn't say anything because he was determined to be brave and good and well-behaved. Hadn't he promised his father that very morning? So he clung to his mother's hand and trotted beside the swish of her black bombazine, and hoped.

They stopped at a high wrought-iron gate and his mother kissed him and tugged his cap into a more suitable position on his dark head.

'So, bubeleh, you'll be a good boy and obey the teacher?' she said anxiously. 'You von't make no noise, bubeleh? You'll be polite? You'll be a good boy, so your Mama be proud of you?' He looked pathetically small against those great gates, small and vulnerable and too tender for the rough world outside their home. She was sure he wasn't strong enough for school yet. He'd barely got over bronchitis. His little wrists were so frail and his legs so thin. Like a cherub he looked, with his heart-shaped face and his dark hair so thick and his eyes so brown, and bigger than ever this morning. He ought to be protected, not sent out to face the world all on his own. But she had to let him go, because he was five and would be six in February. 'You'll be a good boy,' she said sighing as she opened the gate.

The size of the building rising straight off the pavement for three grand red-brick storeys could easily have frightened a child so small, but David recognized it as an adventure, a challenging place full of small shouting shapes, darting kicking shapes, skinny limbs inside rough cloth pre-shaped by another's wear, weighted at one end by the heavy stubs of those black leather boots and finished off at the other by the flat

23

greasy lintel of a cap. The familiar shapes and faces of the Shabbas Walk. Now at last he could talk and play with his own kind. He walked from his mother's protective hands straight into the howling playground, his spine straight with hope, and she, curving her body into its most subservient stoop, crept silently back into the shadows and dared not watch him go.

But he hadn't been there for more than five minutes before he wanted to call her back. He realized now that he was in foreign territory. He could hardly understand anything that was happening, for although everybody seemed to be speaking English it was a quick slurred version of the language and quite unlike the gentle, careful enunciation of his father and the Rabbi. The words flew into the air, sharp as sleet, and were gone before he could make sense of them. He drifted hopefully from one chanting game to the next, but nobody paid him the slightest attention. It was as if he was invisible. Finally he found a group of small boys huddled in a circle beside the steps. They were speaking in low earnest voices and speaking Yiddish. But the wall of their backs excluded him, and when they became aware of his presence they began to whisper so that he couldn't hear. It was cold in the playground and his loneliness made it colder.

Presently, a large man with long black legs appeared upon the top step and blew a whistle, and instantly everybody in the playground, except David, rushed to stand in line before him. The child was left alone and perplexed in the middle of a suddenly empty place.

'Line, boy!' the man barked. 'In line!'

What line? Where was he supposed to go? There were ten or eleven rows of children standing raggedly to attention in front of those long black legs, but the sight of them only confused him. Six of them were lines of big girls, so he knew he didn't belong there, especially as they were grinning at him and giggling behind their shawls. Beyond them was a complicated mass of muddled bodies, boys and girls about the same size as he was, but none of them was giving him any kind of sign at all. As nobody told him what to do, he stood his ground and looked patiently at the man with the long black legs, and waited.

'Line! Line! Line!' Black Legs barked, and the face at the top of his rigid column of flesh grew puce and seemed to be puffing its cheeks. 'Line!'

There was a swish of skirts behind him and a strong hand seized him by the collar and lifted him off his feet so that his boots scrabbled against the asphalt and he found he was being shuffled forward, his shoulders hunched and his heart beating painfully with a sudden and unfamiliar fear. Above his shoulders a fierce fat face was mouthing cross words, 'You do as you're told, the minute you're told, you understand.' But what with the suddenness of the attack, the indignity of his forced march, and the bewilderment of being in the wrong and not knowing how he'd got there, David heard little and understood less. He wanted to explain and to tell her to stop, but the language inside his head was Yiddish, and by the time he'd struggled to find a few inadequate English words, 'I vont I should valk by myself, please,' they were beside the furthest line. The hand scruffing his collar gave him a final jerk that cut off his air supply, Black Legs glowered down at him, and the line shuffled forward towards the step, carrying him with it. It was as though they were being sucked up by some invisible force, up and up, into the awful black mouth of that high door above them. It was an unpleasant sensation. If this was 'education', he didn't like it much.

Once through the door he found himself in an echoing chasm with a ceiling so high above his head that it made him feel squashed and insignificant just to glance at it. But there wasn't time for more than a glance because the horde of small marching bodies was still moving onwards, and this time he was determined to keep with the line and not leave himself exposed to Black Legs and the clutching hand. So he followed the dirty coat ahead of him, watching it sternly, going where it went, waiting in a cloakroom while it hung up its cap and muffler, walking again. And presently they marched through another high door into a room smelling of wax polish and dirty clothes and full of desks, arranged in long straight rows, each one higher than the one in front of it.

It was a very big room, made of red brick and bottle-green tiles. The windows were long and narrow and set far too high up in the walls for him to be able to see out of them, and that made him feel imprisoned, as though he'd been cut off from the world outside. The floor under his feet was covered with wooden boards and above his head wooden girders criss-crossed the roof space. Heavily. At one end of the room a great fire blazed in a black grate, but it was too far away to bring him any comfort. He could see the heat but he couldn't feel it. It wasn't a comfortable room at all. Not a bit like home.

He was briefly aware that there was a figure standing on the other side of the room in front of the fire, a tall black figure with a frowning face, but then alarm stopped any sensation, because the line broke and became individual children again trotting and scrambling towards the rows of desks, all at once and all in different directions, and he was left behind and didn't know what to do or where to go.

He glanced apprehensively over his shoulder at the black figure and saw that it was a woman, a long flat woman, like an ironing board. Everything about her was tight and severe, from the mean little bun of brown hair on the top of her head to the polished points of her narrow black boots. She wore a black skirt, so straight and so tightly buttoned that he could see the shape of the corset underneath it, and a severe black blouse, flat and pin-tucked and embroidered with hard jet beads. Apprehension grew, for this was not the sort of cushiony untidy woman he was used to in the stalls and lodging houses and crowded rooms of Fashion Street. This was a lady. The sort of lady his mother had pointed out to him, the kind you doffed your cap to. Almost instinctively he pulled off his cap and held it in his hands, twisting it nervously. The lady looked down at him, as sharp and straight and steely as a needle. She had a long sharp face and a long sharp nose, and behind a pair of fierce round spectacles small sharp eyes, glittering and black as the jet beads on her flat bosom, and equally uncaring.

'Well!' she said, and the word was a sneer. 'Who have we here?' Her mouth was thin and pale, and turned down at the corners as she spoke. As she lifted her head to look down upon him and disparage him, her throat contracted into long white ridges that reminded him of the icy edges on the piles of cleared snow outside.

He disliked her on sight, because she was ugly and made him feel afraid, and because he knew, instinctively, that she didn't like him.

'Don't tell me it's David Cheifitz,' she said, 'condescended to join us at last. Wonders will never cease!'

He stood mutely before her, aware of all the eyes that were looking at him, rows and rows of hard eyes and sniggering mouths. What was he supposed to say? His heart was beating painfully again, like it had when that other lady dragged him into line.

'Well,' she said again, 'are you David Cheifitz? Or not?'

'Yes,' he said, and began to bite his bottom lip, bowing his head to hide his distress.

'Yes what?'

What did she mean, yes what? Yes was yes, wasn't it? He blinked at her, his eyes shining with the approach of tears.

'Yes, Miss Killip,' the lady said, and her voice sounded very disapproving. 'Didn't they teach you any manners at home?'

'Yes,' he said solemnly, trying to parry her dislike of him by a sensible answer. 'They did.'

She swished across the room to him and seized him by the shoulder, far too tightly. 'Speak when you are spoken to,' she said. '*Don't* answer back.' And she gave him a sharp little shake, so sudden and so vicious that he knew at once that she really wanted to hit him and hit him hard. Then she marched him to a seat in the front row and pushed him down into it. 'There's your seat,' she said, 'and there's your slate,' banging it down on the desk, 'and there's your slate pencil. You copy everything I tell you to copy, understand. And woe betide you if I hear *squeaking*.'

What a terrifying lady she was. Why did she think he would want to squeak? It didn't make sense. But he didn't say anything, because he didn't want to be shaken again, and besides, there wasn't time. She was barking names, one after the other and the children were droning answers.

'Aaronson!'

'Present, Miss Killip.'

'Adams!'

'Present, Miss Killip.'

'Bernstein!'

'Got a fever, miss.'

'Cheifitz!'

'Yes.'

'Yes *what?*'

'Yes, Miss Killip.' If only she wasn't so fierce!

The list of names went on for ever and when the last had been called, an awful bell clanged, and all the children in the room jumped to their feet and stood rigidly and awkwardly to attention. By now he'd learned enough to copy what they were doing so he stood too.

'Lead on!' Miss Killip commanded, and they all filed out of the room again. Which was very odd considering they'd only just filed in. In fact, this education was turning out to be very odd indeed, and not a bit what he'd been led to expect. Mama had promised him he would learn to read and write. She'd never said anything about marching in and out of doors.

They were in another even larger room with a very high ceiling, and they were standing in lines again, long silent lines with all the other children he'd seen in the playground, arm against arm, their dirty clothes very smelly in such close-packed formation. He could hear grown-up feet walking about somewhere beyond the lines, and skirts swishing, but he couldn't see anything except the rough coat of the boy in front of him, and that made him feel captured and vulnerable. Then Black Legs' voice bellowed, 'Face front!' and all the lines turned so that they were facing the north end of the room where Black Legs himself stood silhouetted against the chill white light from a row of very high windows, like a black beetle on a plate. 'All things brights and beautiful!' he barked, and while David was wondering what *this* meant, a piano began to play, and the children started to sing.

Now what was he supposed to do? He took a surreptitious glance to right and left and saw that mouths were open wherever he looked, so he opened his too, and moved his jaw up and down, and tried to look the same as all the others. And that seemed to work, for the song went on and nobody shouted at him or descended to shake him. And when it was over, Black Legs commanded them all to close their eyes, which they did by covering their faces with their hands, and then he spent a long safe time droning on and on in a deep and miserable voice. So that was all right.

From time to time during the drone, David dared an occasional peep through the adaptable shield of his fingers. Black Legs wasn't looking his way, so it was safe enough. In fact, Black Legs wasn't looking at all. He was rolling his eyes about in a very odd way, showing the whites like horses do when they're frightened. And when his voice dropped at the end of each droning pronouncement, he dropped his chin too, right onto his chest, and closed his eyes and sighed heavily. David felt quite sorry for him to be so uncomfortable and so unhappy, standing there in front of them all with the white light dazzling in through the window behind him. Perhaps it was because he'd been made to wear such an uncomfortable collar that morning, a stiff white band encircling his neck. It was hard to swallow with something tight round your neck like that, and it would rub horribly.

The last peep had gone on rather too long, so he closed his eyes again, because he *was* trying to be good, because he *had* promised. And he was suddenly and inexplicably rewarded for his good behaviour by a revelation. He could still see the window. Even with his eyes tight shut. How could that be? He stood quite still, concentrating hard on this unlooked-for image. There was no doubt about it. It *was* the window. He could see the frames as clear and black as though they'd been drawn in charcoal. And he knew what charcoal drawings looked like because he was allowed to draw with it at home. But the light flooding and pulsing between those black frames was bright red, a vibrant shining colour, so satisfying that he felt really sad when it began to fade.

He opened his eyes and peeped again. And there was the white light, patterned by the brown frames just as before. He stared at it for a long time, wondering how it was possible to see things so clearly with your eyes shut, and hoping it would happen again. And when he closed his eyes again, it did. What a marvellous thing.

He was still enjoying the image when Black Legs' peroration came to a groaning end, and the sharp barking voice in which he gave commands returned abruptly. 'Stand! Be quick about it! We haven't got all day. Turn!'

The lines shuffled back the way they'd come, and light and colour and speculation about them were trampled away. The slate was still on his desk where he'd left it. and he did his best to be a good pupil the way he'd promised, patiently copying the letters onto the slate, his teeth set on edge by the scratching and squeaking of slate pencils all around him. So *that* was what she meant! He used his own pencil with great caution, the tip of his tongue protruding with concentration. And he made a good job of it, for copying was easy. He'd been copying letters at home for the last two years and could write both his names, a feat which gave his parents enormous pleasure and invariably earned praise. Today, even the fierce Miss Killip grudgingly allowed that his efforts would 'do', but added with a sneer that he'd better copy everything out again as he'd been so quick. She made him feel as though she was trampling on him. Nevertheless he was beginning to feel more at home in this echoing foreign place. He'd recognized several faces from Fashion Street, and on his way back to the room after the thirty freezing minutes that were 'playtime' they'd shown him where to hang his cap and muffler, and he'd contrived to walk close enough to the fire to garner a little warmth. Copying figures came next, and that was as easy as letters. But then, just as he was feeling that education wasn't so bad after all, everything went inexplicably and terribly wrong.

Miss Killip began a new lesson. 'Drawing!' she commanded fiercely. 'Sit up straight!' and she brisked between the desks, slapping down a small green copy book and half a well-bitten pencil in front of every pupil. Then she stood with her back to the fire and gave them their orders. 'When I give the word, and not *until*, James Murphy, you will open your book at the first page and draw what you see. You will *not* bite your pencils. You will not *lick* your pencils. You will not *talk*. Do you all understand?'

A crowded chorus, 'Yes, Miss Killip.'

'Very well then, you may begin.'

At the word 'drawing', David felt almost as happy as he'd been when he saw the lovely red light. He opened the book eagerly and found that the first page was headed by a border of wide leaves, but contained nothing else except a series of printed lines. He considered them carefully and happily, deciding what he would draw, just as he did at home before he made the first shape with his charcoal. The black lines reminded him of the window frames, and he wished he had a red crayon so that he could fill in the space with red light. If he turned the book round so that the lines rose vertically before him, it would be easy enough to draw round shapes at the top and turn the lines into windows. Which he did, and was pleased with the pattern. But that wasn't enough, of course. He liked a picture with figures in it. His father perhaps, in his flat-brimmed hat, or his mother wrapped in her shawls. He drew heads easily now, with round eyes and a curve for a mouth and a line to suggest a nose, and since the autumn he'd been drawing whole figures, Humpty Dumpty shapes with stick limbs and three-fingered hands, and straight feet both pointing in the same direction. He would draw a figure standing in front of the window. Black Legs. Of course. He set to work quickly, with a long egg shape for the gentleman's head, and his arms raised, their three fingers pointing upwards like forks. If education was drawing, David was going to like it a lot.

He was so absorbed that he didn't notice that Miss Killip was standing beside him, until she made a curious growling noise in her throat. He looked up at her with the slow rapturous smile of satisfied endeavour.

She was pink-nosed with displeasure. 'And what do you think you're doing, may I ask?'

The question puzzled him. He didn't *think* he was doing something. He *was* doing it. The edge to her voice alarmed him. Had he been naughty again? He noticed that all the other children in the room had stopped work and were watching avidly, and that was frightening too. It made him feel that something awful was going to happen.

'Look at it!' she said, sternly. 'Lines all over the place. Dirty smudges. Where are your leaves?'

What leaves? Why did she always ask such silly questions?

'Well, come along, boy. I asked you a question, I want an answer. Where are your leaves?'

'Leaves I have not got,' he said politely.

'Leaves you have not got,' she mimicked. 'I can see you haven't got any leaves. And why haven't you got any leaves, eh? Tell me that. Because you're a naughty little boy!'

Was he supposed to bring leaves to this place? There weren't any leaves in Whitechapel, particularly in the middle of January. 'Cabbage leaves ve have at home,' he offered timidly, trying to placate her because her mouth was growing tighter by the minute.

She bent forward stiffly like a jack-knife beginning to shut and pushed her cold face right up against his forehead so that she was glaring straight into his eyes. 'Just because you've got a pretty face,' she said, 'you needn't think that gives you the right to be cheeky. Where are your vine leaves?' One bony finger pressed down onto his drawing book, stabbing at the border of leaves.

He looked at them with surprise, having forgotten all about them, but he was more frightened than ever now, because the sight of them was making her snort with anger.

'This page is a disgrace,' she said. 'Lines where they shouldn't be. And what's this?' She turned the page sideways and realized, with a shock that was visible to the entire class, that she was looking at a crude cartoon of the Reverend Jamieson, hands raised for the blessing. 'You irreligious little monster!' she screeched. 'How dare you draw the Reverend Jamieson!' She seized him furiously by the shoulder and began to shake him. 'That *fine* man is one of our *benefactors*. He is *not* to be *mocked*.'

David was completely baffled and very upset. He didn't understand what she meant by that hard word 'mocked', for it wasn't a word or an activity he'd ever come across. And he couldn't understand the word 'benefactor' either so it was impossible for him to know what it was he'd done that was so terribly wrong. But he knew he was in serious trouble, for the class had sucked in its breath with anticipation, and he could feel anger tightening Miss Killip's fingers like talons. 'Please,' he said, trying to wriggle his shoulder out of her grasp. 'Please not to hurt me. You hold me too hard.'

'I'll hold you too hard, monster!' she said, pinching him.

32

'You just see if I don't. I knew we'd have trouble with you the minute I clapped eyes on you. Spoiling your book with all this scribble. You're a naughty naughty boy.' She took a large India rubber from her pocket and plonked it down on the Reverend Jamieson's upstretched arms. 'Rub it all out,' she said.

'It is my drawing,' he protested weakly, his eyes filling with tears at the injustice and humiliation of it. Although he couldn't have put his feelings into words, he knew it was quite wrong to destroy the picture he'd created. His parents would never have asked him to do such a thing.

'Rub it out!'

Anger began to uncurl inside his chest. 'I von't,' he said.

Her nose was pinched with fury at such insubordination. 'You will do as you're told!' she shouted. She seized the rubber, and forcing it roughly inside his fingers, began to scrub at the page.

All his lovely drawing being smudged and ruined! It was dreadful. Horrible. He fought against the pressure of her hand, wriggling and squirming, but she continued remorselessly. 'Rub it all out!'

'I von't!' he said, red-faced with anger and struggle. 'I von't!'

She stood behind him, forcing his face down towards the terrible thing she was making him do, rubbing his nose in it. He tried to claw at her hand to make her stop, but she went on, scrubbing the paper harder than ever. There was a hole in the middle of the window now. Just where the lovely red light had been. It was too much to be endured. With an anger so sudden and overwhelming that the whole room was red with it, he bent his head to that awful scrubbing hand and bit it as hard as he could.

She let out one surprised scream. And the class hissed with astonishment. There was a long silence while the two of them looked at one another, eyes locked in hatred and disbelief. Then the teacher walked slowly back to her desk and picked up a long narrow cane and flexed it in her hands.

'I don't like caning boys on their first day at school,' she said, and her voice was icy, 'but you leave me no alternative. Stand over here.'

He stood where she indicated, aware that his heart was knocking against his ribs and that the class was watching him with open-mouthed concentration. After the terror of what he'd done, he was frightened beyond feeling.

She hit him with the stick three times on the tender flesh behind his knees. He offered no resistance at all. Nothing was real now except the pain. 'Now sit down,' she said, 'and let that be an end of it.'

When he got back to his seat, he began to cry, fat tears welling out of his eyes and wetting his cheeks. He was humiliated and hurt and afraid and there were red weals rising on his legs. What would his parents say when they saw them? How would he explain?

'Ai!' his father moaned, rocking in his chair. 'Shame you bring upon this house, David. Your mother you dishonour. Me you dishonour. Vat vill become of us? Ai-yi-yi!'

'Yes, Father,' David said humbly. There was a translucent innocence about this child when he was distressed. He looked like a cherub, his pale face a perfect oval, his cheeks flushed golden brown, his huge eyes luminous with tears, his mouth softer because it was trembling. He had told his father the truth, and now he had to witness the distress he'd caused. It was far more painful than the caning had been, for he loved his parents with the most profound passion. They were kind and patient and long-suffering and they loved him dearly and he knew he should never upset them. And now his mother was crying and his father rocking. And it was all his fault.

'Ve spare the rod vid this child,' Rachel reproached her husband. 'Now see vhat ve got.' She had always been sure the child should have been hit, even as a very little boy, but Emmanuel would have none of it. 'Never rule a child through fear,' he'd said. 'He must obey because he wishes to obey. The Lord will correct him. Whom the Lord loveth He correcteth.' And even when David threw himself about in the most passionate temper tantrums he was held and soothed and never hit. 'Now see vhat ve got,' she said.

'You doubt, Rachel,' Emmanuel sighed. 'Have faith, bubeleh. Ve did right by the boy. I know it.' Then he turned his

34

attention to David. 'Always contain your anger, my son,' he said gently. 'Never strike out. Never ever bite. You vill promise this?'

The promise was given and washed into his heart with hot shamed tears. But deep down inside him, deeper and firmer than the place in his chest where all these strong emotions were shaking him now, was the knowledge that it had all been unfair.

Chapter Three

When they'd eaten what they could of their midday meal, and he'd watched his father stooping back to Mr Goldman's workshop, still pulling his beard with disappointment and worry, David felt worse than ever. He knew he had to go back to school that afternoon because everybody went to school once they were five, unless they were idiots like Moishe Little-head or that funny girl from the corner shop who dribbled all the time. But he wished he didn't have to. What if he did something else that was naughty? Just thinking about it made him feel sick.

He walked as slowly as he could, dragging his feet, and stopping twice to do up his bootlaces, but although his mother looked reproachful she didn't scold and she didn't tell him to hurry. He arrived in the playground just as a plump lady came out onto the top step and rang the bell.

'You vill be a good boy, this time, bubeleh, and keep quiet and obey the teacher?' his mother said anxiously. Worry lines puckered her forehead even though he nodded most earnestly to reassure them both.

Miss Killip was wearing an ostentatious bandage and a very sour expression, but she made no reference to his behaviour and when she took the register and called his name, she didn't even look up when he answered. So that was all right. The afternoon began with another scratching of slates, so he was able to keep his head down too, and when the room grew darker and darker he felt comfortably hidden in the shadows.

At playtime he took his coat, cap and muffler from the peg in the cloakroom he now recognized as his own and crept into the playground, feeling tired and apprehensive. And to his

36

great surprise he was greeted as a hero.

'Was you the kid bit the Killer?'

'Good fer you if yer did!'

'Make 'er bleed, did yer? Serve 'er right!'

Ruby Miller, the girl who sat behind him in class, put her arm round his neck as though they'd been friends for years. 'She didden 'alf wop 'im,' she said. 'Nasty bit a' work that Killer.'

'Poor you! Did yer cry?'

'No he never.'

'Let's 'ave a look-see.'

His weals were examined with growls of hatred and sighs of sympathy, especially from the big girls, and for twenty rewarding minutes he was the centre of admiring attention, allowed to skip first and given a second turn when the rope tripped his legs, taught hopscotch and two dipping rhymes, and fed with shreds of liquorice stick and dips into sherbert dabs and a three-second suck of Ruby Miller's gobstopper. When he filed back into the shadowy classroom, he was warm and comforted. His parents might be shocked and saddened by his behaviour but his new friends approved. Ruby Miller winked at him as they all sat down, and that made him feel at home somehow, as though he belonged.

The room was very dark now, and when Miss Killip distributed a pile of dog-eared reading books, it was almost impossible to see the letters, even the big ones on the cover. He looked at her fierce face, glasses glinting in the half-light, and despite the approval of all his new friends, he was afraid again. Would she be cross with him if he couldn't see? And worse, would she hit him? It was pleasant to be a hero, but he quailed at the memory of that cane.

But before she could be cross with anybody, there was a polite knock at the door and the school keeper arrived in the room carrying a long hooked pole which seemed to be alight at one end, like a long thin candle taller than a man. Now David noticed that there were four huge gaslights suspended from the beams, and he watched, fascinated, as the man proceeded to light them. First he fixed the hook into one of the two chains that dangled from each light, and gave it a gentle tug downwards. Then gas hissed into the mantle and was lit with a plop by the wick at the end of the pole. It glowed faintly at first, like the light at the edge of a candle flame, pale and watery and rather blue, but then it began to swell, rounding out and becoming plump and yellow and filling the mantle. A lovely colour, David thought, enjoying it, as the man moved on to the next. And then the next, and then ...

'I don't know what you think you're gaping at, David Cheifitz!' the teacher said sternly.

He dropped his eyes to his book at once, but as he moved his head he was aware that faces near him were grinning encouragement. And when the school keeper left the room, he looked straight down at him and winked! What a surprise! A grown-up winking like Ruby Miller! And a really friendly wink, almost as though he was showing approval too. What a surprise!

So he found it was easy to settle into this new life after all. Especially now that he had friends to warn him of its dangers. He soon discovered that it was 'cissy' to be escorted to school by your mother, and after several gentle hints and the repeated assertion that he could find his way by himself now with no trouble, see if he couldn't, Mama stayed at home and allowed him the freedom of the streets.

And what a freedom it was! There was so much happening there, and so many games to play. You could swing from the lampposts on a long frayed rope that spun you out into the air as though you were flying; you could skip with all the others in the longest skipping rope in the world; you could play hopscotch and marbles, 'it' and French touch; and when you were just a little bit older and stronger there were all sorts of other games waiting for you, rough dangerous games like Releaso, and British Bulldog, and Jimmy Knacker, where your gang all piled on top of another gang against the playground wall, and you jumped onto the pile of bodies, whooping as you ran towards it and landing with a thud that made your heart leap, even if you were only watching.

It was a new world, with its own rules, its own punishments and its own rewards. A secret world from which all adults, however kindly, were naturally and totally excluded. Within a week he had been absorbed into it and by it. He'd learned to cry 'fainites' when the game was too rough for him to bear, he'd run the gauntlet twice, and won a fine alley playing marbles with Ruby Miller, and even been allowed to 'dip out' for hide an' seek. When the call went out at the beginning of playtime, 'All-y all-y in!' he was the first to run and join.

He soon realized that to make life tolerable in the classroom all he had to do was sit up straight, keep very quiet and do everything he was told, as soon as he'd worked out what it was. He got into the habit of taking a quick glance round at Hymie the Brain, because he always knew what the teacher wanted, even when she gave the most incomprehensible orders.

Drawing was much too dangerous to be done at school, of course. He knew that now. But it didn't matter because he could draw at home. At school he copied leaves and heart shapes, squares and diamonds, working mechanically and almost without needing to think what he was doing. At home he tried to draw people and did his best to make his figures as realistic as he could, concentrating hard and watching his model for long long minutes, absorbed and happy and rewarded. He knew and accepted that they were two quite separate activities, like everything else in this new life he'd begun.

School and home were separate. And so were the classroom and the playground. He behaved in quite a different way when he was in the playground with his friends, as if he were a different person. And of course he was a different person. At home he was quiet and well-behaved and contented, in the playground he was one of a rough, noisy, badly-behaved gang, and if he'd been asked he'd have been very hard put to it to say which of the lives he enjoyed most. At home he was glad to be quiet and loved, and felt it would be admirable to follow his father's example into a life as long-suffering and patient and kindly. At school he enjoyed the racket and the sense of danger, the unexpectedness and excitement and confusion, and felt that what he really wanted to be was the leader of a gang like Alfie Miller.

Alfie Miller was his hero. He was Ruby's brother, and one of the biggest boys in the playground, tougher than anybody. He was eight years old and had his own gang. He walked with a broad-shouldered swagger, his fists thrust deep into the tattered pockets of his cut-down coat and his cap pushed carelessly to the back of his head so that his face could be clearly seen. He had very big feet and very big hands, and his knees and knuckles were perpetually adorned with scars, for he was a prodigious scrapper and never backed down from a fight, or called 'fainites', no matter how much blood was being shed. But it was his face that David admired most, for his face was a war mask, calculated to strike terror into the toughest and inspire total obedience in all his sworn followers. Every time he saw that face, tough and scowling, surveying its kingdom, David wished he could be one of the followers. Such a broad, tomcat face, with hard round eyes, as pale as green glass, and high brick-red cheek bones, a tight mouth to show how brave he was, and a shock of tangled brown hair covering his forehead like a mane.

Spring finally melted the last of the ice ridges, and the tailoring trade picked up, ready for the summer season, and Miss Killip pronounced herself satisfied that David Cheifitz could read. 'He's done quite well for a Jewboy,' she told her colleagues. But it still annoyed her that he had such a pretty face. She preferred her pupils to be rough and ignorant and to look it, bow-legged with rickets, or hollow-eyed with fatigue, or gawping with adenoids, ill shod, shaven headed, badly spoken. She could cope with children like that, and even, at the end of the year, feel a little sympathy for them. But this child had such an unsuitably soulful face with all that dark hair and those big eyes. He looked out of place in Whitechapel. A creature apart, who had to be made to conform. 'You won't like him,' she said to Miss Andrews, who took the next class. 'He's an odd little thing.'

Fortunately the odd little thing had no idea he was being given a bad name, for summer had brought another delight to the crowded pavements of Brick Lane. The first of the hurdy-gurdies had arrived.

It was a splendid hurdy-gurdy, luridly painted, loud and

40

tinny, worked by a young Italian in a high crowned hat, and it was waiting for them when they all came tumbling out of school one Monday afternoon. It could play all the liveliest songs from the music halls, 'I'm 'Enery the Eighth, I am', and 'Any Old Iron', and even 'Knees Up Mother Brown'. So it wasn't long before sufficient pennies and ha'pennies had been collected and the dancing could begin. And for the first rapturous time in his life, David could join in. He'd seen the hurdy-gurdies playing in the street below his window oh so often when he was little, but his mother had always kept him within doors. Now at last he was free to dance.

'Come on, Davey, give us yer 'and,' Ruby Miller said and off they went, jumping and leaping with the rest of the excited crowd, as the music throbbed and clamoured. Petticoats swirled and aprons bounced, hands clapped, arm linked with arm, and down on the dirty cobbles footwear of every kind kicked the dust into the air, boots highly polished, boots pink with brick dust, boots broken and split, boots without laces and boots without toes, and in amongst those crunching hobnails small bare feet, scarred and grey with long-established grime, but lifting and lilting with the best. By the end of the first dance, David was quite drunk with the sheer joy of it. It made him remember the words he'd recited in the *heder* last Thursday. 'Serve the Lord with gladness and come before his presence with a song.' Gladness! Gladness! How right it was! When the last tune had been played and the hurdy-gurdy moved on to bewitch another street, he was panting and dishevelled, but totally happy.

And then Ruby added reward to rapture. 'Me an' Alfie an' our Amy's off up ter the Flowery ternight,' she said. 'Why dontcher come?'

'I vould like,' he said solemnly, hoping his mother would allow it.

'Be outside yer door, five o'clock,' she said as she skipped away.

If only his mother would allow it! That morning they'd started pulling down the old houses on the north side of Flower and Dean Street. He'd heard the thumps and crashes as he dressed, and they sounded very exciting. It would be wonderful to go and see it.

He ate his tea quietly, watching his mother and wondering if it

41

was the right moment for him to open the subject, but she was hard at work, sitting beside the window basting a coat, her head bent low over the cloth and her right hand moving so quickly it looked quite blurred, and he knew from experience that she rarely allowed him out of the house when she was busy.

'Soon you will finish, Mama?' he said hopefully, but her answer wasn't encouraging.

'An hour, two maybe. Oy, so much vork!' She pushed the hair out of her eyes and sighed, and tried to comfort herself. 'For vat I complain, bubeleh? Vork means money, don't I know it!'

'You vould like an errand run, maybe?' he tried. If she sent him to buy or borrow, he could go to the Flowery on the way back, and please her at the same time.

'Such a good boy,' she said, vaguely, but she didn't offer an errand. 'So drink up your tea while it's nice.'

It was very hot in their parlour, especially now that it was crowded with cloth ready for her to baste, and the air smelt of new wool and was full of fibres. He drank his tea thoughtfully, gazing past her busy fingers at the blackened brick of Fashion Street. There wasn't a sound in the room except for the rasp of her needle, and when the three-quarter hour struck, it was so loud the church clock could have been just outside the window.

His mother folded the garment she'd just finished and straightened her back, moving stiffly and grimacing. It was an expression he'd seen so often he knew exactly what to offer. 'You vant I should rub your back?'

'You're a good boy, bubeleh,' she said gratefully. 'You rub, I pin, eh?'

So he massaged the small of her back, rubbing gently with the side of his fingers, while she pinned another coat together, and sighed. And sighed again. Her forehead was quite damp with sweat.

They were banging and thumping in the Flowery. Steady rhythmical thumps like somebody hitting a huge drum. Oh, how very much he wanted to see it! Especially with Alfie Miller. Perhaps she'd let him go now, if he asked very politely. He'd just rub a little bit more and then ...

'So maybe you should run an errand, bubeleh,' she said, wearily.

42

'Yes.' Oh, let it be a nice long way, and then he could come back past the Flowery. He was so excited he hardly noticed how tired she looked.

'Mrs Finkleheim,' she said. 'You know Mrs Finkleheim, in the baker's, corner of Thrawl Street. Tell her no trouble, *has vesholem*, but if she has a minute, I'd be glad to see her.'

'Yes,' he said, ready to leave at once. It must be nearly four o'clock. 'On my vay home, I vatch the men in the Flowery, maybe?'

'Destruction you should vatch,' Mama said, sighing, 'at your age! Oy, oy, vat a vorld!' She was rubbing the small of her back, and her eyes were closed. But she didn't forbid it, so he left the room quickly before she could. It worried him that he wasn't being entirely honest, but he really *had* to go to the Flowery. And besides he was running an errand for her, so he ought to get some reward.

He was just in time. Alfie Miller and his gang were rollicking down Fashion Street as he ran out of the baker's having delivered his message and answered a lot of silly questions from Mrs Finkleheim. Was Mama in bed? At this time of day! What kind of question was that?

'Come on, kid,' his hero said. 'They're knockin' down the chimbley. Be some sport.'

And it was sport! The best sport in the world, like all acts of public destruction, dirty, noisy and totally enjoyable. A team of six men were pounding a side wall with pickaxes, and almost as soon as the gang had arrived and taken up good positions at the front of the crowd, they prized an ancient ivy from its long hold on the brick. It fell slowly, like a curtain, cascading them with dirt and debris, broken brick, red dust, filthy bus tickets, green crusts, fragments of old boot and a stampede of beetles and spiders. A bit further up the road two men were smashing windows with happy abandon, while a second team clattered tiles from the roof. Barefoot gangs scurried from one pile of debris to the next, collecting treasures in their filthy aprons, and an assortment of dusty mongrels ran madly about, barking and growling, or stood with their forepaws on the broken brick wall, rigid with excitement, or fled in sudden and cringeing terror as a particularly lethal object fell from the rooftop in

43

their direction. As a spectator sport it couldn't be bettered, so the road was full of spectators.

David watched enthralled, feeling very small in such a crowd, but rewarded. Very much rewarded. And thinking how odd it was to see the sky in the middle of Flower and Dean Street. A lovely blue sky too, looking very clean beside all those dirty bricks and those heaps of grey plaster.

Then there was a slight pause in the destruction while the roof gang gathered round the chimney stack and considered the best way to bring it down. There was so much pink dust on the pavements that Ruby Miller drew hopscotch squares in it and started a game with her sister Amy.

Alfie was over on the other side of the crowd with two of his cronies. They seemed to be playing some kind of hiding game, dodging in and out among a group of evening shoppers who'd stopped on their way to the Lane and were watching open-mouthed, their heads tilted towards the new skyline. Alfie was wearing his triumphant face and signalling to his friends, sticking his right thumb in the air and grinning, before he ducked behind another back. It must be a good game, David thought, to make him look so happy. And he wished he was old enough to be allowed to join in.

Then his attention was caught by a movement on the other side of the road, and as there was nothing particularly exciting happening just at that moment he turned to see what it was. A young man had arrived with a very odd machine and was arranging it on the pavement. It was a small black box balanced on three long narrow black stilts, like a daddy-longlegs with three legs. He was a well-dressed young man, and he was taking great care with his machine. Happily curious, David wandered across to see what it was.

'Camera, young shaver,' the young man explained. 'I'm a-goin' ter take a picture to put in the paper Thursday.'

This was an incomprehensible answer. Drawing a picture he understood, but taking a picture … 'How you take a picture?' he asked, his eyes quite round with the wonder of the idea.

'Light, young shaver,' the man said. 'Goes in this 'ere haperture, prints on this 'ere plate, and bobs yer uncle – a picture. Quick as a flash!'

'Vithout you draw?'

'Vithout I draw. Miracles a' modern science. Whatcher think a' that, eh? Tell yer what. You go an' get your friends over an' I'll take a picture of *you*. Put that in the paper too, I shouldn't wonder.'

What excitement! To have a picture 'taken'. 'Ruby!' he called, running back to gather the gang.

Ruby wasn't too keen on the idea. 'Better buck up, then,' she said grudgingly. 'They'll 'ave that inside wall down next, an' then we're in after the planks.'

'A picture, Ruby,' he urged. 'He says he take a picture. Of us! To put in the paper, Thursday!'

So she assented. 'Oh all right! Come on gang!'

'I should get Alfie?'

'What?'

'Alfie. For the picture.'

'No fear. 'E's busy.' He certainly wouldn't want to have his photo taken when there were so many pockets to pick.

It was a disappointment, but it couldn't be helped. If they didn't hurry the young man would fold up his machine and go away and the chance would be lost. He peered into the mass of bodies all around them but there was certainly no sign of Alfie. 'Come on then,' he said. 'Ve go.'

The young man took a long time arranging them, in a close group with their backs to the demolition. Then he disappeared underneath the cloth and told them all to say 'cheese' while he counted to twenty. It was a very long time to say one word. By the time he'd finished their jaws were aching. But it was exciting just the same. Even Ruby agreed.

But then the demolition men started to knock down the inner walls. 'Told yer!' she said, and pushed her way back to the front of the crowd. David struggled behind her, wishing she wasn't quite so quick. 'This'll be the last,' she said. 'See if I'm not right. Soon as they're finished we'll nip in fer the wood. You get round the side there, Johnny. There's a good bit under them bricks.'

'Is it stealing?' David asked anxiously. He couldn't take wood if it was stealing.

'Nah! Gawd 'elp us! It's firewood! We're cerlectin' it.'

So that was all right. If it was firewood Mama would be glad he'd come here to collect it too.

They waited patiently until the workmen had put on their coats and gone, taking a lot of the wood with them. And then what a rush there was. For there were grown-ups collecting firewood too and they pushed him out of the way and grabbed all the biggest pieces before he'd had a chance to see where they were. But he got a good armful, just the same. Ruby said it was a good armful. 'Your Ma'll be pleased as Punch,' she predicted.

He walked home, warm with achievement. A hurdy-gurdy, a big bundle of kindling, his picture in the paper, what tales to tell at suppertime! Now he was a scholar how rich life had become!

Aunty Dumpling met him at the top of the stairs. And Aunty Dumpling was cross. 'Where you been, you bad boy?' she said, speaking Yiddish. 'Staying out all hours and your poor mother so ill! You should be ashamed!'

He was frozen with fright, the delights of the day quite forgotten. 'What is it?' he asked, flinging the firewood to the floor. 'How is she ill?' his bottom lip trembled into tears. 'Mama!' He must run to the bedroom at once and see for himself. She was well when he left her. Had she had an accident? Or a fever? What was it?

Aunty Dumpling put out an arm to prevent him. 'You are to come home with me, you bad boy. Your mother is in bed.' Then she took pity on his stricken face, and spoke in English because she could see her use of Yiddish had alarmed him. 'Mrs Finkleheim she got with her. You ain't to go in.'

'She very ill, Aunty Dumpling?'

'No, bubeleh. You ain't to go in though. She got enough without you already.' Her voice was softer now, and her face rounder and more like itself. Now he could ask the question that was filling his chest so painfully.

'She won't die, Aunty Dumpling? *Has vesholem.*' And saying those magical words, hoping they would ward off disaster, he remembered that his mother had said them too – 'Tell Mrs Finkleheim, no trouble, *has vesholem.*' 'Oh say she won't die, Aunty Dumpling.'

'No,' Aunty Dumpling said kindly. 'Suffer she might, die she von't. Not if you come home vid me, like an angel.'

'Where is Father?'

'Vid your moder.'

It was too much. He began to cry, sobbing aloud in his fear, sobbing like baby, 'Mama! Mama! I want to see Mama!'

'Shush! Shush!' Aunty Dumpling scolded, pushing him into the nearest chair, and holding him there. 'You vant she should get vorse?' And at that he sobbed even louder.

But then his father appeared as if from nowhere and wiped his eyes and made him blow his nose and told him his mother was better now and he was to be a good boy and stop making a fuss or he would grieve them all.

'I stayed out. I worried her,' he said between sobs. 'Ai! Ai! It's all my fault. All my fault. I was disobedient, Father. I went to the Flowery. I wish I hadn't.'

'Shush! Shush!' Aunty Dumpling wailed. 'Vat ve do vid this boy? Hush, bubeleh, shush!'

'Take him home, Raizel,' Father said, using her real name for once. Oh, things were terribly serious!

So he went home with Aunty Dumpling, sobbing all the way, and the guilt he carried was heavier than all the firewood in the Flowery.

Chapter Four

Aunty Dumpling lived in Brick Lane, in one room at the top of four flights of stairs above Mr Jones the Dairy. It was a small room and the furniture in it was massive, being the kind made in Worship Street for the high-class trade who lived in double-fronted houses and had rooms large enough to accommodate it. Here, in a room ten feet by twelve, it swelled and creaked, like a fat woman in a corset, filling every space and corner. But David loved it because it was comfortable and familiar, and Aunty Dumpling kept it all so clean, every day polishing the leather, beating the rag rugs, blacking the stove, dusting the ornaments, cleaning out the canary, killing the bugs. There was a place for everything in this room. And a special place for him. Ordinarily, a visit to Aunty Dumpling was a real treat, to be savoured for days in advance and remembered for weeks afterwards. Now he was too consumed by guilt and anxiety to enjoy anything.

They went there in fits and starts, trotting through the crowds in Fashion Street, with David's hand crushed firmly against his aunt's roly-poly bosom, but stopping every few yards to talk to the neighbours, who wanted to know how his mother was. Unfortunately, their conversations were conducted in short unfinished sentences, and often contained more sighs than words, so he learned very little from them even though he listened with straining ears.

'How is she?'

'Oy, oy, poorly.' Sigh.

'Poor soul.' Sigh. 'Did she ... ?'

'Yes. Yes. *Nebbish.*'

'Such bad luck!' Sigh. 'So how many is this?'

'Five, poor soul … ' Sigh.

'I saw you go by, Mrs Esterman. How is Mrs Cheifitz? Has she lost … ?'

'Ai-yi-yi! The pity of it!'

Why were they talking about something his mother had lost? Was that what had made her ill? It didn't seem likely. People lost things all the time, even money sometimes and that was very bad, but they didn't get ill. David sighed heavily, looking at the pavement. There were times when grown-ups were very hard to understand. Why couldn't Aunty Dumpling just tell them what the illness was? Then he would know. Not knowing made him feel so afraid. And yet they didn't sound as though they expected her to die. They were sorry, but not *that* sorry. Vaguely comforted, he trotted on.

They climbed the stairs slowly, as always, and Aunty Dumpling complained all the way up, as always, 'Oy, my poor old legs! Oy, my back! Oy, such heat! Oy, oy, such a climb!' stopping at intervals to catch her breath and lift her skirts away from her feet. And the higher they went the more miserable he felt.

When they got into the room, and the canary was shrilling a welcome to them, and the kettle was on the stove, and the usual pile of dainty blouses was heaped on the table waiting to be trimmed, reminding him of his mother, his misery welled up inside his chest and couldn't be borne. 'Oh, Aunty Dumpling,' he wailed, face wrinkling into tears. 'Vat I done to Mama?'

She sat herself down in her sewing chair beside the window and scooped him up into the cushion of her nice wide lap. 'Vat you done, bubeleh? You ain't done nuttink. She just ill, poor soul. You ain't done nuttink.' And they both cried and howled with abandon, until their faces were wet from eyelash to chin and their misery was all sobbed away. And Aunty Dumpling rocked him and called him 'bubeleh' and told him over and over again that it wasn't his fault. 'Listen, bubeleh, ain't she been ill before? So, she been ill before, an' you come here, vid your old Aunty Dumpling, like a good boy, ain't she got better? So it's the same old story. Same this time as all the others, don' I tell you.' And finally he believed her.

'Ai!' she said. 'If only she got a place in the Buildin's. None a' this happen then, I tell you.'

This was a new idea. 'Vhy not, Aunt?'

'In the Buildin's is all much better, I tell you. I should know. In the Buildin's she vould be happy. Plenty vater. A front door. Give you a nice baby broder, maybe.'

Why would Mama give him a nice baby brother because she had a front door? 'She don't 'ave babies,' he said. Other mothers had babies. Lots of them. But his didn't. It wasn't something he ever gave any thought to. It was just a fact of life.

'You like a baby broder, maybe?'

He shrugged. He hadn't thought about that either. 'No,' he said. 'I vould like a biscuit, please.'

'So, I give you a biscuit, ve get her a place in the Buildin's. Vat you think?'

It seemed an admirable solution.

There were so many nice things about Aunty Dumpling. One was her nice easy emotion which came bubbling up so quickly and washed all over you and used itself up with such a lot of comforting noise, so that you felt quite better afterwards. Another was that she could sew and talk at the same time, even when she was doing the most complicated things, like stitching on frills or ruffles, her plump hands so brown and deft among all that fluffy material. Mama didn't seem to be able to talk and work. She said she had to think what she was doing. But Aunty Dumpling was different. And another nice thing about Aunty Dumpling was that she let you talk about almost anything. All sorts of things. She didn't mind a bit. Things you weren't quite sure you could talk about at home.

Later that evening, when he'd eaten a bowl of borscht, every last drop, and washed his face and hands in Aunty Dumpling's washbasin, which only had a very little crack in it, just in one side, and said his prayers for her like a good boy, he sat up in the middle of her high bed, cocooned inside one of the voluminous nightgowns she kept specially for him, and they talked.

She told him all the old stories, that he'd heard so often and liked so much. About Uncle Solomon, her husband who was too good for this world, and had left her, after four short years, with no children of her own, *'Nebbish!'* but with the incontrovertible status of widowhood and a room full of fine furniture. 'Vorkmanship? You never saw such vorkmanship. So look at the quality of that sideboard, vhy don't you?' And then they got on to his father, who was the best man ever born, and had brought them all out of Poland when they were little more than children, and looked after them all in this cold strange country. 'So young! The baby! And wasn't he farder and moder to us, I tell you. A good man, your farder! And work? You vouldn't believe!'

It was all reassuringly true. But there was still Mama's illness. 'Mama von't die, Aunty Dumpling?' he asked, knowing already that she would reassure him about this too.

'Ain't I told you, bubeleh?' she said as well as she could with a dozen pins between her lips. 'Two-three days you be home again, everything as right as rain.'

'I wish I could get her a place in the Buildin's,' he said earnestly.

'So you go to school,' she advised between pins. 'You learn English good. You get a good job. Nice steady job, good pay. You go to shul, like a good Jewish boy. You marry a nice Jewish girl. No common *shiksa* for our Davey. Nu! So you settle down. Have kids. Vhat a life you got!'

Yes, hadn't he. Dear Aunty Dumpling, to see his future so clearly. He beamed at her over the counterpane, his dark hair so long and thick it was almost in his eyes. But the present and its problems were pressing. 'Aunty Dumpling,' he said. 'Can you be two people?'

'Vhat a boy he is!' she said. 'So one ain't enough?'

It wasn't the sort of answer he wanted. But then he hadn't known what sort of answer he wanted when he asked the question. In fact he hadn't really understood the question. It had grown out of a disturbing sense that he'd unwittingly caused his mother's illness by being two people, one at home and another at school, and that perhaps it wasn't right to be two different people, and he ought to do something about it. Now he was more confused than ever. Scowling, he turned his mind to a more practical problem and a more possible solution. 'I could get a job soon,' he said. 'In the Lane, maybe. That vould help her get a place in the Buildin's, vhat you think?'

'Just a little older you get, bubeleh,' she said. 'At six years old you don't vork yet. Now you sleep like a good boy.' And she bit off her thread in such a sharp determined way he knew he had to obey.

But as it turned out, he got a job a great deal sooner than either of them had imagined possible.

He stayed with Aunty Dumpling for more than ten days. It was the second Shabbas before he went home. To find his mother up and about, wearing her red shawl and presiding over the Shabbas meal, with the candles lit, breaking the Shabbas bread and dipping it in the salt, all exactly the same as always. Back to normal. But when his father returned from the synagogue and said his customary prayer in her honour, 'Strength and honour are her clothing; her children arise up and call her blessed; her husband also, and he praiseth her,' the tears David shed were as much relief as thanksgiving. Whatever else he did, he must never run the risk of making his mother ill again.

All through the long dusty summer holiday he looked after her, restricting the time he spent out in the streets with his new friends and running errands for her, even when it meant returning the heavy coats, glad that it was his arms that were aching and not hers. Yom Kippur wasn't until September, which was *ages* away, and although he knew he would make a special effort to make amends then, he still felt that he'd committed such a dangerous unkindness that it ought to be put right straight away. The fact that she could be ill, and ill so suddenly, made her doubly precious to him. Until this summer, she had spent her time fussing and petting him, now in his six-year-old way, he was fussing and petting her.

But then September came and he had to go back to school again. 'You vill be careful, von't you, Mama,' he said to her solemnly as he left the house on that first morning.

'Vat a boy he is!' she said lovingly. 'Mind you cross the road careful, eh, bubeleh.'

'I'm in the second class now, Mama,' he said, proudly and to show her she had no need to worry. He was quite looking forward to it. No more Killer for a start, and everybody said Miss Andrews was much nicer.

52

Which she was, being a quiet, slow, careful woman, who gentled them when they were in a rush of panic or bad temper, and took them quietly through their chores, praising them whenever she could. Ruby Miller, who'd grown quite a bit taller and very much fatter during the holidays, said she was 'a bit of all right!' And David, copying the tone and style of her quick easy English, was soon saying exactly the same thing. He was learning school English quite rapidly now, and feeling very pleased with himself. Yes, it was true, the second year was better than the first.

Even the fact that his hero had gone up into the big boys and wasn't in the playground any more was only slightly upsetting. He would see him in the streets and, in any case, it wouldn't be long before he was up in the big boys himself. Even now, he wasn't entirely forgotten. From time to time there would be a scrabbling of feet against the wall that divided the big boys from the girls and the infants. Alfie's bold tomcat face would appear over the top, grinning at him. 'Chuck us our ball back, kid!'

But then, just when he'd decided that life at school could actually be quite pleasant, Ellie Murphy arrived.

It was a dank miserable morning, and his mother had insisted that he wear two coats to protect his chest, so he was late getting into the classroom because he'd taken rather longer than the others to struggle out of the top one and hang it on his peg. And there, standing in the gangway as though she owned it, and just where he ought to have been, was a filthy girl, dirtier and more dishevelled than anyone he'd ever seen. Her hair was all tangles and looked dusty like an old coconut mat, and there was a bruise above her left cheekbone and a scab at the corner of her mouth. She wore a long sack-coloured skirt full of holes and a black velvet jacket which had once been very fine but was now frayed at every seam, the cuffs and collar gaping like wounds to reveal a discoloured half-inch of stiffener. Her boots were several sizes too large for her, and grey with dust, and from where he stood he could see her dirty feet through the cracks. Yet she stood proudly, her chin in the air, as though she was important and special, and when she looked across at him he saw that her eyes were a quite

53

startling blue, like the sky that had suddenly appeared in Flower and Dean Street that day when the walls were demolished, a clear, beautiful, unexpected, clean colour. He disliked her at once, recoiling from her in revulsion and annoyance.

'Ah, there you are, David,' Miss Andrews said, smiling her vague smile at him. 'Now we're all here ... ' She turned her vagueness towards the dirty girl. 'You can sit in the seat next to Ruby, dear. She'll take care of you.' Then it was Ruby's turn. 'Her name's Ellie, and I've given her the peg next to yours. If you'll just take her down and show her where to hang her hat ... '

It was a dirty hat too, a flat black straw, trailing a tangled bush of ostrich feathers. Ruby wrinkled her nose, but led the way cheerfully enough, grinning at her friends. But David sat down without a word, scowling and not looking at either of them. He had a seat beside the gangway because he was well-behaved and worked hard and had a ticket for attendance. He knew that because Miss Andrews had told him. And now his hard-earned position was going to be spoilt by a horrible girl.

He prepared himself for the start of the day, still scowling, checking that his slate was clean, and his slate pencil in place, easing his precious slice of prune cake out of his pocket and placing it carefully on the shelf in his desk ready for playtime. It was Aunty Dumpling's special cake and a rare treat. And as always is sustained him through the drone of Tables and the monotony of Arithmetic.

He was waiting at Miss Andrews' desk to have his sums marked when the bell rang for playtime. His mouth began to water at the first clang and he looked up brightly, hoping she'd hurry up and collect in the books.

She caught the glance and responded to it. 'Um ... yes ... Pile your books on the table like good children ... Hymie, you'll collect everyone else's, won't you?'

David was back at his desk within seconds, already savouring the taste of prune cake, his mouth moist with anticipation. And the cake was gone! He couldn't believe it. He knew he'd put it on the shelf. He remembered doing it. All wrapped up in its

54

greaseproof paper, nice and neat, in the corner where he always put it. Could it have fallen on the floor? No. Or in the desk? No. There was no sign of it anywhere, only the dark grease stain on the shelf. And the line was waiting for him. Baffled and hungry and disappointed he marched into the playground.

Fortunately Hymie started calling in the minute they got out of the door, and that took his mind off it a bit, even though his stomach was aching for the food that had been denied it. 'Bags I dip,' he offered, because being busy was the best treatment for hunger. He'd just learned a new dip from Hymie and wanted to try it.

One two three,
Mother caught a flea,
Put it in the tea pot
An' made a cup a' tea.
The flea jumped out
And bit Mother's snout,
Along came Father
Wiv 'is shirt 'angin' out.

The circle was close and warm against the mist, leaning in towards his dipping hand and smelling of fried onions and herrings and burnt bones and coal, nice homely acceptable smells. The new girl was almost forgotten. He decided he'd look for the cake again when he got to the classroom. It must have slipped down somewhere in the desk. That was it.

It was a furious game and occupied the entire playground, spinning them off into every direction like paper chips in a kaleidoscope. Soon both his bootlaces had come undone and he had to call 'fainites' to fasten them again. He knelt beside the steps where there was less likelihood of being knocked over and tied a double knot firmly, concentrating hard. As his fingers tugged the laces he caught a glimpse of a black velvet sleeve and looked up, and there was the awful girl, sitting on the top step, eating something from a piece of greaseproof paper. There was something so surreptitious about her movements that he knew at once that she was eating his cake.

'Vhat you got there?' he asked roughly.

'Nothink.'

'Let's 'ave a look-see.'

'Shan't.'

But he didn't need to look any closer. He could see the filling. 'You got my cake.'

'No I ain't,' she said, and as he climbed the step towards her she crammed the remains of the cake into her mouth all at once, so that her cheeks were puffed with it and her blue eyes bolting.

'You've ate my cake!' he said, enraged.

'Should a' looked after it, then,' she said with her mouth full. He could see the rich crumbs mounded on her tongue.

'You pinched it,' he said, scowling at her.

'No I never, see. Found it on the floor. You must 'a dropped it.'

He hadn't. He knew he hadn't. But she looked so sure of herself, not a bit guilty, and her blue eyes so clear, that she made him doubt.

'Vell ... ' he said. 'Vell ... '

'You're it!' Hymie yelled, jumping onto the step and thumping him in the middle of the back. So the game swept him away.

From then on he kept any titbit he brought to school safely in his pocket, no matter how greasy it was. And he tried to keep well out of Ellie's way. She *had* nicked his cake, and he didn't intend to give her the chance to nick another. But she was always there somehow, tagging along on the edge of Alfie's gang, or worming her way into the best games even though she must have known she wasn't wanted.

Within a week they were calling her Smelly Ellie Murphy. Behind her back, but quite loud enough for her to hear. Poor clothes, patched and darned and faded, were the norm and acceptable at Deal Street School but velvet and ostrich feathers were very definitely not. But even that didn't put her off. Horrid girl!

The months went by and his mother wasn't ill again, the lessons might be boring but they were easy enough, and suddenly it was summer again, his last summer in the Infants.

There were more errands to run in the summer because food

went off so quickly in hot weather and because there was a little more money in the house now that the tailoring trade was busy making clothes for the Season. So he found himself out in the streets more often than he was indoors, running to the dairy in Bell Lane with a little jug to see if Bessie had been milked, or to Jacob the Butcher's in Ruth House or to Mr Cohen's in Thrawl Street with a little dish in his hand for a ha'p'orth of jam or a salt herring. But best of all was a trip down the Lane for a bargain at one of the stalls.

David liked the Lane. You could buy anything you wanted there if you had the money. And it was all on display at his eye level: kosher meat, labelled in Yiddish, or chicken, hung by their scaly yellow legs, their dead eyes bulging; or fish in abundance, slippery herring from Fanny Marks, white dabs and dappled plaice, eels writhing in the barrel; or fruit and vegetables piled high on their green shelves, oranges glossy beside earth-streaked potatoes, apples reflecting the naptha flares from the high polish of their green and red globes, bananas folded against one another in long curved swathes. There was rich cake at Monickendam's, if you could afford it, and bagels hooped through a stick and bread of every colour, from palest yellow to black rye; there were mounds of soap like yellow wax, sacks of coal and boxes full of lacy gas mantles, quiet and clean and unused; there were secondhand clothes hanging from every wall as though they'd been executed, wafting their pungent smell of dirt and sweat with the breeze of every movement below them; there were boots and shoes, scuffed and patched and polished, coils of lace and fluttering ribbons, chipped cups and saucers, pails full of broken eggs, cooking oil like golden water in a vast green vat, even wigs and hairpieces, forlorn on their wooden stands. Anything at all. So much colour, and so much noise, with the stall holders calling their wares in a mixture of English and Yiddish, and such a close warm smell with all those people crushed up against one another in the spaces between the stalls and the shops. You couldn't see the top of the buildings or the pavement for the crush of all those bodies. It was like being in a huge warm bath, only better because this water was brightly coloured and got warmer the longer you stayed in it.

Sometimes he would wander down to Wentworth Street even when he hadn't any errands, just for the pleasure of seeing the sights. And one afternoon in July he saw a sight he didn't expect.

He was loitering beside Flossie Silverman's stall, watching her as she hung belts and braces from the side rail, when a quick surreptitious movement flicked across his line of vision between the dangling colours. It was a small dark hand passing rapidly over the heap of oranges on the next stall. Flick and an orange was gone, hidden in the hand, passed under a dirty pinafore. Then another flick, and an apple was filtched. It was so bold and so quick it took his breath away. He looked up the arm to the face above the hand and saw that the thief was Ellie Murphy.

There was a sweep of thick eyelashes and her blue eyes looked boldly at him for a fraction of a second, recognizing and warning. Then she was gone, skimming off into the crowds, quick as a flea. So she was a thief. He'd always known it. What should he do? He knew you never told your parents anything that happened in the playground, but this was different. This was in the open, in the Lane.

While he was dithering, a hand seized him by the shoulder. He was so alarmed, he jumped. It was Alfie Miller.

'How d'yer fancy a job, kid?' he said, grinning his tomcat grin.

David forgot all about Ellie at once. A job! Wasn't that just what he wanted? A job and the chance to earn money and get Mama a place in the Buildings. 'Yes!' he said, breathless with surprise and pleasure. 'Very much I vould like!'

'Whatcher think?' Alfie said, turning to the man who was standing beside him. ' 'E's a good kid. Straight. Aintcher?'

David nodded his head to show how straight he was, while the man considered him, his thick eyebrows drawn together, and his lips pursed. 'Looks the part, I'll grant yer,' he said. 'Reckon 'e's fly, do yer?'

'Fly? Do me a favour! Quick as greased lightnin' 'e is. Aintcher?'

' 'Ow old are yer?'

'Seven,' David said hopefully. Was that old enough?

' 'E don't look it,' the man said to Alfie.

'More's the better,' Alfie said. And the man drew his eyebrows together again and looked at David for a long disquieting time. 'Come on, Crusher,' Alfie said. ' 'E's as innercent as a babe newborn. Look at 'im, I ask yer! Yer won't get better'n that.'

'Yer on!' the man said, nodding at Alfie, and touching his bowler hat with a thick forefinger. 'Tell 'im what's what. Sunday free o'clock.' And he was gone, his dark coat one of the many shifting and crowding between the stalls.

Alfie took David by the arm and walked him off companionably along the Lane. 'It's like this 'ere, Davey,' he said. 'Nah an' then my uncle cops a bit of a bargain. Some geyser in the trade. Up the ware'ouse. Done 'im a good turn oncest, so 'e sez. So 'e puts a bargain 'is way nah an' then, 'f'yer take my meanin'.'

'Yes,' David said, feeling honoured to be told so much and wondering what his job was going to be.

'On'y trouble is,' Alfie said, looking very serious about it, ' 's'too good a bargain this time. Tha's the on'y trouble. 'E's got these rings, see, real gold rings like yer see in the jewellers. Sell fer 'alf a sov there they would, on'y 'is mate reckons 'e's ter sell 'em in the Lane fer a tanner a time.'

It *was* a bargain. David's brown eyes were quite round with the wonder of it.

'Tried ter sell 'em last week, 'e did,' Alfie went on, 'an' watcher think?'

'What?'

'No takers! Never sold one. They all fought it was a con, I reckon. Well, yer don't sell gold rings fer a tanner, now do yer? Not every day a' the week. An' no one wants ter be the first ter buy, case it's a con. Stands ter reason. Like in school. No one wants ter be first, so you all keep quiet. Well, *you* know that, dontcher Davey? So 'e's got a job on, you can see that cantcher.'

Oh he could, he could.

'So what we want you ter do is this. Stand in the crowd, as if you was interested like, an' when he offers fer the fird time, call out, "I'll 'ave one!" We'll give yer the tanner. Then we got our first sale, an' they can all see what a bargain you've got, an' everythink'll be hunky-dory. Whatcher say? Give yer the tanner if yer do it right.'

Sixpence! It was a fortune! 'I do it,' he promised, and was rewarded by the broadest tomcat grin he'd ever seen on his hero's face.

'Good kid!' Alfie said. 'See yer Sunday. Free o'clock. Wentworf Buildin's. You won't regret it.'

David was so excited he ran all the way home. A job! A real job! He was going to earn money like the big boys and girls. What a help he'd be! And this was just the start. Soon they could afford the rent in the Buildin's. Mama need never be ill again.

Chapter Five

Sunday was a lovely day, pleasantly warm and with just sufficient breeze blowing up from the river to stir the stale air in the chasms between the tenements. The sky was cobalt blue, as David noticed the minute he stepped out into Fashion Street, because it was such a strong satisfying colour it made him lift his eyes to look at it. And the clouds were lovely too, fragile, changing shapes, curled and white like drifting goose feathers.

Good weather and beautiful colour and the prospect of earning his first sixpence filled him with energy. Walking was too tame for such a day. He went to Wentworth Street on the trot, running and skipping as he dodged through the crowds. And what crowds they were. The world and his wife were out in the streets that afternoon and the Lane was so packed with people it was impossible to see from one stall to the next.

Alfie and his massive uncle were waiting in the entrance to Wentworth Buildings. And there was another young man with them, a tall shambling youth with a broken nose and very crossed eyes.

'You took yer time, didn'tcher,' the uncle growled by way of greeting, and he put a dirty sixpence into David's palm and folded the child's fingers down over it as though he were closing a purse. 'There's yer tanner. Keep tight 'old uv it! Speak when I give yer the wink.'

'Is 'e cross?' David asked anxiously as they followed the uncle through the mass of shoppers.

'Ol' Crusher? Nah!' Alfie reassured him. ' 'E's always that-a-way. Bear wiv a sore 'ead, my ol' man sez. You don't wanna pay 'im no mind. Got yer tanner? Be some sport this will.'

But David wasn't so sure, now that he'd arrived. He felt boxed in, cut off from the sunshine and the blue sky by the pressure of sweating armpits, shoving buttocks and jabbing elbows. He couldn't see anything except arms and chests and belts and bottoms, and it was very difficult to keep up with Crusher who was striding through the crowds with the impervious rhythm of a tram. There was an element of danger about this job that David wasn't quite sure about, now that he'd begun it. There'd be thieves everywhere in a crowd like this. Bound to be. What if somebody nicked his tanner? Clutching it tightly in his sweaty palm, he scowled and followed.

But at last they'd struggled to the crossroads and were standing in front of The Princess Alice, and the Crusher had turned and was surveying his customers. The boss-eyed man had acquired an orange box during their progress. Now he set it on the top step, and Crusher climbed up on it and gave the heads below him a wide and peculiarly ugly smile, spreading his thick lips sideways to reveal half a dozen dark brown stumps and the fur-coated mound of a grey-white tongue. 'He' are! He' are! You got the chance uv a lifetime 'ere, ladies and gentlemen,' he boomed. 'Jest you see if you ain't!'

The people below him shifted and rearranged themselves, some walking away as quickly as they could, others stopping and drifting towards him.

'An' when I say a bargain, do I *mean* a bargain?' Crusher continued. 'You never seen nothink like it, missus, I'm tellin' yer. He' are! Take a butcher's. Whatcher think that is?'

' 'S a ring,' a woman's voice answered from the other side of the crowd.

'So it is, missus! But what's it made of? Tha's the question. What you think it's made of, sonny?'

'Looks like gold ter me,' Alfie's voice said, and David saw that he was standing just to the left of the Crusher. Was he helping too?

'An' so it is, my son,' Crusher said beaming at him and the crowd. 'Solid nine carat gold that is. 'Ave a good look. You won't see better'n that outside 'Atton Garden.'

'No good showin' us solid gold, mister. Likes uv us don't go buyin' gold. Ain't got that sort a' mazuma round 'ere.'

62

'I know that, darlin',' Crusher said. 'Tha's why I come down 'ere this afternon ter do y' a favour. Go to a jeweller's, my love, 'ow much d'you reckon they'd rook yer fer that. I can tell yer. Half a sov! Tha's what! Ten an' a kick. An' worf every penny. Every single penny. Well ... they got their over'eads, ain't they, darlin'? They gotta make a good profit, ain't they? Jewellers. I mean ter say.' The audience found this amusing for some reason, and began to laugh and call out. And Crusher laughed with them, showing his brown stumps and holding up the ring between finger and thumb for them to see. 'We don't go fer big profits in the Lane, do we, missus? So I tell you what I'm gonna do. I got these little beauties, 'olesale, I won't tell yer no lies. Got 'em 'olesale, so I could sell 'em to yer fer 'alf the price.'

'Five an' frupence!' the woman said mockingly. 'Do us a favour!'

'I *could* sell 'em to yer fer 'alf the price, darlin'. That don't meanter say I will. I *could* sell 'em to yer fer five bob. I *could* sell 'em to yer fer two florins. You know me. 'Onest Joe, that's me. Nah four bob, tha's a lot a' money. So I tell yer what I'll do. I won't ask yer four bob for 'em, or free. I won't even ask yer *one* bob for 'em. Not even one measly bob. I'm a mug ter mesself, darlin'. Seein' as it's you, I'll let 'em go fer a tanner. One tanner, tha's all I'm askin'. One tanner. Can't say fairer'n that, can I, darlin'? One tanner. Who wants a solid gold ring fer a tanner?'

His audience shifted and muttered and narrowed their eyes, but nobody offered to buy.

'You won't get another offer ter beat this, not in a month a' Sundays,' the Crusher said, looking straight at David. 'A tanner fer solid gold.' And he looked at David again.

It was the signal. Now he had to earn his money. 'I buy one,' he called in his piping voice and he held the sixpence in the air, but inside his closed fist just in case anyone made a grab for it.

'Young gentleman on my right,' Crusher said to Alfie. 'You got a bargain there, son. Who's next?'

But nobody offered. They were all looking at David and the ring Alfie had just delivered into his sweaty hands.

'Tha's never gold,' the woman standing next to him said. 'Let's 'ave a look-see.'

'No,' David said, clutching the ring safely inside his fingers.

The sense of danger was very strong now, and it wouldn't do to let it be nicked when he had to give it back in the end.

'Quite right, sonny,' another woman said. 'S'your ring.' She was a comfortable woman, fat and motherly. 'You stick to it.'

'Who's next?' Crusher tried again.

'I don't buy till I've examined the goods,' a posh voice said.

The boss-eyed man was suddenly at David's elbow. 'I don't reckon tha's gold neither,' he announced belligerently. 'Kid's a mug. 'E's been took fer a ride, tha's what I reckon.'

David was so surprised, his mouth fell open. Why was he being attacked? Surely the boss-eyed man was one of Mr Crusher's friends.

'Whatcher buy it for, eh?' Boss-eyes said, his left eye focusing on a handbag just above David's right ear.

What could he say? If he told the truth he'd give the whole game away, and he knew Mr Crusher wouldn't like that. But if he didn't, he would have to lie and that was wrong, and would upset his father. Caught and confused, he said he didn't know.

'Yer a mug!' Boss-eyes said. 'You want yer 'ead examined. Been took fer a ride, you 'ave.'

'Leave 'im alone,' the fat woman said. 'Wnat's it ter you?'

' 'E wants ter take that to Uncle Three Balls,' Boss-eyes continued, still addressing the handbag. 'Soon see if it's gold then, 'cause yer can't fool Uncle.'

'Yes, why dontcher?' the young woman said. 'We'd all know then.'

Other people joined in, urging him towards the pawn shop, pressing in upon him so that he had to move his feet in the direction they wanted or he'd have been knocked to the ground. He looked despairingly at Mr Crusher, but that gentleman was busy looking the other way. Alfie was grinning at him from the top step of the pub, and almost seemed to be nodding. Was this what he was supposed to do? Why hadn't they told him exactly what he was supposed to do? His feet were still moving and now he was quite near the pop shop.

'Go on in, son,' Boss-eyes said, giving him a shove. 'Or d'yer want me ter to pop it for yer?'

'You leave 'im be, poor little mite,' the fat woman said. 'If anyone's goin' in wiv 'im, it'll be me.'

'You goin' in or aintcher?' Boss-eyes growled, turning his face towards David, left eye flickering, right eye vacant.

He was boxed in with bodies and couldn't see over their heads to where Mr Crusher was standing, but even though he was alarmed, he was thinking fast and with clarity. Even if he pawned the ring, he could always redeem it afterwards, and at least it would be safe in the pop shop. 'All right!' he said, making a decision.

'I'll come in wiv yer, duck,' the fat lady said, tucking her hand into the crook of his arm. And in they went.

He was really quite glad of her presence, because the pawnbroker was brusque and suspicious. He examined the ring through a formidable eyeglass, grunting to himself all the time, and when he put them both down he narrowed his eyes and examined David in the same thorough way. The ring lay between them on the dark counter, butter yellow and gleaming.

' 'E come by it 'onest,' the fat lady said, defensively.

The pawnbroker shrugged. 'Did I say anythink?'

'So?'

'So.'

'Is it gold?'

'Nine carat.'

'So?'

'Five bob,' the pawnbroker offered casually, looking at David.

It was a terrifying amount of money. 'Yes,' he agreed huskily, his heart thumping alarm.

They emerged from the shop to a clamour of questions, from a crowd grown larger and more aggressive and avid for information.

The fat lady enlightened them at once. 'Five bob!' she said, triumphantly. 'Show 'em, kid! Nine carat gold, so 'elp me. The genuine article.'

David held up his two fat half-crowns to show them, but they were already off, pushing their way back to Mr Crusher and his incredible bargain. 'Put 'em away,' she said, as she followed them. 'Got a breast pocket, 'ave yer?' But she was gone before he could answer, and before he'd undone the buttons on his jacket Alfie had replaced her and was standing breathlessly beside him.

'You done a good job, kid,' Alfie said, grinning his approval. 'Give us the five bob, quick, an' the dooplicate, 'fore some fievin' 'ound gets 'is maulers on it.'

David handed the money across at once, glad to be rid of it, and fished the pawn ticket out of his trouser pocket. He was still trying to make sense of Boss-eyes' odd behaviour and wondering whether he was supposed to have pawned the ring or not, but Alfie didn't give him the chance to ask questions.

' 'Ere's yer tanner,' he said. 'Nah scarper!'

It was unnecessary advice, for David was already running home, taking his confusion and his reward with him. He noticed as he went that white hands were raised in the air all around Mr Crusher and that Boss-eyes was handing out rings and gathering sixpences as fast as ever he could. It was nice to think that he'd been the one to show all those people what a fine bargain they were going to get.

And it was a marvellous homecoming, because Aunty Dumpling was there. She'd brought one of her nice cakes and she and Mama were setting the table for tea. The oilcloth had been newly scrubbed, so that all its pretty little blue and white flowers were bright and clearly defined, the kettle was knocking and steaming on the stove, and Mama's work had been folded neatly away in the orange-box cupboard.

'So kiss your old aunt, vhy don't you?' Aunty Dumpling said, holding out her arms to him as he rushed towards the table. And Mama said, 'Just in time, bubeleh,' in the most loving and approving way. But he couldn't greet either of them, not just yet. He was swollen with the pride of his first real achievement. He put the little shining coin in the middle of the oilcloth, just in front of Aunty Dumpling's cake, and stood back to let them see it, his face bright with importance and love.

'This is for you, Mama,' he said. 'My earnin's. In the Lane. For you to 'ave a place in the Buildin's.'

Aunty Dumpling let out a shriek and threw her apron over her head. 'Oy, you ever see such a boy? Seven years old and earning already. A blessing to you, Rachel my dear, don't I tell you. Oy, such a good son.' Tears rolled down her nice plump face, collecting in the creases above her cheeks and running into her open mouth. 'Come an' give your Aunty Dumpling a kiss, bubeleh!'

But Mama had put the kettle back on the stove and run across the room to him, to kneel beside him and throw her arms round his neck. 'He did it for his Mama, Raizel,' she said proudly, holding his face between her hands and kissing him fondly. 'For a place in the Buildin's. Such a dear kind boy ve got.'

He was so happy and so proud, all doubts were forgotten. Then they sat up to the table and drank their tea and ate Aunty Dumpling's cake and praised him all over again.

'So vhat you do, bubeleh? Vhat you do to earn all this money, eh?' Aunty Dumpling asked, her cheeks bulging with smiles and prune cake.

It was a difficult question, but he'd answered it before he realized how difficult it was. 'I ran an errand,' he said, truthfully enough.

'So vhat you *do?*' she persisted.

'I took a ring to the pop shop, Aunt.'

'So young and he runs errands already,' Aunty Dumpling crooned.

'You *pawned* it?' Mama asked, her brown eyes wide with surprise.

'Yes,' he said proudly. 'He give me five bob fer it.'

'Seven years old and he pawns rings!' Mama said trying to sound disapproving. 'Vhat next ve hear?' But her pride was obvious too. Her face was glowing with it, cheeks lifted so that the dark shadows under her eyes spread and lightened, pale mouth stretched so wide she was showing her broken teeth. Normally she kept her lips together except when she had something to say, and even then she spoke towards the ground, her head bowed. It was extraordinary and rewarding to see her head lifted like this.

'Vid a boy like this vhat for you vant others?' Aunty Dumpling asked, patting Mama's hand with her rough gentle paw. 'You got all a mother could vant in just the one boy, nu?'

'Just think, the poor soul, to get a child to pawn her ring for her,' Mama said. 'How she must suffer. We got a lot to be thankful for, Raizel.'

Later that evening, when the cobalt sky had paled to duck-egg blue and the curled clouds were pink as roses, his father came stooping home, tall and tired, to be told of his son's success. And Aunty Dumpling cried all over again, and his mother put the sixpence in the palm of her hand like the precious coin it was and showed it to his father.

'For a place in the Buildin's, he earned it,' she said. 'Ve got a good son, Emmanuel. He vant his mother to live in the Buildin's.'

Emmanuel hung his coat and hat on the door and sat himself wearily in his cane chair beside the table. 'A good son,' he agreed, but there was no pleasure in his voice. 'Nu-nu, ve talk of it later.' His long face was grey with fatigue and his eyes were withdrawn. He gave his beard a tug, sighing deeply, and David saw that his right hand was ringed with red pressure marks from the shears.

'Ai!' his mother sighed too. 'You vork too hard, Emmanuel.' And she put the sixpence in her pocket and, taking his plate from the cupboard, began to dish up the supper. 'Gefilte fish,' she said, offering comfort.

David was so disappointed that tears began to prick his eyes. He blinked them back at once because he didn't want to upset his father, especially when he could see how very tired he was. But the disappointment remained. However rewarding it had been to impress his mother and to enjoy Aunty Dumpling's irrepressible emotion, it was his father he really wanted to please. And he wanted it passionately, even though he had a vague suspicion that his father might ask more probing questions than Mama had done, and might even expose his uneasy suspicion that the transaction hadn't been entirely honest. Nevertheless, he wanted him to know everything about it, to approve his intentions and praise him for a 'good son'. For his father was a good man, upright and righteous, a model of patience and tolerance and endurance, and everybody who knew him valued him and spoke well of him. To be praised by such a man was the greatest good the child could imagine. It was demoralizing that his great effort, his first wage, wasn't

68

good enough to notice.

That night the bugs bit worse than ever, and what with their constant irritation and the discomfort of an emotion that an older child would have recognized as a guilty conscience, David was wakeful. A full moon lit the faded wallpaper above his truckle bed so clearly that once he woke to see a bug crawling down its bright surface towards him, and reaching out his hand defensively he caught it and squashed it under his thumb. It was little consolation. One might be gone, but there were hundreds of others. He scratched at the raised red bumps under his armpits, wondering vaguely whether everybody got bitten in the summer, and as he scratched he realized that his parents were awake in their creaking bed, and that his mother was talking, in Yiddish and in her low apologetic voice.

'We should ask maybe, Emmanuel? Your sister Rivke, she got a place, and she said to me, "Keep on," she said, "you got to ask and ask. Worry them, ask them, keep on," she said. Your sister Rivke.'

'We will wait, Rachel,' his father said. 'They will give us a place in their own good time. You will see.'

'Nu-nu, we never get a place. We don't ask, we don't get.'

'You want we should be *schnorrers*? Begging is not a good thing, believe me. The more we beg, the more they refuse. Better strip a carcase of its hide than be a beggar.'

'Would it hurt to ask just once?' his mother urged. 'Such a little thing!'

'Tenant that worry they don't like.'

'So we ain't a tenant yet. Once, Emmanuel!'

Emmanuel sighed, and shifted in the bed so that the springs creaked and twanged. 'Oy, oy,' he sighed with troubled resignation, 'once then, Rachel. Once, you understand. We don't make a habit of it.'

The great bed creaked and rattled again and David, quiet on his moonlit pillow, strained his ears to hear what his mother would say next. But she was murmuring now and his father was whispering and the words were lost among the covers and masked by the harsh sounds from the street below. He was confused by the undertones of this conversation, because they'd roused a remembered emotion, and it was one he didn't

69

welcome. It was the nagging sub-sense he'd felt when Boss-eyes came striding across to bully him into the pop shop, a feeling that things were not as they appeared to be, and that there were other and less admirable emotions at work just below the surface of the words. But the words he'd been listening to were his father's. Surely his father meant what he said. Always. Because he was a good man. And yet, there was this sense ...

He was still trying to puzzle it out when he drifted off to sleep for the third time that night.

During the next few days the speed of street games and the pounding of rote learning left him little time or energy for perplexing thoughts. His father was the same as always and Alfie was hidden behind the big boys' wall, so he forgot the puzzle he couldn't solve and went back to enjoying his life one day at a time.

But then late one Friday afternoon, just before Shabbas, when he'd gone to Thrawl Street with Aunty Dumpling's little dish for a ha'p'orth of jam, Boss-eyes suddenly barred his way.

''Ang about kid,' he ordered. 'How d'yer like to earn another tanner?' He was stooping so that his face was immediately in front of David's, but he didn't seem to be looking at him, not even with one of his flickering eyes.

'Vell ... ' David said, anxiety and doubt returning, 'I don't know.'

'Worf yer while,' Boss-eyes said. 'Tell yer what. Make it eightpence this time. Whatcher say?'

Eightpence was a very tempting offer, and perhaps he'd been wrong about this man. It was hard to tell if a person was honest when they couldn't look you in the eye. He should ask him maybe. It wouldn't hurt to ask. But that might make him cross, and then again it was very nearly Shabbas, and there wouldn't be time for a long conversation because he had to be home before dusk. It was very difficult ...

'Whatcher say?' Boss-eyes insisted. He was such a very *big* man and the width of his body was making David feel intimidated.

'All right,' he said and was annoyed at himself because he hadn't asked after all, and he was almost certain it was wrong.

He was so deep in his thoughts he didn't notice Ellie

Murphy who was crouched on the steps of the Frying Pan waiting for her father to come out and give her some money for the family supper. But she saw him.

'You're a mug!' she said, getting up from the step and walking towards him.

'None a' your business,' he answered. Trust Smelly Ellie to put her oar in.

She strolled round his averted body until they were face to face. 'You'll end up in quod, you work fer 'im,' she warned. ' 'E's a crook.'

' 'E ain't.'

'End up in quod,' she repeated, nodding wisely.

The nod infuriated him. It was nothing to do with her, and she was horribly dirty this evening, her hands more black grease than flesh, and her hair matted and dusty. 'Push off, Smelly!' he said, glad that his father was nowhere near to hear him being so rude to a girl.

'That's a mug's game, that ol' ring trick,' she said, not a bit abashed. 'We 'ad a bloke up the Flowery used ter work it oncest. 'E got five years. You wanna watch out.'

'Five years in prison?' he said, colouring. She was making him feel afraid now as well as angry. Why couldn't she mind her own business?

'They'll do you an' all, you go along wi' that lot. You ain't got much sense, 'ave yer?'

'I'm earnin' money fer my Ma,' he said proudly, his mouth set and determined because she was making him feel used and foolish now, and he had to try to redress the balance.

'You're a mug, Davey Cheifitz. They've took you fer a ride. An M-U-G.' She was grinning at him, enjoying his misery, beginning to skip and chant, 'Muggy muggy Cheifitz!' Horrible hateful girl!

'I vould rather be mug than thief,' he said. 'You are thief. I seen yer.'

'No you never.'

'I did. You vas nickin' apples in the Lane. I seen yer.'

She gave him a look of withering scorn. 'Oh do me a favour,' she said. 'That ain't nickin'.' How else was she supposed to eat if she didn't help herself to food? '*You* was

71

workin' a con trick and you don't even know it. Brass them rings are. Tuppence ha'penny a dozen. They buy 'em wholesale. Brass!'

'No they ain't!'

'They are.'

'They give me five bob. Fer a *gold* ring. Gold!'

'*Yours* was gold. That's the trick. All them others was brass. You're a mug, Davey Cheifitz! You've been 'ad!'

He ran at her, fists raised as if to strike her, 'Shut your face, you!' as though she was a boy. How dare she tell him things like that? Especially when he knew they were true. But she ducked out of the way behind the thick shawl and wide skirts of a passing street seller, emerging on the other side to chant again. 'Oh-oh, 'it girls, do yer?'

'No!' he yelled at her. 'I don't.'

'Cowardy cowardy custard!'

'I ain't!'

'Y'are!'

People were beginning to look at him, but he was too far gone in rage to care. He was angry at her for taunting him and criticizing him and daring to tell him the truth; and he was angry at Mr Crusher and Boss-eyes for exploiting him and making him feel shamed and feeble; and he was angry at himself for being so weak-willed and so stupid, because she was right, he *had* been taken for a ride.

'Push off!' he yelled at her, backing away, because he was going to cry and he didn't want her to see.

'Cry baby cry!' she jeered, following him to press home her advantage. 'Stick yer finger in yer eye, an' cry baby cry!'

He ran from her, tears welling from his eyes, and he ran headlong, because he knew if he stayed anywhere near her he would hit her. He wouldn't be able to stop himself. He was so hot with anger and shame he had to hit something, and if she was in the way it would be her, he knew it. His outstretched hands touched the wall of Mrs Levy's shop, and at that his anger exploded and he pummelled the brick with his fists until his knuckles were torn, sobbing aloud in an extremity of fury and anguish.

'Great stupid baby!' her voice said disparagingly behind him.

He turned, tear-streaked and furious so that they were face to dirty face. 'I hate you!' he said.

Even that didn't put her off. 'See if I care!' she said, and walked away into the crowds, her spine poker straight and her tatty head held high. Horrible, horrible girl.

The minute he was sure she couldn't see him he began to run home, tear-stained and blood smeared and aching for comfort.

Chapter Six

Ellie Murphy was cross and upset too but, unlike David, she didn't run home for comfort, because hers wasn't the sort of home anybody would run to for anything. In fact she spent quite a lot of her time planning the day when she would run away from it. Now she walked towards it slowly and with dignity, her skirt swinging against her legs and the ostrich feathers on her black straw hat bouncing jauntily behind her.

She knew she was poor and dirty and that the other kids poked fun at her and despised her, but that was no reason to give in. She'd known all her short life that the only way to survive was to fight back, and if you couldn't fight back openly and physically, you fought inside your head. One day, when she was grown up, she would fight her way out of Whitechapel, and right away from her parents too. When she was grown up and she'd 'bettered herself'. She wasn't quite sure what you had to do to better yourself, but she knew she wanted to do it, whatever it was. For she'd seen girls who'd bettered themselves, and she knew that they dressed in stylish clothes and rode about in carriages and always had plenty to eat. Like Mrs Quinton's daughter, who came back to Wentworth Street twice a year, like a lady. One day, she'd be just like that. No matter what happened to her, she wouldn't let them grind her down. She'd fight her way out. Just see if she wouldn't!

Now as she strode through the crowds in Commercial Street pushing past barrows and swaying her skinny body away from loaded baskets and crunching feet, she was thinking furiously. That Davey Cheifitz was a stupid great baby. The idea, calling her a thief! How else would she get fed if she didn't nick things? It was all very well for boobies like him, with aunts to make cakes for 'em and meals all set out nice with a plate for everybody. Oh, she knew. She'd seen it at Ruby Miller's house. All nice and easy for them it was. She had to make shift for herself, because it wasn't like that in Dorset Street.

Dorset Street was a terrible place to live. Worse than the Flowery and that was bad enough. Jack the Ripper had killed two of his victims there, so Ma said, one at No 35 and the other in Miller's Court, right next door to Mrs Fahey's lodging house, where they'd all been for the last six months. And the cops had never caught him. He could start up again any time, Mrs Fahey said. It was enough to make yer flesh creep just thinking about it. She wished they'd hurry up and move on somewhere else. She knew they weren't paying the rent. She'd heard Mrs Fahey asking her mother for it only yesterday. So they'd probably get kicked out pretty soon, or do a moonlight.

In the middle of Commercial Street Ellie had to stop and wait while three trams rattled past, their open top decks crowded with well-dressed passengers, bonnets nodding at bowlers and top hats like chimneys. Her anger faded as she waited, because she could see the corner of Dorset Street from where she stood and the mere sight of it was enough to bring her down from any emotion. By the time she reached the Britannia beerhouse on the corner, her shoulders were drooping with resignation.

Everything about this street was sordid and ugly. The buildings rose forbiddingly from pavements so broken and dirty they looked more like earth paths than paving stones, and a rank black earth at that, and there were kids everywhere, boys kicking and fighting, infants crawling and squalling, and skinny girls bent sideways by the weight of the huge babies they carried on their hips. ' 'Lo Ellie,' they said as she passed. 'Your Ma's been lookin' out fer you.'

She didn't doubt it. Her Ma was always looking out for her, and always for the same reason. She wanted her to look after the babies, and clean their dirty bums, and lug them about with her, and joggle them to sleep when they grizzled. That was an older daughter's lot in Dorset Street and although she did it, to help her mother who was always harassed, she hated it and resented it, especially when her father came home drunk and knocked them all about.

She dodged past the two slatternly women who were lolling against the doorpost, smoking their pipes, and ducked into Mrs Fahey's greasy hall. There was another woman asleep on the stairs, sprawled on her back with her mouth wide open and her neck and cheeks a dull ugly red. Ellie recognized a drunk when she saw one, and stepped round her on tiptoe, careful not to touch her or disturb her in any way. She might not be very good at sums and reading but she knew exactly how to cope with life in Dorset Street.

Her mother was making matchboxes, working with nervous speed and a great economy of movement, folding the fragile boxes with her left hand, flicking the glue brush to right and left, pinching the edges together for a sticky second between thumb and forefinger, fold, flick, pinch, fold, flick, pinch, like a machine. Her face was empty with concentration, and she was surrounded by flies which crawled up the window and the glue-splashed curtain, and circled her head and hands, avid for the paste. The bigger of her two current babies, two-year-old Frankie, was hammering her knees with his fists and screaming for attention, and the smaller, baby Teresa, who was seventeen months old, was busy eating the crushed remains of a box that hadn't stuck properly, but her mother paid no attention to either of them, and didn't even look up from her work when Ellie came in.

In her youth she'd been considered a beauty, a slim, long-legged creature, with thick dark hair, and fine blue eyes 'set in with sooty fingers'. When she first married Paddy Murphy people said they made a really handsome couple, good Catholics both, he so broad-shouldered and wide of face, with a shock of thick brown hair and bland blue eyes and the look of boy, even though he was turned thirty-five, she so petite and feminine beside him. But now their beauty was gone. Drink had removed most of his teeth and thinned his hair and mottled his face with purple. Poverty and incessant pregnancy and the demands of too many children had ruined her. Although she was only twenty-six, her skin was sallow and her teeth bad and all her lissom shapeliness forgotten. Occasionally she would look at young Ellie and wonder if she would grow up to be a beauty too, but for most of her time she

76

was too busy struggling for an existence to think about anything else. Tuppence a gross was the going rate for matchboxes and it took her the best part of a day to earn it.

'Pick our Frankie up, Ellie, will yer?' she said mildly. 'See if you can find sommink ter pacify him. Sommink little fer 'im ter suck.'

It was easier said than done, for there wasn't very much available in their squalid room. Only dirty cups and plates, and the two beds and a collection of orange boxes that served first as chairs and cupboards and then as firewood. And the sack full of matchboxes, of course. Ellie knew that what the kid wanted was something to eat, but there was no food for any of them yet. Food was bought in ha'p'orths and pinches when they could afford it, and only her mother's meagre earnings were really dependable. When the matchboxes were finished she'd be sent to buy bread and marg and a pinch of tea. Until then she'd have to find something else.

Frankie didn't make things easy for her. When she bent to pick him up he threw up his arms and arched his back against her, resisting with all his force, which was considerable, for he was a big boy with his father's heavy bones. She held his stiff screaming body slung across her hip and rummaged about in the tin pail until she found a spoon for him to suck. His trousers were soaking wet and he was even grubbier than she was, but she had long grown immune to carrying damp smelly babies about. It was the natural condition of infants in the Murphy household, and at least it dried in time and didn't have to be wiped off and burnt in the fire like shit.

'On'y another dozen, then I done the gross,' her mother said, flicking and sticking. 'See if they're stuck sufficient ter pack, there's a good gel.'

Ellie set her spoon-sucking brother on the floor and sat on her haunches between him and the pile of finished boxes so that she could test them with her fingers, and he couldn't touch them. Some of them were still quite tacky. 'Not quite,' she was saying when Mrs O'Leary came running in from the next room, wild hair flying.

'Mrs Murphy!' she yelled. 'Look sharp an' clear the room for the love of God. Here's your Patrick out in the street, brawling so he is, an' Amy says he's broke her father's head, an' the pair o' them drunk as lords. Saints preserve us! What'll he say when he sees the state of this room?'

It was a rhetorical question for they all knew what he would say and, even worse, they'd all seen what he could do, particularly when he was roaring drunk. Ellie had the sack open at once. Tacky or not, the boxes had to be under the bed and out of sight before he got up the stairs.

They worked quickly and together, saying little and thinking fast. But the glue was still on the table and at least a dozen boxes still on the floor when they heard him crashing up the stairs and shouting at the drunken woman, 'Shift your ogly carcase out uv me way, woman!'

Mrs O'Leary departed as swiftly as she'd arrived and Ellie crawled under the bed, scooping the sack and the remaining boxes after her.

'Where are me darlin' boyohs?' he roared, lurching into the room, arms outstretched, and with his two filthy mongrels at his heels. 'Let me see 'em. Patrick! Seamus! Come to your Dadda. A finer pair a' boyohs the good Lord never did create. An' I challenge onyone to call me a liar.' Then as he couldn't see his two favourites, despite the most determined effort to focus his eyes, his tone became truculent. 'What've you done wid me boys, woman?'

Mrs Murphy slid the glue pot onto the recess shelf and brushed the table clear of matchbox splinters, her hands quick and nervous. 'Don't start all on at me,' she said, and fear made her voice sharp. 'They'll be out street-rakin' most like.'

'No son of mine should be out in the street when his Dadda comes home,' her husband roared and aimed a blow at his two howling infants, fortunately missing them both. 'Hold your *noise*, will ye!'

The two dogs flung themselves down beside the stove, panting. The air in the room was more rank than ever, with the smell of their dirty fur and their master's beer-laden sweat added to the stink of fish glue and stale piss. Frankie began to cry again. 'Ma! Ma! Ma!' in his incessant deafening way. Pick 'im up quick, Ellie thought, or it'll put Pa in a paddy, sure as fate. But her father was already in a paddy because he'd seen the glue pot.

78

'Woman!' he roared. 'Have I not told ye? Have I not made mesself abondantly clear in this matter? I will not tolerate clotter in me home. A man's home is his castle, so it is. I've a right fer to be obeyed in me own home, and not to come in when I'm weary wi' work and find fish glue all over me table. Clear it from me sight, d'ye hear. 'Tis an abhorrence to me.'

'There you are! It's all hidden away,' her mother cajolled. 'All nice an' tidy. Now you jest sit on the bed an' let me take yer boots off. You'll feel all the better for yer boots off.' She spoke placatingly as if he were a fractious child, and the wheedling note in her voice annoyed her daughter, crouched in her dusty sanctum under the bed.

'An' so I should think,' her father growled, sitting on the bed so suddenly and violently that the springs sagged until they touched her shoulders. 'How mony more times have I to tell ye? I can't abide this work ye do. Can't abide it, y'onderstand. Ye've ter stop it at once, or I shall know the reason why.'

Mrs Murphy ignored the menace in his voice and went on placatingly, 'Jest 'old yer foot up, there's a dear,' as if he were a little boy.

But to Ellie, he was huge and horrible, filling every inch of the room. And so unjust, abusing Ma for working. She only did it because he wouldn't work himself. He was always full of talk about how he was 'on the point of getting the best job that ever was' and how they'd all be rich, but the child knew that all he ever actually did was to go round scrounging, and that he spent the money he cadged on drink and wouldn't give them any for food. Ellie had no illusions about her father. He was a coarse, idle bully and she hated him with a terrified passionate intensity, and pitied her mother for all the dreadful dirty jobs she had to do because of him. Now Ellie sat in the darkness under the bed and aimed her resentment at his boots, brooding but alert, because she knew only too painfully how dangerous he could be when he was drunk. And as she brooded she noticed that a small pile of matchboxes still lay on the floorboards near the table. He'd be bound to see 'em, the minute he looked that way. She'd better make a grab for 'em quick, or there'd be hell to pay.

She put out a tentative hand, and moved it slowly and very

very carefully towards the pile, knowing that a sudden movement would attract his eye. But her caution was in vain. At the very moment her fingers touched the thin wood, her father let out a roar and before she could withdraw her hand he'd jumped up and stamped on her fingers with his one booted foot. The pain was so excruciating she let out a cry despite herself. 'Have I not made mesself clear?' he shouted, kicking the offending boxes into smithereens. 'I will *not* have this clotter in my house. A man's house is his castle, so it is. And another ting! I will have *obedience* in mine! Is that onderstood? Come out from onder that bed or I'll skin you alive.' The dogs leapt about his busy feet, barking with hysterical excitement, and Mrs Murphy picked up her babies, one under each arm, and moved out of harm's way behind the table.

'Oh come on, Paddy,' she tried. 'She didn't mean no 'arm.'

Ellie crawled from under the bed, still wincing, and stood before him, her injured hand under her armpit for a little warmth to ease it. She needed to cry but was afraid of his wrath. The dogs were barking like things demented and both the babies were screaming. Behind her father's back, her mother was mouthing 'Say sorry' at her, but she was rigid with pride and pain and anger, and certainly wasn't going to apologize.

But luckily for her, this time there wasn't any need to say or do anything. Paddy Murphy was already dizzy with beer, and his sudden activity had made him worse. He crashed back on the bed again and closed his eyes, belching and groaning, 'Onfasten me boot for the love of God.' His wife took action quickly, setting Frankie on the floor and handing baby Teresa to her sister. The sooner he was asleep the better for all of them. She removed his boot, unbuttoned his waistcoat and hauled his legs into a more comfortable position, while he belched and farted and grumbled that she was lugging him about 'like a sack a' taters'. But within five minutes he was asleep and snoring, even though both babies were still grizzling, and both dogs yapping.

They gave him another five minutes just to make perfectly sure he wouldn't wake, and then they turned him on his side and went through his pockets. He had three pennies, a ha'penny and three farthings on him. It was enough. 'Nip down the chip shop, there's a good gel,' Mrs Murphy said. 'We'll 'ave fish an' a penn'orth, an' see if you can get 'im ter throw in a pickled onion.'

On her way to the fish and chip shop Ellie examined her aching hand. The flesh was scraped from all four knuckles and purple bruises were already beginning to darken her fingers. 'I hate 'im!' she said to herself. 'Hate 'im! Hate 'im!' When she was older she'd be revenged on him. She'd make him suffer. Just see if she wouldn't. 'I hate 'im!' But just for the moment she'd use her bleeding knuckles to scrounge a few more chips. Old Stan in the fish shop had a soft heart, and if she put her hands on the counter while she waited he'd be sure to notice. Which was more than her mother had, or ever did.

In Fashion Street David had the undivided attention of three adults, even though they were all very distressed and poor Aunty Dumpling was rocking in her seat, her apron in constant fluttering action. When he'd first come rushing home, breathless and dishevelled and bloodstained, there'd been instant concern and uproar. His mother and his aunt took one hand apiece and started treatment at once, scolding and shaking their heads.

'Oy-oy! Davey, bubeleh, how you come to be in such a state? So he'll be the death of me, Dumpling.'

'Such a boy. Don't I tell you, Rachel. Hold your little hand quite still, bubeleh.'

To his great relief, they were too concerned to question him, closely. But when his hands had been cleaned to their satisfaction and sprinkled with boracic powder and bandaged in lint and strips of sheeting, his father came home, and then of course the whole story had to be told and even supper was held up until they'd 'got to the bottom of it'. Now they waited while Emmanuel considered, tugging the sparse hairs of his long straggly beard and sighing.

'Vhy you not tell me all this vhen it begin?' he said at last, looking at his son. His face was very long and very stern and his eyes were solemn, but at least his voice was gentle.

81

Slightly encouraged, David dared an answer. It had to be the truth, because nothing less would do for such a father and such a time. 'Vhen it begin, I didn't know ... ' he stammered, and then stopped for he realized the words weren't completely true. He *had* suspected, even at the start, but he hadn't wanted to believe evil of his friend. He'd put such thoughts away from him, and now they'd caught up with him and he was ashamed and embarrassed. 'It vas a good job. Good money ... '

'Money ain't everything,' Mama said, her face wrinkled with concern. 'Money ve can live vithout. So vhere's your pride?'

'Ai-yi-yi,' Aunty Dumpling wailed, covering her head with her apron again. 'My liddle Davey!' she mourned, muffled under the heavy linen. 'Vorkin' vid a *shtunk*!'

'I *am* sorry!' David said, looking from one to the other of them, mouth trembling. 'I vish I hadn't. I didn't know it vas wrong. Not wrong like a cheat ... '

'Now you know,' his father said solemnly.

'Oh yes. Yes.'

'Ve should be in the Buildin's,' his mother said and the look she gave her husband was like an accusation. 'This never vould've happen, ve got a place in the Buildin's. A nice Jewish community, plenty support, nice Jewish kids for him to play with. Never would've happen.'

Why was she angry with Papa? David thought. What was she accusing him for? Oh dear, this was getting worse and worse, and it was all his fault.

'You get a place some day, Rachel,' Aunty Dumpling said soothingly, giving the little scowling nod that was a sign she was trying to encourage and cheer.

'Some day!' his mother said bitterly. 'Alvays some day. Jerusalem next year! I shall be dead and buried before I'm in the Buildin's. Vhy you don't ask, Emmanuel, I simply don't understand.'

'Ve talk of this some other time,' Emmanuel said, warning her with a quick glance at the child. 'Ve got trouble enough vithout ve go looking for it.'

'Ai-yi-yi!' Aunt Dumpling wailed, disappearing under her apron again. 'Poor liddle Davey! Ai-yi-yi!'

'So vhat ve do about him, Emmanuel?' his mother asked,

her forehead corrugated with anxiety. 'Vhat you think? You got to say, Emmanuel. This time you got to correct him. Ve should've correct him vhen he vas young. Don't I know it! None a' this happen then, you ask me. So you don't ask me, I know, I know. Now you tell me.' And she gave Emmanuel a long, hard, waiting look, and wouldn't even glance at her son. And Aunty Dumpling emerged from her apron for the answer and didn't look at him either.

Emmanuel gave judgement. 'It is summertime,' he said. 'He should be vid other childer, out a' doors, at play. This he must forfeit. A child who is too foolish to know vhich men to trust must stay vithin doors. You understand this, David? You shall go to shul, you shall walk on the Shabbas, you shall run errands. No more than this. No games, for they lead to temptation. This you accept, nu?'

It wasn't a question. It was a statement of conduct expected. But David agreed with it anyway. It was entirely just, and it felt like a protection. If he stayed indoors he wouldn't have to face Mr Crusher and explain why he'd failed to turn up on Sunday. 'Yes, Father,' he said meekly. And his mother smiled at him at last.

Nevertheless it was a hard punishment, for he enjoyed the street games so much and yearned to be out in the sunshine. He ran as many errands as he could, for his mother and the lady along the corridor and Aunty Dumpling and anyone else who asked, but he was always scrupulously careful to run all the way there and back and to stay no longer than absolutely necessary, because he was working out his punishment and it was a matter of pride to do it properly. But he missed his friends with an aching emptiness that made each day longer and longer, and after a week he took to sitting beside the window so that he could watch them in the street below.

'We should let him out for an hour or two, now, maybe?' Rachel urged, for the sight of his pale streaked face peering from the window made her yearn with pity for him. It was a long punishment for a child so young, and she felt worse about it because she'd urged it so strongly.

But Emmanuel was adamant. 'We make a decision, we stick to it,' he said. 'He must learn, Rachel. This time we must be cruel to be kind.'

In the end Hymie the Brain found a solution for them all. Or to be more accurate, Hymie the Brain's measles.

Hyman Levy was the youngest in a large family, and his mother cared for him like a hothouse plant, fussing over his health and constantly anxious. After such a debilitating disease as the measles, there was no question of him being allowed out in the streets until at least three weeks had passed, and even then she would have to think about it most seriously. But she and Rachel saw nothing to prevent him from trotting next door and spending a few hours playing with David, 'Now and then, and providing they are both quiet and sensible, nu?'

Now and then rapidly became every afternoon, for the two boys were glad of each other's company, and soon found that they had a lot in common. They went to the same shul, and had puzzled over the same passages from the Torah, and now they were both waiting for the Day of Atonement, for they both felt they'd offended their parents, one through disobedience which he was sure had led to illness, the other through foolishness which he was sure had led to crime. So they talked, and pondered the difficulty of life, and comforted one another, and their mothers were well pleased by their seriousness.

On the third afternoon Hymie came to the house with a copy of the *Daily Graphic*, and the two boys read the news, which they decided was rather boring, and David discovered a cartoon. He'd never seen such a drawing before and found it intriguing.

'Vhy they draw this man with such a big head?' he asked his knowledgeable friend.

'It's what they do,' Hymie explained. 'It's ter make yer laugh, I think. They always draw the bodies littler an' the 'eads bigger. Some things bigger'n they really are, some things smaller. It's called a cartoon. That one's got a big hooter. Look!'

'I could do that,' David said, studying the little drawing. 'I'll bet.'

So they found pencil and brown paper.

'So who you draw?' Hymie asked, settling himself on the other side of the table.

84

'Guess!' David said, and he began with the straight lines of a small flat body, pin-tucked bodice, straight skirt, pointed feet. The huge oval head took several attempts to get to the right shape, but he didn't rub anything out because he was working so quickly, and presently the face began to emerge, with a small cottage-loaf bun right on top of the skull, and two black dots for eyes set in the centre of a pair of enormous spectacles, and an inverted crescent for a mouth, a very mean inverted crescent.

'It's the Killer!' Hymie said. 'That's ever so good. Let me 'ave a go.'

His Killer was a copy and rather a lopsided one, and while he was busy with it David went on to draw his father, striding legs like black v-shaped scissors, and a long body, stooping forward, and a long straggly beard composed of short wavy pencil lines, and a long nose like a sharp triangle poking out from under the brim of that familiar black hat.

'They're ever so good, your drawings,' Hymie said, with genuine admiration.

David shrugged, because it wouldn't have done to appear proud. If he had a talent it was necessary to be modest about it. But then he smiled. And went on smiling until his face was glowing with the pleasure of praise and achievement. 'We draw some more tomorrow, nu?' he said.

From then on they spent a part of each afternoon drawing cartoons: Aunty Dumpling, bosom like a bolster, two fat chins one under the other, button nose and round eyes; Mrs Finkleheim with that wart on her chin, hairs and all, and her untidy eyebrows, like the spines on a porcupine; Hymie himself, his short dark hair a series of straight pencil lines sticking up in the air, his nose curved like a beak, his brown eyes very close together in the inner curves of his round spectaclesl; the obvious features made bigger, the unremarkable ones ignored.

'This holiday,' Hymie remarked, admiring his portrait, 'can go on as long as it likes.'

But September was approaching fast, and soon they would be back at school and up in the big boys, and David would have to face his hero and explain why he hadn't turned up that

85

Sunday afternoon. Because he *had* given his word, and Alfie *was* his friend, and even if Mr Crusher was doing something illegal, that didn't make Alfie a crook too. Did it? No, surely not. Alfie was one of the best boys in the school. But what could he possibly say about it all? How could he explain? His spirits quailed at the mere thought.

'One thing,' Hymie comforted, 'we shan't 'ave to 'ave nothink ter do with that Smelly Ellie now.'

'Nor the Killer,' David said.

But they were wrong.

Chapter Seven

All through the long bug-bitten days of August while the streets of Whitechapel grew dirtier and more evil-smelling by the hour, Ellie had been looking forward to September and green gardens. Her dreams were sweet with the smell of hop fields, and after a supper of stolen bread and half-rotten fruit, she remembered meals in the open air, sausages tasting of charcoal, fried bread dripping fat, and cocoa made with that odd rich country milk. She would walk through the narrow alleys by Spitalfields Market and be cheered because she knew that in Kent the fields would be wide and the sky high above her head, and that soon she would be there.

The Murphy family went hopping for three weeks every September, leaving their debts and their worries behind them, and for Ellie it was the best time of the whole year. Even when it rained and their makeshift tents let in water, and the adults all around her began the day cold and grumbling, she skipped off to the farm shop for their milk and bread and tea, singing to herself with pleasure. It was a good life out in the fields, sitting astride the bin frame as though it were a horse, and skimming the furry hops from the bines with both hands, quick, quick, oh so quick, and everybody saying what a fine picker she was.

And her father was much better behaved out in the countryside too. He still drank a great deal and came roaring home from the local inn in the darkness, lurching from hedge to hedge, with his dogs yapping at his heels, and then pretended to get into the wrong bed once he was in the tent and made all the other women screech and giggle, but he was more likely to be affable than violent. And although it was annoying to hear him bragging about his country childhood when she knew very well he'd been born and bred in Belfast, she had to admit he worked hard once they sounded the hooter in the morning, even when he had a thick head. Her two brothers, Paddy and Seamus, were as lazy as ever, of course, but here at least they were expected to help and she was allowed to give 'em a whack if they were slacking. Which she did as often as she could and with enormous satisfaction, because they were a right pair a' horrers, proper little toughs, and they needed knocking into shape.

But that September was different, although it began well enough, with two days of warm sunshine and easy picking. Really good days. Too good to last, the old hands said. And although they were mocked for their pessimism, they were right. For many of the families scrambling from the train at Marden Station on that cheerful outward trek were unwittingly carrying an extra item of luggage with them that year, and the item was incubating.

On the third morning, Seamus refused to get up. He lay in the straw bed he shared with Ellie and his two younger brothers and groaned. 'Leave orf, Ellie. I'm poorly.'

'I'll give yer poorly,' his sister said. 'You ain't gettin' out a' your share wiv a trick like that, an' don't you think it. Get up this minute or I'll give yer whatfor.'

But when she pulled him out from under the blanket, he lay on the floor where she'd dropped him, as though he'd lost the use of his legs, and at that Mr Murphy came lumbering across in the half-light to see what was the matter.

'What's op wid me boyoh?' he asked, lifting the child onto his knee.

'Me eyes hurt,' Seamus said, rubbing them.

All the other inhabitants of the tent came gathering round too, and Mrs Shaunnessy brought the kerosene lamp with her and held it over their heads so that the cone of its oily light would illuminate the bed, for it was six in the morning and there was precious little daylight inside the tent. 'Sickenin' for something,' she said, feeling the child's forehead with her rough palm. 'Take my word fer it, Mrs Murphy.'

'That's all we need!' Nell Murphy said, peering at his flushed face with concern. 'Got a pain anywhere, 'ave yer, lovey?'

'Course 'e ain't,' Ellie said scornfully. 'There's nothink the matter wiv 'im. 'E's puttin' it on.'

'Nobody arsked you!' her mother said without looking at her. 'You go an' get the milk. Make yerself useful an' stop being so jealous.' Then changing the tone of her voice from slap sharp to soothing gentle, 'Tell yer old Ma, Seamus, where's it 'urt?'

' 'E'd get up quick enough if it was fish an' chips,' Ellie said angrily as she left the tent.

'Have I to take me strap to ye?' her father roared, displaying his authority for the admiration of the women and children gathered about him. 'Be off wid yer!' And his two mongrels barked their agreement.

It was chilly outside the tent. And spooky too. Silhouetted against the grey sky in the distance she could see the odd peaked shapes of the oast houses, like giants squatting on their haunches, waiting to jump out at her. Even the hop bines looked different in this odd half-light, taller than they did by day, and sinister, shifting and rustling as though they were whispering about her behind her back. She walked past them as quickly as she could, keeping her eyes on the distant envelope of yellow light that was the window of the farm shop, and concentrating her mind on her grievances. Seamus was a lazy little tike, that's all it was. Now he'd be allowed to roll around in bed all day and she'd have to do all his work as well as her own and that wasn't fair. It was bad enough having to pick hops *and* look after those two awful babies. Tessie'd done nothing but grizzle ever since they arrived. If it wasn't for Cissie Henderson and her cousin Polly, there'd be no fun at all.

The Henderson family were working on the next bin along the alley and by dint of sitting on the side of their bins, the three girls could talk to one another while they were working.

'Where's your Seamus?' Cissie asked later that day.

'Pullin' a fast one,' Ellie said and told her two friends all about it.

'That's boys all over,' Cissie said, nodding her tousled head wisely. 'Proper lazy lot they are. I reckon they're jest a nuisance. Worse'n babies, an' that's sayin' something.'

89

All three girls had babies to look after, and they spent quite a lot of their picking time comparing notes on the weight and intractability of their charges.

'I tell you what,' Ellie said, pulling her next bine across her knee, 'you won't catch me 'avin' babies when I grow up. Not likely.'

'You won't 'ave ter get married then,' Polly said, skimming the hops from the bine with both hands. 'You get married you 'ave babies sure as fate.'

It was very true. They'd seen enough of life in Dorset Street to know that. Weddings were always followed by babies. Look at that Minnie O'Malley. She'd only been married six weeks and she had a baby boy already, and a horrible yowly smelly thing *he* was.

'Shan't get married then,' Ellie said. ' 'Cause I tell yer, you won't catch me luggin' babies about all me life. I got better things ter do.'

'Like what?' Cissie asked.

'I dunno jest yet-awhile,' Ellie admitted. 'Better'n this though.'

'You ready for your vittles, daughter?' Mr Murphy called as he returned from one of his trips to the bushes.

' 'Course!' Ellie said. When had she ever been known to refuse food? 'Whatcher bet Seamus'll be there wiv 'is plate,' she said to her friends. 'Just see if 'e ain't.'

But he wasn't. And he didn't eat any supper either, even though it was bangers and mash. So perhaps he was ill after all.

Her mother had no doubt about it. 'D'yer think we ought ter go 'ome,' she said, squinting her anxiety at her husband.

'No, no, Nell,' her husband said, putting their takings into his waistcoat pocket, 'there's no call for to be pre-mature. We will see how the little chap is in the morn, so we will. Onyway, I've a little matter uv business to attend to mesself this evenin', so I have. So it's all out of our hands, d'ye see. There's no question of travellin' till the morn.' And with that he was off, his dogs trotting behind him.

'Business, my eye!' his wife growled to her companions round the camp fire. ' 'E must think I'm daft. Kid could be at deaf's door, wouldn't stop 'im. He's off up the pub.'

'That's men for yer,' Mrs Shaunnessy said. 'A poor lot, so they are. An' never where they's wanted.'

Ellie, watching from the other side of their leaping fire, agreed with her entirely.

The next morning Paddy said he felt ill too, Tessie sicked up her breakfast, and Seamus, who'd been groaning and muttering and coughing and keeping Ellie awake all night, had a rash all over his face.

'Holy Mary Mother o' God, it's the measles,' Mrs Shaunnessy diagnosed, crossing herself fervently. 'An' a mortal high fever, poor little soul. He'll be delirious be nightfall I shouldn't wonder. They always gets worse be night. May the good Lord preserve him, Mrs Murphy.'

Measles, Ellie thought with a flickering of alarm inside her chest. Tha's bad, ain't it? Her mother looked at though it was.

'I knew 'e was sickenin'!' Nell said, smoothing the child's sticky hair. 'We should never 'ave come 'ere, Mrs Shaunnessy. Out in the wilds like this, wiv no doctors or nothink. What's ter become of 'im?' She was tremulous with indecision and worry.

'Sponge him down for a start,' Mrs Shaunnessy advised. 'Nip down the tap, Ellie, there's a good little girl, an' see if you can't get a nice fresh bucket o' water for your poor little brother.'

The way they order you about, Ellie thought mutinously as she trailed through the mud of last night's rain to the tap at the far end of the field. Now that Shaunnessy woman's doing it too. Why does it always 'ave ter be me? It's not my fault the kid's got the measles. Why can't Pa get up and fetch the water for a change? The full pail was extremely heavy. She could only carry it by leaning over sideways, and that made her back ache from her neck to her bum. 'I hate 'em all!' she said between gritted teeth.

But as she drew near to the tent again, she forgot about the measles and hating people and the weight of the pail because her father was shouting like he did when he was going to hit somebody, and the note of violent anger in his voice made her instantly afraid. She fancied she could see his shadow on the canvas, right arm raised to strike, and she struggled on fearfully, with the slopping bucket banging against her legs, until she fell in through the tent flap, her heart thumping. The little space was full of people, all on their feet and all shouting, their shadows mimicking them on the green canvas behind them.

'You will *not*!' her father was roaring. And he *was* threatening to hit her mother. 'How mony more times have I to tell yer? I'll not have my son and heir killed by your stupid folly, not if I have to break every stupid bone in your stupid body to do it. D'ye hear me, Nell? Travellin' is out o' the question. Out o' the question entirely.'

'Oh that's lovely, innit!' Mrs Williams was yelling. 'Stay 'ere, I should. Selfish brute! Give it to all the kids in the camp, I should! We got kids too, yer know. We don't wanna catch your rotten diseases. You keep right away from that bed, Elsie!'

'If you poke your great nose into my affairs, I'll lay one on ye, so I will!' Paddy shouted, menacing her.

'That's all ye'r fit for, Paddy Murphy! Lammin' inter women!' Mrs Williams yelled, standing toe to toe with him, and not a bit afraid. 'Clear off out of it, why dontcher. We don't want yer! That's a killin' disease, the measles. Yer got no business bein' 'ere, none of yer.'

Killing? Ellie thought. It ain't. But the note of hysteria in the tent was unmistakable, and it got through to her, despite her determined opposition to it. Mrs Williams was gathering her things. She meant it. Kids died a' the measles. It was true. They died. Holy Mary Mother o' God, don't let it be me, she prayed, glancing at the two flushed faces on her straw bed.

'It ain't my fault, Mrs Williams,' her mother was saying, in her whining placating voice. 'I'll be off like a shot, the minute 'e gives me the tickets.'

'Do what yer like, mate,' Mrs Williams said. She was busy bundling her belongings inside her shawl. 'Makes no odds ter me. We're off out a' this tent. Come on, kids! Bring yer things. We ain't stayin' ere ter be defected.' She tied the ends of the shawl into a furious knot and stamped out of the tent, pushing her two bewildered children ahead of her.

'Stay 'ere!' Nell begged, running after her. 'You don't 'ave ter go. We're goin' 'ome!'

The tent was full of moving bodies and flailing bundles and

terrifying noises, kids crying and grown-ups shouting and both dogs howling as though it was the end of the world. A killin' disease, lurking inside her two brothers and waiting ter jump out an' get them all. She could see it leaping from their open mouths in sharp blue sparks, springing from the straw, stirred up into the air by every move they made. Sharp, evil, blue sparks that could kill yer, in the air all around her, and being blown her way by all the shouting. She was very frightened. Then she noticed that Pa was taking off his belt, and self-preservation of a different kind urged her into action. She crept round to the other side of the tent to get out of range, lugging the bucket with her.

'You are *not*!' Paddy screamed, flicking at her mother with the belt. 'How mony more times? *I* have the tickets, so *you* will stay where you are, so you will. If that blamed fool woman wants to make an exhibition of herself, then let her do it. *You* will obey your lord an' master.'

'I will *not*!' her mother shouted back, as the belt descended again. 'We're going, an' that's flat! Kids die a' the measles.' Her face was wild, eyes bolting and flesh strained from her cheekbones. 'D'yer wanna deaf on yer 'ands! Two deafs? Free? It spreads like wildfire. They'll all catch it. That what yer want?' She was struggling to force Frankie's stiff arms inside his coat and the child was screaming and threshing about on her lap.

'You are *not* goin' onywhere, Nell Murphy!' Paddy boomed. He threw the belt on the bed and, seizing Frankie's right arm, pulled it out of the coat again so that the child screamed louder than ever from the pain of his pinching fingers and the terror of his voice.

'That's right, pull 'is arms off, I should,' Nell shouted. 'That'll be a fine thing to explain ter the cops.'

The coat was ripped from the child's back and thrown into the corner of the tent, where both dogs leapt upon it and began to worry it. Frankie had screamed himself purple in the face. The tent was leaping with blue sparks.

'God rot the lot o' ye!' Paddy said. And he took his belt and whistled his dogs and went.

Ellie realized that her heart was beating violently and her

forehead was damp with sweat. If I don't get out this tent this very minute, she thought, I shall catch the measles as sure as eggs is eggs. But she couldn't follow her father, because he'd hit her.

'Beecham's Powders!' Mrs Shaunnessy said calmly into the silence. 'That's what you need. Beecham's Powders.'

'What?' Nell asked. Her face was still screwed up against the next expected blow and in the flickering light from the kerosene lamp it looked distorted as though the bones had been bent and the flesh pushed sideways.

'Best thing in the world for bringing down a fever,' Mrs Shaunnessy said. 'Two o' them today, an' you could be travellin' tomorrow. Or the next day maybe.'

Nell caught her breath and gathered her wits. 'Where'd we get 'em in a place like this?' she asked.

'Maidstone,' Mrs Shaunnessy said, tying her shawl over her shoulders. 'Market day today, so it is, an' I've a notion I heard young Jamie say they were taking the cart.'

'Run an' catch 'im, Ellie,' Nell instructed. 'See if 'e'll give yer a lift. Ask 'im nicely mind.' But the child was already out of the tent.

By the time young Mr Jamie had been found and persuaded, the measles and the fear of the measles had spread to several of the other tents. Soon Ellie had been given eleven different commissions for Beecham's Powders and a shopping basket to carry them all home in, and Cissie Henderson had been told to go with her and help her. She was very glad of the company, because Cissie was a sensible girl and knew about things.

They rattled along the narrow earth lane towards Maidstone, between rustling orchards and the long, neat alleys of the hop fields, as the sky deepened to summer blue, and the leaves stretched and spread in the gathering sun, and the pickers buzzed among the bines. It was going to be a lovely day. A lovely peaceful day.

' 'Ark at them birds,' Cissie said.

But Ellie could still see the sparks, rising from their wheels with every jolt, leaping between the horse's ears, darting in the air whenever she blinked. 'You don't die a' the measles, do yer?' she asked her friend, trying to sound casual about it, and failing.

94

'I never,' Cissie said, and her bland round face was suddenly like a shield, shining with sunlight.

'Well, there you are then,' Ellie said, much relieved.

'Izzy Isaacs did.'

'No 'e never. 'E 'ad the new-monia.'

'After the measles. New-monia after the measles.'

'Well, 'e was only one.'

'Oh there was 'undreds uv others,' Cissie said cheerfully. 'Kid at the corner shop. You remember 'im. And Johnnie Andrews' baby'. And the twins ... '

But Ellie didn't want a litany. She'd heard enough already. 'You didn't die though, did yer?' she said.

'No. I never.'

But the knowledge wasn't so comforting now. And the blue sparks followed them all the way into town.

It was market day in Maidstone and the High Street was crowded with stalls, because the hop pickers brought plenty of custom, especially on a Saturday when work had stopped for the weekend, and even in the middle of the week some of them could be expected to wander down to pick up a bargain.

It was just striking nine when the cart ground to a halt outside the Red Lion.

'You got an hour,' young Mr Jamie told them. 'Back 'ere when it strikes ten, mind, or I's'l go 'ome be mesself.'

It didn't take a minute to buy the Beecham's Powders, because they sold them at the Post Office ready wrapped in little packages. They emerged from the darkness of the little low shop into the warm haze of September sunshine like children let out of school. They had a whole hour of freedom, and Ellie knew exactly what she was going to do with it.

'Come on,' she said to her friend, 'let's go shoppin'.'

'We ain't got no money,' Cissie protested.

'Oh do me a favour,' Ellie said, settling her tatty hat so that the ostrich feathers trailed down her back and not across her shoulder. 'Gotta see what I'm doin',' she explained.

She and Cissie joined the crowds ambling around the stalls, now loitering beside a particularly tempting display, now slipping like minnows between earth-stained skirts and leather-thonged moleskins towards a more available prize.

Soon their shopping basket contained a colourful selection of apples and oranges and pears, a rather battered slice of pumpkin, which had squashed in Ellie's quick hand, and two thick rinds of cheese which had been set to one side while the stall holder served one of his friends with more gossip than was wise.

'You're a one!' Cissie said admiringly. 'You'll cop it if they catch yer.'

'I'm fly!' Ellie said proudly. 'Nothink I couldn't nick if I put me mind to it.' And even as the words were in her mouth a daring idea came into her head.

There was an old clothes stall directly in front of them, the usual pile of torn shawls, carefully folded to disguise the worst of their wear, and the usual array of battered boots and shoes on the stall itself, and some quite presentable coats hanging from the rails on either side. One was just her size and hardly worn at all, even though it was very old-fashioned. She wandered forward and after waiting till the stall holder was busy with a customer, examined it carefully. It was made of dark green wool, pleasantly thick between her exploring fingers, and the row of little cloth buttons all down the front of it were in very good condition, not even scuffed at the edges. It was in rather a severe style, with a high collar and very straight sleeves, and the arms would be rather long for her, at least until she grew a bit, but it would do. For both her purposes.

'Nip round the front an' 'ave a look at the shawls,' she told Cissie. 'Pick 'em over. Make out yer might buy. Keep 'im busy.'

'You ain't never gonna nick a shawl!' Cissie said, her eyes round at the audacity of it.

'Never you mind what I'm gonna do,' Ellie said. 'You jest keep 'im occupied. Gi' me the basket.' The clock had just struck the three-quarters, the street was full of people, and her mind was made up. She had thrown out a challenge to fate, and now she couldn't go back on it. If she could steal that coat and get away with it, then the measles couldn't touch her. Until that moment, she'd never tackled anything bigger than a meat pie. A coat would need planning and daring and even more speed than usual, but she was already warm with excitement and hope. This was the way to beat infection.

96

She waited until Cissie had ambled to the other side of the stall and was picking over the shawls, and as she waited, she planned. The stall holder was a slow-moving man, and too fat to run far, even if he saw her. The stall on her left was piled with saucepans, which gave her very good cover from any eyes that might be casually looking at her from that direction. If she crouched down as soon as she'd grabbed the coat she should be able to crawl round to the back of the stall without being seen by anyone. Then she noticed that the stall was covered with a thick layer of green baize, which hung down at the back like a tent flap, and she knew at once how the thing could be done. Go on, she thought, silently urging the stall holder, she's making a right mess a' your shawls. Go an' tell 'er off. And at last the stupid man saw his unwanted customer and rolled across to deal with her.

The coat was off the rail, hanger and all, and slung onto the pavement under the stall. Quick, oh so quick, and no one the wiser. She didn't even have to crawl. All she had to do was walk calmly round to the back of the stall and sit down on the pavement as though she was tired. Then when she was quite sure nobody was looking, she put her hands behind her underneath the green baize and dragged her prize out of its hanger, rolled it into a bundle and shoved it into the basket. It was done. As simple as that.

Once they were safely on their way back to the camp, and Maidstone and the possibility of detection had disappeared behind the trees, she retrieved the coat from under the camouflage of fruit and vegetables she'd arranged on top of it, gave it a quick dust down with her fingers, and put it on.

'You look a real swell!' Cissie said. 'Whatcher gonna do wiv yer old one?' Hoppers usually chucked their old clothes in the hedge the minute they could afford something better.

Ellie was more practical. 'Keep it,' she said. 'That's good enough fer the kids to sick on. This is fer best.' And for protection, she thought, careful to keep her bargain secret.

She wore the new coat all the way home like a breastplate.

Her parents were most impressed, although her mother insisted that the coat be put away at once. 'Wrap it up all nice in brown paper,' she advised. 'Keep it hid. Someone round 'ere might recognize it, an' then what? Yer a real clever gel, yer don't wanna get caught.'

'Chip off the ol' block an' no mistake,' Paddy told his neighbours, chuckling with pleasure. He was easy with beer and had quite forgotten the ill temper of the morning. 'D'you get them powders, girlie? That'll do the trick, you jest see if it don't, Nell.'

But the powders were less impressive than the coat. Nell poured the prescribed dose down each of her son's retching throats night and morning for the next four days, but they didn't improve at all. In fact, Ellie was privately of the opinion that they were hotter than ever, especially in the middle of the night. But at least they weren't dying. And after a week they stopped groaning and rolling about, and Seamus said he was hungry.

'Tomorrow,' Mrs Shaunnessy said wisely, as Nell spooned a plateful of porridge into her son's peaky face. 'An' not a minute too soon, with the weather the way it is, heaven help us. You got them tickets, have ye?'

Nell touched the pocket in her skirt where she'd pinned the return tickets late on Saturday night when Paddy had returned from the pub too drunk to stand and too insensible to know that she was picking his pockets. 'We'll go first thing,' she said. ' 'E can do what 'e likes.'

So they left Paddy Murphy with his beer and his friends and went back to Whitechapel with as much of their takings as they could filtch from his drunken pockets or persuade from the tallyman. And twelve other families went with them. It was a train full of sickness. Ellie sat by the window nursing Tessie with one arm and trying to stop Frankie from trampling on the invalids with the other. Her new coat lay in the luggage rack above her head, and she was still perfectly fit.

It was pelting with rain when they arrived at London Bridge, long rods of white water falling vertically out of the sky, and with such force that they bounced off the cobbles straight up into the air again, sharp and white as sleet. The gutters were awash with a grey-brown torrent and the choppy surface of the River Thames was full of little black pits.

'We'll take a horse-bus,' Nell decided, lifting baby Teresa onto her shoulders and doing her best to cover the child's inadequate dress with her shawl. 'We got the money.'

But there were many other passengers with the same idea, and although several buses came dripping up to the kerb it was more than ten minutes before there was room for all the sodden Murphys on one of them, and by then both the invalids were shivering, Tessie was wet to her skin and Ellie's ostrich feathers were trailing a stream of ice-cold water down her back.

'Ne'er mind,' Nell tried to comfort. 'Soon be 'ome, eh? Chaff 'is fingers for 'im, Ellie, there's a good gel.'

Ellie took Seamus's lifeless fingers into her hands and tried to rub a little colour back into them. 'I don't 'alf feel bad, Sis,' he said.

'Soon be 'ome,' she said echoing her mother.

But the home they'd left so cheerfully just over a fortnight ago was occupied by someone else, and anyway they owed Mrs Fahey nearly three weeks' rent, so they couldn't go back there. They squelched up Commercial Street, stopping at every shop corner to read the advertisements, and growing colder and wetter and more depressed by the minute. The two boys were ghastly pale and the babies were grizzling. 'Drowned rats, the lot a' yer,' Nell teased, trying to cheer them up. Ellie's hair was stuck to her forehead and water ran down the straggly ends of her curls as though it was pouring from a tap. 'Aintcher found nothink yet?' she complained as her mother scanned the cards for a rent they could afford.

'There's a basement in Thrawl Street,' Nell said. 'Four bob a week. It's a bit steep but it might do a turn till yer Pa gets back. You stay 'ere an' I'll see what I can fix.' And she left them dripping in a doorway while she went off to try and negotiate a lower rent.

It was a square brown room which had once been the kitchen of the house when the house was a family home. It still contained the black kitchen range and a chipped butler's sink and even a cupboard in the chimney corner, but it was dark and damp and stank of rotten vegetables and cat's piss. The window was little more than a slit below the ceiling and the only furniture, apart from the fittings, was a rickety bed with a very damp straw mattress set squiffily across the springs.

Nell smudged the rain from her face with the back of her wet hand and tried to encourage them. 'Soon 'ave this fixed up lovely,' she promised. 'Don't lie on the floor, Seamus, there's a good boy.'

But Seamus felt too ill to care whether he was good or not and stayed where he was. 'We'll get a fire going,' Nell said, opening the coal hole hopefully, and finding only dust and a strong smell of mice. 'Nip up the corner, Ellie, quick as yer can. We oughter get them kids in bed.'

For the next hour and a half Ellie ran one errand after another, for coal and kindling and Beecham's Powders, to the pawn shop to redeem the blankets, and three times to the market to scrounge orange boxes, until she was so wet that the rain was running down the small of her back and her sodden shoes had rubbed blisters on both her heels. Back in their squalid room Nell coaxed their obstinate stove to light and propped the mattress in front of it to steam off the worst of the wet. She stripped her two shivering sons of their soaking clothes and wrapped them in her newly redeemed blankets and laid them on the springs. Then she sent Ellie for bread and marg and a twist of sugar and a pinch of tea, and they transformed their orange boxes into a table and four chairs, unpacked the mugs and the kettle and the teapot and made themselves a meal. The mattress was still steaming like a great straw horse and it was taking all the heat from the stove, but at least the tea was warm.

'We shall be all right now we're 'ome,' Nell said, wiping Tessie's nose on the edge of her shawl.

But Ellie felt so cold she didn't think she'd ever be all right again.

During the next few days she and her mother did what they could to transform their underground cell into a home, but it was a hard task. They cadged more boxes and bought more coal and even redeemed the table cloth and the curtains. But at night the black beetles came rustling out in their hundreds to scuttle over the hearth and the cupboards and their makeshift furniture, devouring as they went. The mice were so daring they scampered across the blankets and crawled up the bedpost, whiskers twitching in the dusty light dropping down into the room from the street above. And Ellie, lying in the damp bed while her mother snored and her brothers coughed and groaned and burned with renewed fever, missed the green fields and the smell of the hops and thought how unfair it was that she should be dragged to Whitechapel just because her brothers had the measles.

The next morning she made a bid for partial freedom.

'I oughter go ter school, Ma,' she said, as she scraped a spoonful of jam over the remains of the bread. 'Whatcher think?'

Nell didn't think much of the idea. 'Whatcher wanna go ter school for?' she said. 'You never learn nothink. Frankie, leave yer sister alone, yer bad boy. Eat yer own slice.'

'I'm s'pposed ter be up in the big girls,' Ellie said. 'You'll 'ave the School Board round.'

'Don't know where we are though, do they, lovey? Don't you go worryin' yer 'ead about school. I'll see ter the School Board. You're more use ter me 'ere.'

Which she was. It couldn't be denied. And on that awful day she was particularly useful.

By mid afternoon their dank room was growing dark and the fire was beginning to give out quite a pleasant heat. Seamus and Paddy had been sponged down, Frankie was snoring at the foot of the bed and little Tess was sitting by the hearth, playing with a string of old cotton reels. Perhaps her mother was right after all and things really were going to improve.

But then suddenly and without warning, Seamus began to rave, sitting bolt upright in the bed and clawing the air with both hands, wheezing for breath and coughing and shrieking, 'Get 'im off! Get 'im off. Don't let 'im get me, Ma!' over and over again. Nell tried to comfort and sooth but he was far beyond her, burning with fever, in a private terror she couldn't touch.

'Get Mrs O'Malley! Quick as yer can,' she said to Ellie. 'Run! Say 'e's delirious.'

He had pneumonia, of course, as Nell knew without being told, and even though Mrs O'Malley came back with Ellie as

101

quickly as she could, there was nothing she could do to help. 'This is the crisis, Nell dear,' she said, 'an' there's no medicine on earth can help him through the crisis. You know that, don't you? We must wait and pray. That's all we can do. Poor little man.'

' 'E'll be all right, won't 'e?' Ellie asked anxiously, feeling ashamed of the way she'd blamed the poor kid for dragging them back to London. It wasn't his fault any more than it was hers, and she knew that now, and regretted her black thoughts.

'If he turns the corner, he'll get well again,' Mrs O'Malley said. 'If he doesn't ... It's up to the good Lord now. You say your prayers for him. That's the best thing you can do.'

But Ellie couldn't pray. It didn't seem appropriate somehow when her brother was so obviously fighting for his life. She and Nell sat beside him all through the evening and late into the night while he struggled for breath and the phlegm knocked and bubbled in his congested lungs and he threw off the blankets and muttered incomprehensibly. And his brother lay beside him in the tousled bed, coughing and choking and almost as hot. 'Oh my dear good God,' Nell said over and over again as the hours passed horribly. 'What we gonna do?'

Soon after two o'clock Ellie fell asleep where she sat, her chin on her chest and her back propped against the side of the bed. When she woke, daylight was falling into the room in a dusty column and her mother was asleep on the floor and both the boys were quiet. I'll sneak under the covers for a bit, she thought. Her neck was very stiff and it would be bliss to lie flat. As she climbed cautiously over Tessie's sleeping body, Paddy stirred and groaned, but he didn't wake and Seamus made no sound at all. He was lying on his back with his mouth open and looked really quite peaceful. It wasn't possible to stretch out her full length in the bed after all, because there were so many people in it and she had to avoid at least two patches of wet, but she curled herself into a relatively comfortable position and was asleep again immediately.

When she woke for the second time her mother was wailing, an odd, high-pitched, wordless noise, 'Aaaaagh! Aaaaaaagh!' more like a cat than a woman. Ellie was very frightened and scrambled out of the bed at once to see what was the matter.

' 'E's dead! 'E's dead!' Nell wailed. 'My poor Seamus! My poor little boy! Aaaaagh! Aaaagh!'

'He can't be!' Ellie said, looking across at the bed again to where Seamus was still lying on his back with his mouth open, exactly the same as he'd been during the night. ' 'E's asleep, Ma, that's all. Asleep.' He couldn't be dead.

' 'E's cold!' her mother said. She was sitting on the floor with her arms round her knees rocking with distress.

' 'E ain't!' Ellie said stoutly. She wouldn't believe this death. It wasn't real or true. ' 'E ain't!' She simply couldn't endure it. She'd made a bargain about this measles, hadn't she? Back in the country when she nicked that coat. It all seemed such a long time ago she could hardly remember it. What had God done with her bargain? ' 'E ain't. I can't bear it, Ma.'

But he was. And they all had to.

Paddy Murphy came home for the funeral and made a great deal of fuss about how much he loved his 'darlin' boy', but he didn't pay for it, and went off to the pub the minute it was over, as Ellie noticed with the new cold eyes of grief, and then came home late and roaring drunk just as if it were an ordinary day.

'You'd 'a thought 'e could a' stayed 'ome jest once in a while,' Nell complained as they turned out his pockets and removed the boots from his drunken feet. ' 'Is own son's funeral.'

'I 'ate 'im,' Ellie said, feeling she could risk the truth now. ' 'E don't look after us or nothink. 'E drinks all the money. If you ask me, it's 'is fault poor Seamus died. More'n anyone's.'

'You mussen say that,' her mother reproached. But she didn't sound cross. Only weary. ' 'E's yer father.'

'I know. I 'ate 'im.'

'Don't get married, gel,' Nell advised, lugging her husband onto his back. 'It's a mug's game.'

'Don't you worry, Ma,' Ellie said, looking at her mother solemnly in the candlelight. 'I never ever will!'

Chapter Eight

Mr Torrance, the headmaster of Deal Street Boys, was a very patient man and, as such, a rather unlikely leader for such a tough school in a very tough quarter. Everything about him was grey, but whether with age or chalk it was difficult to say.

When he first took office, back in the idealistic days of his early forties, he had considered himself a man with a mission. Somewhere in amongst those filthy hordes he felt sure there would be boys with hidden intelligence or special talents, boys who could be nurtured and rescued, sent on to secondary schools, turned into gentlemen. And he would be the one to do it. But the boys didn't materialize, and as the years passed his dream gradually receded. He grew weary with disappointment and the daily grinding task of forcing the three Rs into unwilling minds. Four years ago, in 1893, the directors of the People's Palace in the Mile End Road had opened a secondary school, right on his doorstep, so to speak. For a few quite heady months the dream had reasserted itself, but the quality of his pupils remained inexorably low. In all these years he'd found only four candidates to send up for the preliminary examinations, and all four had failed. It was very dispiriting.

Sighing, he stood beside the high window of his dusty study one afternoon in April, watching the boys in the playground below. Such a boisterous lot, he thought, and all so ordinary. He really ought to do something to lift the tone a little, especially now it was Jubilee year. A display of work perhaps, and a Jubilee party. After all, the dear Queen, God bless her, *had* provided them all with a splendid opportunity.

Rachel Cheifitz wasn't the least bit interested in the Diamond

Jubilee, although the newspapers were full of it and the *Daily Graphic* predicted that the nation was heading for a spectacular jamboree.

'So she reign sixty year,' she said shrugging her shoulders. 'She ain't got a place in the Buildin's!' It was later that afternoon, and for once school and work were both over for the day. She and her family were pushing a loaded handcart up Flower and Dean Street, greeting their neighbours as they went. They were moving house.

At long, long, joyful last her dream was coming true. Rivke and Raizel had got her a flat in Rothschild Buildings. A lovely two-roomed flat and right next door to Rivke's own. At six shillings and thrupence a week it wasn't exactly cheap, but it was there for the taking and it had its own scullery and its own W.C. and it was Jewish.

'Vid our own kind!' Rachel said happily, plunging forehead first through the triumphal arch of the entrance into the Jewish kingdom of the inner courtyard.

'Ve find the rent somehow,' Emmanuel said to David, as they pushed the cart after her. 'Ve von't vorry your mother, nu?'

'No, Father,' David agreed. 'Two years an' I work too, don't forget. We manage.'

'Ai yi!' his father sighed. 'Ve manage.' But he didn't sound at all sure about it.

The inner courtyard was bigger than David had imagined it, and it was full of people he knew. The buildings rose for six stern storeys on three sides of it, the fourth being blocked off by the blank walls of a seven-storey warehouse. Their brickwork had once been the usual London colour, soft buff sand with two courses of red brick between the windows and terracotta keystones to the window arches, but smoke and grime had long since blackened away most of the original colour and now they resembled nothing so much as three dark forbidding cliffs, pocked with busy windows and climbed by ironwork staircases, revealed behind their open galleries. But it was the life in the buildings that mattered, and the life in these buildings was familiar.

Clotheslines stretched from one side of the courtyard to the other, most of them sagging under the weight of heavy washing, like a line of ships labouring under full sail, and in between, eddying and swirling, the kids from school occupied every space with rough games and cheerful quarrels. There was Izzie Perlman picking sides with young Benny Lipschitz for 'Jimmy Knacker', and there were all the Levy boys, and Schneider and Raingold and Morry Schwartz. They called to David as he passed, bent over the cart, and he chirruped back happily. There'd be some sport playing here. And what a lot to draw, so many faces, everywhere you looked. Old men pondered at smoke-wreathed card tables close to the walls while their womenfolk called to each other from the windows in Yiddish or broken English, or gave singing commands to the children in the yard below them. The familiar smells of family life rose pungently from every open window, fish and fried onions, burning bones and over-ripe oranges. It was a marvellously lively, homely place and he felt at ease in it at once, and couldn't wait to get the furniture upstairs so that he could come down again and join in the games.

Aunty Dumpling was already on the balcony two floors above them, stouter than ever in her sacking apron, and with her sleeves rolled up above her elbows, ready for action; and Aunt Rivke and her daughter Becky were waiting at the foot of the stairs to kiss them all welcome and assist with the chairs. Her two solid sons were following with the second cart, so they were all eager to get the first one unpacked before they arrived.

Rivke began to give orders before her kiss was dry, brisk and forceful as always. 'So, you take the table, Manny! You help your father, David! Becky! Rugs! Ve on our vay up, Dumpling!' And they all obeyed her without question.

As he struggled backwards up the narrow staircase, and was pinned into corners by the rigid length of the table, David watched his father's long anxious face and thought yet again how very odd it was that he and his two sisters should be so very dissimilar. Aunty Dumpling was as fat and easy as a cottage loaf, and much the same shape, with her roly-poly bosom, her wide hips, short rounded arms and little fat fingers. There was so much extra flesh on her face these days that her brown eyes seemed to be sinking and her mouth looked ridiculously small

106

between the mounds of her two folded chins and the rough red balloons of her cheeks. But she was so loving and chuckly, her eyes were so bright and full of life, and her curls so plump, you forgot how fat she was and expected her to laugh and cry and romp as though she were a child.

Aunt Rivke, on the other hand, could never have been mistaken for a child. She looked as grown up as anybody possibly could be, dour and rather hard done by, with her pear-shaped face and her pear-shaped body, and her air of indomitable effort. Being exceedingly froom, she wore a black curly wig under her shawl whenever she went out, but in the buildings she went bareheaded, and bare was really the most accurate word for her appearance. Her hair was so sparse and grey it was no more than a thin covering for her skull, even though she parted it just above her left ear and did her best to spread its inadequacies over as much of her forehead as she could. Beneath it, her features were lopsided too, the left eye bigger and lower than the right and the left side of her narrow lips turned down as though she was sneering. She looked like a woman who bore the world a grudge, and for most of her waking life she behaved that way too, attacking the most trivial chore with such energy and aggression it was quite alarming to watch her. Herring would be slapped onto the table, bread thudded onto your plate, chairs crunched into position. Now it was the turn of the rag rugs which were being hurled before the stove as though she had just defeated them in battle. And yet she never actually complained about anything, and was always most willing to help. 'There, bubeleh,' she said lovingly to her sister-in-law. 'Ve soon be settled.'

Rachel was in the scullery and tearful with happiness. 'Oy, oy, oy, a scullery all to myself!' she said enraptured. 'Such luxury! My own tap, Emmanuel! My own sink! No more I should carry vater! Oy, oy, oy!' She touched the tap reverently, lifting a drip of water onto her forefinger. 'Vater ven ve vant it!'

David and his father stood outside the scullery door, looking in at her delight. The little room was too small to hold them all at once, but she was right about how convenient it was. It had a sink, and a tap, and standing in one corner a fine fat copper to

107

heat water and wash the clothes in. True, the brick walls were clammy, and there were flies crawling across the whitewashed ceiling, but what of that? It was *their* scullery, opposite *their* W.C., inside *their* front door.

'Ve don't share vid anyone ever again,' she said rapturously. 'Oy, Emmanuel, bubeleh, you are *so* good to me!'

He bent his head towards her shining face, smiling quietly. 'I vould give you the vorld, my Rachel, if I had it to give,' he said. And the look that passed between them was as close and loving as a kiss.

Watching them, David felt his heart contract with an odd almost painful pleasure, because they were so fond of one another, and so happy. And yet he knew his father hadn't really done anything to get this flat. It was Aunty Dumpling and Rivke who'd done all the work, fretting and worrying until they got their own way. He'd been too timid to make demands. If it had been left to him they would still have been in Fashion Street. And Mama must know it too, and yet here she was behaving as though it had been all his doing, and here he was basking in her love as though he completely deserved it. It was all very puzzling and complicated, like so much about life these days.

'Vhat you vaiting for?' Rivke asked. 'You think you stand here vid beds in the yard? Oy, such a boy!'

As he sped off down the iron staircase he tried to sigh his doubts away. Whatever else, it was wonderful to be in the Buildings at last, with all his friends, and particularly now with the Jubilee coming. There'd be some sport in London this summer and no mistake.

And sport there was.

It was one of the best summers anyone could remember, with perfect weather, just as though the old queen had commissioned it. The decorations were put up early and by the end of May every high street in London was twittering with bunting and forested with thick ropes of evergreens. It was a month for elaborate parties and glittering parades, and that meant new clothes and nonstop work for the tailors of Whitechapel. Emmanuel and Rachel worked as long as there was daylight to see by, and David helped them whenever he could, even though he was aching to go out into the streets and join in the fun. On his way to school he stopped to watch the trams and buses as they passed, packed with sightseers, and noticed that the draymen had taken to wearing buttonholes, like lords at a wedding. 'Sixty glorious years,' the banners triumphed. Sixty glorious years of peace and prosperity in the biggest empire the world had ever known. It was something to celebrate. If only he could.

'There's three hundred and twenty million people in the British Empire,' he told Aunty Dumpling one evening, very much impressed by the *Graphic*'s latest dazzling statistics.

'So you ask me, there's three hundred tventy million here in London,' she said, biting off the last thread of the day. 'You never see such crowds!' Then she made him an offer that made his heart leap. 'Ve go see 'em tonight, after supper. Vhat you think! I done enough vork for vonce.'

'I should have to ask Mama,' he said dutifully but his face was shining at the mere thought. And at last Mama gave her permission, 'seeing he vas vid Dumpling'.

So they put on their Shabbas best and went.

London was unrecognizable. It had become a hanging garden. Every street in the City was draped with ropes of evergreen, looped and twirled and intertwined, or woven into shields and crowns, and the Mansion House was lit up like a palace in a pantomime, with 'God Bless our Queen' written right across the front and a huge Star of India hung above the pediment.

In the West End, the scent of potted palms and crushed foliage was almost as strong in the sultry evening air as the usual aroma of horses, and St James's Street was so closely overhung with greenery that strolling along it was like walking through an arbour. Aunty Dumpling said she felt quite done in by it and was glad to be out in the air again in Piccadilly but David thought it was marvellous and had half a mind to go back and experience it all over again. There were buskers everywhere, and men selling everything and anything you could possibly want, ice creams, paper flags, baked potatoes, Jubilee programmes, anything.

In Trafalgar Square an impromptu party had begun. The

109

crowds were singing 'Ta-ra-ra-boom-de-ay', and a circle of cheerful characters was inventing a leaping dance that almost fitted the words and required an exhilarating display of frilly petticoats and buttoned boots. So they joined in at once and danced until Aunty Dumpling was completely exhausted and had to sit down on the pavement to recover. Then she said her feet were killing her, so the two of them limped off along the Mall to the lake in St James's Park, where to David's delight she took off her boots and stripped off her stockings and dabbled her swollen feet in the water. And nobody seemed to mind. Not even the coppers, two of whom strolled by and only grinned at them. Things *had* changed this season, and no mistake.

'Vhat larks ve have, bubeleh!' she chuckled, her face rosy in the evening sunlight.

And David, watching her with love and admiration, wished he'd brought his sketch book with him. 'I can't wait fer the Jubilee,' he said. 'D'you think this weather'll hold?'

'Ain't nothink von't stop it,' she assured him, beaming at him from the water's edge.

And she was right.

From then on they went to the City or the West End every evening, to see the sights and enjoy the entertainment, and David grew steadily more excited. Sometimes Aunty Rivke came with them, with Becky or the boys, and sometimes they took Hymie along, but David's parents stayed at home, saying they still had far too much work to do, which was true enough, for they were even working by candlelight now.

'You will come Jubilee Day,' David begged. 'You mussen miss Jubilee Day.'

Jubilee Day was promised: 'Vork be over by then,' Emmanuel said, smiling at his son's breathless excitement. 'Ve come vid you. If only to keep you calm!'

Jubilee Day dawned in a blaze of hard-edged sunshine and patriotic fervour. By six o'clock in the morning the sky over the Buildings was pale lilac, the drains smelled really strong, and David and his parents were already sticky and uncomfortable in their Shabbas best. Aunty Dumpling arrived with a canvas bag full of biscuits and pancakes, protesting that she was melting away, and at that her sister-in-law wondered whether it wouldn't be more advisable to stay at home, and was laughed to scorn. 'This,' Aunt Dumpling said with the solid determination of fourteen stone, 'I vouldn't miss for all the vorld.'

Then Rivke knocked on the wall to signal that her family were ready and off they all went down into the bubbling courtyard and out to the excited streets.

Whitechapel was quite unlike its usual work-a-day self for there was no trade, and cleared of stalls and carts and custom the streets looked peculiarly empty and a great deal wider, especially as the crowds walking along them were all going in the same direction and with the same cheerful purpose. The trams were all running in the same direction too and there were plenty of them, and more horse-buses than David had ever seen, but even so it took a very long time and three separate buses to get to the City. But eventually they all arrived at the corner of Ludgate Hill with a fine view of steps of St Paul's and a line of dismounted Hussars already in position beside the kerb.

Rivke wasn't at all pleased. 'So vhat ve vant vid the soldiery?' she asked, thwacking her basket down onto the pavement behind the blue legs of the six-footer immediately in front of them.

'Pertection, missus,' the Hussar said cheerfully. 'Crowds can get werry wiscious, believe you me.'

'Humph!' Rivke snorted. 'I never *see* a crowd more better behaved then this one. Soldiery!'

The Hussar turned his head slightly, so that he could grin down at her. 'Tell the truth, missus,' he said, 'I come ter see the percession. Best way ter get a front seat, this is.'

'Just vhat I thought, young man,' she said and suddenly cracked her dour face into a grin. 'Vhat a day ve got!'

The crowd around them grew by the minute and soon they were so tightly packed together there simply wasn't room for anybody else. The road was completely empty except for three piles of horse dung and the occasional mounted policeman who clopped along as casually as if he were out riding in the countryside. They seemed to have been waiting for ever, squashed in behind the giant Hussar. Even the distribution of Aunty Dumpling's biscuits only occupied them for a very short time, and left David feeling hotter than ever and very thirsty.

But at last there was a muffled roar from the crowds in Fleet Street and looking back David could see that handkerchiefs were fluttering all along the street like white petals in a gale, even though the road itself was still completely empty. A few minutes later they could hear the clatter of hooves and the rattle of accoutrements. Then, to great excitement, the first contingent swung into view, Canadian Mounties, stiff-spined in their red jackets and grinning at the crowds. 'Fine body a' men,' the Hussar said. 'Mounties. Always get their man, so they say.'

'Same as me!' Aunty Dumpling said, rolling towards the kerb to get a better view. 'So vhere's the ol' Queen?'

'Do me a favour!' the Hussar said. 'That percession's six miles long. Troops from all over the Empire. You won't see the Queen fer hours an' hours. You ain't seen the like a' this anywhere in the world.'

David was amazed to see his own Aunty Dumpling flirting with a soldier, but there were so many amazing things happening on this amazing day that perhaps the rules for proper behaviour had been suspended. He glanced at his father and was relieved to see that he was smiling as he watched the passing troops.

'So vill you look at that!' Rivke said, excited and awed. 'There's a load a' blackies next.' And so there was, their brown faces surprising above the green and gold of their elaborate uniforms: the Jamaican artillery, no less. Behind them came Maoris and Malays, Sikhs in crumpled turbans, Chinese soldiers wearing white caps like inverted pudding basins, and a formidable troupe of lancers from India with stern unsmiling faces and fierce beards. The parade went on and on and on, scarlet and gold, emerald and gold, turquoise and gold, black and gold, bright and loud and larger than life. Band vied with band, their drums and trumpets echoing in the stone canyons of Fleet Street and Ludgate Hill, while David cheered himself hoarse, dazzled and overwhelmed.

Standing safely and happily among his family, thrilled by the throbbing noise and the extravagant colours of the parade, he was a boy bewitched. Everything about this day was totally unlike anything he'd ever experienced before. He'd never seen horses so fat and sleek, or carriages so impressive, or men so tall, or women so magnificently gowned. The dazzle of their diamonds made him blink, and their smiling well-fed faces were visions from another world. Even the buildings were splendid here, with their columns and pediments and their high decorated windows full of faces, and red, white and blue flags draped over all the sills. St Paul's Cathedral was simply overwhelming, blocking the sky before his eyes, like some huge stage set, its blackened columns a foil to the blaze of colour below them. Scarlet barricades had been erected like a bright skirting all round the edge of it and on either side of the steps, and the steps themselves were crowded with extravagantly costumed extras, troops in red, black and gold, choristers in white robes and clergy in magnificent red academicals. It took his breath away just to look at them, they made such a marvellous picture.

There was a sudden decline in the volume of sound around them as one by one the thousands in Ludgate Hill stopped cheering long enough to say 'There she is' and crane their necks to get their first glimpse of the Queen. Then, and at an appropriate distance from the flamboyant coaches of the other royals, a red-wheeled landau appeared, drawn by six cream coloured horses caparisoned in gold and scarlet and purple. And sitting in the middle of that splendid coach like the black centre of an exotic plant was a short, fat, ordinary old woman, with a plain black hat on her sparse white hair, and an old-fashioned black crinoline belling around her over the seat. He couldn't believe what he saw.

'Is that the Queen?' he asked. So plain and ordinary in the middle of all this?

'It is. God bless her!' the Hussar said, and David noticed that fat tears were coursing down the man's brown cheeks, even though he was smiling. Then there was no possibility of hearing anything that anybody might be saying, because the Queen's coach was immediately in front of them, and hands

113

and handkerchiefs were being waved with total abandon and the cheering was a full-throated nonstop roar, and he simply had to join in. The old lady, flushed and uncomfortable in her bulky black clothing, nodded and smiled as she passed, and he cheered and wept with the rest, caught up in a sudden upsurge of emotion that he wasn't expecting and couldn't understand. Then the coach swung round behind Queen Anne's statue and he lost sight of her, and knew he was sighing with disappointment like everybody else.

'I vill draw this,' he said, his upturned face shining with passion and tears. And even though nobody could hear him, it was a solemn promise. Somehow or other he had to catch this moment, the colour of it, and the noise, and the crowds, and the glorious weeping emotion.

Over on the other side of Ludgate Hill, squashed among the crowds that ringed Ludgate Circus, Ellie Murphy was wiping the tears from her eyes too, surreptitiously, of course, and right on the edge of the sleeve of her special green coat, because she didn't want to stain it. It was very hot in the green coat, but she couldn't have worn any other garment, even if she'd possessed one. For this was a special occasion. She'd been up since four in the morning and had walked all the way to her chosen spot, because she hadn't any money for a bus fare and she wanted to be certain of a good position. Her mother was still hard at work with those dreadful matchboxes and she knew that by now her father would be in the nearest pub, 'drinking the old Queen's health', but she was having a day off, on her own, and glad of it, her brothers and sisters left behind to plague someone else.

The parade had been a giddy marvel. She'd tapped her feet in time to the bands, and cheered the troops, and drunk in every detail of all the ravishing gowns that had passed, shimmering and glittering, before her eyes. And she'd cheered the old Queen too, even though she hadn't seen very much of her because she'd opened up a large white parasol just as her coach was passing. It was a day an' a half an' no mistake.

To her left four young women were blowing their noses and wiping their eyes and adjusting their hats. They were very interesting young women and she'd been watching them all through the morning, trying to listen to their conversation and admiring their clothes and wondering where they came from. They were just the sort of young women she wanted to be like, nicely dressed and well fed and all so sure of themselves. From time to time during the morning she'd wondered who they were and where they lived and how they managed to look so fine. Now, as the crowd began to shift and stir, ready to disperse, one of them enlightened her.

'We'll have some tales to tell the girls back in Barkers tonight,' she said, patting her chignon.

They worked in Barkers. They were shop girls in Barkers. That's why they were all wearing the same skirts.

'D'you think they really will shut the doors like they said?' the second asked, anxiously.

'At ten, d'you mean?' Chignon said. 'Nah! On Jubilee Day? Never on your life. We could stay out till midnight, I'll bet.'

'I wouldn't like to risk it, Vera,' Anxious said. 'What if they was ter lock us out? What 'ud we do? We'd 'ave ter walk about all night. Think a' that!'

They live in, Ellie thought. They're girls and they live in! Fancy that! They work in the shop and live in the shop and get fed in the shop an' all. I'll bet.

And to prove her right, the third girl smoothed down her long black skirt and said, 'Well, I'm for going back on time. I don't know about you others but I shall be ready for my supper.'

That's what I'll do, Ellie thought, watching them. The minute I'm thirteen, I'll leave home an' work in a shop. I won't be Smelly Ellie no more, I won't. I'll be a shop girl then, an' dress like them, an' go back ter the shop fer supper. That's 'ow I'll better mesself. What a bit a' luck I came ter the Jubilee!

It was a jubilant promise. And a solution.

Chapter Nine

The minute he got back to the Buildings, David started work on his drawing. He was glowing with excitement and inspiration and he couldn't wait to get started. His exhilaration was infectious. Aunty Dumpling was bubbling with it and his parents were beaming and Aunty Rivke and Uncle Ben and his three grown-up cousins, who'd never seen him draw anything before, were huge-eyed with admiration as they pulled their chairs up to the table to watch him. Aunty Dumpling spread a large sheet of grey sugar paper reverently across the table while he ran to collect his gear, the paintbox he'd bought from the money he'd earned running errands, brushes, pencils, clean rags, eggcup full of water.

He worked at speed, before the vision could fade, using three brushes and three colours for the first rapid outline: Prussian blue for the huge pram shape of the landau, with a long mudguard curved over the high back wheel, and just the suggestion of a lamp at the front; scarlet lake for the wheels and the shafts and the beginning of the reins; grey for the cream horses; and right in the middle of the paper the first smudgy outline of the old Queen with her white parasol high above her head and her dress spreading out from her shoulders like a bell. He talked as he drew, in short staccato phrases, as quick as his fingers, 'Skirt – so – no – a bit more on that side, I think, – face – little hat – too much – that's better.' And his family watched him, proud and impressed.

'An artist in the family ve got,' Uncle Ben declared, hooking his thumbs into his waistcoat pocket and giving his head a little sideways nod of satisfaction.

'A boy vid talent, don't I tell you,' Aunty Dumpling beamed.

'That's the ol' Queen to the life,' cousin Becky said. 'How d'yer do it, Davey?'

116

David neither knew nor cared. It was enough that it could be done and that he was doing it, tumbling his vision onto paper as quickly as he could, scowling with concentration, his face dark with pleasure. When the women went off to the scullery to prepare supper, he worked on, forgetting that they needed the table, racing against the fading light. It took the clunk of a penny into the gas meter, the scraping of matches and the sudden glow of the gas to bring him back to the ordinary world.

'Ve got a scholar at our table, Emmanuel,' Aunty Dumpling said, giving her brother's arm a loving pat.

'A table is not blessed unless it has fed a scholar,' Emmanuel said, happily quoting the old proverb. 'Alvays providing the scholar take time from his vork to eat. Sit down, sit down, all the family. Ve got plenty chairs. Ve got plenty food. Ve even got the table back. Now ve celebrate, nu?'

His long face was creased into its gentle smile, and there was no rebuke in the tone of his words, but David nevertheless suddenly felt ashamed. He'd been so absorbed in his painting he hadn't given any of them a thought. He'd forgotten about supper and how hungry they must be, and he hadn't offered to help his mother, and worse than all that he'd kept everybody waiting. 'I'm sorry, Father,' he stumbled, his cheeks flushed. 'I should've ... I mean, I'd have stopped long ago. I wish you'd said, see.' He was clearing his things away as he spoke, working awkwardly, wishing he hadn't been so thoughtless.

'Vhat a boy!' Aunty Dumpling said lovingly. 'Of his family he thinks. In the midst. An *edel* boy, don't I tell you!'

At such a very high compliment, David blushed more furiously than ever. Then they were all caught up in the cheerful ritual of the meal, and his embarrassment passed. But twenty-four hours later he was back at the table, brushes in hand, and had again forgotten all about them.

Hymie Levy came back with him every day from school, just to see how it was progressing, and the two boys spread the painted sheets all over the table, arranging the procession in order, remembering and re-savouring.

'You oughter put this up on old Torrey's wall,' Hymie said, when the ninth sheet was finished. 'It's ever so good.' Mr Torrance was gathering a display of work to pin on the main

117

wall of the assembly hall, compositions and samples of handwriting inside a border of newspaper cuttings. He called it 'our visual celebration' and made daily appeals at assembly for more contributions.

'Take up a lot a' room,' David said, trying to find reasons against the idea because he liked it so much and it was making him feel so proud.

' 'E wouldn't mind,' Hymie said. 'A wall that size! It could go in the middle. Be a real centrepiece then.'

'Well ... ' David said, picturing his huge painting in the middle of the display, and wanting to see it there more every second. 'Only if *you* tell Sir.' And then, just in case he was appearing too eager, 'Bet 'e sez no.'

But 'Sir', their class teacher, Mr Williams, was very taken with the picture and had it put up immediately, even in its unfinished state. 'It's very good, Cheifitz,' he said. 'I never knew you had a penchant for Art.'

' 'E draws all the time, sir,' Hymie said with immense pride. 'Got a great stack a' drawin's at 'ome.'

'Really?' Mr Williams said vaguely. 'A great stack you say? Well, well.' And he made a mental note that he must tell the headmaster that this Cheifitz lad had talent. 'When do you think you'll finish this drawing, Cheifitz? Mr Torrance wants the wall covered by the end of next week.'

'By Thursday,' David promised. And by Thursday it was.

On Friday morning the last sheets of sugar paper were trimmed and pinned to the wall and the drawing was complete. It caused a stir. 'You seen what Cheify's done? Ain't 'alf good.' Groups of boys gathered all day, to inspect and tease and secretly admire, and even the teachers told one another it wasn't 'half bad for a nipper'.

But David was miserably and perversely ashamed of it. He'd wanted to capture the emotion he'd felt as the Queen passed by, that glorious uplifting sense of affection and pride and tribal power. And he hadn't done it. He'd painted a pattern, that was all, and not a particularly good one. The horses were all unreal, their legs stiff and square like toys, and the carriages were too big, and their occupants distorted, and the crowd looked like rows of pink balloons. Oh, it was horrible! He was

118

overwhelmed with shame at how bad it was. And now everybody was looking at it, and everybody knew he'd painted it, and he wished the ground would open up and swallow him from sight.

'What's up?' Hymie said at his elbow.

'It's so bad!' he said, still looking dolefully at his creation, all his splendid pride in it deflated into shame.

But Hymie was too thrilled to recognize his disappointment and thought he was fishing for compliments. 'It's a bit of all right, Davey,' he said, banging his friend between the shoulder blades, 'an' that's a fact.'

But the facts were otherwise, David thought, oblong of fetlock, balloon-faced, grotesque and clumsy and inadequate. His terrible sense of public failure cast a gloom over the rest of the day, and even when school was over and they all went running home ready for Shabbas he felt no lifting of the spirit, not even when the candles were lit and the room grew golden in their haze. He ate the ritual meal, silent under the babble of talk from his Aunt Rivke and his Uncle Ben and his three loud cousins, and on Saturday he dressed in his Shabbas best and went for his usual walk with his parents, dutifully answering their questions, behaving properly, as a Jewish child should. And all the time he was carrying his failure about with him like a great stone in his chest.

Why hadn't he seen how bad it was when he was painting it? Then he could have hidden it away and altered it later maybe when he felt a bit better about it, instead of parading it in front of everybody on that awful wall. How could he have been so stupid? But he knew the answer to that question and it was a very uncomfortable one. It was because he'd been so full of his own importance, David Cheifitz the artist, wanting praise and applause, feeling special and set apart. It was because he had been proud.

He could have worked that out for himself, even without the Shabbas to point the way. But the reading from the Torah that Shabbas seemed to have been chosen specially for him and he listened to it with a sinking heart, recognizing his faults, and hearing them named. 'Lord, my heart is not haughty nor mine eyes lofty: neither do I exercise myself in great matters, or in things too high for me.' Who was he to imagine that he could

119

draw the Jubilee? His prayers stuck in his mind, mere words that wouldn't rise, and the stone filled his chest, dragging him down and down.

By Monday morning he was quite bleak with shame. And the picture was still there, right in the middle of the wall, awkward and inadequate and exposed. He couldn't bear to look at it and he certainly didn't want to talk about it, even though all his friends were full of teasing admiration, and every teacher he met, all through the day, made a point of passing some comment upon it. By the end of the afternoon his shame had become a triple-headed rage, against himself and his stupid pride and his ugly picture. And a plan had formed itself alongside the rage. A dark, hot, angry plan. He would sneak back into the school that night, as soon as it was dark, and tear the wretched thing off the wall and destroy it.

The school always emptied immediately the last bell went, but it was early July and the weather was still warm and the skies still clear, so he had to wait for more than four hours before it was dark enough to return. And even then the sky above the school building was still distinctly blue even though the first pearly stars had risen. He was just about to sneak into the playground when he saw the dark shape of the school keeper outlined against one of the upper windows. Now what? he thought, irritably. Silly old fool! What's 'e doing, wandering about in the dark? The place should a' been empty! Now he'd have to wait even longer, hours and hours probably, because he'd never known the school keeper hurry for anything. *Nebbish!*

So he hung about just outside the gates, scowling with impatience and suppressed anger, while that steady gentleman made his nightly inspection. It was a very long time before the side door finally opened and his shadowy figure emerged to cross the playground and crunch home to his house and his supper.

Heart pounding like a hammer, David ran across the asphalt. The cloakroom window was still open, just as he'd left it, and just about wide enough for him to squeeze through. Which he did, feeling adventurous despite his anger and scratching his knees on the sill.

It was surprisingly dark inside and looked unfamiliar with

120

the pegs all as empty as meat hooks on a Monday, and only the faintest flicker of light to show him where the door was. The uncanny absence of sound made his footsteps ring and echo. Daunted by the noise he was making, he took off his boots, tied their laces together and hung them round his neck. Then he tiptoed out of the shadows of the cloakroom into the comparative brightness of the Infants' hall, where chairs stood in dark rows against the walls and the moon dropped pools of white light onto the polished parquet. It looked strange and enormous, and it made him aware that school was really rather a forbidding place. But there was no turning back now.

Up the stone staircase. Silently, in his stockinged feet. Along the corridor between the classrooms where the enclosed air smelled of sweat and dirty clothes and wax floor polish. Gently through the squeak of the hall doors. And then he could see his target, and his anger rose swift as a flame in a furnace and he ran, forgetting the need for caution, and threw himself at the wall and ripped the first sheet away from its restraining pins and threw it on the floor. Then he stretched for the second, his hands moon-white and eager, and a quiet voice spoke behind him. 'What *are* you doing, boy?'

He was startled but he didn't stop, because he couldn't. His rage was extreme now, too hot and fierce to be doused by a voice, even though the voice belonged to Mr Torrance, and somewhere in a deeper part of his boiling mind he knew it and knew he should obey it. He tore the second sheet from the wall, shaking with fury, and then a solid body was wedged behind him and iron hands were gripping his wrists and he was being pulled backwards, sobbing and struggling, 'I 'ave ter do it. I 'ave ter! I can't bear it!' And then, somehow or other, his legs were walking in a perfectly reasonable way, and he was in Mr Torrance's room where the gas was lit and the curtains drawn. The headmaster was lowering him into a chair, as gently as Aunty Dumpling would have done. He began to feel that perhaps he was asleep and dreaming, because nothing felt real any more. His spine was stiff with arrested fury, and his fists were clenched and the scowl was set on his face, but there was nothing in his mind to move him on to the next thought or the next sensation.

'Now then,' Mr Torrance said mildly as he walked to his seat behind the desk, fumbling into the sag of his chalk-lined pocket for his pipe and his matches and his tobacco pouch. 'Let's have a look at you, young man. You've got some explaining to do.' And then, when David lifted his head and looked straight at him across the desk, 'Why bless my soul, it's Cheifitz!'

For a few seconds neither of them could think of anything to say, David because his mind seemed to have turned itself off, Mr Torrance because he was still coping with surprise. Catching a vandal in the act was nothing new in Deal Street, but to discover that this particular vandal was young Cheifitz put such a strain on his credulity it made his head ache. For a start, he quite liked the boy. He always looked clean and well cared for, and that was invariably a good sign. Not well-fed, of course, because none of his pupils could really be considered well-fed, but wholesome at least, and well-formed. Quite a handsome lad, in fact, especially now that he'd lost the babyish look he'd had when he came up from the Infants. Fine brown eyes, quite honest looking, really, and you noticed them more now that his eyebrows were thicker. And then of course a well-defined nose made such a difference to a boy's face, even when he was scowling. No, he'd always considered young Cheifitz as one of their better boys, and when Mr Williams told him about the painting, he'd really felt quite gratified. And now here he was actually destroying it. What on earth had got into him?

'You were tearing down your own painting,' he said, and the word 'painting' was quite shrill with disbelief. 'You were, weren't you?'

'Sir,' David said, using the word in the customary expressionless way, like all boys in the presence of an accusing teacher, even though the scowl was still chiselled between his eyes.

'I don't understand it,' Mr Torrance said, filling his pipe. 'Your own work.'

'Sir.'

'I ought to cane you,' Mr Torrance said, but his tone was still reassuringly mild. He was packing tobacco into his pipe, comforted and pleased by the rough strands under the ball of his thumb, and the familiar pungency his pressure was releasing. 'What made you do it?'

'Weren't no good,' David said, wincing and looking across at the teacher as though he was squinting into sunshine.

'Ah,' Mr Torrance said, settling his pipe between his teeth and reaching for the matches.

The room was very calm and very quiet, so that the slightest sound became significant and musical. Between them the gaslight was burning in rhythm, throbbing and purring like a cat, and when Mr Torrance scraped his first match and began to draw its fire down through the tobacco, the sharp suck, plop, suck of his breath was like the sound of eggs breaking. To David it was as if they were both suspended in some other world, quite apart from home and school and family and friend. A world without time where emotions didn't exist.

'I thought it good,' Mr Torrance said. 'Tell me what was wrong with it.'

The scowl dissolved into earnestness. 'I vant to show vhat ve felt, sir. It vas in my head, so clear. I knew vhat it vas,' he said, speaking quickly and forgetting to be careful about the way he pronounced the words. 'It didn't come out, you see. Not the vay it vas.'

Why, the boy's an artist, Mr Torrance thought, drawing the smoke into his mouth as David detailed all the deficiencies of his painting. 'Things rarely come out the way they were,' he said when the catalogue was finished. 'You would need to be a very great artist to achieve that. And training of course.'

Smoke columned out of his nose while they both considered this.

'Would you like to be trained as an artist?' Mr Torrance said.

In normal circumstances it would have been a question beyond comprehension or consideration. Boys from Deal Street didn't leave to become artists. Tailors, yes, or cutters, porters, dockers, street sweepers, labourers, burglars, drifters but never artists. But now, in this odd peaceful limbo, David knew at once that that was exactly what he wanted to be.

'Yes, sir,' he said. 'I would.'

'Very well,' Mr Torrance said, 'we will start by restoring your painting to its pristine condition. Then you will gather all your drawings together and we will put them in a folio. Then I will see your parents, and if they are agreeable I will enter you for secondary school.'

It was a dream come true.

123

Chapter Ten

'An honour, don't I tell you,' Aunty Dumpling said, her plump face damp with delight. 'Technical school, Emmanuel! Think a' that! The East London Technical School.'

Emmanuel was thinking of it, and his thoughts were making him bite his lips. It *was* an honour. Of course it was. To have your only son marked out as a scholar for all the world to see. A very real honour and David was worthy of it. But it had to be paid for, that was the trouble, and the price was high. Fees of a shilling a week meant fifty shillings a year, and if the boy were accepted they'd be committed to paying it for the next four years, unless he won a scholarship, which they really shouldn't count on. Nu-nu, it was a lot of money, and the tailoring trade was more uncertain than he'd ever known it. And then there was his keep. Ai yi! It would be very very difficult. A less devout man would have said impossible.

'Can ve do this, bubeleh?' Rachel asked him. She spoke so softly her voice was almost a whisper, and her confidential tone revealed her understanding of what this commitment would mean. 'Ve should say no, maybe? Vhat you think?' If they were going to say no they should decide now, while the boy was at school and out of the house.

'Nu-nu, ve manage,' he reassured them both. 'Such an opportunity, Rachel. It don't come twice.' He looked at the headmaster's letter lying on the table before them, and smiled ruefully. The choice had been made the moment it arrived. 'He vin a scholarship maybe.'

'Don't I tell you!' Dumpling agreed, descending upon him to reward him with kisses. 'Ve manage. Ve save. Ve make his liddle suits. Such an honour!'

124

A voice was calling excitedly from the courtyard. 'Mrs Cheifitz! Mrs Cheifitz! Such news ve got, you never believe! Mrs Cheifitz!'

It was Mrs Levy, waving a letter at them, her face glowing in the soft light of late afternoon. 'From the school,' she explained. 'Our Hymie they vant to send to the Tech.'

Rachel seized her letter from the table and waved it in answer. 'Our Davey also,' she said.

'*Mazel tov!*' Mrs Levy called. 'So they go together. Two scholars. Vhat better ve vant! Oy-yoy! Great is our God and greatly to be praised for His loving kindness.'

'First they got to pass the examination,' Emmanuel warned. 'Ve don't count chickens before they hatch, nu?'

But none of the women paid any attention to him at all. With boys so clever! Of course they'd pass.

David and Hymie were't quite so confident. Wanting to go to the Tech was one thing, winning a place was quite another. They did extra work for Mr Williams every diligent evening from then on, and they hoped they were improving, but they couldn't be sure. A scholarship examination was a daunting thing and they both knew, only too well, that all the boys from Deal Street who'd ever attempted it had failed.

'How d'you reckon our chances, then?' they would ask one another as they walked home from school together at the end of each day. And the answer was invariably the same. 'Slim an' gettin' slimmer!' Then they would sigh and grimace if they were feeling anxious, or punch one another if they were feeling fairly confident, but neither of them would admit to hope. That would have been evidence of pride, and their God was a little too prone to chastize pride with failure.

So they went meekly to the examination, both of them tense and pale and pretending unconcern, and for the whole of one very hot day sat in a gymnasium that smelt of tarred rope and old rubber and sweaty feet, and did heart-juddering battle with Mathematics and English Language.

Then they had to wait for more than a fortnight before the plain important envelopes arrived with the good news. Both of them had been accepted as scholars at the East London Technical College and David had won a scholarship from the

Drapers' Company worth £10 a year.

Then what celebrations there were. Aunty Dumpling wept and wailed for a good ten minutes and covered him with tears and kisses, and his mother smiled and smiled, and his father's long tired face was lifted with pleasure. The two families invited each other to special meals at which their clever boys sat in the place of honour and were praised until their cheeks burned scarlet. And they were praised and petted all through the summer until September arrived and David and Hymie put on their special school suits and caught the tram rattling along the Mile End Road to the People's Palace.

They settled into their new life as scholars very quickly and made new friends and grew accustomed to a new pattern. And a very demanding pattern it was, with new things to be learned at every minute of the day, and several new vocabularies to be acquired, and notes and homework to be completed every evening. There were rewards in this new life, David thought as he did battle with his first set of mathematical problems, but you certainly earned them. But never mind, tomorrow was Friday, and on Friday afternoon he would have his very first Art lesson.

It was a crushing disappointment. The Art master, Mr Eswyn Smith, was a mild looking man, stooped and untidy, with a thick fringe of grey curly hair ringing the pale bald dome of his skull and a long, uncombed, brindled beard, speckled tawny and grey and white, and dotted with scraps of paper and flecks of paint and pencil shavings. He wore a pencil behind one ear and two paintbrushes behind the other, and the kangaroo pocket in his linen apron bulged with rags and brushes and squashed tubes of paint. He had a soft untidy voice too, and a trick of addressing his class with his body turned slightly away from them, so that he was looking at them sideways on. David liked him at once.

'My function in this establishment,' he said, 'is to introduce you to the delights of Art. Now I am not such a fool as to imagine that any of you will actually wish to become artists when you leave this school. No indeed. I'm sure you will all end up as scientists or engineers, but that is no reason why you shouldn't learn about perspective and balance or acquire some

126

appreciation of colour and line. In short, it is my job to ensure that you do not leave this place as complete barbarians. No matter how you may have arrived. Very well, we will begin this afternoon by drawing a pencil sketch of that window. Without using a ruler. Rulers are for mathematics. In Art we draw freehand.' And he set off along the rows of desks to distribute pencils and paper.

Nu-nu, he's wrong this time, David thought happily, *I'm going to be an artist.* Won't he be bucked when 'e knows. And he took his folder of cartoons out of his satchel and laid it on the desk ready to surprise and please.

'Oh yes,' Mr Eswyn Smith said mildly when he saw the offering. 'What's this?'

'My drawings, sir,' David said proudly. 'I want to be an artist.' And he watched with happy anticipation as the teacher opened the folder.

'Um,' the man said flicking through the pile, much too quickly. 'Cartoons, I see. Have you got anything else?' He wasn't impressed, as David could tell at once from the flat tone of his voice. 'Well, you've learned one trick, I'll grant you that. Let's see how you get on with all the others. You've got a long way to go, young man, so the sooner you start the better. There's your pencil.' And he gave David a vague smile, settled his pencil behind his ear and moved on.

He wasn't impressed with the drawing of the window either. 'Yes, that's the frame,' he said mildly. 'Now what do you see *through* the frame, eh? That's the problem. Filling the frame. Quite a good start but only a start, eh?'

I'm glad I didn't show him the Jubilee, David thought as he drooped back to his desk to fill the frame. 'Cos 'e wouldn't think much a' *that.*

During the next few weeks they learned the rules of perspective and drew boxes and houses and tree-lined roads and streets full of shops. But although David did his best to do exactly what was required of him, he was never praised and rarely noticed. It was a chastening experience and left him demoralized and unsatisfied. He'd come to this school to learn about Art because everybody said he was good at it, and now it seemed he was only ordinary, and his special talent wasn't

127

special after all. Nevertheless he worked hard, and strove to please, even though he couldn't see the point of most of the things he was asked to do.

Until the day he saw the rats.

Mr Eswyn Smith had set them a special task that Friday afternoon, a subject in two tones, brown and grey, which was to display as many textures as they could contrive. As David walked home along Commercial Street through the grey mist of a steady drizzle, his mind was busy turning over possible ideas. What sort of things were grey and brown? Horses, maybe. But horses were very difficult. Boots? But they'd done boots, and there weren't a lot of different textures in a boot. Oh, why couldn't they use as many colours as they liked?

At the corner of Shepherd Street a gang of workmen were laying drains and a small crowd had gathered to watch them do it. Idly curious he drifted towards them. The pavement was gouged by a long deep trench, and the drainpipes were stacked beside it, mud-smeared but ready. There were over twenty men in and around the trench, some digging with varying degrees of energy and enthusiasm, some resting on their spades. They and the trench were all exactly the same colour, the heavy dark brown of wet London clay. Their waistcoats and trousers were stiff with the stuff and even their caps were daubed with it, although their boots and spades and the puddles of water under their feet were grey as iron.

'Mind yer feet, son,' the foreman warned. 'Better not come too near the edge. Lot a' rats this morning.'

'Rats!' David said, shivering a little at the idea.

'Dozens a' the beggars,' the foreman said. 'Just broke a nest up. Be bitten ter death we would if our legs wasn't tied up proper.'

David looked down at the man's legs and the stout leather gaiters that protected his calves. Then, as if to prove him right, two fat damp creatures squirmed out of a nearby culvert from among a tangle of cables and slithered through the mud no more than three feet away from him. Rats, David thought. Great fat rats running about Whitechapel in broad daylight, their mud-brown fur spiky with water, and their tails trailing behind them like cables, iron grey cables and iron grey claws.

128

A picture in two tones. I could draw that fur with lots of short straight pencil lines, and the eyes would be black with just a curve left white to show the reflected light, and the claws smudged grey inside a narrow outline.

Two of the workmen set about the scurrying vermin with their spades, the broad iron thwacking into the mud with an echoing thump, and soon two were dead and the remainder vanished. Then as he watched, both horrified and fascinated, he realized that the mound of damp brown objects near his feet, which he had carelessly imagined to be a pile of old rags, was in fact a heap of dead rats, tied by their wiry tails. Their flesh was battered and flattened and their fat cheeks deflated, but their vicious yellow teeth and protruding claws were still chillingly obvious. Their fur was as flat as leather. He could show that by smudging again. But above their muzzle he could see the sharp spikes of wet fur – little pencil lines, very close together. I could leave the teeth white and give 'em a really heavy outline. A picture in two tones and a variety of textures.

'D'you mind if I sit by the side 'ere, an' jest make a few sketches?' he asked the foreman. 'I'll keep out yer way, I promise.'

'Suit yourself, son,' the foreman said, tossing the latest victims onto the pile. 'On'y don't blame me if yer gets bit.'

He sketched for over an hour even though the drizzle smudged his notebook and the crowds jogged his elbow, and when he got home he started his picture. The two live rats running from bottom right to top left, boots and spades grouped around them, grey puddles outlined beneath them, brown clay behind them and the pile of dead rats suspended like leather rags from the righthand corner. All the things he'd learned, about the variation of line and the use of light and shade, came effortlessly into his mind to help him. It was more than four days before the picture was finished to his satisfaction, but the work was a pleasure.

And at last his effort earned real praise.

'Now that's what I call a picture, Cheifitz,' Mr Eswyn Smith said when he handed it in. 'You're making your line work at last. Better than cartoons, eh?'

'Yes, sir.'

'Now you can see the possibilities, I think?'

Yes, oh yes, he could.

'You've caught that wet fur very well indeed.'

David didn't blush, because he'd gone beyond childish pride by now. He knew he had a talent but he also knew what an effort that talent would always require of him.

Oddly enough and although he didn't expect it, from then on Art became enjoyable again. They were still working in two tones and still struggling to make mere pencil lines express texture, but he knew he was winning the struggle. Now he drew whenever he got the chance, covering pad after pad with sketches, absorbed and happy.

'Such a boy!' Aunty Dumpling said, admiring his enthusiasm. 'Alvays he draws. Such a scholar, don't I tell you.'

'How you gettin' on in school?' Aunt Rivke asked when she met him on the stairs.

'Good!' David told her. 'I'm gettin' on good.'

'So you like it, nu?'

'Like it! It's the best thing I ever 'ad 'appen to me, in all me life. I tell you, Aunty Rivke, I'd like ter stay there fer ever an' ever.'

130

Chapter Eleven

'I've 'ad enough a' school,' Ellie Murphy said to her great friend Ruby Miller. 'I'm goin' after that job in 'Opkins an' Peggs Sat'day.'

'Never!' Ruby said, much impressed. Hopkins and Peggs was the local drapers and a most prestigious place. It ran the full length of Shoreditch High Street from Church Street to Bethnal Green Road, and it sold high-quality goods like they did in Barkers or Peter Robinsons in the West End. 'That's 'igh class, 'Opkins an' Peggs.' She'd been there twice with her mother and still felt overawed by it, all those rolls of expensive cloth and shop girls with snow-white collars and cuffs, and immaculately clean hands. She couldn't imagine Ellie Murphy in a shop like that. 'You'll never get took on in 'Opkins an' Peggs.'

'Just you watch!' Ellie said. 'Be thirteen Monday, then I'm off. I'm gonna better mesself. Job like that 'ud do me fine. They live in, yer know, at 'Opkins an' Peggs.'

It was a Thursday evening early in May and the two girls were on their way back to work in the Lane, Ellie to wash dishes at the pie and mash shop, Ruby to help her brother sell herrings. They'd been working after school for more than three years now, and ever since the Murphys had moved to Heneage Street they'd got into the habit of walking there together.

'I know what yer thinking,' Ellie said, catching the dubious expression on her friend's plump face, 'and yer wrong. I'll get took on, you'll see.'

'Trouble is,' Ruby said honestly, 'you don't exactly look the part, do yer? Not really. Not when all's said and done.'

'I'll get mesself a new rig,' Ellie said, her jaw hard with determination. ' 'Ave a rub down. Brush me barnet.'

But Ruby wasn't persuaded, and the expression on her face was beginning to undermine Ellie's rather limited confidence. Fortunately they'd just reached the corner of Lolesworth Street and the Lane, and that gave her an idea.

'We'll ask the innercent bird,' she said. 'That's what. Then we'll see.'

The 'innercent bird' was a bedraggled blue budgerigar who hopped dolefully about in a small wicker cage balanced precariously on a ramshackle trestle table with a label above its head proclaiming that it would take a planet from the box telling your past and future life for one farthing. Its owner, a fat affable Gypsy with a face like a flat iron, stood beside it in a bundle of old skirts and tatty shawls beaming toothless encouragement at her potential clients. 'Tha's right, darlin',' she approved as Ellie proffered her farthing. 'You just choose your question, my lovey, and let the innercent bird look into your future.' And she handed Ellie a greasy card full of badly written questions. 'Which d'yer want, dearie?'

Ellie read the card as well as she could through its coating of grime and brown grease. 'Shall I be happy in love? How many husbands shall I have? Ought I to grant that which he asks so ardently? Have I any rivals? Shall I do well to confess all?' What odd questions, she thought, and wondered who would ask them, but as she was wondering she saw the question she wanted to ask. Number 27, 'Shall I be successful in my enterprise?'

'Number 27, dearie,' the Gypsy confirmed, and she raised a cardboard partition at one end of the birdcage to reveal a stack of miniature shelves, each containing an equally tiny card. The innercent bird was scratching its head, and had to be prodded with a straw to remind it of its duty. Eventually it hopped to the shelves and after two or three tentative pecks at the woodwork it contrived to push one of the cards through the slot behind it and out of the cage. 'Come round the side, dearie,' the Gypsy said, making way so that Ellie could stand beside her. 'There's your answer, my love.'

Ellie took the card in her hand and turned it over.

132

'Cleanliness is next to Godliness,' she read. 'What's that supposed ter mean?'

'Means you gotta wash,' Ruby said.

'Bloomin' sauce!' Ellie was very annoyed by the impertinence of the innercent bird.

' 'E don't lie, darlin',' the Gypsy soothed, coming to the defence of her soothsayer. 'Jest a feathered finger a' fate, that's all 'e is. Aintcher, my chuck?'

Ellie growled away from her fortune and its teller. ' 'E'll end up in a pie, 'e goes on saying things like that.'

But despite her initial indignation the message took hold, and when she considered it coolly lying in her truckle bed that night with Tess and Maudie, the new baby, kicking on either side of her, she could see the sense of it. She'd been planning to nick herself some clothes from the secondhand stalls in the Lane. Perhaps the bird was trying to tell her secondhand wasn't good enough. Perhaps she ought to go for something brand new. Be a darn sight more difficult of course, but this was worth it.

But then again there was the business of Godliness. That meant doing the right thing, didn't it? And she knew it wasn't right to steal. Tell yer what, she said, partly to herself and partly to that vague God she wasn't sure she believed in, if I can get mesself the clothes for this job, I'll turn over a new leaf an' never steal another thing so long as I live. I'll keep mesself nice and clean, earn me own way. How about that? It seemed a fair bargain so she turned her attention to the practical business of how it could be done. I'll 'op school termorrer, she thought, an' go an' 'ave a look-see. I'll pop round Ruby's first thing an' see if she'll give me a lend of 'er Ma's old carpet bag, an' I'll take a few coppers jest in case. I'll bet I can do it. Be nice to 'ave really new clothes fer once in a while.

Ruby's Ma said she could have the carpet bag providing she didn't get caught with it, and providing she brought it back before three o'clock. And Ruby said she'd tell Miss Silverman she'd been sick or something, and would she be back in time for work? And then it was seven o'clock and time for her shopping expedition to begin, so they came to the door to see her off and wish her luck.

133

'Poor little blighter,' Mrs Miller said, watching her as she ran off towards Brick Lane. 'I 'ope she gets 'er job, Ruby. Be the making of 'er if she could leave 'ome. She deserves a bit a' luck wiv an ol' man like that Paddy Murphy. If she gets 'er new clothes you tell 'er ter come round 'ere termorrer an' 'ave a good wash afore she gets dressed. Tell 'er she can use the tub if she's early. Afore six mind, or yer Dad'll 'ave sommink ter say.'

'Ta, Ma,' Ruby said. 'I'll tell 'er.'

Shoreditch High Street was a classy place, presided over by the bow bell chimes of St Leonard's Church at the northern end and just up the road from Liverpool Street Station to the south. It was full of fine shops and well-to-do shoppers, there was a cut-glass pub on every corner, and the London Music Hall did a roaring trade next door to Rotherham's. Even the stalls were classy here, Ellie thought as she walked towards Hopkins and Peggs, clutching her carpet bag. The fruit was a sight for sore eyes and the jellied eels fair made her mouth water. But there wasn't time for food this morning. There was too much to be done.

By dint of standing outside the shop and peering through the windows it didn't take her long to establish that the women who worked at Hopkins and Peggs all wore black skirts and blouses, and dressed their hair in the most sober style, with the merest suggestion of a fringe across their foreheads and the neatest of buns at the nape of their necks. I shall need 'airpins, an' a brush an' comb, she thought, making a mental list. Black skirt, black stockings, garters, black boots. I'll 'ave a white blouse fer termorrer though, all that black looks like a funeral. An' a straw boater ter top it all off. That Morrie Isherman bloke sells boaters. Gaw dearie me, I shall 'ave me work cut out ter get all that lot.

She looked wistfully through the plate glass at all the tempting goods on display. Clothes for other women in another world. She knew they were beyond her, but she couldn't help lusting after them just the same. One window was curtained with elegant skirts, in serge and grosgrain and cravenette with neat little bolero jackets to match, waterfall skirts and mermaid skirts and gored skirts, with box pleats and

134

pin tucks and elaborate braiding; another was tiered with fine blouses, milk white and cream and very pale lavender, in chiffon and ninon, lawn and muslin and embroidered linen, with high, boned neckbands and pouter pigeon bosoms frothing with lace. Right in the middle was an elegant creation in cream muslin with long Renaissance sleeves, puffed at the wrists, and dear little lingerie buttons all the way down the front between the lace panels and the fine tucks. Ellie found she was licking her lips at the sight of it. How the other 'alf live, she thought. Lucky devils! Fancy bein' able ter dress like that.

Then the bow bells struck half past eight and a gentleman in a dress suit opened the doors for custom so she thought she'd better make herself scarce. Moochin' about 'ere'll never do, she scolded herself. Better cross over the road and get cracking, straight away. There was no hope of nicking anything from the shops, but the stalls were far more likely.

It took her all morning to collect her outfit, for the men who sold new clothes were a great deal more careful of them than the secondhand sellers, and they watched their merchandise like hawks. She had to wait more than half an hour for the chance to lift a blouse, and by then she was so impatient and so cross she took two as a sort of revenge. Stockings were easy because someone had pushed three pairs right off the stall onto the pavement and all she had to do was pick them up, but boots were impossible. The crafty devils hung 'em outside the shops, right enough, but never in pairs, and what was the use a' one boot? In the end she had to settle for a secondhand pair after all, which was a bit of a disappointment. But by midday Mrs Miller's carpet bag was full to the brim, and Ellie was feeling well pleased with herself. She'd even pinched a pair of scarlet garters and two cakes of scented soap. Now she was loitering near Morrie Isherman's hat stall in the Lane, fingering the boaters.

'Tanner!' Morrie said, creeping up behind her so suddenly it made her jump.

She recovered quickly and gave him a bright smile. 'Aintcher got nothink fer frupence?'

'Do me a favour,' he said. 'That's 'ats we're talkin' about.'

'Tell yer what,' she tried. 'I'll give yer tuppence an' a cake a' scented soap. How about that?'

'Nicked it, aintcher?' he said amiably. 'Holy terror, you are, Ellie Murphy.' Then as she went on looking at him imploringly, 'Oh, all right then. Go on. You can 'ave it. Where's yer tuppence?'

She fished the coins and the soap from the pocket of her old green coat and handed them across.

'Good gel,' he approved. ' 'Ang on a tick. You can sling that in an' all.' And he opened a battered hatbox and fished out an enormous hat.

It was a Floradora, weighed down with plump red roses that curled and curved above a brim even wider than her shoulders. The flowers were dusty and the rim bent but it was the most luxurious hat she'd ever seen. She couldn't believe her luck.

'Cor!' she said. 'You're a pal, Mr Isherman! Ta.'

' 'S a pleasure,' he said grinning at her and admiring her pretty blue eyes. 'Now you cut off 'ome like a good gel an' don't you go nickin' nothink else.'

'I won't,' she promised happily, and her expression was as honest as her vow. She'd nicked all she needed now.

She wore the Floradora all the way back to Mrs Miller's, feeling pleased with her prowess and happily aware that she was causing a stir. Well, I earned it, she thought. I done a good job a' work this morning.

Mrs Miller was impressed too, and told her she could leave her 'shopping' in Ruby's bedroom till she needed it, which was a great relief because she didn't want to take it home for fear of the bugs and all those grubby kids. Then she thought she might as well go to school for the afternoon, seeing it was the last time she'd ever have to.

Nobody said goodbye to her at the end of the day, but that didn't surprise or upset her, because they'd never said goodbye to anybody as far as she could remember. Miss Silverman gave her a certificate that said she'd achieved an adequate standard in English and that her arithmetic had earned a credit, and then she was out in the sunshine and free to start earning her own living. She was so happy she danced all the way home.

She slept very little that night, what with the bugs and the babies, but that didn't worry her either, because she knew it was for the very last time, and anyway she had to be up early to get to Ruby's in time for her wash. At five o'clock her mother creaked out of the double bed and began to stir the ashes in the stove, and at that Ellie extricated herself from the babies and got up and dressed.

'You off out?' her mother asked.

'Um.'

'Get us a pinch a' tea, will yer.'

'I'm off after a job, Ma. Shan't be back fer a while.'

'Oh,' her mother said. 'I shall 'ave ter send Tessie then. Give 'er a shake, will yer.'

'Is there anythink to eat?'

'Not till someone goes an' gets it.'

'I shall 'ave to 'ave air pie then, shan't I,' she said, shrugging her hunger away and wondering whether she'd have time to nick something. 'I'm off then. Tat-ah.'

'Mind 'ow you go,' her mother said automatically. But she didn't look up, and Ellie had a sinking feeling that she didn't mean it.

Mrs Miller was far more welcoming. 'There you are, lovey,' she said. 'You're in nice time. Go an' get yer things,' The tin bath was already in position on the rag rug and there were two kettles and a large saucepan heating on the stove and a towel warming on the clothes horse.

'Nobody won't come in, will they?' Ellie asked nervously. She'd never had a bath in a tub before and the thought of standing naked to wash herself, even in a kitchen as warm and welcoming as this one, was suddenly very daunting.

'No fear a' that, duck,' Mrs Miller reassured. 'Back door's locked an' I'll draw the blinds for yer. You'll be quite private, don't you worry. Men ain't due back till past six. You look sharp, we'll be over an' done long afore that.'

Even so, as she sped upstairs to collect her new clothes Ellie's heart was thumping with a most uncomfortable embarrassment. She'd got to have that bath, cleanliness being next to Godliness an' everything, but she wished having a bath didn't mean showing herself up. Her old clothes were little more than smelly rags and now they'd be left on the floor for Mrs Miller to see. It made her feel ashamed just to think of it. And besides that, they'd see her wiv nothing on, and she'd got titties coming. 'You got ter do it, gel,' she told herself sternly as she picked up her bundle. 'You wanna get on, you got ter do it.' But embarrassment was making her eyes bolt.

She needn't have worried, for Mrs Miller was a tactful woman and sensitive to the fears of a thirteen-year-old. When Ellie got back to the kitchen, the bath was ready and steaming and the clothes horse had been arranged around the tub like a towelled screen. She crept behind it gratefully and removed her tatty clothes.

'If I was you, gel,' Mrs Miller's vioce said calmly from behind the towel, 'I'd get shot a' that lot, now you got all new. I'll burn 'em for yer if yer like.'

'Oh yes,' Ellie said, lowering herself rather gingerly into the warm water. 'I would like, please Mrs Miller.'

So the old clothes were wrapped in brown paper and put on one side to be burnt and the old dirt was scrubbed away, and ten minutes later the new Ellie emerged from the steam, pink and pretty and wrapped in a white towel ready to face the world.

And realized that she hadn't got any underwear.

'Oh Ellie!' Mrs Miller said, laughing out loud. 'If that don't beat all! Ne'er mind, duck, our Ruby's got an old chemise we was keepin' fer Amy. Nip up an' get it, Rube, an' a pair a' drawers an' all. We can't 'ave 'er goin' fer a job wiv no drawers.'

'You're ever so good ter me,' Ellie said gratefully. 'I'll bring 'em back, I promise.'

'You 'ave a good rub down, and get yourself dressed quick as yer can,' Mrs Miller advised tactfully. 'I'm off ter make the beds. I'll bring yer down a lookin' glass if yer like.'

The new clothes were lovely, soft and clean and smelling so fresh. The boots weren't a very good fit, but what a' that. Everything else was just right. She pulled the belt as tight as she could and looked down happily at the smooth cloth of her new black skirt, her two neat black ankles, and her hands emerging from her neat white cuffs, so clean and pink she hardly recognized them.

'You look a treat,' Ruby said. 'Whatcher gonna do wiv yer barnet?'

'Give us a lend a' your scissors, I'll show yer.'

138

Ten minutes later, the transformation was complete. Her long curly hair had been brushed and combed and pinned into a bun on the nape of her neck and she'd cut herself a curly fringe. 'Well, you *do* look a swell,' Mrs Miller said. 'If you don't get took on this morning, I'll go ter Jericho.'

But the nicest moment came two minutes later when Mr Miller came home for his breakfast and didn't know who she was.

' 'Oo's the young lady, mother?' he asked, and Ellie was gratified to notice that he looked quite uncomfortable at the sight of her, as though she was someone special. A young lady, eh? she thought, and she took another glance at her new clean face in the looking glass on the dresser.

'Well, blow me down!' Mr Miller said when he'd been enlightened. 'I'd never 'a know'd. Never in a month a' Sundays. Where's me breakfast then, woman?'

'I'd better be off then,' the young lady said, because Mrs Miller was putting a loaf of bread on the table and the sight of it was making her mouth water.

'Good luck!' they all said as she pinned on her boater. And Mrs Miller gave her a kiss and a neat brown paper parcel. 'I've wrapped up all yer new things for yer.' And Ruby came to the door and launched her into the early morning sunshine. 'Remember the innercent bird?' she giggled. 'I'll bet yer get took on now.'

'Fingers crossed,' Ellie said, because it didn't do to tempt Providence. Then she set off on her adventure.

Shoreditch High Street was still empty when she arrived and the shops hadn't opened yet, although the assistants were all in position behind the counters and the windows were washed sparkling clean, like a line of dazzling mirrors all along the street. A line of reassuring mirrors, reflecting her new, clean, pretty, grown-up image everywhere she looked. By the time she reached Hopkins and Peggs, she'd almost grown accustomed to it.

The porter at the staff entrance didn't even look at her. 'You an' all the others,' he said when she'd explained why she'd come. 'Straight up the stairs. Second door on the left.'

It was a small brown waiting room, with an empty table in the centre and a collection of odd cane chairs set rigidly against the walls. Half a dozen of them were already self-consciously occupied by an even odder collection of girls, all of whom made a point of not looking at her when she came in, although they looked up at once when she went to sit down, and barked at her almost with one voice, 'Not there!' indicating with their eyes that she was to sit on the seat at the end of the line. It wasn't very encouraging.

Then there was nothing to do but wait. Three more girls arrived and were barked into the right seat and presently an apologetic woman with wispy grey hair put her head in at the door and whispered 'Next'. The girl nearest the door got up and tiptoed out. Time passed. More new girls arrived and four more originals were whispered away, never to return. The silence was oppressive.

I shall 'ave ter say sommink soon, Ellie thought, or we'll all go barmy. 'They don't come back, do they,' she tried, looking at the girl beside her. 'I reckon someone's ate 'em.'

They all looked up at once, shocked and anxious, and one or two said 'Shush!' very fiercely. So that was a waste a' time. They'd better give me this job, she thought, after all this.

But at last, after more than half an hour, the grey-haired woman called her and trotted her down the narrow corridor into a carpeted office where a very grand lady sat behind a desk, a fierce pince-nez dangling on a chain round her neck and a pile of papers on the blotter before her.

'Name,' she said as Ellie came to a halt before her.

Until that moment it hadn't entered Ellie's head to change her name, but now, as the woman looked up at her with calculating eyes, she took a deep breath and a new identity.

'Ellen White, ma'am.'

'Address?'

She gave Mrs Miller's address so effortlessly she could have believed it herself.

'References?'

What does she mean by references? Ellie thought. Was it that certificate they gave her at school? She took the little paper from her skirt pocket and handed it across hopefully, but when the lady read it she gave her a very odd look.

'It says here that your surname is Murphy and that you live in Heneage Street,' she said.

Ellie opened her blue eyes as widely as she could and prepared to lie her way out of trouble. 'That was me mother's name,' she said. 'I used me mother's name at school yer see, ma'am.'

'Ah!' the lady said and she wrote something on the certificate and pinned it to the top of the pile. Illegitimate of course, she thought. We would have to watch this one if we took her on. Then she fixed her pince-nez firmly on her nose and stared at the girl.

'Tell me why you want to work in Hopkins and Peggs.'

That was a lot easier. 'Because it's the best store in the district, ma'am.'

The answer pleased. 'And if we take you on, I'm not saying we will mind, but if, what would you have to offer us?'

The new Miss White was taken aback for the second time, but while she was gulping towards an answer the door opened and a tall man strode into the room, coat tails flapping behind him. 'Sorry to disturb, Miss Elphinstone,' he said. 'Must have those accounts, d'you see.' And then he noticed Ellie, and his eyes flickered and lit up, and held their glance for quite a lot longer than was necessary. He put his hand on the desk and stopped rushing and stood still.

He likes the look of me, she thought, and hard on the heels of that realization came another, even more pleasant. He thinks I'm pretty.

'Well,' he said, still looking at her. 'Who have we here, eh? New recruit, Miss Elphinstone?'

'Yes, Mr Hopkins.'

Mr 'Opkins? He couldn't be *the* Mr 'Opkins, surely? He didn't look old enough.

'Let's try some adding up, shall we?' he said, still gazing. 'Two yards at two and eleven three, three at one and eleven three, and a yard at – oh, say four and six.'

You don't catch me wiv that sort a' stuff, Ellie thought delightedly. That's jest mental arithmetic. And she did the sums quickly. Six an' six an' four's sixteen. Sixteen an' six take away five farthings, 'Sixteen an' fourpence three farthings.'

He beamed his approval. 'Just the sort of girl we want, eh Miss Elphinstone?'

The pince-nez glittered. 'If you say so, Mr Hopkins. Here are the accounts you wanted.' He clutched the folder to his linen bosom and rushed out of the room again.

I've got the job, Ellie thought, with excitement rising into her throat like a fountain. But she stood still and waited, looking down at the carpet so that Miss Elphinstone couldn't see how triumphant she was feeling.

'We pay two and sixpence a week to start with,' that lady said, 'laundry deductable, board and lodgings found. When can you start?'

'Now, if yer like, ma'am.'

And now it was. Miss Elphinstone rang the bell and the grey-haired lady put her head obediently round the door and instructions were given.

'Dress lengths with Miss Morton.'

Ellie was so excited she grinned all the way down the corridor. I've done it! I've done it! she thought. I've left 'ome. I've got a job. I'm on me way! From now on Smelly Ellie was gone and forgotten. Ellen White had arrived.

It was a long first day and a very hard-working one, especially on an empty stomach. First she was taken upstairs to the attic and introduced to another Miss Elphinstone, who looked even more formidable than the first one and read her such a lengthy list of rules and regulations it made her head spin. 'We rise at six sharp when you will be expected to sweep the shop and clear etcetera, in your *own* clothes, of course. Breakfast is at seven thirty, after which you will wash and dress properly, dinner at one, supper at eight, except for Saturdays, when it is usually nine, depending on our closing time. Laundry is sent out at seven o'clock on Thursday mornings and returned on Monday at the same time. Wednesday half day, when you are not allowed on the premises, and Sunday of course. We serve breakfast and supper on Sundays but apart from that we don't expect to see you at all. Those who are late for meals go without. You will always use the north stair to get to the

142

dormitories. The south stair is out of bounds for female staff. I trust that is clearly understood. We have our reputation to consider. Doors are locked spot on ten o'clock at night and the gas in this dormitory is put out at half past. This is your bed. You may leave your parcel in the cupboard.'

Then she was provided with the regulation black blouse and three sets of white cuffs and collars. Suitably attired, she was sent down to the shop and her duties. It was like stepping into another world. The dormitory had been a spartan place, smelling of damp and carbolic soap, with its bare walls distempered yellow and floorboards underfoot, the bedsteads iron and the cupboards cheap white deal. The shop was luxurious. Here the walls were covered in thick flock paper and the floors in polished linoleum, the high counters were made of fine carved oak, and above their head a complicated network of miniature rails and points buzzed the all-important cash from customer to cashier in a series of drum-shaped containers. It was an exotic place, smelling of new cloth and the expensive scents of its expensive customers. The old Smelly Ellie might well have found it daunting, but the new Ellen White took it all calmly, as though she was accustomed to it.

Miss Morton turned out to be a wisp of a woman who did everything at speed, flicking material from the roll so rapidly that the counter was draped with it in seconds and ripping off the required lengths with a whip-crack alacrity that was most impressive. Ellie spent the morning tying up parcels, holding up lengths of cloth for the customers' inspection and tidying up after the sale, which meant re-rolling all the materials that had been displayed and carrying the heavy rolls back into their original positions again. She was mightily relieved when one o'clock came and they all trooped off to the basement for their dinner.

As she suspected that there would probably be a hierarchy in the dining order in this place, just as there was in everything else, she stood beside the door and watched, hoping that somebody would enlighten her, or that she'd be able to work out what it was. Presently she was joined by a girl she recognized from the waiting room that morning, a pale skinny girl with a fuzz of straw-coloured hair and pale grey eyes. 'They

143

took you on an' all,' she said to the girl, grinning a sort of welcome.

'Never thought they would,' the girl said. 'They're ever so sticky. Where are we supposed ter sit?'

By now Ellie had noticed that the important people had already settled themselves at the tables in the middle of the room and that the oilcloth on the tables nearest the wall was chipped and stained. 'Likes of us by the wall, I reckon,' she said, so by the wall they went, and waited hungrily while steaming plates of meat and potatoes were served to the centre tables.

'You're sharp, intcher?' the new girl said admiringly. 'Where d'yer come from?'

'Whitechapel.'

'That accounts,' her new friend said sagely. 'You gotta be sharp you live round there.'

True enough, Ellie thought. And was glad of it.

They introduced themselves, and the new girl, who said her name was Maud, tried to catch a glimpse of the meat as a tray full of plates was carried past them. 'Hope it ain't mutton,' she said. 'I got a sensitive stomach.'

Ellie didn't mind what it was. 'I'm so 'ungry I could eat a horse,' she said.

'You probably will,' her new friend said.

Ellie laughed, but secretly she was counting her good fortune again. Meat and potatoes served up to you piping hot in the middle of the day. This is the life, she thought.

She was still of the same opinion at half past seven that evening when the store had finally closed and she was covering the goods with dust sheets. Her arms ached and her feet were sore, but what of that? Presently she'd be going down for another meal, and tonight she would sleep well in a clean bed all on her own. And on top of all that there was the marvellous moment when she would tell her family what she'd done.

After supper she bought a stamp and a postcard and wrote a thank you note to Mrs Miller. 'I got the job. 2/6 a week and my keep. Not so dusty. Thank you ever so much for all you done, especherly the bath. I will come and visit on my day off Wednesday and return the things, Love from Ellie. x x x.'

144

Then she went to Heneage Street.

Her mother was hard at work pulling fur so the room was full of drifting fibres and the smell of rotting flesh. There was no sign of her father and the kids were all over the place as usual. She noticed that Tessie had already taken her place as substitute mother and was carrying the baby about on her hip, poor kid. After a day spent among the refinements of Hopkins and Peggs, they all looked dreadfully dirty to her but they were pleased to see her and thought she looked 'a real swell'.

'Where's Pa?' she asked. Trust 'im ter be out.

'Up the pub,' Paddy told her. 'Where d'yer think?'

'D'yer manage ter get anythink to eat?' her mother asked, looking up briefly from a rabbit skin.

'I live in, Ma. Meals an' bed an' all. I just come down ter say goodbye.'

Nell sighed heavily. 'You're a good gel, Ellie,' she said, 'an' I'm glad yer got out of all this, but I shall miss yer, lovey, an' that's a fact.'

'You takin' your green coat?' Tessie asked hopefully.

'No. I got all the clothes I need. You can 'ave it if yer like.'

'Be my turn ter leave school next,' Paddy said, stung to a momentary jealousy by all the attention she was being given. 'Jest you wait then!'

'I shall 'ave ter be off in a minute,' Ellie said. 'They shut the doors at ten o'clock. Don't wanna be locked out me first night.'

But just as she put her hand on the doorknob, Paddy Murphy came rolling home from the pub. He was dramatically amazed at her appearance and his amazement gave Nell the chance to scramble the skins out of sight before he could complain. 'Well, will ye look at that!' he said. 'Here's me daughter all dressed up like a lady, so she is. Wonders'll never cease.'

'She's got 'erself a job,' Nell told him, throwing the sack under the bed.

'An' not before time, child. We could do with the money, an' that's a fact. When d'ye get paid?'

Gaw, 'e's ugly! Ellie thought. Crafty old thing, and she began to smile, thinking of the shock he'd get when she told him. 'It's *my* money, Pa,' she said. 'I ain't livin' 'ere no more.

145

I'm livin' in. My wages. My keep. You ain't gettin' a brass farthin' out a' me.'

He was furious. 'You mind yer mouth, gel,' he roared. 'Remember who ye're talkin' to.'

But she laughed at him. 'Yell all yer like. Don't make no odds ter me. I don't live 'ere no more.'

'It's come to somethin' when your own daughter won't help you,' he said, whining and assuming his 'hurt' expression. But she ignored him, feeling her power, despising him. He narrowed his eyes and looked at her craftily for a few seconds. Then he changed his tone and his line of attack. 'Very well, daughter,' he said. 'I'm not a man to bear a grudge. I'm a loving man, so I am. So I'll give you a word of advice. You wanna watch those fingers.'

'What's 'a matter wiv 'em,' she said hotly.

'They're light so they are,' he said and now his grin was malevolent. 'An' light fingers end up in quod. Ye've been warned! Now I can't say fairer than that, can I?'

'Fair!' his daughter snorted contemptuously. 'You don't know the meaning a' the word. You never been fair in all yer natural.'

'You just mind your mouth, missie,' her father growled again. 'You're not so big that I can't take me belt to ye.'

'You ain't never takin' that belt ter me no more,' Ellie said looking him straight in the eye, her expression icy. 'You done that fer the last time. You ever lift a finger ter me ever again, and I'll kick you from 'ere to the middle a' next week. So you can put that in yer pipe an' smoke it!'

She was aware that the kids were huddling together in the furthest corner of the room, their eyes wide with amazement at her daring, and that her mother was sitting back on her heels enjoying it, and that her father's face was turning puce with extreme rage.

'Nell! Nell!' he cried. 'Will ye hark at the girl! Have I to be spoken to in this way by me own daughter? Sure she'll make me ill so she will. Me that's given her the most priceless commodity known to man.'

'What cermodity?'

'Why life, daughter. Life!'

146

'What a load of old guff an' gubbins. You never gave nothink ter no one.'

'Oh, oh,' her father wailed, holding out his hands to her mother and trying to look appealing. 'Will ye stop her, Nell. She's makin' me ill!'

'See if I care,' Ellie said.

And on that note she left them.

Chapter Twelve

Regular meals and uninterrupted sleep soon began to have a marked effect on the new Miss Ellen White. By September when her brothers and sister were starting another miserable school year she had grown more than an inch taller and was half a stone heavier. The extra flesh suited her, rounding her limbs and plumping her cheeks and giving her a new air of womanly assurance. Her eyes were bright, her hair well brushed and gleamingly clean and for the first time in her life her conscience was clear. She hadn't realized what a relief it would be not to have to steal or tell lies any more. 'This is the life!' she told herself as she lead her friends down to the canteen for supper. To be housed and fed and paid and approved of was little short of luxury. And she knew she was approved of. Miss Morton actually told her so and even Miss Elphinstone was pleased with her, as she could tell from the little nod the lady invariably gave her when they passed.

Unfortunately, the young men in Mr Hopkins' employ did rather more than approve. And that was a nuisance.

'Hello, beautiful!' they would say, making eyes at her as they scurried into the shop first thing in the morning. She would try to keep them at their distance with an icy politeness, 'Good morning, Mr Tiffin. Good morning, Mr Jones.' But that only made them laugh. It wasn't long before they'd nicknamed her Miss Ice White, and although none of them understood that her hauteur was caused by fear, it made a good topic of conversation and speculation. Soon they were laying bets on which of them would be the first to steal a kiss from this challenging young person.

'Bet I could!' Jimmy Thatcher bragged. He was a thickset

sandy-haired boy who worked in the basement packing, and fancied himself as a ladies' man.

'Never on yer life!' they mocked. 'She wouldn't look at you. Not wiv your ugly mug!'

'You watch!' he promised. And from then on he laid siege, sitting at the table next to hers, walking through the shop as close to her as he could get, and lurking on the landing in the hope of catching her as she came downstairs. And at last one cold morning his determined patience was rewarded. She was late down to the shop, and they were alone on the stairs together.

Never a man to waste time on preliminaries, he seized her round the waist at once, grabbing at her belt with his big blunt fingers. 'Give us a kiss!' he said shoving his face into hers. 'Quick! No one's looking!'

She drew herself up to her new full height and tried to pull his hands away from her belt. 'Take your dirty maulers off me this instant!' she said furiously.

'Give us a kiss then!'

She was so angry and so frightened she acted without thought, almost instinctively. She stamped on the toe of his boot, and as he shifted his balance wincing she swung a fierce kick at his shins.

It hurt him so much he forgot all about being amorous, and while he was rubbing his shin and swearing at the top of his voice, she ran off down the rest of the stairs as fast as her shaking legs would carry her.

Down in the shop her friends were alerted by his roars, and rushed to comfort her. They were delighted to hear how brutally she'd dealt with him. 'Serve him right,' Maud said. 'He's 'ad that coming to 'im fer ages.' He'd tried to pin her in a corner once too. By the end of the afternoon Thatcher was a laughing stock and Ellen was a heroine, and from that moment on her little group of friends looked to her, young as she was, as their leader.

Early one November afternoon, when a battalion of the Royal Fusiliers came marching down the High Street, she was the one who went to ask Miss Elphinstone to give them permission to watch the procession from the upper windows.

The British Army was embarking for another war in some out of the way part of the Empire, and the Fusiliers were on their way to Fenchurch Street Station and the troup train to Tilbury. They were preceded by a drum and fife band, drums in thunderous unison, fifes squealing like pigs, and they wore full dress uniform and determined expressions because they knew they were being admired. They were led by a resplendent sergeant with a face as red as his coat and a chest like a pouter pigeon, and they drew a long dark straggling crowd behind them, like a magnet trailing iron filings. There were clerks with self-important expressions, grimy boys in grubby rags, elderly gentlemen stepping out boldly in time to the music, and down beside their well-polished boots a flea-bitten collection of Shoreditch mongrels, yapping themselves silly with uncontrollable patriotism. It was very exciting.

Ellen and Maud, cheering them on from the upper windows of Hopkins and Peggs, with most of the other girls from the shop, enjoyed it all very much and thought the Fusiliers looked very handsome in their fine red coats.

'Fine lookin' body a' men,' Maud approved as the column passed beneath them. 'Funny ter think a' them fighting a war though.'

'Tha's what they're for, innit?' Ellen said reasonably. 'They wouldn't a' joined the colours else.'

'D'you think any of em'll get theirselves killed?'

'Don't ask me. Anyway we shan't know nothink about it if they do. 'S down South Africa way. Nothink ter do wiv us.'

'I think they look just lovely in them red coats.'

'Shop!' Miss Elphinstone warned them, swishing into the dormitory. 'Three minutes, Miss White. Three minutes to be downstairs and ready!'

'Be there in two an' a half, ma'am,' Ellen assured her, and stood back from the window at once.

Miss Elphinstone gave her usual half-hidden smile of approval as she moved on to chivy the second dormitory. No matter how silly and excitable the other girls might get, you could always depend on Miss White. She'd turned out to be quite an addition to the staff, invariably bright and cheerful and very well groomed. She kept her cupboard in immaculate

150

order and her clothes were always spotless. And a natural leader, too. They could do with more girls like her. Surprising really that such a pretty girl should be so sensible. Usually the pretty ones were silly and flighty. But this one was different. There was no nonsense with any of their young men. She was never rude to any of them and they all seemed to like her, but she kept them all at arm's length, most commendably. Yes, they'd struck very lucky with Miss White.

Back in the first dormitory Ellen was leading her own troops back to work, with a saucy imitation of Mr Fenway the floor walker. 'Come along, ladies! Look lively!'

'Them red coats was lovely,' Maud said following obediently. 'I wouldn't mind one a' them mesself.'

'I'd rather 'ave the feller inside it,' Polly said, laughing.

'Wouldn't do yer much good wiv 'im marchin' off ter war,' Ellen said, straightening a curtain on her way out.

In the street below them the crowds were walking away too. The excitement was over. But had they known it, the story of those red coats had only just begun.

Out on the sun-scorched plains of the veldt they weren't quite so lovely as they'd been in the streets of Whitechapel. In fact they were a conspicuous nuisance and it wasn't long before the army had decided to discontinue their use in battle and to dress their troops in a colour that would give them some camouflage. They called it khaki, and its arrival had a profound effect on the casualty rate.

It also had an unexpected effect on the tailoring trade and women's fashions at home. Khaki costumes with scarlet trimmings were all the rage that year, and Hopkins and Peggs soon had a window full of them. Not to be outdone by the gentry, Ellen and Maud bought several yards of striped ribbon from haberdashery and having trimmed their boaters and the collars and cuffs of their white blouses went off in style to the London Music Hall of a Wednesday to sing patriotic songs in their patriotic colours.

And down in Whitechapel the tailors were working all hours to fulfill a rush of orders, for all those fashionable costumes, and officers' uniforms in fine worsted, and the new heavy battle dress for the infantry. Khaki for the troops was an awkward

151

material to work, being thick and cumbersome and very, very heavy. It exhausted Emmanuel Cheifitz, and tore Rachel's fingers, and reduced Rivke to growling. But at least the work paid, which was just as well because the rents had gone up again and so had the price of bread. 'So that's var for you,' Aunty Dumpling said. 'The var begin, the price go up.'

It was a bad winter. Emmanuel grew more gaunt with each cold day, his thin chest wracked with coughing and his eyes haggard.

'A doctor you should see, maybe?' Rachel suggested, but he wouldn't hear of it. Doctors cost money and there was little enough of that for food and coal.

'No. No,' he sighed. 'It vill pass, bubeleh.'

But it didn't pass. It got worse and worse, until finally when the sleets of February had chilled him to the bone he began to run a high temperature and was too ill to get out of bed. This time his sisters were adamant and the doctor was called. 'Inflammation of the lungs,' he said, and advised complete rest until the fever subsided, 'otherwise he'll end up with pleurisy and we don't want that.' It was a blow to the entire family.

'I *must* work,' Emmanuel insisted, struggling to sit up and finding even that impossible. 'I shall be well tomorrow, Rachel, I promise you.' To be ill when there was so much work!

'Rest, bubeleh,' Rachel said. 'Don't you worry. Ve manage.'

But it was easier said than done. With the breadwinner's wage lost to them, they wouldn't be able to afford the rent. And even if the Board of Guardians gave them a loan to tide them over, it would still have to be paid back. And how was that to be done? Women might work every bit as hard as men, but they didn't earn the same kind of money. The three women thought and planned and agonized, but however often they asked one another what they should do, the blunt answer remained the same. There was nothing within their power.

To David there was no problem. He knew exactly what had to be done and who had to do it. He was nearly fourteen and Bar Mitzvah, with his own phylacteries to use at morning prayer, an adult member of the community. 'Don't you worry, Mama,' he said when Rachel finally admitted defeat and began to weep, 'I will take care of you.'

'Such a boy!' Aunty Dumpling admired, removing her apron from her head, to give him a watery smile. But she burst into tears again when he told them what he intended.

'I shall leave school,' he said calmly, 'and go to work and pay the rent. I am Bar Mitzvah now. A man. It is high time I worked.'

'But your education, bubeleh!' his mother protested. 'Your drawing!'

'I can draw any time,' he told her gently. 'Now we need a wage.'

Emmanuel said he wouldn't hear of it, and wept tears of disappointment and weakness. But the boy was determined.

That afternoon he went to see the principal and explained his situation. 'I must go to work. The rent has to be paid. I am the man of the family now.'

And the principal, who had heard this story from so many of his students, sighed and agreed, but with the proviso that he become apprenticed to a good trade and that the remainder of his scholarship should be transferred to pay the premium. 'It will mean a smaller wage,' he said, 'at least to begin with, but it will be secure work, and it could lead on to better things. When you are sixteen you can come back to evening school here. By then you should be earning a fair wage and things should have sorted themselves out for you. It would be a pity to discontinue your education, having come so far. Go and see Mr Tranter. He will know what apprenticeships are available.'

David came home that afternoon with his future settled, clutching the address of a bookbinder in Shoreditch High Street. And Emmanuel, who felt too weak to argue, agreed that if this had to be done, an apprenticeship was the best way to do it, and comforted them both that bookbinding was at least an artistic trade. 'But you go back to the school when you sixteen,' he urged. 'This you promise?'

David had every intention of going back. Life at the Tech was too rewarding to be relinquished for ever. And besides, he was drawing better now than he'd ever done, and he was secretly hopeful that if he could only study just a little longer, he might become an artist. Even Mr Eswyn Smith said his work was 'quite good' nowadays, and that was praise indeed. So one day. When things weren't quite so difficult.

In the meantime, there was a job to be done, and if he had to earn his living, binding books seemed as good a way as any.

He went to Mr Woolnoth, Bookbinders, the very next morning. It was a very small shop on the west side of Shoreditch High Street, and at first sight it didn't look at all promising, but once inside, he could see it was a thriving establishment. Behind the green baize window was a long busy workshop, so long and so busy that he couldn't see what was going on at the other end of it. It was mounded with paper and full of apprentice boys stacking and packing and counting. In one corner a spiral staircase corkscrewed upwards, and the boy who'd opened the door to him gave him a grunt and led him towards it. At the top was a small archway that led to the upper workshop.

Here men were painstakingly stitching pages together, or carving coloured leather with a battery of curious tools, or working with fragile gold leaf, and all round the edges of this skilled occupation boys were watering glue pots and cleaning tools and sweeping. He'd certainly be kept busy here, if nothing else.

He waited patiently while the boy went off to fetch Mr Woolnoth, and presently a man in a brown suit put down the leather he was handling and walked across the workshop towards him.

'Mr Tranter tells me you write a fair hand,' he said, 'and are on your way to becoming a competent draughtsman. Is that so, would you say?'

'I hope so, sir.'

'There's pen and paper,' Mr Woolnoth said. 'Write your name and address. Take as long as you need. It's quality we're after, not speed. When you've finished, take a second sheet and draw something.' And then he was gone, moving delicately between the desks, as soft-footed as a cat.

David wrote obediently and in his very best copperplate, and drew a careful sketch of the row of glue pots on the shelf beside him, and after a while the boss returned to consider his efforts. By now, such was the inescapable sense that he was being tested David was feeling and looking more nervous than he knew. But the sight of his bitten lip pleased Mr Woolnoth. His writing

154

and drawing were both pronounced 'fair enough' and he was told to report for work in ten days' time and to provide himself with a good quality linen apron in the meantime. It was as quick and easy as that.

Although he'd always imagined he would feel terribly excited when he first started work, he went home in a state of calm so profound it was almost as though he was walking in his sleep. Now nothing remained except his farewell to the Tech.

Saying goodbye to his friends was easy enough. They all lived locally and knew they would see one another in the Buildings or down the Lane or at one of the music halls. But the teachers were more difficult, for several of them were annoyed at his sudden departure and said so, and Mr Eswyn Smith was furious.

'It's always the same story,' he said when David came to see him at the end of his last Friday. 'Just when I've got you into some sort of shape. Well, don't blame me, boy, if you never amount to anything.' He was so annoyed he was snorting.

David tried to assure him that no blame would ever be attached. But that only made him worse. 'God damn it!' Mr Smith roared. 'Why you? I could have made a fine artist out of you, given the time. What sort of world do we live in, I ask you.' And he tore his paintbrushes from behind his ear and threw them at the wall.

'I will come back, the minute I'm sixteen,' David promised ardently. 'You have my word of honour.'

'You'd better, God damn it!' the art teacher said. 'And don't you stop drawing for a minute. You're one of the best pupils I've ever had.'

This was news. 'Am I?' He'd never said anything like this before. Never. 'Am I?'

'You didn't know it? Yes, God damn it, you are. And now this! Well, go if you're going, before I throw something else.'

This time David went home in a highly emotional state. To have discovered how much he was valued just at the very moment he had to leave was an irony he hadn't expected. Until then he'd been buoyed up by the knowledge that he was doing the honourable thing, supporting his parents and earning his living, and he hadn't stopped to think beyond it. Now he

155

couldn't escape the feeling that he was throwing an opportunity away. I'll go back, he promised himself. On my sixteenth birthday, I'll go back. No matter what it costs. I'll have earned it. And that thought was comforting.

The next Monday he started his apprenticeship, with the best of intentions and three pennies in his pocket. And although he missed his friends and felt cut off from all the things he'd enjoyed so much at school, he was resolutely uncomplaining. He was a man now, at work and supporting his family, and men didn't complain.

In the first week he was set to unpack the printed pages, in the second he was taught how to collate them. In the third he was told to make the glue and keep it watered, which he didn't enjoy at all. But he learned fast and could see that Mr Woolnoth was pleased. Six weeks later when his father was finally well enough to return to work, he was learning how to make endpapers, and how to set up the frames and how to mark up for sewing. By the summer he was sewing simple stitches and gluing up spines. And by then the work was enjoyable. He still missed school, but there were rewards in this crowded workshop among the quiet sounds of sewing and carving and the intermittent conversation of the men and the clowning friendship of the boys. It was hard work, just as he'd known it would be, but there were pleasures attached to it too. He liked the warm smell of new leather and the crisp scent of a new-printed page, and after a time he even enjoyed the smell of the gluepots, sweet and fishy though they were.

And whenever he had a minute to spare he drew sketches. Of Mr Woolnoth pondering, and Mr Steinway carving, and old Mr Martinson burnishing the gilded edges of a huge book held between his knees, of Tom and Jem and Fozzy and Abe and Dickon, the other apprentices, sweeping and setting up frames and stacking and stitching and grimacing at the smell of the glue. And every sketch was a step nearer the time when he could go back to the Tech.

Chapter Thirteen

Aunty Dumpling had found herself a gentleman friend. The shock waves *that* caused in the Cheifitz family! To be keeping company with a Jew would have been bad enough. But a goy! Rachel and Rivke were scandalized.

'At her time of life!' Rivke said scathingly. 'She should be so stupid!'

'I never hold my head up again!' Rachel wailed. 'The shame of it, Rivke. Vhy she do this?'

'Ai-yi-yi!' Rivke howled. 'Forty-nine years old to take up vid a goy!'

Emmanuel tried to be reasonable. 'So he takes her to the theatre vonce in a vhile, a meal maybe. It ain't a marriage yet.'

'Great oaks from little apples,' Rivke said, her face more lopsided than ever with disapproval.

'*Has vesholem*!' Rachel prayed. 'How could she spend her time vid such a *schlemiel*?'

David didn't know how he should react. It was certainly a most deplorable thing for a Jewish woman to marry out of her religion. He'd always known that. But this Jewish woman was Aunty Dumpling, his own roly-poly Aunty Dumpling, with her marvellous capacity for fun and affection, and he couldn't help thinking she'd hardly be likely to choose an unsuitable man, even for a trip to the theatre. And as to getting married, why that was really ridiculous. She couldn't possibly get married. He wouldn't even think of it.

'What's 'e like?' Hymie asked as they settled down to their weekly game of cards in the empty parlour above the Levy's shop.

'Haven't seen 'im,' David admitted, dealing the cards.

157

'They're in love, maybe,' Hymie said. He was already sixteen and had been out at work with the Gas Company for more than two years now so he considered himself an expert on love, as on many other matters. He was a solid looking individual with thick black hair and the makings of an equally black moustache, but as ugly as he'd ever been, his eyes too small behind those heavy horn rims and his nose too big and his wide shoulders awkward.

David on the other hand had grown steadily more handsome. When he'd left school he'd been a little boy, pale and anxious and undersized. Now he was a grown man, five foot ten inches tall, with a silky moustache and fine brown eyes and the confidence born of knowing that he was quite good-looking. Certainly the young women he passed on his way to and from Mr Woolnoth's were gigglingly aware of him, and some of the bolder ones had taken to making eyes at him from beneath their hats or, even worse, fishing for him with saucy remarks flung more or less in his direction. 'Mind you don't tread on the nice young man's feet, Elsie!' or 'What I wouldn't give fer a nice strong arm to 'old on to.' He didn't find them particularly attractive or interesting, and he knew, from everything he'd been taught at home and in the synagogue, that a brazen woman was best avoided. But that left him in a difficult position. He simply didn't know how to respond. Occasionally he was flattered by their attentions, when the hint was just a little too broad, he was shocked and couldn't avoid showing it. Then they laughed at him until he could feel the blushes spreading flame into his cheeks, and he would fall over his feet in an effort to get away from them. At home among modest Jewish women he'd always felt safe and comforted. And now his own modest Jewish aunt was courting a goy.

'She can't be in love,' he said scowling at the idea. 'She's forty-nine.'

Hymie grinned. 'Can happen any time,' he said. 'Take my word fer it. I fall in love every Thursday.'

'You don't.'

'Straight up! Every Thursday. I only have to be in that theatre five minutes and I'm in love. You never saw such girls

as there are in that theatre of a Thursday. You got to admit it.'
He and David went to the Pavilion nearly every week to see a
Jewish melodrama, and now it was pantomime time which was
even better.

David laughed at him. 'That's not love, Hymie. You never
even speak to 'em.'

'I would if they gave me half a chance,' Hymie said ruefully.
'Don't even see me, that's the trouble. Wait till it 'appens ter
you, then you'll know what I mean.'

'Unclean thoughts!' David warned, laughing at him again.
'You're supposed to keep yer eyes to the ground and resist
temptation, like a good Jewish boy.'

'And miss all the fun!' Hymie said. 'I should co-co. Have a
gasper.'

David took the proferred cigarette and they both lit up,
feeling very grown up and manly.

'No seriously, Davey,' Hymie said. 'Don't yer want ter fall in
love?'

David stung his nose by exhaling the smoke too quickly, so
for a few minutes he had to blink back tears and couldn't
answer, which was just as well, because he wasn't sure about his
feelings at all. Of course he wanted the comfort and happiness
of a good marriage, and he supposed he would fall in love like
everyone else, but there were fears too. What if the girl he
loved didn't love him? Or what if his parents arranged a
marriage for him and he couldn't love the girl? The whole
subject was fraught with difficulties. Better to avoid it.

'I'm going up Brick Lane termorrer,' he said. 'If 'e's there
I'll do a sketch, show you what's 'e's like.'

Hymie flicked ash from his cigarette and grinned, and let the
subject pass, like the good friend he was. 'Good idea,' he said.
David's sketches were always worth looking at, and this one
should be particularly good.

The next day was clammy with fog licking long, sulphur
yellow tongues against the windows and curling through every
crack to chill and choke. Rachel wasn't at all happy about her
David going off to Brick Lane in such weather. 'You catch your
death a' cold, bubeleh,' she warned. 'Some other time, nu?'
But curiosity was stronger than cold weather.

'I knew you vould come, bubeleh,' Dumpling said wrapping him in the fondest embrace as soon as he stepped inside her room. 'Nothing don't keep my Davey away from his old aunty. Vhat you think of my Davey, Mr Morrison? He's a fine boy, nu?'

The man sitting beside the stove had risen to his feet when David entered. Now he stood nervously holding out his hand in greeting, a short slender man, with sleek brown hair greying at the temples, and the narrowest moustache David had ever seen. It was little more than a line, but very neatly trimmed. He must have a very steady hand shaving, David thought, and shook that steady hand, surprised at how cold it was.

'Fred Morrison,' Dumpling said, doing the honours. 'He has the flat across the road. Mrs Renshaw's, you remember. Such a nice woman. Oy yoi! Vhat a life ve lead!' Mrs Renshaw had suffered a heart attack last summer and died before anyone could get to her. 'Vhat a life! Ve eat now, eh Davey?'

David sat opposite the infamous Mr Morrison all through the meal, and by the end of it he really rather liked him. He was such a very correct man, calling Aunty Dumpling Mrs Esterman all the time, and passing the dishes most politely, and talking so seriously. He said he worked as a despatch clerk for the *East London Weekly Pictorial*, and was gratifyingly interested in Mr Woolnoth and his bookbinding. 'It being all part an' parcel a' the same trade, so to speak.'

David started his first sketch of the man as soon as he got home that evening, but although his clothes were easy enough, the suit so dark and uncreased and the shirt so white with its high wing collar and its fat neat tie, the face was impossible because he couldn't remember any of its expressions. The pencil-line moustache, the thin nose, the sleek hair, yes, but not how Mr Morrison looked. It took four more meetings and six more sketches before David came anywhere near a likeness.

And then one afternoon in January he suddenly realized what it was he'd missed. Aunty Dumpling had just turned down the gaslight and they were settling round the fire to read the latest copy of the *Weekly Pictorial* when Mr Morrison glanced up sideways at her. His face was lit by the firelight and it wore such an odd expression that David found himself

160

staring, much longer and harder than was polite or proper. Nervousness, he thought, observing the taut lines etched into the man's cheeks. He wants to please. And then he noticed the dog-like anxiety in the man's eyes, and understood something else. He thinks he's inferior. Inferior to us. How very odd, when he's so well-dressed and proper. The idea that a grown man could feel inferior to a woman and a sixteen-year-old was new and extraordinary. Absorbing it, David felt that he liked Mr Morrison even more.

That night's sketch was much better, for he'd caught the tilt of the head and the taut cheeks and the lustrous anxiety of the eyes. This one was good enough to cover with tissue paper and put away in his folder, ready to be shown to Mr Eswyn Smith. For in twelve days' time his long exile would be over. In twelve days' time he would be back at the People's Palace. And I *have* earned it, he thought, looking at all the sketches he'd amassed.

In the grand emporium of Hopkins and Peggs the staff were preparing for the January sales, and Ellen was being observed. Miss Morton needed a new assistant, and she and Miss Elphinstone were thinking of promoting Miss White.

'She's been with us three years now,' Miss Morton said. 'She's nearly sixteen. A dependable young woman. Good head for figures. Quick.'

But promotion couldn't be rushed. 'I will keep an eye on her,' Miss Elphinstone decided. 'See how she does.'

Ellen knew nothing of this, for just at the moment she was fully occupied keeping her eye on somebody else, a quiet, undersized, scruffy little girl who was walking very slowly past the counter, deliberately not looking at the off-cuts of ribbon and lace trimming that were piled so temptingly in the sales baskets. She was watching a thief.

It was a disquieting experience, for the child reminded her of her earlier self, and it was a self the thought she had forgotten. She knew so exactly what that girl was thinking, and what she would do next. And sure enough, almost to the predicted second, a small rough hand reached out to tweak a length of velvet ribbon out of the nearest basket. But Ellen White was quicker than she was.

161

'That'll be sixpence,' she said, holding hand and ribbon in a equally sudden grip.

'I was only looking, miss,' the girl said, bold with fear.

'You wasn't thinking a' nicking nothink?'

' 'Course not!' The lie was easy and wide-eyed.

'You wasn't thinking a' buying nothink neither, was yer?' Ellen said pleasantly. And when the child stared back and didn't answer, 'Tell yer what, I'll walk you to the door, shall I. See you safely on yer way.'

They walked together, Ellen's hand lightly on the girl's shoulder. 'I'd stick ter the Lanes if I was you,' Ellen advised as they parted.

And the girl gave her a cheeky grin, agreed and fled.

'Most diplomatic,' Miss Elphinstone approved, having watched the entire incident. 'Yes. I think she will do, Miss Morton. I will recommend her promotion after the sales.'

David's return to the Tech was quite a pleasurable occasion, although most of his friends had left by now, like Hymie. But the teachers were the same, and Mr Eswyn Smith hadn't changed at all. He was standing in his favourite corner of the room, busily cleaning the brushes on a multicoloured rag, and the walls around him were covered with designs and drawings and examples of handwriting. His bald head was spattered with white paint and there were pencil shavings in his tatty beard, just the same as always. When he saw who'd arrived he threw the rag onto the table and strode forward to welcome him back.

'David Cheifitz, my dear boy, they said you'd enrolled. Just at the right time too. We're off to the Tate next month to study the masters. Did you bring your sketches? Good! Good! Well, let me see them.'

It was a lovely moment. Like coming home after a long journey. He signed up for both Art classes, on two evenings a week, and after the first week he felt as though he'd never been away, and on the fourth Thursday evening they went to the Tate Gallery to study the masters.

It was an overwhelming experience. There was so much to look at that David forgot how to look. He drifted from canvas to canvas in a stupor, saturated by the painted beauty all around him and overawed by the terrifying competence of all those artists. He would never be able to paint like that. Never. Not if he studied for a hundred years. Such hands, white and relaxed, their elegant nails as pink as pearl; such eyes, gleaming with the most intelligent light as though they were set in flesh and blood. He was lifted and demoralized by the power of it all.

Mr Smith was bubbling with cheerfulness. 'This way for the Pre-Raphaelites!' he said. And they all trooped after him.

The Pre-Raphaelite paintings were in another imposing saloon, only this one was empty and silence hung in the air to press them all into good behaviour. Girls with pale dreaming faces gazed to right and left from every canvas or looked soulfully at the viewer, and these were not the grubby faces of Whitechapel nor the corseted bodies of the West End. These angelic creatures wore flowing draperies that clung to their bodies, and their bodies were as perfect as their faces. They stopped David in his tracks. He had never seen anything he liked so much or thought so beautiful.

That is, until he saw the Lady of Shalott, glowing towards him from the far end of the gallery. It was a painting of a calm blue-green river bordered by spiky reeds and willows and luxuriant trees, and in the centre of the picture was a dark boat with an unlit lantern at the prow, a drifting, silent, ominous boat. And sitting in the boat was another beautiful dreaming girl. She was dressed in white and had long, straight, red-gold hair that framed her face and fell in unbrushed profusion almost to her waist. Her face, or rather the expression on her face, made his heart contract with a sudden and entirely new emotion as if somebody were nipping at it, squeezing and pinching, but in an odd pleasurable way. Her chin was raised, so that her head was tilted back and her long slender neck was in shadow. All the light in the picture fell on the beautiful oval of her face, on the fine curve of her cheek and the straight nose ever so slightly tip-tilted, the full red lips ever so slightly parted and the huge eyes anguished, lids drooping. Even at this distance he knew that her eyes would be blue, but he had to walk right down the gallery before he could be sure, and as he

163

walked, and the beautiful girl grew closer and closer, he forgot all about paint and painting, all about shape and colour, all about his need to acquire a better technique. This was the face of a damsel in distress, and if he could have done it he would have jumped straight into the canvas to help her. He had fallen in love with a picture.

From then on he visited the Tate Gallery whenever he had the time, walking there if he couldn't afford the fare, to stand happily alone before the lovely vision. Mr Smith found him a copy of Tennyson's poem so that he could read the story of the Lady of Shalott, and now he knew that she had died for a glimpse of love, which was romantic and beautiful and terrible. And when the lady of the poem, forced to view the world through that awful mirror, caught a glimpse of those 'two young lovers lately wed' and cried that she was 'half sick of shadows' he knew so exactly what she was feeling it was as if she were in the room and speaking to him.

From time to time as the spring eased into summer he tried to draw his vision, but the finished picture was always flat and unrealistic. 'You draw better from life,' Mr Smith observed.

'Try the coronation,' Hymie said. 'You'll see all sorts then. Do a great big picture like yer did a' the old Queen's Jubilee, d'you remember?'

But the coronation didn't inspire him either. He and Hymie went to see the procession, and he took his sketch pad and filled several pages with rapid sketches, horses, guardsmen, fashionable ladies in their huge hats, people in the crowd eating and cheering, even the new fat King, smiling benignly, but none of them pleased him. They were good enough, that was all. But there was something more to be found. He was sure of it. If only he knew where to look.

All through that long hot summer and the mild autumn that followed, he prowled and brooded and dreamed, restless and dissatisfied, as though he was waiting for some great event.

But nothing much happened. Aunty Dumpling and Mr Morrison still went out to the theatre once a week, but there was no sign of a romance, and his mother seemed to have forgotten she ever thought it likely. Hymie fell in love every Thursday, and Rivke's son Joe got married. Three flats in the

164

Buildings fell vacant and were filled by new arrivals from Russia, who couldn't speak a word of English. But life was just the same. The tailors were all kept very busy making gowns for coronation parties and there was plenty of trade for Mr Woolnoth too, as London schools awarded special editions of *Edward Our Sovereign* and *King Edward's Realm* to the most subservient of his subjects. Winter cracked a few more paving stones, January gave them all chesty colds, and on David's seventeenth birthday rain fell from the sky all day as though the gods were emptying buckets. But nothing changed.

Then it was June again, and Mr Eswyn Smith was organizing another exhibition of his pupils' work in the Winter Garden. 'Pull out all the stops this time, lads,' he urged. 'We've got a good audience, particularly over the weekends, two symphony concerts and an opera. We might just hook a few buyers or a nice fat commission or two. The principal seems hopeful. You never know.'

So they gathered their work together, from pencil sketches to full-sized portraits, pictures of every kind in every medium, charcoal, Indian ink, pastels, watercolours, even oils. David took pains with his choice, because he could understand how important it was, even though his feelings weren't engaged. And when the display was mounted on tall screens all around the Winter Garden among the potted plants and the elegant fretwork of the galleries, he was pleased with his drawings and felt he'd arranged them to advantage.

The centrepiece was a large painting of the Building on a dark Shabbas evening, with the brickwork indigo blue, shadowed black, and every living room lit by the fuzzy golden bloom of candles, one above the other in seven-storey columns, and the grey courtyard below them full of vague blue figures, bent forward, hurrying home. He'd liked it very much when he'd first painted it, and his pleasure in it hadn't diminished because it reminded him of the quiet and peace of the Shabbas, and the gentle moment when the family were gathered together and the meal began. Around it he'd grouped a collection of sketches and portraits, of stall holders in the Lane, of Mr Woolnoth and the apprentice, of Aunty Dumpling and Mr Morrison, of Hymie playing chess, and the King in his

165

carriage and cousin Joe standing under the *chuppah* with his bride.

Yes, he thought, standing back to get a good view, it was a creditable collection. It looked professional. If he did feel just a little pride it was justified. This was his best work.

He wanted to know what other people thought of it and took to visiting the gardens every evening, loitering in the galleries while the visitors were promenading, so that he could watch their reactions. One or two stood before his pictures for quite a long time, which was really quite exciting, and one lady actually said they were 'well executed', but nobody offered to buy any, despite Mr Smith's optimism. By the final evening of the exhibition he'd resigned himself to artistic obscurity.

But he and Hymie went to the Winter Garden for the last time anyway. And it was the best evening of the lot, crowded with well-to-do people who all seemed genuinely interested in the display and stood around among the screens drinking champagne and talking to one another in their easy drawling voices.

'Wherever 'ave they all come from?' David wondered.

'It ain't from,' Hymie said knowledgeably, 'it's for. They've come fer the opera, whatcher bet. Be all right if one of 'em wanted ter buy one a' your paintings, nu.'

'It 'ud be more than all right,' David said. 'It 'ud be a miracle. That's what.'

The first bell was ringing for the return of the audience and sure enough the gardens began to clear. They had come for the opera. It was rather a disappointment. 'Well, that's that,' he said. 'Let's cut off fer a cup a' coffee.'

'No, 'ang on a tick,' Hymie said. 'There's a lot more people coming in the other end. Look.'

And he was right. The gardens were filling again, and this time with working men and their wives and families, and groups of girls, and sweethearts arm in arm. They entered cautiously as though they'd been waiting for the nobs to leave and weren't quite sure the coast was entirely clear. And a lot of them were looking at the pictures.

'See what *they* think,' Hymie said.

166

So they stood and watched as the new crowd circled the stands, chattering and exclaiming and giggling, faces raised and hands pointing.

And David suddenly saw the Lady of Shalott.

She was standing right in front of his exhibition looking up at the picture of the Buildings, a small slender girl with a mass of dark curly hair caught up in a bun at the nape of her neck under the brim of an absolutely enormous hat. He had a vague impression that she was wearing some sort of costume in a pale colour, dove grey or lilac, but it was her face that caught his attention. Her head was turned so that he had a heart-stopping view of her lifted profile, wide brows and huge blue eyes, a short straight nose ever so slightly tip-tilted, full red lips ever so slightly parted, the slender stem of a white neck and an exquisite curve of cheek. The Lady of Shalott, beautiful and perfect and here, in the flesh.

For a few seconds he stared at her in admiration and disbelief while his heart drummed against his ribs as though he'd been running, then she turned her head so that her lovely face was hidden by the brim of that ridiculous hat, and he remembered he had legs and began to walk towards her. He hadn't got the faintest idea what he would say to her. He only knew that she was the most beautiful girl he'd ever seen in his life, and that he simply had to stand beside her and talk to her.

A hand clutched his sleeve and pulled him to a halt. It belonged to Mr Smith, who was grinning so widely his mouth was like a slice of melon. Oh not now! Not now! What does he want?

'Allow me to present our Mr Cheifitz,' the Art master was saying, looking over his shoulder at the person beside him. 'David, this lady is Mrs Fulmington of Finsbury Square. She would like to commission a portrait.'

She was a huge fat woman in purple, and she was grinning too, displaying a row of hideous false teeth, all identical and unlikely. A commission, David thought, a real commission, and he knew he ought to be feeling excited, because it was a piece of extraordinary good luck. But the Lady of Shalott was walking on to the next screen. Oh why now?

Nevertheless he shook hands politely and listened while the

167

fat lady told him how very good she thought his drawings were
and what a very pretty girl her daughter was. 'You'll enjoy
painting her, I'm sure,' she gushed. 'The prettiest curls,
although I say so myself. An artist's delight.'

'I shall look forward to it, ma'am,' he said politely, but
craning his neck to see where the beautiful girl had gone.
Hurry up or I shall lose her. No, there's that hat, curving
before John O'Connell's pictures. Oh she's all curves, and
what lovely thick hair she has. Hurry up, do.

But nothing could hurry Mrs Fulmington. She gushed and
bridled, and held his arm with her fat gloved hand, and told
him what a great lover of art she was, and wouldn't get to the
point, no matter how hard he and Mr Smith endeavoured to
inch her there. It took nearly half an hour before she finally
gave him her card and suggested a time for the first sitting.
Nearly half an hour, as he knew with anguish, because he'd
been watching the great clock all the time, when he wasn't
looking for the Lady of Shalott.

Nearly half an hour, and when she'd finished the beautiful
girl was gone.

Chapter Fourteen

David was frantic. He danced and dodged from one end of the Winter Garden to the other, narrowly missing the patrons and the potted plants, taut with eagerness and anxiety.

Hymie trundled after him, puzzled and complaining. He could hardly believe his eyes. Could this really be David Cheifitz rushing about like a lunatic, jumping and panting and treading on people's feet? Gentle David Cheifitz? David Cheifitz the artist? 'Steady on, Cheify!' he said. 'What's got in ter yer?'

David couldn't stop to explain. 'She must be 'ere,' he muttered. 'Must be. She can't be gone. Ai yi yi! She can't be gone.'

But she had, and finally after nearly an hour searching the same walks and corners over and over again, he had to admit it.

Hymie tried to comfort him. 'Don't yer want ter get 'ome and tell yer Ma about the commission?' he asked. 'I know I would.'

But David hadn't the slightest interest in the commission. 'All my life,' he said, with the dramatic extravagance of seventeen years, 'all my life I been waiting to meet a girl like that. And now this! Why oh why did that silly woman have ter come up with her commission then? Of all times! She 'ad the rest of the evening. The rest of the fortnight even. Why then? It's too bad, Hymie.' He looked as though he was going to cry.

'Plenty more fish in the sea,' Hymie said helpfully, nodding his shaggy head to encourage his friend. Who'd have thought old Cheify would get smitten like this?

'Girls ain't fish!' David shouted. 'How'm I gonna find her,

Hymie? Where d'you think she's gone?'

'Off 'ome I 'spect,' Hymie said. 'Same as we should.'

Everybody had gone home. The place was almost empty and so quiet their voices echoed. There was only one old gentleman left in the gardens, quietly examining the paintings and looking tetchily at the two boys whenever they raised their voices.

'I find 'er,' David said. 'I come back 'ere every Saturday, till I find 'er. I vow it. I find 'er somehow or other.'

' 'Course,' Hymie said comfortingly. 'Only we go home now, nu?'

Emmanuel was thrilled to hear of the commission. 'Our son a portrait painter,' he said. 'Vhat you think a' that, Rachel?'

Rachel was more interested in Mrs Fulmington. 'Vhat she look like, Davey? She dress good, nu?'

'I don't know. I suppose so, Mama. She was fat.'

'Fat? Oy-oy, Davey. Vhere's your manners? You don't call a lady fat. So tell your Mama all about her.'

'Later, Mama,' David said, kissing her vaguely. 'Now I got ter do a sketch.' His brain was swollen with images of his beautiful girl and he wanted to commit them to paper before the memory began to fade.

Rachel sighed her resignation as she cleared the table to make way for him. 'So he's an artist. *Nebbish*! He ain't got time for his Mama.'

There was truth in her complaint that night, and he knew it, but couldn't respond to it. The vision was too imperative.

It was an excellent drawing, one of the best he'd ever done, although it didn't satisfy him. He'd caught the delicate curves of her cheek and her chin and the fullness of her parted lips, and he'd managed the gleam of those blue eyes, and the texture of that heavy hair. Other details were lost. He remembered that the neck of her blouse was unbuttoned, and that her arms were slim and her waist delectably slender, but he couldn't recall the colour of her costume nor what flowers decorated the brim of that enormous hat. Never mind, he thought. When I find her again I'll get her to pose for me in exactly the same clothes. And the thought was both comforting and upsetting, for it brought his sense of loss into the keenest focus.

From then on he drew at least three pencil sketches every day, mostly head and shoulders, because her face was so clearly printed on his memory and he still couldn't draw hands. And in his Tuesday class he started a full-length portrait, with her lovely eyes gazing dreamily out at him from above the Pre-Raphaelite draperies he liked so much and drew so well. By now he'd drawn her so often he felt they were already acquainted. He tied three of the best sketches to the foot of his bed, so that her face was the first thing he would see when he woke in the morning and the last thing to occupy his thoughts before he drifted off to sleep at night. Oh he *must* find her. He *must*.

That Saturday, the minute Shabbas was over, he dragged poor Hymie off to the People's Palace to search. They were there every week for the next month, regardless of what was on, but there was never any sign of the beautiful girl. And then it was July and the first of the sketches was beginning to curl. The sight of it made him morose. 'I don't reckon I shall ever find 'er, Hymie,' he sighed. 'She's the one girl in all the world fer me. I shall never love no one else. Never.'

Hymie thought that was carrying things a bit too far, but he had too much concern for his friend to say so. 'We go on looking, nu?' he said. 'Maybe she came fer the opera. We'll come 'ere fer the next opera. Whatcher think?'

But David only sighed profoundly and looked more miserable than ever.

It's just as well he's got ter go an' draw that portrait termorrer, Hymie thought. Sommink ter take 'is mind off it. An' not before time!

David hadn't given his first commission a single thought. It was a job, that was all. Like binding books. He would do it because he'd given his word, but it meant nothing to him. It didn't even make him feel excited.

His eyes acknowledged that Finsbury Square was an impressive place, with its high town houses set well back from the genteel luxury of the well-trimmed park at its centre. But that was all. In normal circumstances Mrs Fulmington's house would have made him feel gauche and out of place, but now, with his head full of dreams and despair, he climbed the steps to the front door as easily as though he were climbing the staircase in the Buildings, and when a supercilious butler admitted him, he announced himself as 'Mr Cheifitz, portrait painter' boldly, as though he was a Royal Academician.

Mrs Fulmington was fatter than ever in heliotrope satin, and her daughter Fifi turned out to be a tubby three-year-old with thin mouse-brown curls and a fat pasty face. Being an only child and very spoilt she had no intention of sitting still to be painted. She squirmed and wriggled and whined and complained, 'I's bored! I's hungry!' and even though her mother tried to bribe her with lemonade and chocolate biscuits, it was almost impossible to draw her. Nevertheless he did what he could and made several quick sketches while she smeared chocolate on the cream brocade. Then he promised to return for a second session in a week's time, and made his escape.

Mr Eswyn Smith was highly entertained by his account of the sitting and laughed immoderately.

'It's all very well you laughing,' David said ruefully. 'I tell you, sir, I wish I'd never took this on.'

'Let's have a look at your sketches then,' Mr Smith said deciding to be helpful. But when he saw them he laughed even louder. 'You've made her look like a pig,' he said.

'She is like a pig.'

'Oh dear me!' The Art Master said, still laughing. 'Her mother won't think much of that. I suppose her hair *is* scraggy? Yes, of course. Trust you to be accurate.'

'That's what she's like,' David said stubbornly, 'and it was hard enough doing these. I told yer, sir. She wouldn't keep still. Ai-yi! I don't think I'll ever be able to draw her.'

'Then draw someone else,' Mr Smith advised. 'There's plenty of kids round here would sit still for tuppence.'

'That'ud be cheating,' David protested.

'Not a bit of it, you dreadful young Puritan. That's good artistic practice. All the best portrait painters do it. As long as you get the face right nobody notices the rest of the figure, you mark my words.'

So as it was good artistic practice David asked his cousin's little girl Naomi to sit for him. She was four years old and a

172

good deal skinnier than Mrs Fulmington's awful Fifi, and very much better behaved, so after three busy half-hours he had produced several commendable sketches, most with blank faces but one with an approximation of the original sitter. The next week he took them all back to Finsbury Square so that proud Mama could make her choice.

She was quite charmed. 'Why that's my little Fifi to the life,' she said. 'How very clever of you, Mr Cheifitz! Just look at those dear little feet. She's always had such delicate feet, Mr Cheifitz. She takes after my side of the family when it comes to the matter of feet, you know.'

And David looked from Naomi's narrow bones to the podgy appendages scrambling over the sofa in front of him, and decided to keep quiet. Mr Smith had been quite right.

So the portrait was finished, and a flat uninteresting untruthful thing it was. Mrs Fulmington was delighted with it. 'I shall recommend you to all my friends,' she gushed, handing across the promised two guineas. 'I think you are so very clever, Mr Cheifitz.'

But her friends didn't appear to share her opinion and no further commissions were forthcoming. By now David was so cast down by the loss of his beautiful girl he hardly noticed this lesser disappointment. Evening classes had stopped for the summer and now there was nothing in his life but work and useless dreams. It was very hot and the streets of Whitechapel smelt worse every day, pungent with the sweat of labouring men and animals, of stale piss and hot horse dung and the decomposing accumulations of the outdoor privies. And to make matters worse, there was no breeze to carry away the smell of its industries, the sour fumes from the breweries or the fleshy stink from the tanneries or the prickling scent of rotting oranges from Spitalfields Market. Flies and bluebottles worried the horses and crawled over every stall, and at night the bugs bit so often and so furiously that sleep was impossible. David took to sitting out on the gallery during the worst part of the night, and when morning came he was pale and lethargic in consequence.

'Vhat ve do vid him?' Rachel worried. 'He don't sleep. He don't eat nothink. You think he's sickening maybe?'

173

'Nu-nu,' Emmanuel said. 'He vell enough, bubeleh. It the heat. Ve all suffer.'

'So maybe he's in love,' Dumpling suggested cheerfully, setting down her teacup and wiping the sweat from her forehead with a large handkerchief.

'Never on my life!' Rachel said. 'Such a thought vouldn't enter his head.'

'So vhy not? You ask me he's just the age.'

'So ve don't ask you, Raizel. The idea. He's a good Jewish boy, I tell you. He don't think such thoughts.' She was very annoyed, her hands trembling among the teacups.

'The heat, bubeleh,' Emmanuel said, trying to calm them, because they were both pink in the face and alert with anger.

'So ve ain't all like some people,' Rachel said, looking at her sister-in-law sharply.

'Ai-yi-yi!' Dumpling wailed covering her head with her protective apron. 'Me she means, Emmanuel. Your own sister!'

'Some people,' Rachel continued regardless of the wails and her husband's anxiously placating hand, 'vhat don't behave like good Jewish vomen. Some people vhat ain't got no modesty vorth the name.'

'I should live to hear such things!' Dumpling's high-pitched voice mourned through the shroud of her apron.

'Love, she says, Emmanuel! You hear her. Love! The shame of it! Courting vid a goy and she calls it love!' Tears fell down Rachel's cheeks like rain on a window.

'Rachel! Raizel! Please!' Emmanuel begged. 'Ve don't say these things!' He turned from one to the other in such agitation he looked like a spinning top. 'Please!'

Dumpling pulled her apron down beneath her chin, smearing her tears as it descended. 'Goy he may be,' she said. 'Lover he ain't. So you got a dirty mind, Rachel Cheifitz!'

Now it was Rachel's turn to howl her outrage. 'I should live to hear such vords!'

It took Emmanuel the rest of the evening to restore them to an approximation of reasonable behaviour, and even then they could only bear the sight of one another if he sat between them and held a hand from each. When David came home from his chess game with Hymie they were both so extravagantly affectionate towards him that he knew there'd been a row. And when his father wouldn't tell him what had upset them, he knew it must be something serious.

'Was it to do with Mr Morrison, maybe?' he asked tentatively.

Emmanuel sighed profoundly. 'Ai-yi, David! Vhat a vorld ve live in! Too much vork, I tell you. Too liddle play. And so hot! Is no vonder ve *kvetch*.'

And he was right. The heat was intolerable. Perhaps his mother and Aunty Dumpling wouldn't be so prickly with one another once it got cooler. But in the meantime everybody in East London seemed to be fatigued and short-tempered. Mr Woolnoth snapped at the apprentices and the apprentices quarrelled witih one another. His father and Uncle Ben spent more and more of their time gambling, and weren't comforted. And out in Brick Lane the gangs were beginning to spar.

The two most formidable of the local gangs, who used to live in the Nichol before it was demolished, were spoiling for a fight, insulting one another and putting the boot in at every opportunity. So no one was surprised when the knives came out and the street was loud with shrieks and screams. This time the whole thing started with a bottle fight between two women, but within minutes the street was full of running figures waving knives and bottles and chair legs and lengths of piping. Less than an hour later three people were in hospital with stab wounds and the police had arrived and made ten arrests, with considerable difficulty and despite vociferous opposition.

David, watching from the door-locked safety of Aunty Dumpling's upper room, was excited and appalled. The fighting figures made excellent models, but the mindless violence of it all was more puzzling than ever this year.

'Why they fight?' he asked his father as they walked home from the synagogue that Friday evening. 'Why they don't talk, argue it out maybe, like we do, instead a' just thumping? Don't make no sense ter me, none of it.'

Emmanuel couldn't say. 'Ve live in a violent vorld, nu.'

'Someone ought ter stop it.'

'I known vorse violence vhen I vas your age. Ai yi! In Varsaw they kill us, systematic, house by house, street by street. Thank the good Lord they don't do that at least.'

'An' dishonest too,' David went on, head down, brow furrowed, watching the tips of his own boots as he walked. 'I seen Alfie Miller in the Lane yesterday, floggin' cheap trays, makin' a killin'. Gold rings on his fingers an' all, an' all the poor old things flockin' ter buy.' He could see Alfie's well-fed tomcat face so clearly, and hear the chink of the coins as he dropped them into his pocket. 'He used ter be my hero, Alfie Miller, an' he's a crook.' It was demoralizing. Oh, London was a horrible place, furnace hot and stinking and full of thieves and thugs. Was it any wonder he couldn't find his beautiful girl here?

'Alfie Miller ain't your affair no more,' Emmanuel said solemnly. 'In any case it ain't for us to judge. God vill judge.' And he quoted the Yom Kippur prayer. ' "Verily it is Thou alone who art judge and arbiter, who knowest and art witness; Thou writest down and settest the seal; Thou rememberest things forgotten." All ve got to do is fear the Lord and obey the Commandments.'

He spoke with such quiet pride that David was comforted, for his words implied that Jews were different, and that was reassuringly true. They didn't run riot in the streets and attack one another with knives. They were quiet and peaceable and God-fearing, a cultured civilized people who could be trusted to uphold the law and be kind to one another. And gladness made his heart swell so that warmth spread from the centre of his body to his skin, because he was Jewish, and belonged irrevocably to such a people.

And that night his last conscious thought was not a dream of his beautiful woman, but a prayer of thanksgiving to his God.

Nevertheless the heat and bad temper went on.

Hymie and his family were going to Southend on Bank Holiday Monday. Now that all three of them were earning and all his brothers and sisters had married and were living away from home, there was money to spare for outings. 'Be some sport there,' he said happily to David. 'Southend. Imagine the sort a' girls there'll be! Why dontcher come with us?'

David wished his old friend luck, but the thought of girls, at Southend or anywhere else, didn't entice him.

'Sickening, don't I tell you,' Rachel said, when she heard he'd refused such an offer. 'Vhat ve do vid him?'

It wasn't in Emmanuel's nature to think of doing anything to anybody, and he could only shake his head and sigh and pluck his beard tatty.

In the end it was Rivke and her husband Ben who found a solution for her. Ben and his son Josh were both porters in a big department store in Shoreditch, and every year the store ran a staff outing for the workers and their families. This year charabancs had been hired to take them all to Wanstead Flats for the day and according to Ben there was a seat vacant on his particular charabanc, because one of the other porters had fallen ill. 'So come vid us vhy don't you?' he asked. 'Day in the country. Do you good. Plenty to eat, plenty to see, plenty to draw. Vhy not?'

For most of the year the Wanstead Flats were nothing but a windswept common, a flat unkempt heath, spiked with gorse and inhabited by rabbits and the occasional wagons of wandering Gypsies. But on Bank Holiday Monday it became a huge open-air theatre, with a fairground, a freak show, donkey rides and fortune tellers, wrestlers and travelling players, and stalls and barrows from all over North London, gathered for the best day's trading in the entire year. There would certainly be plenty to see and sketch.

'Well ... ' he hesitated.

Rivke and Josh both added their voices and so did Josh's two little girls, Naomi the model and her three-year-old sister, Ruthie. 'They got donkeys, Uncle David,' Naomi said. 'It's ever so good.'

So to his mother's intense relief, David agreed to join them.

They had a fine day for it, for overnight rain had broken the hold of the long hot spell and cooled tempers and freshened the air. The charabancs arrived in good time and even though they picked up their passengers from all over Shoreditch and Whitechapel, they were in Wanstead Flats long before half past nine.

'Vhat a day ve got!' Rivke said as the driver opened the door. 'Put yer bonnet on, Ruthie.'

'Can I 'ave a go on the swings?' Naomi said, following the others down the gangway.

' 'Course,' David said. 'Soon as we get out. I promise.' He was immediately behind her, guiding her by the shoulders to make sure she didn't trip, and as they reached the step he looked up to check that their way was clear. And found himself gazing straight at the Lady of Shalott. His surprise and pleasure were so intense he was frozen to the spot. She was climbing down from the second charabanc, wearing the same lilac-coloured costume and a smart straw boater, and talking to a short plump girl with fuzzy fair hair. And she was even more beautiful than he remembered her.

Then he realized that Josh was standing just outside the charabanc, his arms raised to lift little Ruthie down. Josh would know who she was.

'See that girl there, Josh,' he said eagerly. 'Just walking off. By the red tent. See? D'yer know who she is?'

Josh set his daughter on the ground and straightened her ruffled skirt before he looked. 'Oh yes,' he said slowly. 'That's our Miss White. Dress materials. For vhy you vant to know?'

'I've seen 'er before,' David said, and even to his ears the explanation sounded lame. 'She's very pretty.' And that made him blush. But how marvellous! She worked in Hopkins and Peggs, just across the road from Mr Woolnoth's.

Josh looked away tactfully. 'Yes, I s'pose she is,' he agreed. 'Lots a' young fellers fancy 'er, and that's a fact. Don't make no difference one way or the other, I tell you, 'cos she's a proper man-hater, our Miss White.'

'A man-hater?'

'Keeps 'em all at arm's length. So you ready, girls?'

A man-hater, David thought, and the idea pleased him. There was an admirable pride in it. She was too pretty to cast herself away on any old Tom, Dick or Harry, and she knew it. He loved her more than ever for having such good sense. But she was walking away! 'See you in a jiffy,' he said to Josh as he ran. 'Shan't be long!'

He was out of breath when he caught up with her beside the coconut shies, so he had to stand where he was for a minute or two to recover. But he didn't mind this little delay, because he'd found her again, and she was there, almost beside him, and he knew her name and where she worked, and anyway he could admire the delicate line of her cheek and the thick black eyelashes fringeing her blue eyes while he waited, and that was pleasure enough for the moment.

'I'll 'ave a go, shall I?' she said to her companion. And he liked her voice too, a clear bold voice, he thought, but womanly. She was paying her penny for the three wooden balls. What a chance!

He eased in beside her and paid his penny quickly, so that they could throw together, and even though he was watching her, or perhaps because he was watching her, he threw so luckily he dislodged a coconut. She glanced at him as the prize was put into his hands, her eyes smiling at his good fortune. It was the perfect moment to speak, always providing she could hear him above the hooting and drumming of the roundabout.

'You can 'ave it if yer like,' he offered, and then blushed furiously because his voice sounded so rough and the offer so crude.

But she went on smiling. 'D'yer mean it?'

' 'Course.'

'No, I couldn't. Go on, it's yours. You won it.'

'I'd be honoured,' he said, offering the coconut with both hands. 'Really. Anyway you oughter've won one. You throw ever so straight.'

'Well, ta,' she said, taking the coconut. 'I wish I 'ad an 'ammer. We could share it.'

'We'll 'ave a go on the rifle range,' he dared. 'P'rhaps I could win one. You never know.'

'Well ... ' she said again, and now she was looking serious, as though he'd gone too far and been presumptuous.

'We oughter be introduced,' he agreed to still her doubts. 'If my cousin was 'ere he'd introduce us. I know who you are.'

She looked at him with such a sharp expression on her face that he blushed again. 'Do yer?'

'I seen yer before,' he explained. 'At the People's Palace. You was lookin' at the exhibition. The art exhibition. In the Winter Garden.'

179

'Yes,' she said, relaxing a little. 'I was. I went there wiv Maudie 'ere. Yer right. Was you there an' all?' But her eyes were still guarded.

The pride of what he was about to say made him stand tall. 'You was looking at *my* paintin's,' he said. 'I was exhibitin'.'

'Fancy!' Maudie said, most impressed.

But Miss White took it calmly. 'I know who you are an' all then,' she said. 'You're David Cheifitz, aintcher?'

He was so surprised his mouth fell open. He hadn't expected fame quite like that. How did she know?

'My name's Ellen White,' she said, smiling at him again. 'An' this is my friend, Maudie Fenner.'

They shook hands. He was so happy he wanted to jump about and shout. But he tried to be calm. 'Let's win an 'ammer,' he said.

They didn't win a hammer. Or a goldfish, which Ellen said was just as well. But they went on the roundabout, and saw the freak show and didn't think much of it, and had rides on the donkeys. And that reminded David of his family.

'I promised ter treat my cousins to the donkeys,' he said as they dismounted.

By now Maudie was beginning to flirt with him. 'An' how old are they when they're at 'ome?' she said, making eyes.

He took flirtation solemnly as always. 'Four and three,' he told her.

'Then we'd better find 'em,' Ellen said. 'If you've promised, they'll be lookin' forward to it. Poor kids.'

It took a lot of walking and talking to achieve, for the fairground was so crowded it was impossible to see more than a few yards ahead whichever direction they looked.

'You'd see more if you was up in the swings,' Ellen said, and that was such a very good idea they all agreed to act on it immediately. And there, standing beside the showman as if they'd prearranged it, were his cousin Josh and Naomi and little Ruth.

He introduced his two new friends, shyly and hoping he wouldn't blush too much, but before any of them had a chance to feel awkward Naomi moved in to the attack.

'Where've you bin?' she demanded. 'We waited an' waited.'

'*I* bin on an 'orse,' Ruth told them proudly. 'Wid reins!'

'No you never,' her sister corrected, as the crowds milled around them. 'You bin on a donkey, silly.' Then she turned her reproachful eyes to David again. 'We waited an' *waited* fer you. An' you never come.' She wanted him to know how much he'd been missed.

Her reproach shamed him. He felt he should try to make amends. 'Take you on the swings,' he offered. 'How about that?'

'Both?' Ruth asked hopefully.

'Well, if you're goin' on the swings, I'm off,' Maudie said, waving at her current young man who was lurking for her beside the rifle range. 'Me an' swings don't agree. See yer later, Ellen.'

So David and Ellen took the two children on the swings and they all enjoyed it very much. I've found her, David thought, pulling the furry ropes through his hands. I've found my beautiful girl. And he laughed aloud as their bright carriage swooped into the sky, and the moon-faced figures below them dipped in and out of their sight. And how pretty Ellen was, with her dark hair flying behind her as they rose and falling forward to frame her face as they descended, her blue eyes shining with laughter.

When their turn was over, Josh and his wife Maggie were both waiting to take their daughters on the roundabout, and there was no sign of Maudie or her young man.

'Let's go on the helter-skelter,' David said, thinking, quick, before anybody else can join us.

So they did, and after that they bought pie and mash and sat on the scrubby grass to eat it, talking and talking. They talked so much they hardly had time to swallow. He told her all about Mr Woolnoth and how particular he was, and took out his sketch pad to show her a portrait of the gentleman, and she was very impressed by his sketches and wanted to see them all. Then she gave him her famous impression of Mr Fenway, the floor walker, with pursed lips and folded arms, stabbing his alarm cry at his ladies, 'Look lively, ladies! Look lively!' From then on they entertained one another without a pause, drawing and mimicking every odd and eccentric character they could remember or discover around them.

181

Then they realized that their laughter had made them dry, so they had to go off to the beer tent to 'wet their whistles'. And after that there was Indian toffee to be sampled and hokey pokey ice cream at a penny a lump, which was so rich it made David feel quite sick for half an hour afterwards, although he didn't admit it.

And the sun shone on them all day.

When the evening began to draw in and the first of the naptha flares were lit above the stalls, they were quite surprised by how quickly the day had gone. But by then the Music Hall had opened its tent flap, so they went in to the first house and enjoyed it all so much they decided to catch the last performance too.

'I like the sing-song,' Ellen said. 'Don't you?'

Oh he did. They had to sit so close together in the crowded tent they were almost thigh to thigh, and that was a pleasure so exquisite he would have sat through any performance for the sake of it. He was so happy being with her, breathing in the musky, powdery scent of her flesh, and drinking the sight of her, like a man long parched of vision. Her cheeks glowed like peaches in the heat of the tent, and now that they were so close together he could see that they were brushed with a fine down of tiny soft hairs, and that the pale skin above her upper lip was beaded with miniature pearls of sweat. And he remembered the Song of Solomon, 'Behold thou art fair, my love; behold thou art fair, thou hast doves' eyes within thy locks; thy lips drop honeycomb, honey and milk are under thy tongue; and the smell of thy garments is like the smell of Lebanon.' And he knew he wanted to stay beside her for ever.

But even the longest and happiest of holidays have to end, and at last the ' 'Opkins 'Op' was on its bedraggled way back to the charabancs, the men shirt-sleeved and jovial, the women flushed with beer and idleness, girls giggly, young men oggly, kids sticky-mouthed, sleeping babies sausaged into shawls and draped over their mothers' shoulders, acknowledged lovers arm in happy arm. And among them came Ellen and David, still talking, still laughing and still locked eye to eye.

All through the evening David had been waiting for a chance to ask her to walk out with him, but it seemed so presumptuous and they'd been talking so much he hadn't found the moment. Now, with all her friends gathered before the second coach, he began to panic. If he didn't ask quickly, she'd be gone.

'We're – er – I mean – er – I'm – er – I mean,' he stuttered, glad that it was too dark for her to see how much he was blushing. 'There's a good play on at the Standard. Beauty an' the Beast. I was thinkin' a' goin' Thursday. Or Tuesday if you'd like. What I mean is, would yer like to see it with me?'

She didn't answer for a very long time, but stood, considering his face seriously, her blue eyes dark in the faint light from the charabanc. She was remembering her mother's voice, 'Never get married, gel!' and her own heartfelt answer, 'Don't you worry, Ma, I never will!' and wondering whether this really was her standing beside this handsome young man and knowing she was going to say 'yes'. But he was different, a young gent, almost a swell. Not a rotten old roughneck like her old man, nor a soppy ha'p'orth like them fellers in the shop, all sheep's eyes and stupid remarks. *His* eyes were serious and very handsome, and he was watching her with such a touching anxiety she really couldn't resist him. He'd be different, she was sure of it.

'Yes,' she said. 'I would. Ta. Thursday'd be lovely.'

'I meet you outside the store,' he said, smiling fit to crack his face. 'Quarter past seven, nu?'

It was a marvellous journey home. He was so happy he wanted to jump about and dance and run up and down. It took all his concentration just to sit still as the charabanc rattled towards Stamford with its singing cargo. How beautiful London is, he thought, with the street lamps shining like beads of polished amber and the trams streaming yellow light and the pavements blue as the night sky. And as they went racketing along the Mile End Road, past the white glimmer of the People's Palace and the black shadows of the young plane trees, he knew he was lucky to be alive in such a place.

Chapter Fifteen

'You should a' see your David at the fair,' Rivke said to Rachel. 'Don't you never tell me he ain't got an eye for the girls!'

'I knew it!' Dumpling said, pinning a frill deftly to the front of the blouse she was sewing. 'Didden I say so, Rachel?'

Rachel said nothing, but her face was sour and she was tacking with quick angry stitches.

The three women were working together in Dumpling's room, with lemon tea to sustain them and the window open wide to admit what little air there was. It was very hot and they were all tired and sticky and working harder than they should under the pressure of the orders they had to finish in that shortened week.

'A boy so handsome vhat you expect?' Dumpling said, fitting another row of pins between her lips. 'Onny nat'rul.'

'A pretty girl he took on the svings,' Rivke informed them, slapping a skirt seam into position ready for machining. 'Best looking girl in the shop, according to Josh. All the young fellers vant her, an' off she valks vid your Davey. So vhat you think a' that, bubeleh? Good taste in vomen, nu?' She gave Rachel a lopsided grin to show she was half teasing, but her sister-in-law wouldn't receive it.

'I tell you vhat I think a' that,' Rachel said crossly, 'idle gossip, that's all it is. I vonder you ain't got nothink better to occupy your mind.'

'My Josh ... '

'Your Josh!' Rachel interrupted. 'Alvays first with the gossip, your Josh. So ve don't listen to your Josh.'

'A better boy don't tread shoe leather,' Rivke said driving the material through the machine as though she was planing wood. 'Good vorker, good son, don't give himself airs, like some I could name. So you vatch your mouth, Rachel Cheifitz.'

'A *meshuganer*!' Rachel accused. 'Nothing, he don't know, if he says my David's after the girls. My David's a good Jewish boy. He don't chase girls, I tell you.'

Dumpling removed the last pin from her mouth and mopped her forehead with her apron. 'So they all chase girls, dolly,' she said, giving Rachel a little placating nod. 'All the young men they all chase girls. Come the spring, the fine weather, you know vhat they say.'

'I don't vanna hear,' Rachel said stubbornly. 'My Davey ain't like all the others. My Davey's an artist.'

'Umph!' Rivke snorted, and she and Dumpling exchanged a quick glance that expressed their disbelief, their annoyance and their pity for her pig-headed blindness.

'I make more tea, maybe,' Dumpling said bringing their uncomfortable topic to a halt. 'Oy oy such heat!'

But later in the week when she and Rivke took their finished garments back to the sweat shop they told one another with considerable satisfaction that their sister-in-law was being a poor blind fool. 'So vhat a shock she get vhen she know the truth,' Rivke said. 'My Davey's an artist! Oy oy oy! Pride before a fall, Dumpling, don't I tell you.'

'Vhat the eye can't see!' Dumpling said wobbling her chins vehemently. 'Ain't no good ve tell her.'

'Ve should talk to Manny maybe?'

'Nu-nu! Time enough vhen it ain't so hot. Oy, my back!'

But Emmanuel already knew and wished he didn't. Rachel had come home incoherent with tears and distress that afternoon, vowing she would never work in Dumpling's room again, and it had taken him more than an hour to comfort her into a better frame of mind.

'They don't mean it, bubeleh,' he said drying her eyes.

'They mean it,' she sobbed. 'So spiteful, just because he's an artist, a cut above that Josh, may he be forgiven.'

'So you forgive him, bubeleh, nu?'

'My David's a good Jewish boy. He ain't got one impure thought in his head. Ve know that, Emmanuel?'

Emmanuel wasn't at all sure he knew any such thing but he

nodded and murmured as though he agreed, and comforted himself that David was kept so busy with his work and his classes that he really wouldn't have very much time for courting even if he wanted to. And besides, he was young yet.

At that very moment, had he known it, David was at the Standard Theatre sitting as close as he could to his beautiful Ellen. It was a very good play, with a slim dark-haired hero beset on every side by unspeakable villainy, and winning through to fame and fortune in the spotlit ring of the National Sporting Club. And even though the actor who played this gullible innocent looked far too fragile to prevail in a boxing ring, they followed his progress with sighs and cheers, and when the villain was finally forced into the ring to confront him and was then instantly felled, they clapped and cheered and booed until the curtain fell too. When they emerged into the smoky evening, they were glowing with satisfaction because virtue had triumphed and they'd been sitting side by side for such a long delightful time.

They ambled, very slowly, along the few hundred yards that separated the Standard Theatre from the staff entrance of Hopkins and Peggs. And they told one another what a good play it was and how much they'd enjoyed it, and she thought he was much more handsome than the hero, but of course she didn't say so, and he thought she was the prettiest girl he'd ever seen and that she was getting prettier by the minute and that he'd give anything to kiss her, but of course he kept his thoughts to himself.

They stood together in the doorway as the theatre-leaving crowds chattered past them along the pavement and a fleet of trams buzzed and rocked along the rails in the middle of the road. And they were so absorbed in each other they didn't notice any of it, not even the noise.

She's only about two inches shorter than I am, David thought, and only about three inches away. And it occurred to him that if they were just to sway towards one another, just a very very little, they would be mouth to mouth. And the thought made him weak at the knees.

'What d'yer do of a Sunday?' he asked, huskily.

'We 'ave ter stay out all day,' she said. 'We're supposed ter

186

go ter church an' visitin' an' such like. Ain't allowed in till eight o'clock supper.'

'D'you go ter church?'

'No.' She sounded surprised at the question, and he, remembering how secure he always felt at the synagogue on a Sabbath evening and how happy, was surprised at her surprise. The fact that she wasn't religious registered somewhere at the back of his mind, but faintly, because there were other more important things to occupy him just at the moment.

'I s'ppose you go visitin' then,' he said, hoping she didn't. 'Family an' such.'

'Some gels do. Not me though.'

'Whatcher doin' this Sunday?'

'Nothin' much really,' she said, her eyes widening most beautifully as the same thought entered her mind.

'We could go ter the country. Epping Forest. Take a train.'

'Yes,' she said, and now her voice was husky too. He was much encouraged by the sound, and was just beginning to think he might offer to kiss her after all when there was a scraping of locks behind the door, and at that she panicked and pushed the door open quickly, making excuses to the shadowy face behind it, and with two quick paces and a fleeting smile was gone.

He was so happy he skipped all the way to the tram stop.

He was the first customer to walk into Hopkins and Peggs at half past eight the next morning, looking very proper in his dark working suit and his cloth cap covering that thick dark hair. 'Morning, Miss White,' he said, touching his cap as he passed her counter. So they smiled at each other for a brief happy second before their working day began.

Miss Morton was charmed. 'What a polite young man,' she approved, and looked quizzically at her assistant for an explanation.

'We was at school tergether,' Ellen obliged. ' 'E's an artist.' And it was a great satisfaction to her that she could be claiming his friendship. An artist. It was a cut above a shop assistant, an' no mistake.

The next morning he stopped beside the counter long

enough to pass her a small much-folded note. And three aggravating customers followed him in and had to be served with chintzes, and curtaining, and took for ever to choose two perfectly ordinary dress lengths. Stupid women! It was more than twenty minutes before she could read what he'd said.

'Dear Ellen, Don't forget tomorrow. I shall be outside the main entrance eight thirty sharp. They say the fair is very good this year. Kind regards, David Cheifitz.'

Correct and formal though it was, it felt like a love letter. She tucked it inside her blouse and kept it there all day – when she wasn't reading it again.

The next day they took a train to Chingford, along with several hundred others, and walked in a chattering crowd along the well-trodden path through the woods, among the grey-green columns of the beeches and the fluted boles of the famous hornbeams, their feet rustling the heaped copper leaves and their heads brushed by the low boughs of hideously pollarded trees, until they came to Queen Elizabeth's hunting lodge and the fairground. Old women in feathered hats and old men in bowlers, costers with gaudy neckerchiefs under their dirty faces and their pockets crammed with bottled beer, misshapen mothers with tribes of skinny kids and various babes in arms, a gallimaufry of bonnets and baskets and trampling boots, all on their way to sample the delights of the countryside, donkey rides, swings, shies and roundabouts, ice cream and Indian toffee, cockles and whelks and winkles.

It was a friendly familiar place, much smaller than the Bank Holiday fair but every bit as good and splendidly noisy. They went on the donkeys and had two goes on the roundabout, and walked arm in arm through the crowds like a real courting couple, while the organ pipes fluted their tinny tunes and the drums and cymbals crashed their incessant rhythm and the showmen bellowed their wares. And presently they came to the flying trapeze, which by general agreement was reckoned to be the best and most dangerous thing at the fair.

It was a simple construction, consisting of a long metal frame from which hung a series of dangling ropes, each ending in a handle or a loop, and above them six wide metal hoops which served to give marginal support to the flyers as they swung from rope to rope along the frame. It was an irresistible challenge to the young men and their girls, and there was always a large crowd below them to mock or egg them on. When David and Ellen arrived, two girls were happily screaming their way along the ropes towards the point where their boys were eagerly waiting to catch them from their final leap.

'Would yer like a go?' he asked, watching the first girl as she squealed down through the air towards the welcoming chest of her escort.

'If you go first,' she said, and it struck him that she had two quite contradictory expressions on her face, her blue eyes bold but her mouth soft and vulnerable. And he was intrigued because he hadn't thought of her as bold or vulnerable before that moment. Only as beautiful.

He'd only been on the trapeze once before, and that was last year, with Hymie, but he climbed up as though he was a veteran and swung with foolhardy audacity, jumping high into the air before he landed, so that the crowd would cheer and she could admire.

And then it was her turn. She tied her boater round her neck and set off, swinging like a lilac bell, her dark hair lifting on either side of her face like wings, and her boots treading the air. She didn't scream like the other girls but swung steadily, hand over white hand, concentrating and purposeful, and as he watched her he realized that she was a little afraid and he called out to encourage her, 'Nearly there! I'll catch yer!' And the crowd gave him a mocking cheer and some ribald advice. And at that he knew he'd made a mistake. He'd been so eager to hold her in his arms he'd forgotten how public all this was. It wasn't the right time or the right place, and he was ashamed of the desire that had driven him to suggest it,

But she was already dangling from the last rope and there was nothing he could do to stop her. She dropped like a diver, her fists clenched on either side of her face and her eyes tight shut. Her fall was so precipitate and so swift that she knocked him off balance, and even though he caught her they fell backwards together and rolled over and over on the straw, laughing and gasping, with relief and desire and excitement.

189

He could feel the full length of her lovely body against his, her breasts soft above the hard bones of her stays and her long legs rounded and warm, and the desire to kiss her was so strong it made him groan. But then they'd rolled to a halt and had to disentangle themselves, because the crowd was cat-calling and mocking again, 'Go on boy, give 'er one!' and he was ashamed because they were making a public spectacle of themselves, and the moment should have been private. She looked at him shyly as she scrambled to her feet, and he saw the flush on her cheeks and the moist gleam in her eyes and knew that he loved her.

'Let's have sommink to eat,' he said.

They had beer and cheese in an old-fashioned pub just along the road. While they were eating it, there was a sudden rush of noise from the road below them, a rattle of wheels, and laughter and chattering voices. They stood up at once to see what it was. And a cycling club passed by on its way to one of the Riggs Retreats, the men in Norfolk jackets and knickerbockers, the women in tweed cycling dresses with their bonnets firmly netted underneath their chins.

Ellen watched them enviously. 'We got a cycling club at 'Opkins,' she said. 'I wouldn't 'alf like ter join. I been savin' up fer a bicycle, months an' months.'

'We could both join,' he said, making up his mind about it at once. 'Free ter ride wherever we like. Just the thing!'

She looked up at him with that odd mixture of confidence and uncertainty. 'Take a bit a' time,' she warned. 'Bicycles cost money.'

'Secondhand's cheaper,' he said, beaming at her. 'I'll get 'em, shall I? Leave it ter me. I bet I could get two good 'uns in the Lane.' The offer made him feel manly and responsible and protective, particularly as he still had some of his commission left.

And to his great delight she agreed. 'Be fun,' she said.

And fun it was. Greatly daring, she invested a week's wages in a length of pale blue serge and paid Maudie's mother to run her up one of the new bloomer suits. It was a stunning creation and she looked extremely pretty in it, as she knew because she'd crept down to the shop after lights out to get a full-length view of herself in the long mirrors in the dress department. The high puffed sleeves nipped in at the elbows and the full bloomers nipped in below the knee were high fashion and very feminine. With a broad red ribbon trimming her boater and a broad red cummerbund emphasizing her waist, and new black stockings and neat button boots to complete the outfit, she looked like one of the swells. And that pleased her because she wanted him to see her at her best. For all her initial doubts about him, she had to admit he was becoming more and more important to her.

When he came into the shop the next day he gave her a note to tell her he'd 'bought the bicycles, real bargains. I will tell you about them Thursday at the Music Hall. It is Little Tich and Gus Elan to top the bill. You will come, won't you? From David.'

'I can't wait fer Thursday,' she said to Maudie when they went down to the canteen for their mutton and potatoes. 'We're going to the Music Hall, Little Tich an' Gus Elan.'

'An' David Cheifitz an' all!' Maudie teased. 'You was supposed ter be a man-hater!'

'So I changed me mind.'

'You can say that again!'

On Friday morning, after a riotous evening at the Music Hall, he delivered her bicycle, which cost her less than she'd already saved, and that Sunday they joined the Hopkins and Peggs Cycling Club and went off on their first jaunt across London Bridge, through Bermondsey, and into the Kent countryside. They were very decorous, riding carefully along beside each other because they had to concentrate on the difficult business of steering and keeping upright. When they got back to Hopkins and Peggs just before supper time, they both said what a nice day it had been but they were both secretely disappointed with it. The bicycles were all very exciting but they'd actually kept them apart. They hadn't held hands once all day.

However, the next Sunday was an improvement, for the club went to Epping Forest and by now they'd mastered the art of riding their awkward steeds and felt rather less self-conscious among their new friends. They stopped for a meal at Riggs Retreat, and ate on the wooden veranda among the potted

191

palms with all the others, still behaving properly, but when the tour continued they contrived to dawdle behind all the rest until they were on their own. And after a while they stopped cycling and dismounted to get their breath back.

'I'd like to do a sketch of you in that bloomer suit,' David said as they rested on the handlebars, admiring one another. 'You look ever so pretty in that bloomer suit.' And the compliment made him blush and delighted her.

'I don't mind,' she said.

So they propped their bicycles against the hedge and walked into the woods to find a suitable setting. Because it was rough underfoot and the twisted roots of the beeches were half hidden by all those long dead leaves, he offered his arm like a gentleman, and she slipped her nice warm hand into the crook of his elbow, and they were touching again.

Presently they found a secluded corner among the hornbeams. She found a comfortable place to sit and he settled down to draw his first sketch from life.

She'd already seen several expressions on his face, all of them handsome and all of them young somehow. Now, watching him as he drew, she saw another side of his character. His face darkened and looked older, and he scowled and stared, or smiled an indrawn, private smile. It was a passionate foreign face. The face of a man apart. And she admired it, and was excited by it.

It was so quiet among the hornbeams she could hear the scratch of his pencil and her own heart beating. Sunshine filtered through the green leaves to dapple her new blue suit with pale discs of silver and somewhere in the branches above her head a bird was fluting 'peeep-a peeep-a peeep-a', over and over again with a joyous echoing insistence. I shall remember this moment all my life, she thought, because I think I love him.

Then the sketch was done and his expression changed and he came rustling through the dead beech leaves to show it to her, eager and shy and young again.

'I shall make a painting a' this,' he said.

She stood up at once and took the sketch book into her hands. 'It's ever so good,' she said. 'Do I really look like that?'

He'd drawn her half asleep, with the blue costume draped over her figure in the most revealing Pre-Raphaelite curves. Perhaps I ought to 'ave sat up a bit more.

'You do ter me,' he said, and then he was afraid that the drawing might have shown her too much about how he was feeling, and he put the little book back into his hip pocket, quickly. But they were still standing within an inch of one another, and they were alone, and the scent of her lovely dappled flesh was making him feel quite lightheaded. 'You're the most beautiful girl I've ever seen,' he confessed.

They were so close together she could feel the breath of his words. 'It's a lovely drawrin',' she said, looking straight into his eyes. What a warm brown they were and so tender.

'Lovely Ellen,' he whispered, and her face was so meltingly beautiful he couldn't resist any longer. He leaned towards her, ever so slightly, and put his mouth gently onto her parted lips. It was a moth's kiss, the merest brush, soft and tentative and gentle, a signal that he meant no harm, a touch of adoration. But it made them both tremble.

'I love you,' he whispered, putting his arms round her, but gently so that she could move away from him if she wanted to.

She swayed towards him. 'I love you too,' she whispered. 'Oh David, I really do.'

And at that he kissed her again, as though he was in a trance, moving his lips languidly against hers, sipping the most exquisite pleasure from her mouth, his heart drumming more violently than ever. And she put her arms round his neck and returned the kiss, following his movement and increasing its pressure until they were both panting. 'Oh Davey! Davey!' she said when they finally paused for breath.

'I could stay 'ere for ever kissing you,' he said. 'I love you so much.'

And this time she kissed him.

'You give us the slip this afternoon an' no mistake,' Fenny Jago said as she and Ellen and the other live-in girls were getting ready for bed that evening. Her voice was tart with disapproval. 'Where'd yer get to, you an' that David Cheifitz a' yours? As if we didn't know!'

The bare brown room was mellowed by gentle gaslight and langorous with the accumulated heat of the day and the relaxed fatigue of its occupants. It was full of girls in various states of cloud-white undress, pale arms lifted above tucked chemises, petticoats discarded in a froth of frills, nightgowns billowing, bare feet ambling, long hair tumbled from all those restricting pins, bellies rounding away from the rigidity of all those hard boned stays. A drowsy, easy room, drifting towards sleep. And until that moment, the conversation had been as gentle as the setting.

Now tousled heads turned towards the speaker, some shocked, some frowning, but all alerted by the unpleasantness of her innuendo.

' 'E drew another picture,' Ellen said mildly. 'I posed fer 'im an' 'e drew.'

'An' the rest!' Fenny mocked. 'An' the rest!'

It was a direct insult but Ellen shrugged it away. She was still warm and content, well loved, much kissed and proof against the unkindness of envy, almost as if his arms were still round her, containing and protective. She went on brushing the tangles from her hair, and spoke to the girls gathered round her bed. ' 'E's gonna make a paintin' a' this one,' she said. 'I'll show you when 'e's finished.'

'Paintin', my eye!' Fenny said, and she walked across to Ellen's admiring circle and pushed through until her sharp face was inches away from her adversary. 'All that carry-on wiv poor Jimmy Thatcher. I remember. Don't you think I don't! An' I tell yer, you never fooled me! Not fer an instant. Ice white! Load a' rubbish that was. Ice white! You're no better'n the rest of us.'

'Shut yer face, you!' Maudie said, springing to her feet and the defence of her friend.

But Ellen was still calm, to everybody's surprise, including her own. She put out a hand to restrain Maudie and spoke directly to Fenny's fierce face. 'Never said I was,' she said. 'I put 'im in 'is place, that was all. 'E shouldn't a' tried 'is luck. Was 'is own fault.'

Fenny was too angry to hear her. 'All that carry-on,' she continued. 'Ice white, my eye! Jimmy Thatcher was my feller.

We was walkin' out till you came along, I'll 'ave you know. Walkin' out. You 'ad no business taking my feller away, Ellen White, and then pretendin' you was snow white. Pure as the driven snow, my eye! Well, you'll come to it in the end, same as all the rest of us, you mark my words. Down on yer back you'll be, same as all the rest. If you ain't been there al-a-ready.'

The insult was so crude it caused an outcry. Ellen's circle of friends protested loudly. 'Oh, what a rotten thing ter say! You oughter be ashamed, Fenny Jago. Wash yer mouth wiv soap an' water!' And they glanced anxiously at Ellen and were intrigued and angered and excited to see that she was blushing.

The insult had been like a blow to her stomach. She was remembering the tenderness of his kisses and her sense of being loved and protected, and she was so furious to hear him being compared to that coarse Jimmy Thatcher that her calm mood was ruptured and gone in the instant. Her hairbrush was still in her hand and she stood up and swung it into Fenny's sneering face, suddenly, like a fierce spiked weapon.

'You jest watch yer mouth, that's all,' she said, 'unless you want a clip round the ear'ole. I never took your precious Jimmy Thatcher. You can 'ave 'im an' welcome. Much good may 'e do yer.' Her friends growled approval and Fenny put up a hand to defend her cheeks. But she didn't retreat, even though they were standing almost toe to toe.

'N'yer!' she sneered. 'True colours now we're seein', Ice White!'

'I'm warnin' yer,' Ellen said. 'Put a sock in it.'

'Can't take the truth!'

'I'm warnin' yer! We don't like smutty talk, none of us.' Another chorus of approval.

The golden air was quivering with bad temper and Ellen's face was a blaze of anger, her blue eyes steel hard, her jaw set. She was a good head shorter than Fenny Jago and considerably slimmer but she looked as though she would wield that brush and knock her enemy to the ground. The girls waited breathlessly as she and Fenny glowered at one another.

'N'yer!'

'Pack it in!'

'N'yer!'

Then there was a flutter of nightgowns near the door and feet pattering and a whispered warning. 'Miss Elphinstone!' The hostilities came to an abrupt and immediate halt. By the time that redoubtable lady made her entrance, all her girls were safely and properly beneath the covers, and the room seemed calm, if a little too hot.

The gas was turned down, polite goodnights were murmured, and Ellen was left alone with her thoughts.

And very uncomfortable they were. For there'd been an element of truth in Fenny's venom, and now it expanded in her mind and poisoned her joy. To be loved so tenderly and so unexpectedly was a happiness past any she'd ever been able to imagine, something apart and something different from anything she'd seen or suspected in the rough world of her childhood. Most of the grasping males she'd met at work or out in the Lane had been brutally and unashamedly after one thing and one thing only. They were coarse and selfish and she disliked them instantly. But David was different. David was gentle and sensitive. He offered her love as she'd always dreamed it could be, not a squalid grabbing with no concern, but a protective enriching tenderness. And yet the horrid phrases stuck in her mind, 'On yer back. Like the rest of us.' Oh it mustn't be like that! she thought. It mustn't! That was dirty, smutty, horrible. Love was beautiful. And she remembered how very beautiful it had been. With David, she promised herself, things would be quite different. But ugly thoughts troubled her dreams.

Fortunately David was the very first person in the shop that morning and the sight of his handsome face, lifting and rounding into the most loving smile, restored her balance and her hope.

He had a letter in his hand, which he passed quietly across the counter so that their fingers touched, briefly but pleasurably. A faint familiar smell of leather and glue rose from the cloth of his working suit, and as he bowed his head towards her a swathe of dark hair fell from under his cap to lie softly across his forehead. His eyes were very dark and tender, but he remembered to be circumspect. 'Good morning, Miss White.'

Outside the shop window the street was bright with sunlight. 'Good morning,' she said, 'Mr Cheifitz.' *Dear* Mr Cheifitz.

This time it really was a love letter although quite a short one. 'Dear Ellen,' he wrote, 'I meant every word I said yesterday and I hope you did too. I am so happy I can't believe it. You are the dearest girl in all the world. Will you come to the Tate Gallery with me tonight? There is a picture there I would very much like you to see. Only if you want to of course. With love from David, x x x.'

How could she refuse?

So after supper they took one of the new Underground trains to Westminster, and sat side by side beneath the new hard electric lights while their odd caterpillar of a train rocked them along. It was the first time Ellen had ever travelled by tube and that was an excitement in itself. When they emerged from the sulphurous darkness into the bustle of Parliament Square, the sun was beginning to set and the sky above St James's Park was streaked with rich colour, lilac and orange and salmon pink.

'I shall put a sky like that in my paintin' of you,' he said. 'Behind yer head, so as ter show up yer hair.'

'There was a tree behind me 'ead,' she said. 'Bet yer couldn't even *see* the sky.'

'You will in my paintin',' he promised.

'That's cheatin'.'

'That's artistic licence.'

'Oh 'ark at you!' she laughed, teasing him because she was very impressed and wasn't sure yet that she wanted him to know it. 'You an' your artists!'

'Wait till you see what I'm goin' ter show yer.'

They walked along Millbank towards the gallery, arm in arm, beside a choppy sky-blue Thames, and as they walked, the spreading colour in the sky dappled the water with leaf-shaped patches of lilac and pink and gold. It was a magical evening.

Ellen was unprepared for the impact of the paintings she was about to see. They overwhelmed her.

'They're so big!' she whispered, tiptoeing after David through the huge galleries.

'Ain't they jest!' he said happily. 'This is real art, you see,

Ellen, real art. We'll stop an' see some a' the others next time. Onny they close in half an hour, so we'll 'ave ter look pretty sharp ternight.' They had arrived at the entrance to the Pre-Raphaelite gallery. 'Close yer eyes. Don't open 'em till I tell yer.'

She smiled at him and closed her eyes, and he led her by the hand until they were both standing in front of the Lady of Shalott. 'There!' he said. 'Whatcher think a' that?'

There was something about the quality of his voice that alerted her, a sense of strong emotions kept under control, and an anxiety she hadn't expected. She looked at his face before she looked at the picture, and she didn't really understand either of them, he so dark-eyed and strange, hopeful and bashful at the same time, the picture telling a story she didn't know. She gazed at it for a long time, thinking carefully before she said anything, because there was no doubt that it was important to him.

'It's a lovely paintin',' she said at last, and then added practically, 'Why's she lookin' so upset?'

So he told her the story of the poor bewitched lady, and how she'd been forced to view the world through a mirror, and how she was drifting to her death because she'd dared to disobey.

'That accounts,' Ellen said, looking at the anguished face again. 'Why couldn't someone've smashed the mirror for 'er when she was a kid? I know I would've.'

'Oh Ellen,' he said laughing with admiration and affection. 'You're priceless! Smash the mirror. I'll bet you would've an' all.'

' 'Course,' she said, recognizing his admiration and basking in it.

He glanced from the beautiful face in the portrait to the even more beautiful face before him, and knew that the only emotion the portrait was stirring in him now was dulled and distant, a remembered pang of longing, no more. And he was suffused with happiness because he'd found his Ellen, his lovely, lively, practical, passionate Ellen. 'Before I met you,' he told her, holding both her hands and looking straight into her welcoming blue eyes, 'I used ter think she was the most beautiful woman in the world. Now I know it's you, my

198

darling, darling Ellen.' He wanted to kiss her, but was aware that the attendants were on the prowl because it was so near closing time.

'I ain't a lady,' she said feeling she ought to warn him a little. 'I was born in the Nichol, 'fore they pulled it down. An' yer know the sort a' place that was.'

It didn't seem to worry him. 'I was born in Wilson Place,' he said. 'They pulled that down an' all, ter make way fer the Buildin's. I don't reckon it matters where you was born. It's what you do counts. You'll always be a lady ter me, always, no matter where you was born.'

When she began her confession she'd had a vague hope that she had found the moment to tell him who she really was. Now she knew it couldn't be done. Not then anyway. 'I *ain't* a lady though,' she repeated sadly, and looked at the lady on the canvas.

'Nor was she neither,' he comforted. 'She was only a model posing as a lady. So I tell you, if I was ter draw you an' do a great paintin' like that, you'd look like a lady. Every inch a lady. Just like her.'

'Is that what you'd like ter do, a big paintin'?' The eagerness in his voice was so touching she forgot her need for confession.

'I used ter think so. Ain't so sure now. Cost a precious lot a' money a canvas that size. Ter say nothing of the paint. Oils, you see. Cost the earth. No, I reckon I'm better as I am. A draughtsman. I'm a good draughtsman, though I sez it as shouldn't.'

'If I *was* a lady I'd buy you all the paint and canvas you wanted,' she said, and smiled so lovingly into his eyes that he simply had to put his arms round her.

'None a' that!' the attendant said, sneaking up behind them. 'Closin' in ten minutes. Time you was on yer way out.'

That night, when the dormitory was still and all her friends were fast asleep, Ellen returned wakefully to the moment when she'd so nearly confessed. It was very flattering to be compared to a lady, especially that lady, who really was very gorgeous, but the comparison was a difficulty too. How could she tell him she was really Smelly Ellie Murphy, who'd nicked his cake and been the class joke, when he thought of her as a lady and told her it didn't matter where you were born, only what you did? And then another even more alarming thought entered her busy brain. What if they were to meet Ruby Miller one evening and she were to let the cat out of the bag without knowing? Ruby was working as a lady's maid for a family called Winstanley over in Bethnal Green. Ellen saw her nearly every Wednesday, or at least whenever they both had the afternoon off. And Ruby didn't know anything about him. Well, nobody did yet. Except the people in the cycling club. And Maisie, of course. Perhaps she ought to warn Ruby. Just in case. Next Wednesday, she thought, as sleep finally sucked her away, I'll tell her Wednesday.

Ruby was washing her hair in the sink when Ellen arrived that Wednesday afternoon. 'Goin' up West this evening,' she explained, peeping at her friend from behind a swathe of wet hair. 'They're all off out ter some do, so we got the evening off. Bit of all right, eh? Why dontcher come wiv us?'

'Well ... ' Ellen said, trying to think of a tactful way of refusing. 'It's like this ... I've promised.'

'You're walkin' out wiv David Cheifitz, aintcher?' Ruby said affably, returning to her tussle with the soap.

'She seen yer, last Thursday, up the Standard,' Mrs Miller explained, lifting a jug full of clean water from the draining board. 'You ready fer this then, Rube?'

'Not yet! Not yet!' her daughter said, waving a wet hand wildly above her head.

'Well, buck yer ideas up, do,' Mrs Miller said cheerfully. 'There's all the washing up ter do. You ain't got all day.' She was warm and bustling and friendly, and there wasn't a trace of unkindness in her voice at all. Not for the first time, Ellen envied her friend Ruby and wished she could have had a mother even half as loving.

'We're walkin' out, me an' David,' she said. 'I should a' told yer before.'

'Said so, didn't I, Ma?' Ruby said from under the soapsuds.

' 'E's a good-lookin' lad,' Mrs Miller said. 'What's yer Ma think?'

'Ain't told 'em yet.'

'No,' Mrs Miller said and the word was an agreement. 'You wouldn't, would yer. Not really. Can't say I blame yer, duckie.'

'I go 'ome once a month,' Ellen said, because she felt she ought to justify herself. 'When the ol' man ain't there. Take 'em some food. Bits an' bobs. No point givin' 'em money. 'E'd only drink it.'

'Quite right, duck,' Mrs Miller said. 'I'd do the same messell.' She was clearing the dirty dishes from the table onto a tray.

Ellen joined her beside the table and began to help her. 'I think I love 'im,' she said.

Mrs Miller held the teapot against her chest and expressed her approval by patting it, but Ruby rose from the sink like a naiad, streaming water and soapsuds, and threw her arms round Ellen's neck and kissed her over and over again, rapturously and very wetly. 'I think that's lovely,' she said. 'Lovely! Oh Ellie, that's lovely!' until Ellen's blouse was soaking wet and she had to beg her to stop.

'Daft ha'p'orth,' Mrs Miller said. 'Put yer 'ead back in the sink, do, an' let's get the soap out of it, or we shall never 'ear the last. There's a towel on the airer, Ellie love. Give yerself a rub-down. You're soppin' wet.'

'Thing is,' Ellen said, pulling the towel down from the drier and mopping the front of her blouse. ' 'E don't know who I am really. 'E thinks I was born Ellen White. I ain't told 'im I changed me name or nothink ... '

'No,' Mrs Miller said mildly, pouring the clean water over her daughter's soapy head. 'You wouldn't a' done. 'Course not. I can see that. Can't you, Rube?'

'I'll tell 'im in the end,' Ellen promised, glad that they were too busy to be looking at her face. 'When it's the right moment like. It's not ... I'm not bein' deceitful. Not really. It's just I've never 'ad the opportunity.' And she realized that her excuses were making her blush, and knew that she was ashamed of them. She *ought* to have told him.

'Don't worry, duck,' Ruby said from under the smother of falling water. 'Your secret's safe wiv me. I won't say nothink, never fear.'

'Ta,' Ellen said, and busied herself with the towel again.

201

'Sounds serious,' Mrs Miller said, reaching for a second towel from the drier. 'You wasn't thinkin' a' gettin' wed, was yer?'

'Not jest yet-a-while,' Ellen said, blushing again. ' 'Spect we will in the end though.'

' 'E's a Jewboy, Ellie,' Mrs Miller said, handing the towel to Ruby and turning to give her guest her full attention. 'Jews marry Jews as a rule. You know that, dontcher?'

Oh yes, she knew it. She knew it so well she'd been steadfastly avoiding the knowledge ever since that first day at the fair. ' 'E's different,' she said, and she raised her head, eyes flashing and chin in the air.

'Well, I 'ope so, fer your sake,' Mrs Miller said, mildly. 'What do 'is folks say?'

' 'E ain't told 'em yet. We ain't told no one yet. They'll be all right. They're nice.' But she wasn't sure and the expression on her face showed it.

'Pot a' tea,' Mrs Miller decided, turning their conversation to easier matters. 'Aintcher gaspin' fer a pot a' tea? I know I am.'

'So vhere's your Davey?' Rivke asked her sister-in-law when they met on the stairs, some days later. 'Sunday an' he ain't home again. Ve never see him these days.'

Rachel was flustered by her interest but she explained about the cycling club and hoped the explanation would satisfy. 'So healthy, Rivke. Fresh air. Good healthy exercise. Just vhat he vant.' They climbed the next flight together, panting a little in the heat of their exertions.

'You vant ter vatch him,' Rivke advised when they reached the second gallery. 'Young man like that out all hours. That club could be just an excuse for chasing the girls. If I vas you I should think a' gettin' him married, maybe.'

Rachel snorted. Trust Rivke to say the one thing she shouldn't. 'Married! Such an idea! Vhat next?' she said. 'He's a boy yet, Rivke. How many more times I got ter tell you? He don't think a' such things.'

'They all think a' such things,' Rivke said. 'How many more times I got ter tell *you*? He's a grown man. He needs a wife.'

'He ain't!' Rachel said stubbornly. 'He don't!'

'For vhy you don't see the truth about that boy of yours is

202

more than I can comprehend,' Rivke said, hooking her door key out of her skirt pocket by its long string. 'He needs a vife, I tell you, bubeleh.'

'He don't!' Rachel shouted, losing her temper suddenly. 'You hear me, Rivke, he don't, he don't!'

'So ve hear you all over the Buildin's,' Rivke said, taking care not to raise her voice because their neighbours down in the courtyard were obviously listening. 'So don't shout. You don't change human nature shouting, bubeleh.'

'My Davey's a scholar,' Rachel shouted. 'He ain't like any old *meshuganer*, crazy for women. An artist, I tell you. A good boy. A cut above ... '

'Yell all you like but don't say I don't varn you,' Rivke said sternly, preparing to do battle with her key. Her black wig was over one eye, but she still looked fiercely disapproving. 'Find him a vife, I should, dolly.'

'You! Dumpling! Josh!' Rachel yelled, too far beyond herself for caution. 'All the same you are. Every one. Ain't you got nothink better to do than criticize my Davey? He's a good pure Jewish boy, I tell you.' And then, seeing the faces avidly watching her in the courtyard, she yelled down, 'So mind your own business, vhy don't you!'

'You yell, ve listen!' Mrs Guldermann said, grinning malevolently up at her. And at that Rachel fell upon her door and after several tear-smudged attempts to get the key into the lock and turned she stumbled into the comparative sanctuary of her home. Oh what if they were right? Surely he couldn't be chasing girls? Not her Davey. He wouldn't do it.

Chapter Sixteen

And so the summer continued and a rapturous summer it was, even though Ellen never found the right moment, and David didn't tell his parents. But he walked through the shop every morning to give her a smile and a letter, and they cycled every Sunday, and every evening except Friday they went out together, to the theatre or the Music Hall when they had the money, for a stroll around the City when she had only an hour off or they were broke. But either way they were together and that was all that really mattered, for by mid evening it was dark enough for kissing, and with autumn coming it was growing dark earlier and earlier. It wasn't until September began that he realized he hadn't seen Hymie for weeks. It made him feel quite guilty.

He made amends at once, cycling round to the shop early one Sunday morning before he went to Shoreditch to meet Ellen and the club.

'So what's the news?' Hymie said, welcoming him affably. 'I thought you was dead.'

'I'm in love!' David said.

'Oy oy! So what happened to the Lady of Shalott?'

'It's her. I found her!'

'Some fellers have all the luck!' Hymie said when the tale was done.

'Yes,' David agreed seriously. 'It *is* luck! I never thought I'd find her again, an' that's a fact.'

'What's yer Dad think about it?' Hymie asked.

'I ain't told him yet.'

Hymie gave him a quizzical look and took out his packet of cigarettes. 'Why not?' he said offering one.

'Ta,' David said, glad of the pause while they both lit up. 'Well ... ' he said finally. 'She ain't Jewish.' It was a painful fact to be forced to face. He'd been avoiding it all summer. But there it was. Spoken and admitted. She wasn't Jewish. She ate bacon and thought the Sabbath was comical and hadn't even heard of the Commandments. And because she wasn't Jewish he hadn't said a word about her to either of his parents. And he ought to have done.

'My life!' Hymie said understanding at once. 'They won't like that. What yer gonna do?'

'Not much I can do,' David admitted. 'I love her, Hymie. I want ter marry her.'

'If that's the case,' Hymie said, 'you'll have to tell 'em sometime.'

'At Yom Kippur,' David said, making his mind up at last. 'I should've told them at the start, Hymie, so for that I got to attone. Then I tell them – I think.'

'My life!' Hymie said again. But he agreed to come to the theatre on Thursday to be introduced. 'Trust you ter fall fer the wrong girl, Cheify!' he said as they parted.

'She ain't,' David said earnestly. 'She's the only girl I'll ever love. Ever. I told you when I first saw her, nu?'

'Your Ma'll have a fit,' Hymie warned.

David didn't doubt it, and the thought of what she'd say when Yom Kippur began and he finally plucked up enough courage to tell her made him scowl all the way back to Shoreditch. But then he saw Ellen sitting astride her bicycle in her delicious bloomer suit and he forgot everything except the joy of being with her again.

September came, and a new term at evening school and Yom Kippur. But David still didn't confess to his parents. Several opportunities presented themselves during the fast but he dodged them all. For what if they forbade him to see her again? It would have been well within their rights as Jewish parents, and the more he thought about it, the more likely it seemed. He stood beside his father in the crowded synagogue brooding and doubting and feeling horribly ashamed of his cowardice. Because that was what it was, and he knew it. But he couldn't run the risk of being forbidden to see her. He loved

205

her too much now. She was part of his life, and more important to him than either of his parents, dearly though he loved them. She occupied his every dream and he thought about her all day long, continually and obsessively, so that her laugh rang above the scuffle of the workshop, and her face shone at him from every page, and her dark hair eclipsed the stitches. The hours they spent together were too swift and too precious and too blissfully happy to be curtailed or altered in any way. So although it troubled his conscience he decided to say nothing for just a little longer. It wasn't really deception, he tried to persuade himself, just delay. It would give him time to think of the right way to break the news, an acceptable way that wouldn't outrage them.

He didn't enrol for any more Art classes either, although he did go down to the People's Palace on enrolment evening to see Mr Smith and explain why.

'I thought I'd take a year off, maybe,' he said, recognizing the lame excuse even as it left his mouth. 'I'm getting stale. Don't you think so, sir?'

'The siren's song!' Mr Smith said mildly if enigmatically. 'You cut off into the world, Cheify. Enjoy it while you can. Life is short and art is long, eh?'

'I'll come back an' see you, sir, I promise.'

Mr Smith crossed David's name from the list on the table between them. Then he pushed his pencil into the thicket of hair above his right ear and grinned. 'I hope she's a beauty,' he said.

David felt his cheeks burn, but he looked his teacher in the eye and admitted, 'She *is*.'

'I'm glad to hear it,' Mr Smith said as they shook hands to mark their farewell. 'A beautiful model is the most necessary adjunct to an artist. Perhaps you'll bring her to see me some day.'

As he walked back to Whitechapel past the pavement stalls of the Mile End Road, David was deliberately storing their conversation in his memory, resavouring it like the precious exchange it was. If only he could talk to his father like that, easily and openly, admitting his love and being approved of simply because she was a beautiful girl. But in his father's eyes

206

she would be unsuitable, however beautiful, and the longer he loved her, the more surely he knew it. It was against his nature to be secretive. But that was what he had become. Oh why couldn't she have been born Jewish?

It was a bad winter that year, a cold secretive season, obscured by fogs from November till February, chill and dank and dirty, coughing diseases into all the crowded tenements of Shoreditch and Whitechapel. There was an epidemic of measles in October, followed almost immediately by two even worse, diphtheria and scarlet fever. Soon, white coffins were an all too familar sight in the Buildings, and there was a general air of frozen sorrow about the place. Trade was bad and getting worse and work was hard to find and difficult to keep.

But despite bad weather and guilty consciences and the sickness and unemployment all around them, David and Ellen led charmed lives, contained and sustained in the little world of their love for each other. They didn't even catch cold, which was little short of a miracle when they spent so much of the season walking about in the raw night air or sitting in stuffy theatres and crowded music halls being coughed over by their less healthy neighbours.

Now and then, when the fog lifted and it wasn't raining, they put on their overcoats and took out their bicycles and rode to Epping Forest where the hedges were a damp black tangle of dead leaves, brambles and winter-revealed litter, and the overhanging boughs dripped on their passing heads. But they didn't notice any of it, they were so wrapped up in each other, talking and teasing and playing their own private version of kiss-chase, for four scampering feet and two ardent mouths.

And that was how they found the white house.

They'd cycled deep into Epping Forest that Sunday morning, following the path north towards Great Monk Wood and Wake Valley Pond, riding side by side and at a leisurely pace because they were deep in conversation. It was a chill afternoon and the sky they glimpsed between the sodden branches was a sombre grey, so when they reached the Riggs Retreat at High Beach and saw that it was open, David was tempted to stop and buy hot drinks to warm them both up.

But Ellen was restless. 'We'll 'ave sommink on our way back,' she said. 'Let's leave the bikes here an' go off exploring. I got itchy feet.'

'Fleas, I 'spect.'

'Sauce!' she said, propping her bike against the veranda. 'You coming or aintcher?'

'Two intrepid explorers a' the wild wood set off on their dangerous mission,' David said, posing in front of the veranda as though he were having his photograph taken. Then he grinned at her and settled his own machine against the wooden railings. 'After you, Miss Livingstone!'

The ground behind the Riggs Retreat fell away steeply in a series of terraced rose gardens, but now the roses were cut right back and the earth was black and bare. Ellen paid no attention to any of it but went skipping down the stone steps, her cape billowing behind her like a train, and David followed, admiring the rhythm of her quick feet and the easy grace of her movements and wishing he could catch them on paper. Several sketches, he thought, one after the other, to show a sequence, set side by side. And then she was gone, plunging between the trees like a fawn, her cape licking the branches.

'Wait fer me,' he yelled, crashing after her.

Her voice came echoing back from the thicket in front of him. 'Catch me if yer ca-an!' He could hear beech leaves scuffling and twigs cracking and her feet running further and further away, and he followed the sounds happily, ducking to avoid branches and kicking the dead leaves into the air as he ran. Just ahead of him the trees were thinning and he could see the grey sky and a patch of smeared whiteness. He shouted her name and she called back at once. 'Come an' see what I've found!'

It was a wide clearing and she was standing in the middle of it, gazing up at a huge old-fashioned white house. It had evidently been empty for a very long time, for the windows were curtained with dust and grass was growing from the cracks in the front steps and the stucco was stained and chipped. But it had been a splendid place in its day, two storeys high, with a line of attic windows under the eaves for the servants, and flanked by outhouses and stables.

'What a place!' he said, standing beside her with his arm about her shoulders. 'What say we explore?'

'Be a lark if we could get inside,' she said. 'I'd love ter see the inside.'

'Come on then. I dare yer!'

The front steps led to an inner balcony that stretched along three-quarters of the frontage, past the central front dor which disappointingly, was locked, and four of the six high French windows, which were equally secure. The balcony was screened by elaborate wrought ironwork now weather-blackened and rusty, but the floor was almost in its original state, tiled in a geometrical pattern of blue, green, buff and white, which they both thought very pretty.

'No way in here,' David said. 'Let's try the back.'

There was a yard at the back of the house, much overgrown with moss and ferns and leading to a very dirty window and a grey door set askew under a warped lintel. 'I don't reckon that door's on its hinges,' David said as they approached. 'You ask me it's just propped up.'

It was.

'What a bit a' luck!' Ellen said, her hands already tugging the handle.

It took considerable strain and strength to lift the door, because although it wasn't shut it was wedged tight. But they were both full of determined energy and ardent with curiosity, so at last the job was done and they'd turned it far enough on its axis to make a gap big enough to squeeze through.

The kitchen was dark and cold and very dirty, with a greasy ceiling and brown walls and hard stone flags underfoot, but they explored it just the same. They poked their noses into the pantry and the wine cupboard, investigated the wash house with three deep sinks and a broken washboard, and a small square cosy room that was obviously the cook's parlour. Then they found a flight of narrow stairs at the end of the corridor, beside the servants' bells, and scrambled up, hand in hand in the darkness.

There was a door lined with green baize at the top of the stairs, and when they opened it they found themselves in the hall, and another world. It was a very grand place indeed, surprisingly warm, and spacious, and full of white light, with an elaborately carved ceiling high above their heads and the same pretty tiles under their feet. The staircase was made of oak with intricately carved balusters, and the panelled doors that led out of the hall to right and left were painted with leafy branches and spring blossom and perching birds.

' 'S like a palace!' Ellen said, unbuttoning her cape in the warmth. 'Bet they 'ad some sport 'ere in the old days.'

David took off his cap and stuffed it into his coat pocket. 'Just look at them paintings,' he said.

But she was already running up the stairs ahead of him. 'Last one at the top's a cissy!'

She allowed him to catch her at the top of the first flight where there was a landing lit by a Venetian window. And he was artist enough to spend two seconds thinking what a perfect setting it would be for a portrait of lovers kissing, even before their kiss began. He held her lovely face tenderly between his hands and kissed her mouth lingeringly and langorously, moving his own dreamily from side to side, as waves of delicious pleasure spread through both their bodies. 'Ellen, bubeleh,' he said softly when they paused for breath. She was smiling her love straight into his eyes and her lips were so full and so red with kissing he couldn't resist kissing them again.

The house was silent all around them and as their lips touched in that second kiss he rejoiced that they were alone in this private place and had no need to rush or pull apart abruptly for fear of passers-by. But privacy and time were mixed blessings, for the longer they kissed and the more pleasurable their kisses grew, the more instinctive their love-making became. As they drew apart for the seventh time, or was it the eighth? he was holding her about the waist, his thumbs the merest fraction of an inch away from the lovely inviting curves of her breasts. The desire to touch her was so overwhelming his face was strained with it. She bit her lip, hesitating, wanting him to continue, but a little afraid of sensations so strong and so compelling. And the sight of her face, flushed and perplexed, halted him. They stood close together but very still, she hoping and fearing, he knowing,

210

even with passion urging him on most powerfully, that he should only continue if she gave him permission. 'May I? May I, Ellen?'

She lifted her head very very slowly, and closed her eyes. It was a movement so meltingly tender and yielding that no other permission was necessary. Breathless with gratitude and anticipated pleasure, he cupped her breasts in his hands for the very first time and began to stroke them, kissing her neck where her flesh smelled of salt and talcum and musk. 'Oh Ellen! Bubeleh!'

'Davey!' she whispered. 'Davey, Davey, Davey!' the words crooning in her throat, vibrating underneath his lips. The pleasure in her breasts was so intense she couldn't bear it. But when he paused, just long enough to lift his head and find her mouth again, she couldn't bear him to stop either. 'Oh don't stop! Don't stop!'

And then, to her surprise, her legs began to tremble. And that made them both stop and filled him with remorse. 'What is it? I ain't hurt yer, 'ave I, Ellen? Sit down, nu?' his eyes all tender concern.

They sat on the top step cuddled close together until the trembling stopped. 'P'raps we shouldn't 'ave,' he said, anxious and contrite. 'I'd never do nothink to hurt you, Ellen, you know that dontcher?'

'Yes,' she said. Of course she knew it. Wasn't she here with him, trusting him?

This was the moment to ask her to marry him, he thought. But he couldn't, could he? Not till he'd told his parents. 'I do love yer,' he said.

'You won't never leave me, will yer?' she said, and it hurt him that she sounded so anxious about it.

'Never ever,' he promised. 'Not now. Not after ... We belong together now. Fer always.'

'Yes,' she said. 'We do, don't we? I'd never a' let no one else do ... that. You know that, dontcher?'

' 'Course!' Oh he really ought to ask her. It was the proper thing to do, and cowardice not to.

'I'm all right now,' she said, soothing him because he looked so worried and loved her so much. 'I dunno what came over

211

me.' But the trouble was, that uncontrollable trembling had made her remember Fenny Jago and her ugly jibe, 'Down on yer back, same as all the rest.' Perhaps you were bound to feel ashamed like that unless you were married. She gave her head a little shake to push her thoughts away and stood up, pulling him to his feet after her. 'I'm off ter see the rest. Catch me if yer ca-an!' And she ran before anything more could be said or done.

Sudden movement lightened their mood. They played kiss-chase all over the top floor of the house, through bedrooms and dressing rooms, in and out of cupboards, hiding mouse-still behind doors and kissing langorously in corners, until they were quite out of breath and their sudden, serious commitment to one another had been absorbed and accepted. Then they came downstairs again, arm in arm and still panting, and a pale sun broke through the clouds to column through the Venetian window and lighten their way.

David looked back up the stairs to the little landing. 'I'd like ter paint a picture a' this place,' he said. 'Two lovers with the winder behind 'em, maybe.'

She understood at once. 'You an' me,' she said. 'Kissin'.'

'We'll have a look round downstairs,' he said, 'an' then I'll come back here an' do a sketch. Whatcher think?'

The first door on the right led to a series of rooms, one leading out of the other and all quite empty and rather chill and dull, but the first door on the left led to an enormous room which stretched for the full length of the house. It had high windows filling three of its walls and a huge fireplace made of mottled marble in the centre of the fourth. The moulded ceiling was picked out in powder blue and white, there were elaborate carvings above both the doors, and enough blue and white striped wallpaper still left on the walls for them to see how beautiful it had once been. Even without furniture and curtains, and with the floor bare, there was a grandeur about this room that overawed them. The fireplace was so big there was room for them both to sit inside it. Which they did, with their backs against the side walls and their feet where the fire should have been.

'It's like a little house,' Ellen said. 'You an' me on either side

212

a' the fire. All warm and cosy.'

He was more interested in her than the fireplace. She looked so very pretty with that white marble behind her dark curls and her eyes shining love at him from the shadows. Prettier than he'd ever seen her. And he knew he had to draw her. Now. Just as she was. He took his pencil from the top pocket of his jacket and tried to fish out his notebook too, but his cap was still stuffed in the way, and after a useless tussle, which was an aggravating waste of time, he gave up the effort and simply drew an outline sketch of her head and shoulders on the wall beside him. And found he was quite pleased with it.

'Whatcher think?' he asked proudly.

'Very life-like,' she said laughing at him. 'Takin' it home, are yer?'

Now he wished he'd persisted in his efforts and that the sketch was in his notebook and retrievable. 'I shall leave it here fer posterity,' he bragged happily, and signed it with his initials.

'Daft ha'p'orth,' she said lovingly.

Crouching beside the wall to draw had made him feel cramped. He crawled out of the fireplace to straighten his spine and stretch his legs. 'I wonder who lived here,' he mused.

'They must a' been swells.'

'Why'd they leave?' he said. 'That's what puzzles me. If I had a place like this, I'd stay in it for ever, wouldn't you?'

She was still sitting in the fireplace, with her knees under her chin, gazing dreamily in front of her, but she didn't answer him. He walked to the windows and looked out into the wilderness that had once been a garden. They'd had a lot of horses, he thought, whoever they were. There were stables on both sides of the house. And how green the woods were. Even in the middle of winter. He sat on the sill of the central window wondering if he had sufficient artistic technique to draw such a complication of green tones and varying textures. It would be lovely to do a painting of Ellen against such a setting. And as always, wondering led to attempting. This time he retrieved his notebook, and soon he was busily sketching, absorbed in the impossible task he'd set himself. He even forgot his lovely Ellen for the moment.

The first two sketches were useless but the third was better. In fact he was really quite pleased with his efforts, for the second time that day. 'Reckon you've inspired me, bubeleh,' he said, looking at the sketch pad and speaking to the quiet figure he could just see out of the corner of his eye. But she didn't answer him then either, and this time her silence made him feel just a little uneasy. He walked across at once to show her his work and apologize for neglecting her.

She was sitting where he'd left her, with her arms clasped round her knees, but she was unnaturally still. Still as a statue, staring straight ahead of her, with an expression of such horror on her face that the sight of it froze his blood. 'Ellen!' he said running to her. 'What's the matter? What's up?'

Her eyes were glazed and withdrawn, looking inwards, transfixed by some internal horror and her face was as white as paper. She wasn't aware of him at all, but when he put his arms round her in a clumsy effort to comfort her, she began to moan, and then to rock backwards and forwards. 'Oh! Oh! All them poor fellers. Oh, they're in such pain. Them poor fellers. An' all the blood.'

He was very frightened. First that awful fit of the shakes, and now this. It was as if she were possessed. What if there was a *dybbuk* in the house, and it had got into her somehow or other when he wasn't looking? *Has vesholem!* He knew about such terrible spirits, because Aunty Dumpling had told him. Oh what should he do? 'Ellen!' he begged. 'Look at me, bubeleh. Please!' But she went on staring into space. He ought to shake her, maybe. But that might give her a shock.

'They can't 'elp groanin',' she said, and he was relieved that she was speaking with her own voice, even though he couldn't understand what she was saying. 'Oh the pain. It's everywhere. All round. They can't bear it. Can't bear it.' Then her eyes swam into focus and he knew she could see him again, and she threw herself into his arms and burst into passionate weeping. 'Never leave me!' she begged. 'Oh Davey, never ever leave me. I couldn't bear it.'

'Never ever!' he promised with equal passion. 'I told yer. I never ever could. Not now. I love you. I'd do anything for you. Anything!' And at that she wept more wildly than before.

He held her and patted her back and made soothing noises and let her cry, because he couldn't stop her and he didn't know what else to do. And she cried for a very long time, with the tears running off the end of her nose and her cheeks blotchy and her blue eyes bloodshot.

But at last the worst was over and her sobs were gradually subsiding. He held her hands very gently and ventured to ask her what had happened. It couldn't have been a *dybbuk*, could it?

'I dunno what it was,' she said, wiping her eyes. She looked wan and bewildered. 'I get these sort a' moments sometimes. Like a dream, only I'm wide awake. I sort a' see things. Hazy sort of. Like yer do in a dream. Onny it ain't a dream. I'm certain sure a' that. I *feel* things really, more'n see 'em.'

A dream, he thought, taking comfort from her explanation. That didn't sound like a *dybbuk*. Perhaps she was a seer, like Hannah, who spoke so clearly in her song of thanksgiving, or Huldah the prophetess, who was consulted by the priests. 'You was talkin' about pain,' he said, wondering if she could remember it now.

'This room was full a' men,' she said. 'Shufflin' about on crutches, an' bandaged up, an' groanin'. An' lines a' beds too. They was in terrible pain. I could feel it. An' I was lookin' fer something. I'd lost something. That was it. I *had* ter find it, an' I didn't know where ter look. I was searchin' all over. Oh dear, oh dear. It was awful.' Her face was beginning to crinkle towards tears again at the memory.

'D'you often see things like that?' he asked, partly to take her mind from the present vision and partly because he had to know more.

'Not like that. I never seen nothink as bad as that. Mostly I jest see things fer a minute or two, an' then I don't know *what* they are after.'

'When you see things,' he said, speaking very carefully because he didn't want to offend her, and because this was so very important he had to know the truth, 'do you know it's *you* seein' them? Or do you feel you're someone else?' He was breathless with apprehension. Oh she couldn't be possessed! Not his lovely Ellen.

215

'Oh no,' she said, easily. 'It's always me. I wish it wasn't. It's like a dream, but it's always me dreamin' it.'

He was weak with relief. And now sympathy for her flooded back. 'Does it scare you?'

'It did then.'

'My poor love,' he said tenderly, and kissed her, holding both her hands in his. 'Your hands are like ice.' It must have been a terrible experience for her, this waking dream.

'Cold 'ands, warm 'eart,' she said trying to make a joke of it. And failing.

'It's this place,' he said, touched by her attempt to recover herself. 'What say we go back to Riggs an' have a slap-up meal an' warm ourselves up?' The sight of her stricken face made him feel protective and ashamed of his questioning. If she was a seer, a prophetess, she was very very special. Now he felt honoured to have been chosen to protect her. 'We'll go to Riggs, nu?'

It sounded like a very good idea. And although he wasn't quite sure he had enough money for a really slap-up meal, that's what they did.

It was growing dark by the time they cycled back to Shoreditch. As they kissed goodnight outside the staff entrance to Hopkins and Peggs, they realized that they were both exhausted. It had been an extraordinary day. And much longer than twenty-four hours.

Chapter Seventeen

It took Ellen several wakeful nights and a good many thoughtful days to digest all the events of that Sunday. For a start, she felt she was irretrievably committed to him, now that they'd gone beyond kissing, and the thought made her feel rapturously happy, and yet at the same time frightened her. Sooner or later she knew they would get married, and that was right and proper and what she wanted. But she could still remember her mother's warnings somewhere in the childish recesses of her mind, 'Don't you let 'em touch yer, gel!' and the words roused a sense of wrong-doing and risk-taking that wasn't easy to ignore. It had been sensible advice at the time, when she'd been coping with the crude advances of young men like Jimmy Thatcher, but it didn't apply to her gentle David. 'Course not. David was different. He was an artist, sensitive and delicate and not a bit like all the others. Look how marvellous he'd been when she had that terrible waking dream. He'd taken it all so calmly, and he hadn't loved her any less because of it. Quite the reverse, in fact, which wasn't what she'd really expected. Not if she was honest about it.

It was the waking dream that had upset her more than anything else, partly because it had been so vivid and frightened her so much, but also because David had seen her during it. Until then she'd taken great care not to let anyone know when she had one of her 'moments' and so she'd managed to persuade herself that they weren't really very important. They were just an odd private trick she'd learned somehow or other without trying to. A way of receiving messages. That was all. Most of them came from her family and could be acted on and forgotten quite quickly. She would 'know' when her mother was upset or one of the little 'uns had taken a pasting from the old man, and then she would buy something tasty for them to eat and pay them a surprise visit to comfort them. It was useful, but she preferred it to be unremarkable. Now and quite suddenly it had become something far more important. For this dream simply wasn't the sort of thing she could push to one side and ignore. It had lasted too long and affected her too deeply. The terror and the awful sense of loss returned at dead of night to frighten her all over again and she found herself asking David's anxious question, 'What was it?' and following that with a second, even more anxious, 'Why did it happen to me?'

On nights like that it was a relief when the day began and she knew he would soon be walking through the shop with his daily love letter, his nice normal daily love letter. Unfortunately, he wasn't the only one to be paying court to her these days.

Love was making her bloom, plumping her cheeks and rounding her breasts, thickening her hair and bringing a glow to her skin. At first she was delighted with the improvement, especially as David noticed it and responded to it so lovingly. But after a while Jimmy Thatcher noticed too, and took to loitering in the dress department again, just like he'd done when she first arrived, leering at her in the most unpleasantly knowing way. He had a score to settle with Miss Icy White and this was a good chance.

She did her best to deflect him, but he was persistent.

'An' how's Miss Ice White this loverly mornin'?' he would say, leaning across the counter to ogle her.

'Busy. 'Op it!'

'Little bird told me you was in love. Not quite such an icy white now-a-days, eh?'

'Aintcher got nothing better ter do than loll around 'ere makin' silly remarks?'

'Got the taste fer it, aintcher? You wanna try *me* now yer got the taste fer it.'

'You wanna clip round the ear.'

'Naughty, naughty!' he said, mocking her.

And off he'd go, whistling. It infuriated her.

218

'I'll give 'im such a fourpenny one if he keeps on,' she said to Ruby as they laid the tea table that Wednesday afternoon. ' 'E don't take a blind bit a' notice no matter what I say.'

'Saucy beggar!' Ruby sympathized, emptying a twist of sugar into the sugar bowl. 'Don't 'e know you're walking out?'

' 'Course. Fat lot a difference that makes!'

'You told David?'

' 'Course.'

'What's 'e say?'

'Ignore it.'

'That's all very well,' Ruby grimaced. ' 'E don't 'ave ter.'

'I'll fix 'im come the New Year,' Ellen promised. 'I got an idea.'

'Cor,' Ruby said impressed. 'Tell us! Whatcher gonna do?'

'Invite David to the party.'

Hopkins and Peggs always gave a New Year party for their staff and although trade was bad and takings low they saw no reason to make an exception this year. Ellen and Maudie had been looking forward to it since November. Particularly as this year they'd completed five years' service and earned the right to invite a guest. Maudie was bringing her sister all the way from Bethnal Green.

'I know they don't celebrate Christmas, the Jews,' she said. 'But New Year's a different thing, ain't it?'

'Quite different,' Ruby said. 'Cor! Fancy 'aving a feller ter bring ter the party fer everyone ter see! Wish it was me!'

But Ellen's feller wasn't at all sure he wanted to be taken to the party for everyone to see. 'I'll come if you really want me to,' he said. 'I'd rather go to the Standard though. They got Marie Lloyd top of the bill.'

'It's important,' she urged. 'That Jimmy Thatcher's gettin' worse an' worse. I want 'im ter see I'm spoken for.'

'*Are* yer spoken for?' he teased, stroking her top lip, to make her shiver.

'Ain't I?' Shivering.

His kiss was an answer to both questions. 'So who wants ter see Marie Lloyd?'

'We'll 'ave some fun, I promise,' she said. 'They do us proud, New Year.'

Which was true enough. But it didn't help him to explain yet another night out to his parents. There was an edge about his mother's comments these days that made him feel guilty. 'So vhy you don't spend a liddle more of your time vid some nice Yiddish friends.'

'It's 'Opkins and Peggs,' he tried to explain. 'Josh and Meg'll be there.'

'Nu-nu, I vonder you don't vork there yourself,' she said tartly. 'The time you spend.'

Preparations for the party began as usual as soon as the shutters were put up at seven o'clock, and within an hour the dining room had been transformed. There was a Christmas tree blazing with candles in one corner, the ceiling was festooned with a network of paper chains, wreaths of holly hung from every door and the tables had been set with white linen, for once, and decorated with mounds of evergreens.

'It'll be fun, you'll see,' Ellen tried to reassure him as they walked in to supper. He was looking far too pale, and his serious expression made her realize that it was an ordeal for him to be put on display like this. I shouldn't've done it, she thought, and was ashamed of an emotion that now looked far too much like selfishness.

But he smiled at her lovingly, and anyway, it was too late for second thoughts.

Supper was a raucously jolly meal, because they were all a little ill at ease and talking excitedly. But the food was appetizing if not abundant and there was plenty of ale to wash it down, so it wasn't long before cheeks were flushed and tongues eased. David sat between Ellen and Maudie and although the food wasn't at all to his taste, at least he contrived to pass his slice of ham to Ellen while Maudie's current 'feller' was playing the spoons, and the conversation was cheerful enough.

Then the gaslight was turned down low and all the tables and chairs were cleared to the edges of the room to make a space for dancing, and the real business of the evening began. The managers and floor walkers were all in extravagant good humour by then, booming at one another at the top of their voices, parading about the room in their customary evening

220

dress pressing fruit punch and the compliments of the season on all the excited employees. But the assistants gathered self-consciously round every table, girls to the left and men to the right, of course, as was only right and proper, and hoping that they weren't overdressed now that they were no longer half-hidden by the table cloths. And that left Ellen and David feeling rather exposed among the older couples. They stood awkwardly together as the errand boys sped about the room pretending to be waiters, with beer for the plebs and brandy for the gentry, and tobacco smoke billowed from all those once-a-year cigars. And David wished he hadn't come, knowing he didn't fit in at such a Christian celebration.

At the far end of the room a square had been roped off for the band who were now arriving, music in hand. They were rather an odd collection of instrumentalists, consisting of a pianist of sorts, two shrill violinists who hadn't the slightest intention of playing in harmony, or even together, Miss Morton brisk as ever on the squeezebox, and Mr Fenway, resplendent in a tartan jacket and an old fashioned cravat, rattling a kettledrum. But at least, David thought, they signalled the hope of activity. All that standing around watching one another was embarrassing.

'Which one's Jimmy Thatcher?' he asked Ellen, as the band rearranged their seats and adjusted their music stands.

'Down the other end,' she said. 'Drinking the dregs! 'E would!'

David examined his rival, who was busily drinking all the dregs from the discarded brandy glasses. He could see why Ellen wanted to be rid of him. What a coarse looking creature, with his face too wide and his eyes too small. Like a pug. And fancy drinking other people's leavings! 'Don't think much of him,' he said.

'Nor me!' she said, beaming at his good judgement. 'Let's 'ope 'e takes the hint.'

Then young Mr Peggo clapped his hands for attention and requested the company to be so good as to take their partners for the first waltz. And from the moment the dancing began, there was so much noise and such cheerful activity that doubt and embarrassment and the deplorable Jimmy Thatcher were

221

temporarily forgotten. David and Ellen danced every dance bar two, and when they weren't dancing they were drinking fruit punch and joking with Maudie and the cycling club. And neither of them paid any attention to Jimmy Thatcher, who was now rolling drunk and making clumsy passes at any girl within range. Unfortunately, despite the fact that he was having considerable difficulty focusing his eyes, he finally saw them, and blundered across the room to make his presence known.

' 'Trodush me to your friend, Miss Icy White,' he said thickly, grabbing hold of Ellen's sleeve to steady himself.

'Go away!' she hissed at him. 'Mr Peggs is lookin' at yer.'

'So thish ish the famous Ikey Mo,' he said, narrowing his eyes to look at David. 'Mr Schnozzle! Yer very own Yiddle-iddle.'

David went ashy white under the insult and his mouth closed as if it would never open again. And Ellen was so torn with guilt and distress she forgot to be angry. 'Davey!' she whispered, reaching out for his hand and not finding it.

'Oh-oh! Davey ish it?' Thatcher sneered. 'Yiddle-iddle Davey!' And he poked a finger into David's chest. 'Jewboy!' The cycle club had gathered around them, but David was too angry and Ellen too numb with distress to notice.

'Sling yer 'ook, Thatcher,' Maudie's feller warned, moving into the attack. And he turned to David, feeling he ought to explain, ' 'E's tight. 'E don't know what 'e's saying.'

'He knows,' David said suddenly and bitterly. 'He means it.' And he caught his adversary's blunt fist in mid-poke and threw it aside with such force that it pulled them both off balance. Thatcher toppled backwards into the nearest table, removing cloth and decorations as he fell. David stumbled into the steadying arms of Maudie's feller. And the cycling club took action, because Mr Peggs was striding thorugh the crowds towards them, and if something wasn't done soon, they'd all be in trouble.

'Dance!' Mr Galsworthy instructed, as he and three of the others seized one Thatcher limb apiece and prepared to carry him from the room. Luckily he was still too dazed to offer any resistance and although David was still trembling with fury, he followed Ellen and the others into the dance, which was a lively

222

version of 'The Dashing White Sergeant' and soon pulled them into the crowd. By the time Mr Peggs arrived even the table had been set to rights and if the evergreens *did* look a trifle battered, he decided not to comment upon it.

'I'm ever so sorry,' Ellen said, when 'The Dashing White Sergeant' was over and the noise of the dancers returning to their seats gave her sufficient cover to apologize. 'I wouldn't've 'ad that 'appen fer worlds. I never thought 'e'd go for yer. I'm ever so sorry.'

'I should've hit 'im,' he said, scowling. He'd endured an insult that shouldn't have been endured and he felt diminished because of it. They should have been left to fight it out. Then at least his pride would have been satisfied.

'Oh David,' she said. 'I *am* sorry.'

And this time he looked at her and saw how very upset she was. 'It ain't your fault,' he said, but it was a grudging admission and didn't sound like forgiveness to either of them.

Nevertheless the ugly moment receded as the dancing continued and Thatcher didn't come back. They couldn't stay miserable for very long when they were in each other's arms and their feet were moving in rhythm. The band played with increasing abandon, the gaslights were turned down to the merest flicker, and in no time at all it was midnight. The crowded room grew gradually still while the party waited breathlessly, and at last the grandfather clock, which had been wheeled into the corner specially for the occasion, struck its twelve reverberating notes.

' 'Appy New Year,' she wished him, kissing him softly under cover of all the riotous greetings and smacking kisses around them. Was she forgiven? He looked as though he'd forgiven her.

'You too, bubeleh,' he said lovingly.

'Wonder what it'll bring.' Could they even dare to think of marriage? She'd better not mention it. She'd caused enough trouble for one evening.

'Who knows?' Oh if only she was Jewish. They could marry in the spring. They ought to marry in the spring. Then she'd never have to put up with louts like that Jimmy Thatcher ever again.

'Auld Lang Syne!' Mr Peggs announced.

The New Year had plenty of surprises in store for all of them, but at its start it was no more propitious than the old. January brought more fog and several days of sleet and an outbreak of flu. And at the end of the month, the Rothschild Buildings were a-buzz with rumours of a terrible massacre. The poor of St Petersburg had taken a petition to their Tsar, marching to his winter palace 200,000 strong in five huge processions, led by their priests and carrying their religious ikons, and their loving father, the Tsar of all the Russias, had ordered his troops to open fire on them, unarmed and defenceless as they were, and they'd been mown down in their thousands.

Russian Jews like Hymie and Morrie Leipzich spent all their evenings mourning their one-time countrymen, and debating the consequences.

'Killed in their thousands,' Hymie said, over and over again. 'Ai-yi! Bread they ask for, bullets they get. The Tsar-murderer!'

'Now there will be revolution,' Morris predicted. 'Ain't nothink to stop it. An' high time too! I shall go back the minute it starts.' He'd been born in Whitechapel, but now he felt more Russian that his parents.

'Terrible, David, nu?' Hymie said.

And David agreed that it was terrible. A crime against humanity. But he couldn't take it to heart and feel enraged about it the way Hymie was doing. It was all too far away, and he was too happy.

But it looked as though they were right, for within a week news filtered through that a wave of strikes had begun, and not just in St Petersburg either, but all over Russia, wherever there were mines and factories and dockyards to gather the workers together. More than half a million of them had downed tools according to Morrie Leipzich's cousin. And that wasn't all. Apparently the universities were joining in too, revolutionaries were making speeches to the students and 326 professors had signed a petition demanding a change of government, free elections and the power to make their own laws.

The nightly debates in the Rothschild Buildings grew more

heated than ever as Jews from Eastern Europe, young and old, crowded into their neighbours' cramped living rooms to relay the latest news and give loud voice to their hopes. They smoked and talked at speed, eyes glistening, arms waving, faces burning, while the samovar steamed on the sideboard and smoke clouded the ceiling.

Their passion reduced Emmanuel Cheifitz to beard-plucking anxiety. 'Vhere's the good?' he asked Rachel after one particularly noisy evening. 'Vid Mother Russia over the other side of the world. So they talk and talk, bubeleh. It don't do nothing.'

'Don't you vorry your head, Emmanuel,' Rachel soothed. 'Ve let them talk, nu? They're young yet.' A revolution so far away was no concern of theirs.

Unfortunately revolutionary fervour was in the air in London too, and by mid February the cabinet-makers in Worship Street and even the tailors and operatives of Whitechapel and Spitalfields were holding union meetings and drawing up a list of reasonable demands, a working week no longer than fifty-eight hours, government contractors to pay wages at union rates, the right to eat their meals off the premises. By the end of the month, when the bosses had denied all their demands and looked set to ignore them for ever, they followed the blazing example of the Russians and discarded their meekness and refused to work.

Emmanuel was distraught. 'For vhy they do this thing?' he appealed to David. 'To refuse to vork! Such madness! Ai-yi-yi! Vhat they vant to do to us? They get us all sacked. Ve strike, they sack! Ai-yi-yi-yi!'

For the first time in his life David found himself questioning the values he'd always accepted, and wondering whether the Jewish capacity for endurance wasn't occasionally a disadvantage. The cabinet-makers had actually gained an improvement with their strike. The bosses wouldn't increase their pay, but at least they'd cut their hours. And that couldn't be bad.

'What do you think?' he asked Ellen when they were strolling back to the store from the Standard Theatre later that night.

'One thing I will say,' she told him, grinning, 'it's done us a

225

bit of good at the shop. We 'ad roast beef fer supper Sunday. And sprouts!'

'Yes, but going on strike,' he said. 'D'you think it's right ter go on strike?'

'I think you oughter stand up fer yer rights,' she said. 'If you got a chance to better yerself, why not?'

'An' not obey the boss?' It was a new thought and a dangerously exhilarating one. 'My Dad says they'll all get the sack. He's worried out of 'is wits.'

'There is that,' she said but she didn't seem at all concerned.

'What about your Dad … ?' he tried tentatively. She never spoke about her parents, and until now he'd never tried to make her, but now it suddenly seemed possible.

'Oh 'im,' she said and laughed.

'Would he go on strike, d'yer think?'

That made her roar with laughter. 'Not likely,' she giggled. ' 'E's been on strike all 'is life, my ol' man. Never done an honest day's work as long as I can remember.'

David was rather shocked at this, and his face showed it, but by now they'd reached the shelter of the staff entrance and the chance to kiss goodnight, so the tricky topic was set aside.

But not for long.

Four days later Ellen had an urgent note from her sister Tess. 'Plese coem and see ma. Bad news Love from your ever loving sister tess.' Considerably alarmed she went to Whitechapel immediately after supper.

The family were living in one damp room in the basement of a terraced house in Chicksand Court. Ellen had only been there twice before and hadn't thought much of it. She thought even less that evening, and David, who'd gone with her despite a vague feeling that she didn't want him to, was appalled.

Tess had been watching out for her sister through the narrow basement window and as soon as she saw her boots on the pavement she ran up the area steps to greet her and thank her for coming. 'I been at me wits' end, Ellie,' she said. 'I couldn't leave me new job, could I?' She'd just started work as a scullery maid in a big house in Hoxton, and was eager to make a go of it.

'This is my friend, David,' Ellie said, picking her way down the broken steps of the area. 'What's up?'

226

'Hello,' Tess said vaguely, without looking at him. 'I been at me wits' end, Ellie.'

What a dreadful place, David thought, following them. He'd never seen so much dirt.

The door to the Murphys' room was missing. It had been chopped up and burnt in the stove since Ellen's last visit, and now the smell from the privies filled the place with noxious fumes. Inside the room an elderly woman sat on an orange box by an empty stove weeping grey tears into her grimy hands, and two dirty children were huddled on a bed in the corner, greedily eating chips from a pile of greasy newspaper.

'I brought 'em sommink,' Tess explained proudly to Ellen. 'Out me wages.'

'Good gel,' Ellen said automatically, as she looked anxiously at David's shocked expression and wondered what was wrong with her family and where she ought to begin. There was no sign of their father, which was a blessing, although his dogs were in their usual place on the rag rug, biting their fleas and stinking the place out.

'Hello, Ma,' she said. 'This is my friend David. Where's Pa?'

'Is that you, Ellie?' her mother said, raising a tear-streaked face to peer at her. 'They've took 'im, gel. 'E's inside. In stir, pour soul. They give 'im a carpet. Three months. 'Ow we shall all make out, three months without the hope of a wage, I do not know!'

Oy oy! David thought, his heart sinking even further, a mother filthy dirty and a father in prison. What sort of family was this? But Ellen was delighted.

'Never!' she said. 'What d'he do?'

'Wen' off ter some strike meetin',' Tess said, grinning. 'Nothink ter do wiv 'im, it wasn't. Dockers or some such. Anyway 'e got tight apparently, an' started throwin' 'is weight around, you know the way 'e does. Onny this time he bashed a copper. An' they done 'im.'

'Serve 'im right!' Ellen said, and Maudie and little Johnnie looked up at her from their bundle of grease and nodded to show they agreed.

' 'Ow we shall all make out, I do not know,' their mother said, weeping again.

'Best thing that ever 'appened,' Ellen said. 'Chance of a lifetime, this is, Ma. I'll tell you 'ow you'll make out. You'll make out lovely.' Plans were marshalling themselves inside her busy brain. 'First we'll get you out a' this bug-'utch. Then you can get a proper job. No more pullin' fur an' matchboxes. You can make ciggies up the factory in Worship Street. They pay good money, Florrie says. Then I'll find you a nice clean room, somewhere right away. New school fer the kids. It's the chance of a lifetime.'

'Oh dear,' her mother said, only marginally comforted. 'I don't know.'

'You'll see,' Ellen promised and she looked at her mother's bent head with loving pity. How grey and old she was, poor thing, with her cheeks quite caved in. Had she lost some more of her teeth? 'You're rid of 'im,' she said. 'Just think a' that. You're rid of 'im fer three whole months.'

And at that her mother looked up again and gave her a watery smile. 'You're a good gel, Ellie,' she said. 'Always said that, ain't I? A good gel. She's a good gel, mister.'

The good gel was frowning at the dogs. 'They can go an' all,' she said. 'I'll take 'em up Club Row, Sunday.'

'Sell 'em, you mean?'

' 'Course.'

'You can't do that, gel. They're yer fathers. What 'ud 'e say?'

Ellen gave her mother a devilish grin. 'Don't matter what 'e sez. 'E can't do nothink about it, can 'e? Not where 'e is. Come on, Tess, come on, Davey, we got work ter do.'

'Oh dear,' their mother was saying as they sped off towards the door, 'I don't know, I'm sure.' But even in the half-light she looked relieved.

'First things first,' Ellen said as they cut through the back streets towards the Whitechapel Road. 'We'll get 'er right out of 'ere. Nice place down the Mile End Road. They got decent 'ouses down there. I seen 'em on me way out wiv the cycle club. She's only got Maudie and young Johnnie ter look after now you an' Frankie are away. They don't eat much, an' Maudie could get a little job Sat'days to 'elp out.' Maudie was quite old enough to be bringing in some money.

She was so absorbed in her plans that David felt quite left

228

out. 'You don't need me now, do yer?' he asked stiffly.

But she didn't even notice how he was feeling. 'No!' she said cheerfully. 'Me an' Tess can manage.'

'All right then. I'll go an' see old Hymie.'

'Good idea,' she said, smiling at him briefly.

He left them at the tram stop and strode off to Hymie's feeling disturbed and dejected. It was terrible to think that his lovely Ellen had come from such squalor. And it made him wonder what sort of a wife she would be. What if she didn't realize how awful it was? What if she couldn't keep their house clean? And that made him feel worse than ever, riddled with shame for betraying her with such a thought. This is prejudice, he scolded himself as he strode towards Brick Lane. But the idea stuck like a burr.

Ellen and Tess took a tram to the London Hospital, planning all the way. And the houses there were very nice, rows and rows of neat two-storey terraces with white lace curtains at the windows and a respectable white arc scrubbed in the middle of all the front doorsteps. Ellen was impressed.

'One a' these'll do a treat,' she said, scanning the advertisements in the nearest corner shop. 'Cor! Look at that! Large bedrooms, scullery, use of copper and W.C., six bob a week. Didden I say she'd be better off 'ere? An' there's another. Two rooms, six and six.'

'You don't get sommink fer nothink, don't you tell me,' Tess said with the lugubrious solemnity of the thirteen-year-old. 'There'll be a snag, sure as fate.'

There was, as the two girls discovered when they read further. The flats were certainly cheap, but they all required key money, usually a guinea and payable in advance.

'That's torn it!' Tess said.

'No it ain't.'

'Oh give over, Ellie. Where's she gonna get that sort a' money? There ain't a penny in the place.'

'You an' me an' Frankie. 'E earns enough at that ol' buildin' site of 'is. It won't 'urt 'im to cough up once in a while. An' Paddy, soon as 'e gets back from Geordieland.' Paddy was a deckhand on a collier that plied between Newcastle and the Thames.

229

' 'E ain't due back till Monday next.'

'That'll do,' Ellen said, rather absently, because she was doing sums in her head. 'One guinea between three's seven shillin's, four's only five an' thrupence. We could all run ter that, surely.'

'Well ... ' Tess said, doubting but tempted.

'I'll write ter Frankie the minute I get back. 'E'll chip in, I know 'e will. Come on, Tessie. We can do it.'

Her determination was so infectious Tess had to agree. 'I shall be skint fer a fortnight, I'll 'ave you know,' she grumbled. 'Still I s'pose it's worth it.'

It took them nearly an hour to find exactly what they wanted, but when they did they were very pleased with it. Two nice clean rooms on the top floor of a house rented by a widow called Mrs Nym and her grown-up daughter Lisa. They gave the widow half a crown as a holding fee and promised to be back with the rest within two days. And the matter was concluded.

That Sunday she sold the dogs at Club Row and then went to Ilford to tell Frankie and persuade him to part with five shillings and thrupence.

Paddy came home from Newcastle the next Monday with his pockets bulging with cash. She and Tess took him off shopping before he could get to the pubs and spend it all, so their mother had two secondhand beds to start her new life with, one for her and one for the kids, which she declared to be the last word in luxury. 'You're so good ter me,' she said tearfully as her six children met for the last time in her squalid basement to tell her how the move was to be arranged.

And it went well. She and the widow took to each other at once, just as Ellen had hoped; the boys moved the furniture and the girls scrubbed the floors; Frankie said he was a dab hand at fires and proved it by lighting a really splendid one; and they all had fish and chips together at their nice scrubbed table to finish off the day.

'Best thing I've ever done in me life,' Ellen said to David when they met the next evening for their trip to the theatre, and she told him all about it.

'You're a giddy marvel,' he said, secretly relieved that she'd made such a good job of cleaning the flat. She did have all the virtues after all. 'Where'd yer like to go?'

She chose the theatre but the theatre was shut and a placard outside informed the crowd that had gathered around it that the management apologized for any inconvenience to their customers during the industrial action currently being taken by 'a few music hall artistes' and suggested that they might care to attend 'The Britannia' where an alternative programme had been arranged.

'It's ol' Marie Lloyd,' a man in the crowd explained. 'Brought 'em all out on strike, she 'as. Ain't been a proper show round these parts fer nearly a week.'

'They got a demonstration outside the Britannia ternight,' another man said. 'What say we go an' 'ave a look-see?'

'Why not?' the woman with him said. 'Better'n nothink. They say all the stars come out on the pavement an' sing.'

David and Ellen were very disappointed. They'd been looking forward to the show that evening. The crowd began to move away. 'We could go an' see the demonstration if you'd like,' he suggested.

'Why not,' she said grinning at him. 'Least it's free!'

It was a very big demonstration. They could hear the noise of it long before they reached the theatre, even above the clatter of hooves and the continuous growling of wheels. And what a crush there was in the High Street, and what emotion. It was like being in the middle of a storm. Laughter crackled all around them and everywhere they looked people were on the move, hands gesturing, heads turning, breath billowing from open mouths in white clouds, and bodies swirling abruptly from side to side like weather cocks in a gale. And right in the eye of the storm, on the topmost step and cunningly lit by the blaze from the foyer, was the great Marie Lloyd herself, a small dumpy figure hung with furs.

As they arrived the manager came out onto the theatre steps with a paper in his hand, and from the anguished expression on his face and the pious position of his hands he seemed to be begging to be heard. Nobody paid any attention to him until Marie Lloyd pretended to plead his case. 'Give the poor beggar a chance,' she said cheerfully. 'They might 'ave give in. Yer never know!'

231

The manager gave her a venomous look and began to read from his paper. The management had not capitulated, he was glad to say. On the contrary, they'd gone to considerable trouble and expense to provide quality entertainment for their customers tonight, as usual.

This provoked a roar of laughter and some ribald interest.

' 'Oo's 'e got then?'

' 'E ain't got our Marie, or Gus!'

'Or Little Tich.'

'Or Florrie Forde.'

'Perhaps it's 'is old woman.'

' 'E ain't got an old woman. 'Ave yer cock?'

'No one would 'ave 'im!'

The manager tried not to be deterred. He had a job to do and he proceeded to do it, doggedly, although his paper shook in the gale of their mockery.

The management was pleased to announce the evening's programme, he told them. Then he read the list, one long-forgotten unfamiliar name after another. The crowd was enraptured. ' 'Oo's 'e when 'e's at 'ome?' they roared. 'Never 'eard of 'im! You should a' left 'em in mothballs. We're in the twentieth century. Ain't nobody told yer?' They gave him a round of applause laced with moistly blown raspberries and derisive whistles, but none of them were tempted to buy a seat for his show. Their favourites were all out on the pavement so they were happy where they were.

Presently some of the original audience began to drift out of the building, bored by the sixth-rate entertainment inside and attracted by the racket they could hear from the street.

'What's it like?' the crowd asked as they emerged.

'Load a' rubbish!' one man yelled back, and was roundly cheered for his honesty.

'Told yer!' Marie Lloyd said. 'We'll 'ave 'em on their knees in no time. Take a leaflet, darlin'! Support the Federation!'

The turncoat took his leaflet happily and was cheered again.

'Give us a song, Marie,' a rough face urged from the crowd.

'You give us a sub!' she retorted grinning. 'Support the Federation, an' you can 'ave as many songs as yer like.'

'Give us a dirty look then,' another man called.

232

'You've already got one!' she said.

It was better than the real thing, as David and Ellen told one another on the way back to Shoreditch. Who'd have thought a strike would be like that? And what faces! David couldn't wait to draw them; Marie Lloyd open-mouthed and fur-hung, the manager with his hangdog look and his begging hands; faces snarling and cheering and shouting and laughing. A feast of faces.

'You ought ter send 'em to the papers,' Ellen said, as they sat in the Lyons tea shop on Saturday evening and he showed her his first sketches. 'Betcher they'd print 'em.'

But he wasn't sure. 'No,' he said. 'They ain't good enough yet.'

'Them two,' Ellen urged, picking out the pictures of Marie Lloyd and the manager. 'Nothink venture, nothink gain. Ask that nice teacher a' yours. I bet 'e'd say send 'em. Go on, I dare yer.'

'You trying to organize me now?' he asked, laughing at her.

'On'y if yer want me to,' she said, perfectly confident that he did. 'You gotta admit I'm good at it.'

That was undeniable and as he couldn't kiss her in a crowded tea shop he agreed to pay Mr Eswyn Smith a visit and see what he said. Perhaps they were worth a try.

Mr Smith was very pleased to see him and quite agreed with her judgement. *'Essex Magazine,'* he advised. 'They're on the up. Not a bad company to join. And on the look-out for new talent, so they tell me. What would you do if they took you? Aren't you on an apprenticeship?'

David admitted that he had another two years to run. 'They won't take me though, will they?' he said. That would be too much to hope for.

'I would,' Mr Smith told him. 'But then I'm prejudiced.'

That Wednesday David was going to supper with Aunty Dumpling and Mr Morrison, and on a sudden impulse he took his drawings along to ask their advice.

Mr Morrison thought they were very fine. 'A sight better'n anythink in the *East London Weekly Pictorial*,' he said, stroking the thin line of his moustache with his forefinger. 'Your nephew's a real artist, I tell you, Mrs Esterman.'

233

'You think I don't know it!' Aunty Dumpling said delightedly. 'So send them, bubeleh. Vhat you got to lose?'

David looked at his sketches again. 'I don't know ... ' he said. It would be too painful to offer them and have them rejected. On the other hand they were the best he'd ever done, and he had to start somewhere.

'So vhat *she* say, that nice young lady of yours?' Aunty Dumpling asked. The question was so sudden and unexpected and personal it made him blush to the roots of his hair. Fancy Aunty Dumpling knowing about Ellen!

'A nice young lady,' Dumpling approved, smiling hugely. 'Ve see you at the Standard, three four wccks ago. I say to Mr Morrison, vhat a nice young lady. Ve don't say nothink to your mother, you understand. Nu nu,' shaking her head till her chins wobbled.

He was only partly reassured. 'She ain't Jewish, Aunty Dumpling,' he felt he should explain.

She shrugged the explanation away. 'So the whole vorld should be Jewish? Vhat she say about the drawings, bubeleh? Don't she say send them?'

He admitted that she did, and her good sense was applauded. 'So you send them, nu? Vork so fine, vhat you vaiting for? You send them, they take them, you an' your young lady come and have supper vid me and Mr Morrison, nu?'

Put like that it all seemed perfectly possible, even Ellen's partial introduction to his family. And so, despite misgivings and the fear of failure, he sent his drawings to the *Essex Magazine*. Then there was nothing he could do except wait, proudly pretending unconcern. But after a week, to his surprise and Ellen's delight, a letter arrived with the news that they had accepted both drawings and were sending him a guinea each for them. And what was more and better, they asked him to come up to the office in ten days' time and see their Mr Palfreyman, 'to discuss the possibility of a short-term contract'.

'Who'd've thought it?' he said to Ellen, amazed at such good fortune.

'I would,' she said.

'You're a girl an' a half,' he said. She had such faith in him. It made him feel confident just to look at her. Oh if only he could find the right way to tell his parents about her! If he got a job, perhaps that would be the moment to tell them. A job as an artist! How proud they'd be! A job as an artist, a meal with Aunty Dumpling. Nothing but good could come of it.

Chapter Eighteen

Essex Street was an insignificant, cobbled alley that ran steeply downhill between the Strand and the Embankment. It was invariably dark and dank and uninviting, for the houses that hemmed it in on either side were too tall and overbearing and full of their own importance to allow entry to anything as frivolous and unnecessary as sunlight, and the street itself was so narrow it acted as a funnel to all the moisture both above and below it, drawing mists up from the Thames morning and evening, and sucking fogs down from the fumes of the Strand and the obfuscations of the Law Courts all day long.

Ordinarily David would have avoided such a place, and probably been more than a little deterred by it, but now, with his precious letter safe in his pocket and an undeniable hope burgeoning in his brain, he trotted happily down the hill over the wet cobbles, and soon found the office of the *Essex Magazine*.

He knocked politely, once, twice, three times. And waited. But as nobody took any notice he pushed open the door and walked in.

He found himself in a narrow vestibule that led to a panelled office, so small it was really little more than a cupboard and only just big enough to contain one roll-top desk, two cane-bottomed chairs, a thriving office plant and a drooping office boy who was slouched on one of the cane chairs with his legs on the other and his chin on his chest, fast asleep.

David coughed. Politely. But the snoring continued and it didn't look as though a paroxysm of coughing would rouse the sleeper.

The front door was flung open with a bang and a huge man

in a grey topcoat and a green bowler hat strode into the room and gave the office boy such a crack across the back of the skull it was a wonder his neck didn't snap.

'Look alive, young Shaver!' he said mildly. Then he saw David. 'Who are you?'

David explained.

'First floor, Mr Palfreyman. An' if he sez you're late, tell 'im the Shaver was asleep.'

'Can't a feller close 'is eyes?' the Shaver grumbled, adjusting his collar and relocating his neck.

'Never know'd you with yer eyes open,' Green Bowler said, stirring the papers on the desk. 'Any messages? You don't know, do yer? Useless pudden.' Then without looking at David he addressed his next remark to him. 'Door at the top a' the stairs.'

This time one timid knock brought an instant reply. 'Pray do come in.' David did as he was told and walked into the room trying not to look too self-conscious or feel too nervous. It was a calm, well-ordered room, and remarkably dry considering all the dampness outside the building. A red fire burned brightly and neatly behind the black bars of the grate in the corner. 'Do sit down, dear chap,' the voice said, and it was a dry voice, but welcoming. Very welcoming indeed. 'You are Mr Cheifitz, I take it. Yes, yes, of course. Did you bring your work?'

David handed his folder across and watched as Mr Palfreyman carefully undid the ribbons and exposed the top sketches to scrutiny. His heart was beating most uncomfortably. Would they be good enough? Perhaps he should have brought some of the others. Making the selection had been very difficult.

Mr Palfreyman examined the folder slowly and methodically, without looking up. He was the most orderly, dapper man David had ever seen. Everything about him was clean and correct, from the immaculate stiff collar propping up his little round chin to the well-buffed nails on the plump fingers he was using with such care and precision among the sketches. His suit was made of very good material and was silvery grey, like the fringe of neat hair that ringed the bald dome of his head.

He wore a gold watch chain neatly across the centre of his waistcoat and a gold pin neatly in the centre of his cravat, and a pair of gold-rimmed spectacles were perched neatly on the bridge of his short snub nose. A round, friendly face, David thought, watching it hopefully, and noticed that the muddy light from the long office window shone on the gentleman's pink skull as though it had been polished.

'Yes,' Mr Palfreyman said, laying the last sketch exactly on top of all the others. 'Yes, yes, of course.'

David felt as if he was suffocating. What did he mean? Yes, he was going to offer him the job? Or yes, I like your work? He shifted his damp feet to warm them a little and looked hopefully at Mr Palfreyman, his brown eyes eager.

'Well now, Mr Cheifitz,' Mr Palfreyman said, smiling benignly. And then his expression suddenly changed as though his face had been transformed to India rubber and somebody was screwing it into a knot. 'Good heavens above! Will you look at that?'

He was staring at the window, and before David could turn his head to see what was the matter, Mr Palfreyman had leaped to his feet, seized a duster from the top drawer of his desk and rushed across the room to attack the window with it. 'If there is one thing I cannot stand,' he said scrubbing at the glass, 'it is a damp window. Ugh! Ugh! I will *not* stand it!' He worked furiously while David watched and the red coals shuffled in the grate. It took a lot of effort before the gentleman was satisfied, and as he returned to his desk, tossing the wet duster into the waste paper basket en route, he still sounded aggrieved. 'Moisture in the open air is deplorable enough,' he said, 'but within doors it is an abomination. Don't you agree?'

Would a nod be the right answer?

'Now then, my dear chap, how long do you think it will be before you can give me an answer?'

'An answer, sir?'

'Yes, yes, of course. To our offer. To our offer.'

'Are you offering me a job, sir?' David was so excited he could hardly breathe.

'Yes, yes, of course. Did I not say so? Dear me! I do apologize, dear chap. Very remiss of me. All that moisture, you

238

see. Quite sets my teeth on edge, moisture. Well now, I will explain our terms.'

They were princely. Twenty-five shillings a week and all materials found. A trial period of three months, then a review, then the job proper, all things being satisfactory. It was miraculous.

'If I gave in my notice today, I daresay I could start Monday, sir,' he said breathlessly.

'What is your trade?'

'Apprentice bookbinder, sir.'

'Ah!' Mr Palfreyman said thoughtfully, and he looked at David for quite a long time, straight through the centre of his spectacles. 'How many years do you have to run?'

'Two, sir.'

'Ah! Then we have matters to consider. This must be weighed up. Yes, yes, indeed.'

David's heart sank. Was he going to reconsider the offer? An apprenticeship was nothing. Not compared with a chance like this. 'Mr Palfreyman, sir ... '

'We will consider this carefully,' Mr Palfreyman said, smiling his benign smile. He had taken a large box of matches from the second drawer of his desk, and now it was being opened and the first match picked neatly from the pile.

A pipe, David thought, to aid concentration.

But he was wrong.

'These matches,' Mr Palfreyman explained, 'will represent the pros and cons. Pros to the right, cons to the left, you understand. Very well,' selecting a matchstick from the righthand pile, 'we will begin. We will pay you twenty-five shillings a week, which is more than you could earn as a bookbinder. However,' selecting another matchstick from the lefthand pile, 'bookbinding is a steady trade.'

There was a pause while they considered the two little shreds of wood now lying so reasonably on either side of the desk.

'Secondly. You will meet many interesting people if you work for the *Essex*. Yes indeed. On the other hand, you will miss those friends you have already made.' Now there were four matches on the desk, neatly opposing one another, two by two. 'Thirdly ... '

What a very kind man he is, David thought, watching as the matches were lined up in thoughtful and eccentric order, taking all this trouble just for me. He had no doubt at all now that he wanted to work on the *Essex* with Mr Palfreyman, but he waited politely until six pros and cons had been explained and aligned, and when he was finally asked, 'Now, me dear chap, what do you think?' he took his time to answer, as befitted such an important moment.

'I should very much like to accept your offer, Mr Palfreyman,' he said. 'Very much. I'll go straight back to Mr Woolnoth's now, an' see how soon he'll release me, an' I'll write an' tell you just so soon as ever I know. I give you my word.'

'I'm sure you will, dear chap. Welcome to the firm.'

The next half hour blurred like a dream. They shook hands solemnly. Mr Palfreyman rose from his seat and took a walking stick from the stand in the corner of the room and gave three sharp raps with it in the centre of the carpet. The summons was answered by the Shaver who presently arrived, blinking and confused, and was despatched to 'fetch Mr Quinton'. Mr Quinton turned out to be the man in the green bowler and the journalist whose work David would be illustrating, and as boisterously friendly as ever.

'Welcome to the madhouse, young'un,' he said affably as they shook hands. 'I shall be down your way in a day or two. Doin' a piece on Spitalfields in the small hours. You know the sort a' stuff. London by night. Plenty a' local colour. Come an' see the print shop.'

By now excitement and success were making David's head spin, but he followed Mr Quinton obediently down the stairs and along a dark corridor into an echoing barn, where four huge printing machines crouched on the stone flags, black and oily like brooding dinosaurs. A half-wall of wooden partitions had been erected along three of the walls to form a series of cramped, badly-lit offices. Mr Quinton had his name on the door of his particular den. He led his new colleague into the gloom and introduced him to a filing cabinet bulging papers and a desk bent sideways under the combined weight of a library of books, several tons of newsprint, three clotted inkwells, an old shoe and a variety of paperweights.

'A poor place, but mine own,' he said, obviously very proud of it.

And David nodded and grinned at him because he was too overwhelmed to do anything else.

'You're next door,' Mr Quinton informed him. 'When d'you start?'

'Soon as I can,' David said. He'd have started that very minute if he'd been able to. 'I got ter see my boss first, you see.'

'I'd get cracking then, if I was you. Strike while the iron's hot, eh?'

And it was hot. Scorching hot. Charging him with energy. He ran downhill to the Strand and jumped aboard a moving bus, full of daring and wellbeing. He was going to be an artist! A real artist! Working on a newspaper! Making his mark! It was too good to be true.

By the time he got to Aldgate pump, reason was beginning to cool him a little and he knew it would be difficult to break this news to Mr Woolnoth. But Aunty Dumpling would be as thrilled as he was, and as her home was only a short tram ride away and there was a tram waiting most providentially at the points all ready to take him there, he decided to tell her first.

'Vhat a boy!' she said, kissing him moistly over and over again. 'Vhat I tell you? Great is our God and greatly to be praised for His loving kindness.'

David was smiling so widely his jaws ached. 'Good, nu?'

'Now you bring your young lady to supper, nu?'

Yes, yes, of course he would. 'When, Aunty Dumpling?'

'Tonight,' she said. 'So vhy not? Something ve got to celebrate.'

Everything was happening as he'd hoped it would. Great is our God, indeed.

'Now I got ter see Mr Woolnoth,' he said, putting on his cap.

'Talk meek,' she advised. 'This he ain't gonna like much.'

Which was an understatement. Mr Woolnoth was furious. To take three hours off work on a damp spring morning was bad enough, but to ask to be released from his apprenticeship! 'The very idea!' he said. 'Five good years thrown away. A good trade lost. And all for what? A quick profit. The lure of the

241

City. Sheer folly! What on earth possessed you to do such a thing?'

His anger made David stubborn. 'I want to be an artist, Mr Woolnoth, sir,' he said. He'd quite forgotten Aunty Dumpling's sensible advice. His tone wasn't meek and neither was his expression. He was all pride, hair bushy, moustache bristling, perky as a cock sparrow. 'It's the chance I've always wanted.'

'Your fee is not returnable, I trust you understand.'

He understood and wasn't the least deterred.

The other apprentices were most impressed. 'Have yer really given in yer notice?' they said.

'I have!' he bragged. 'And I'm takin' my girl home ternight.'

'Some fellers 'ave all the luck!' they envied.

And that was certainly how it seemed.

It was a charmed day. Even their timing was perfect. She came skipping out of the staff door just as he turned the bend in the road. And she knew what had happened at once, just from the sight of his face.

'You got it! You got it!' she sang, running towards him with that skimming, lilting movement he loved so much, arms outstretched. 'Didden I tell yer?' And then he caught her in his arms and lifted her off her feet in triumph and delight.

'Best bib an' tucker,' he advised when the first news was told and they'd got their breath back. 'You're coming ter supper with my Aunty Dumpling.'

That was a sobering thought and required an immediate retreat to the dormitory for a clean blouse and neat curls and a great deal of cheerfully unnecessary advice from her excited friends.

When she emerged from the brown doors of the empty emporium half an hour later, David couldn't see any difference in her but he'd learned enough by now not to say so. When she asked him, rather anxiously, how she looked, he kissed her and told her she was a 'sight for sore eyes'. And they walked off arm in arm to their first meal with the family.

That was a great success too, despite an awkward start when they all got in one another's way among the clutter of heavy furniture. But as soon as they were seated round the table and

Aunty Dumpling's famous chicken soup was steaming most succulently in the dishes before them, and Mr Morrison had declared that no one was 'a patch on Mrs Esterman for cooking', the meal became a party and a time for congratulation and approval. David's new job was approved of as the best thing he'd ever done, and Ellen was approved of too. Not in so many words, of course. Aunty Dumpling was much too discreet for that. But by glance and smile and loving voice and agreement, and all the age-old implicit signs so long used and so subtly recognized between one generation and the next.

They stayed round the table, drinking tea and making companionable conversation, until nearly a quarter past ten. Ellen thought the tea was most peculiar, served with a slice of lemon. What a funny idea! And so sharp it made her lips shrink. But she drank it politely and even ventured a second cup, because David's nice plump aunty was being such a dear.

Now, they told each other as they kissed a final goodnight in the empty porch of that familiar staff door, now there was nothing to stand in their way. He had a good job. She'd been accepted. Now they could plan their wedding. The form and style the ceremony would take were matters that simply didn't enter their heads. In their present state of enraptured satisfaction it was enough that marriage was possible.

'Soon you will be Mrs Cheifitz. Whatcher think a' that?' he asked, after what they'd promised themselves would be the very very last kiss of the evening.

'Yes, yes, yes,' she said and kissed him again.

It was nearly half past eleven before he got home to the Buildings, but his excitement was stronger than ever. For now he was running towards the last and happiest triumph of the day. The moment when he would tell his parents all his plans, about his new job and his lovely Ellen, the moment when they would rejoice in his success as a son and welcome Ellen into the family as a daughter. Just like Dumpling had done, only better.

He charged through the archway into the empty courtyard where the yellow gaslights bloomed one above the other like misty roses on the long square trellis of the windows, and the old men sat on the balconies smoking the last pipes of the day, and the courtyard echoed with the crooning Yiddish of late evening. And he knew how much he loved this building and what a reward it was to be part of it. And now he would be more than just part of it. He would be taking his place in the community, founding a family, raising children, bringing joy to his parents, an artist, admired and respected and honoured.

He ran up the stairs two at a time, and burst into the living room breathless with good news.

His parents were sitting on either side of the table, waiting. Their faces were composed and quiet and so massively angry they froze him where he stood. After all the noise and excitement of his day there seemed to be no sound in the room at all. Only the tick of the clock on the mantelpiece and a thrumming in his ears that he gradually recognized as the beating of his heart.

'What is it?' he asked, and his voice was gruff.

There was a letter lying on the table, stark white against the brown of the chenille cloth. A letter with familiar writing on it. His father picked it up with both hands and held it out before him, and David was appalled to see that the paper was trembling.

'So this is the way I must hear bad news from my own son?' Emmanuel said, speaking Yiddish and sighing from the most profound sadness. 'A letter from his master. What have I done to deserve such unkindness? Do sons hide behind their masters now? Do sons lie to their fathers?'

'No, Father, no. I do not lie!' He was anguished by such a sudden terrible accusation. What did he mean? Surely he wasn't talking about the job. Not his marvellous job.

'You lie,' Emmanuel said with the same terrible sadness. 'You take another job. You leave a good apprenticeship. You tell me nothing. You lie.'

'It is a good job, Father,' David tried. 'Drawing for a newspaper. A good job. I swear it.'

'To tell me nothing!' his father mourned. 'Your own father. Nothing. I hear it from a letter.'

'I meant to give you a surprise,' David said miserably. 'It *is* a good job. Nu-nu, I will make a success, I promise you.'

244

'We bred a *schlemiel*,' his mother said bitterly. 'A *schlemiel*. How the neighbours will pity us. Poor dumb fools, they will say, to breed a *schlemiel*. *Has vesholem!*' Her face was pinched with fatigue and fury and disappointment. 'For why you don't say nothing?'

'For why you don't ask advice?' his father wanted to know. 'You ask me I could have told you, don't do it.'

'I did ask advice,' David said earnestly. How could this be so terribly wrong? He'd been accepted as an artist, a man to be honoured, a man set apart by his calling. Surely his father should be proud. 'I asked my teacher, Mr Eswyn Smith.'

'Your teacher told you to accept this job?' There was disbelief on his father's face now, as well as that awful sadness. The two of them sighed lengthily, locked in incomprehension and hurt pride.

'A *shaygets* he asks advice,' his mother said sharply. 'He don't stay with his own kind. That's the whole root of the trouble. May he be forgiven.'

I can hardly tell them about Ellen now, David thought. Not in this mood. Oh how did it happen? Why aren't they pleased? 'I'm going to be an artist,' he said stubbornly, but the words sounded truculent.

'What is done is done,' Emmanuel said after another sighing silence. 'What you have undertaken, you have undertaken. There is no more to be said.' And he took Rachel by the hand and led her into the bedroom as though they were part of a most solemn procession.

Left on his own in the empty room David suddenly felt weak and deserted. His legs buckled beneath him as though he could no longer support his own weight and as he crumpled heavily onto his truckle bed he began to cry.

It was a most miserable night. He lay in his familiarly uncomfortable bed checking and re-checking the puzzle of his father's response. And coming back time and time again to the same barrier to any understanding. He was going to be an artist, and surely his father ought to be as happy as he was about it. He simply couldn't understand how his loving triumphant surprise could have been received as an insult. If he'd suddenly told them about Ellen, he could have

245

understood their anger. He'd known all along that they would need a lot of persuading to accept a *shiksa*, but to react so angrily when he'd got a fine honourable job ... After all, asking to be released from an apprenticeship was nothing nowadays. Lots of boys did it. And some of them with no excuse at all.

When the first streaks of grey sky released him, he got up and dressed as quietly as he could, and crept out of the flat, easing the door shut behind him without a sound. There was only one person he could turn to for advice at a time like this, and that was Aunty Dumpling. He was too distressed to wait till evening. Or even till the poor lady woke up.

Fortunately Raizel Esterman was a light sleeper, and his persistent tapping and rattling outside her door soon roused her. She wrapped herself in her old dressing gown and opened a chink in the door to see who it was. 'Davey is it?' she said, peering through the crack like an owl in a tree. Then she saw the tears glistening on his cheeks and threw the door wide and seized him at once into a bearhug of an embrace, imploring him to tell her what it was, and assuring him he was her own dear, dear Davey, and giving herself over to a torrent of companionable weeping so loud and so extravagant that all words were lost under the wailing of it. It was very comforting and just what he needed.

It took until seven o'clock to tell the story in enough tear-stained detail to satisfy them both. Then Aunty Dumpling settled her two plump hands on either side of her teacup and gave judgement. 'So you do good vid the paper, bubeleh,' she said. 'You vork hard. You do good. You don't say nothing about your nice young lady yet. So maybe I get a chance to talk them round. Maybe not, Ve see, nu. In the meantime you vork, vork. Make a name. Manny ain't a stern father. So. Sooner, later, you see vhat he says. So proud he'll be yet.'

'D'you think so, Dumpling? D'you really think so?'

'Ain't I just said? Vhat you vant, a testimonial?'

It was sound advice, he thought, trailing to Mr Woolnoth's, Dumpling's prune cake still sweetening his tongue. If only he could be certain she was right. But then there was Ellen. He hadn't said a word about Ellen and now she was waiting for him in the shop expecting good news. How could he possibly tell her what had happened? He hadn't written her a letter and he didn't know what to say.

She was stacking new rolls of cloth on the stands and looked up brightly when she heard his approach. The expression on his face told her the news at once, but there wasn't time for more than a few snatched words. 'Cheer up!' she said. 'We'll manage, whatever it is.'

'I love you,' he mouthed, when Miss Morton was looking the other way. But it didn't cheer either of them.

They were still cast down that evening, despite their most determined efforts to 'look on the bright side'. They walked back to Hopkins and Peggs dolefully, even though they were arm in arm.

'It all seems so bloomin' daft,' she said. 'All this fuss 'cause you've give up an apprenticeship, an' I'm not Jewish. I ask yer! I'm as good as they are any day a' the week.'

'Better!' he said, meaning it. 'Oh, why's life so beastly difficult?'

'Things'll look up when you start at the *Essex*,' she comforted. 'You'll see.'

And although he didn't really believe her, she was proved right. It was fun working with Mr Quinton. He liked the man's wry humour and his quick spidery handwriting, and the way he went rushing off after a story, leaping on and off moving trams as if that were the natural way to behave, or holding a snatched conversation with a man on top of a bus going in the opposite direction, or lurking behind pillars, taking notes, like an informer. He said he never knew what they were going to do from one day to the next, and didn't want to. And after a few days in his company, David believed him. It was undeniably exciting. 'Draw that chap by the lamppost,' he would say. 'What a titfer! And the old girl with her head in the bucket. Must 'ave her.'

Then they would set all the sketches out on the floor in Mr Quinton's clobbered office and choose the best, and David would be sent away to polish them up for the print. He would make an elaborate etching of the chosen ones and the finished plates would be fed into the maw of the largest machine and presently reappear on the pages of the magazine, looking so handsome and professional he had to pinch himself to make sure it was all really happening.

Within two weeks he felt so at home in the place it was as if he'd never worked anywhere else. The weather improved, Ellen was as loving as ever, even though she knew they'd have to wait for quite a long time before they could think about marriage again. It was good to be alive after all.

Soon it would be the festival of the Passover, when the family would gather together for the ordered meal of the Seder, and they would eat the *charoset* with its apples and nuts and spices, and three *matzos*, those special loaves of unleavened bread, and the Song of Solomon would be sung in the synagogue to hónour the new season. Surely they would forgive him then.

And in a way they seemed to have done, for the meal was eaten in the same affectionate way, and the four questions asked by the youngest member of the family, and the last piece of the middle *matzo* hidden for the children to find, and everything was exactly as it had always been. Except that nobody referred to his new job or said anything about it. Not even Dumpling, which was a terrible disappointment.

But the words of the Song of Solomon were as beautiful and moving as ever. Standing beside his father in the synagogue, David couldn't help feeling that all was as it should be, no matter what might be thought and unspoken. 'For, lo, the winter is past, the rain is over and gone; the flowers appear on the earth; the time of the singing of birds is come, and the voice of the turtle is heard in our land; the fig tree putteth forth her green figs, and the vines with the tender grape give a good smell.' Yes, he thought, God has given us a beautiful world, and he knew that his Ellen was part of the beauty and not to be denied. 'Arise, my love, my fair one, and come away.' Old Aunty Dumpling knew what she was talking about. It was simply a matter of biding his time until just the right moment. Then they would agree. How could they do anything else when she was so beautiful and he loved her so much?

Actually Aunty Dumpling was finding it almost impossible to get her brother and sister-in-law to talk about their son at

248

all. When he started work at the *Essex Magazine* they made no comment, although they did look at his drawings and noted, but privately of course, that they were being published in larger and larger numbers as the weeks went by. But she couldn't persuade them to praise him. And as to talking about a young lady, that was totally impossible. Rachel was adamant. She wouldn't hear of it, not even when Rivke and Dumpling arrived together one Thursday afternoon to try and make her see sense.

'Von mistake he make, that I grant you,' she said. 'Von mistake, ve chastize him, he make atonement. Von mistake. Now ve got our own good boy again. So you don't talk dirty to me. He vant a vife. Maybe a girl he got. He don't. He ain't. I know. A boy so young he don't even think such things.' Her voice was shrill with impending hysteria. 'So leave me alone, the both of you.'

Finally Dumpling lost patience. Soon she would be going to Salford to visit the Estermans, as she did every year at the beginning of June. This time, she told Rivke, she would leave David in charge of the canary.

'I give him the key, nu? Then ve see how young he is.'

Rachel's overbearing rigidity was too ridiculous for words, and she hadn't forgotten how unnecessarily poor old Fred Morrison had been censured for keeping *her* company. 'I give him the key.' The decision pleased her although she couldn't have explained why. She had a vague feeling that she was striking a blow for her nephew's independence but otherwise her motives were muddled. It would be nice for Davey and his young lady to have a little privacy away from the critical eyes of his mother, particularly when his mother didn't know it. And it would serve Rachel right for being so stiffnecked.

'I leave a pinch of tea, bubeleh,' she said to David as she gave him her last-minute instructions, 'and there's a lemon in the jar, then you can make a nice glass of tea vhile you clean the cage. Some time Sunday will do. You know to use the new gas ring, nu?'

So David agreed to keep an eye on things for her, because she'd been so kind. And Ellen agreed to go with him because she couldn't have borne to be without him, even for the brief half-hour he reckoned it would take.

'I'll go an' see me Ma Sat'day night,' she decided. 'Take her a few things. See how she is. Then we can feed the bird an' 'ave the rest a' Sunday to ourselves, all nice.'

'Good idea,' he said.

But the governor of Wormwood Scrubs had other plans.

Chapter Nineteen

It was a perfect day for an outing. Even at seven o'clock in the morning the sun was quite warm and the sky a most satisfying blue. The cycling club were gathering in Shoreditch High Street as David arrived, and a brightly coloured, busy crowd they were, giggling and gossiping, adjusting haversacks, pulling up socks and pumping up tyres. At first he couldn't see Ellen, but that was hardly surprising with such a turn-out. He wheeled his bicycle carefully through the tangle of machines and riders looking for her, greeting friends, and agreeing with the universal opinion that they'd 'got a good day for it'. But when he caught sight of that pretty blue suit, he was surprised and upset to see that the face above it was smudged with tears.

Mr Galsworthy, the club secretary, was comfortingly at his elbow. 'Nothink serious, Cheify. Little family matter, that's all.'

But he wasn't reassured at all, and propped his bike against the kerb to rush off and see for himself. Maudie was standing beside her, talking earnestly, and when she sensed his approach, she looked up at once and gave him the first garbled news before the concern on his face could provoke further tears. 'It's 'er ol' man. They let 'im out last night. 'Er Ma took 'im back.'

'What's up, bubeleh?' he said, taking her hands.

'They give 'im remission fer good behaviour,' she said bitterly. 'Good behaviour! I ask you. 'E ain't been 'ome more'n five minutes an' he's wreckin' the place. All my good work ruined. 'E's been sick all down the curtains, an' swore at Mrs Nym, an' spent all 'er money down the boozer. An' now 'e's gone off ter Club Row ter buy hisself a dog. Makes me spit.'

251

'Oh Ellen,' he said, wiping the furious tears from her cheeks with his fingertips. 'I dunno what ter say.'

'Nothing you can say,' she told him angrily. 'They should never a' let 'im out. 'E oughter be locked up fer good an' all.' The unexpected sight of him the night before had filled her with such loathing she still couldn't contain it, sprawled across the bedspread she'd bought and cleaned, spitting on the floor she'd scrubbed, with his beer on her nice clean table and his boots beside her nice black-leaded stove, and her Ma grovelling and the kids snivelling. It was more than human flesh and blood could bear.

'You ain't never took 'im back, surely ter goodness,' she'd said to her mother in furious disbelief.

'An' why not, girlie?' he'd answered massively and easily, puffing his horrible bad breath in her direction. 'Sure 'tis me own hearth an' home, so it is, an' haven't I the right for to be in it?'

'No you ain't,' she said. 'You ain't paid a penny piece a' rent. An' where d'yer think the key money come from?'

'Shush! Shush, Ellie,' her mother said, giving him a placating squint out of the corner of her eyes. 'Don't rile 'im, fer Gawd's sake. 'Ave a bit a' sense.'

'Sense!' Ellen stormed. 'You stand there an' talk ter me a' sense!' And then the tears had filled her chest and risen in her throat, and she'd had to run before they brimmed out of her eyes and gave him a reason to mock her.

'I hate him,' she said to David. 'Great idle lump. What they want ter go an' let 'im out for? She was doing all right without 'im. Now 'e'll drag her right down in the muck again. What a waste!'

'She *is* his wife,' David pointed out.

'More fool 'er to stay with 'im! She should 'a left 'im years ago.'

Such a very trenchant opinion upset him. 'It ain't fer us to tell our parents how ter live,' he said. 'Surely?'

'It's all right fer you,' she said. 'You got good ones.' Her blue eyes were flashing with such anger that for a second he felt they were going to quarrel. But fortunately they were rescued by Mr Galsworthy calling his troops together from the other

252

end of the line, 'All set?' The sudden movement all around them broke the mood, as club members wheeled their bicycles into the road and began to mount.

'Dry yer eyes,' David urged. 'No good cryin' over spilt milk, nu?'

And she did her best to smile for him and that encouraged them both.

'Off we go!' their leader chirruped, and the cavalcade rattled off southwards along the Sunday emptiness of the Shoreditch High Street. The sun was already quite warm on their shoulders. 'We got a lovely day for it!' they said. 'What price blazin' June!'

Above the long green sheds of Liverpool Street Station the sky shone pale yellow, and David noticed that the horses toiling up the ramp into the station with their holiday carts and carriages were already blackened with sweat. 'It's goin' to be a real scorcher,' he said to Ellen. She looked much more cheerful now they were cycling along together.

'Be nice in the country,' she said, and she *was* more cheerful. 'Won't take long ter feed the bird, will it?'

He'd almost forgotten Aunty Dumpling's canary. 'Ten minutes. No more.'

'We'll cut through the back,' she said, because they were at Petticoat Lane already. 'Shan't be a tick, Maudie.'

It took them a great deal longer than a tick to ease their bikes through the crush of the market. There was so much going on there. The first customers were busily searching for the best buys, while the more tardy stall holders were still arriving and unpacking, so the street was crowded with frantic activity. Clothes hung in serried fringes from every wall, untidy canopies of bright colour against the blackened brick, and the stalls were hemmed in by cardboard boxes and obscured by rails trailing coats and jackets and skirts and trousers. They inched their unwieldy machines through any gap that presented itself, although at times it was quite impossible to move in any direction at all, and difficult to see where they were going. The stall holders didn't approve of their presence, and were quick to tell them they were 'committin' a public nuisance wiv them things' and that 'it didn't oughter be allowed'. By the time

253

they'd pushed their way to the corner of Cobb Street they knew they'd made a mistake coming down the lane in the first place.

'Let's cut up Cobb Street and double back,' David said. 'We shall get lynched we keep on here.'

So they wheeled their bicycles into the comparative peace of the side street and followed it north into a cinder alley no bigger than a pathway that divided the back yards and privies of one row of narrow terraces from the front doors and living rooms of another. The smell there was so foul that they pedalled through as fast as they could. There was no one else in the alley, only three empty stalls propped against the fence, and a trestle table outside the pub on the corner of White's Row, so they had a clear ride.

'We could nip down White's an' cut through Fashion Street,' Ellen was saying, when a gang of roughs kicked their way out of the pub and occupied the cobbled yard immediately between them. They looked ugly and they looked drunk, standing with their moleskinned legs balanced astride and their caps pushed back from the heat of their faces.

David stopped, and Ellen hesitated, one toe on the ground, estimating their mood.

'Straight through,' he decided. 'I'll go first. You stick close be'ind. With a bit a' luck they won't even see us.'

They rode quickly but as steadily as they could, and for a second it looked as though they were going to get past without abuse or interference. But then one of the roughs lurched across the cobbles and made a grab at Ellen's handlebars. And she found herself looking into the ugly leer of Jimmy Thatcher.

'Well, well, well,' he said. 'Wash thish? Miss Icy White an' 'er Ikey Mo. 'Ere's a turn up fer the books.'

Fear stiffened her spine. 'Let me pass,' she said and was pleased that her voice was cold and calm. She could see David out of the corner of her eye and knew that he'd stopped and was propping his bike against the wall of the corn chandler's next to the pub. 'Don't stop, David,' she called. ' 'E's lettin' me through. Ain't yer?'

For answer Thatcher grabbed her by one arm and pulled her off the bike so that she fell with one leg still over the saddle and quite unable to defend herself. As she struggled to sit up,

Thatcher and his friends moved in, ugly faces grinning. 'Thash what we do ter bints what muck about wiv Jewboys,' he said. 'Wan' any more, do yer?'

Then things happened at such speed and with such passion that she couldn't register half of them. David's hands were round that thick neck pulling it backwards and the roughs were roaring. Fists punched from every direction as she scrambled from the bike. She could hear oaths and grunts and baying laughter and the harsh sound of hobnails scrunching the cobbles. And by the time she got to her feet, David and Thatcher were fighting, both bareheaded and red-faced, their arms flailing. As she caught her breath, two of the roughs joined in. David was grabbed by the arms and pinioned, and he was struggling and kicking, and Thatcher was punching him in the face.

She had a vague sense that there was a stick of some kind hanging outside the corn chandler's, and she ran and pulled it from the wall, not caring what it was and growling with anger. She knew that the corn chandler was running after her, protesting that he'd call the cops, but she didn't care. They were hurting her Davey and she was going to stop them. Her first blow thwacked across a bent and moving spine. It was a glancing stroke she hardly felt, but her second landed right across the bridge of Jimmy Thatcher's nose.

For a split second he looked at her with total surprise, then his nose began to bleed, spurting red gouts in a regular pulse, like a fountain, and spattering everywhere, all down the front of his clothes, sideways onto his friends and David who were still fighting furiously, even onto her bloomer suit. He put up his blunt paws in a vain attempt to staunch it, while David knocked one of his mates to the ground and kicked a third, and all four turned tail and ran off down the alley, leaving Thatcher on his own. 'Look what you done,' he said to Ellen. Blood was dripping through his fingers onto the cobbles.

She was delighted. 'Serve yer right, great bully!' she shouted.

'I'll 'ave the law on you,' the corn chandler said, puffing up behind her. 'That's my broom you got there, I'll 'ave you know.'

' 'Ave it an' welcome,' she said, thrusting the broomstick

255

into his hands. 'I done all I want wiv it. Unless you want some more,' glowering at Thatcher.

David was keen to go on fighting too. 'Well?' he threatened. ' 'Ad enough, 'ave yer?'

'You can 'ave 'er, mate,' Thatcher said, still dripping blood. 'She's a reg'lar hellcat, tha's what. Wouldn't catch me wiv a bint like that. You can 'ave 'er. Wish I'd never set eyes on 'er.'

It was a splendid victory, but it wasn't until they'd cycled triumphantly through White's Row and Fashion Street and arrived at Mr Jones the Dairy in Brick Lane that they realized what a price they'd paid for it.

They'd propped their bikes in the yard and were tiptoeing up the stairs to Aunty Dumpling's room at the top of the house when Mrs Smith, who lived in the first floor back and was the self-appointed guardian of the staircase, put her head out of the door to see who they were.

'My stars!' she said. 'You been in the wars, aintcher! Whatcher been doing?'

'Gang a' drunks,' David explained, and he put up his hand to feel the side of his face where the direction of her eyes and the delighted shock on her face told him there must be some damage. Then he noticed that Ellen's pretty blue suit was spattered with dark red spots of blood, and that one side of her face was smeared with it too.

'Did 'e hurt you?' he asked, suddenly anxious and concerned. ' 'E didn't hurt you, did he, Ellen?'

But she was looking at his torn knuckles and didn't answer.

'Iodine. That's what yer want,' Mrs Smith informed them. 'Best thing out fer cuts, iodine is. I'd give yer some a' mine, onny I just this minute run out. My stars, you 'ave been in the wars! I'd get on upstairs an' clean all them cuts if I was you. Might turn septic else. Iodine's what yer want.'

She quite alarmed them. 'We'll get cleaned up straight away,' David reassured them all. 'Don't you worry. I'll see we don't turn septic.' And he and Ellen made haste up the stairs.

'Salt's good,' Mrs Smith called after them. 'I got some salt you could 'ave. I'd bring it up for yer, onny I can't get up the stairs wiv me legs.'

'My aunt's got salt, ta,' he called back to her as they reached the second-floor landing.

'It's the stairs, you see,' she said. 'Can't get up the stairs no how.' But she managed to get across the landing to tell her neighbour. They could hear her voice, rising up the well of the stairs, loud with importance. '... I've jest this minute seen 'em. ... terrible state. Fightin'. Oh yes! Gangs, I shouldn't wonder. ... I've given 'em salt ...'

The canary was rapturously pleased to see them and began to pipe and call the minute they opened the door but he was wasting his time, for by now they were so concerned about one another they didn't even hear him.

'I didn't realize we was in such a mess,' Ellen said, looking at the red splashes on her suit. 'We oughter soak all them stains. They'll never come out else. Look at the state a' your shirt. It's smothered. 'As yer aunty got a basin?'

She had three. And a jug full of cold water. And the remains of a bar of soft soap in the soap dish. 'Take yer shirt off,' she said. 'I could 'ave that clean in a jiffy.'

'Shirt can wait,' he said. 'I want ter see if 'e's hurt your face.'

So although she protested that she wasn't hurt at all, she allowed him to sponge the bloodstains from her cheeks and rolled up her sleeves so that he could clean the graze on her elbow and dry it most tenderly on Aunty Dumpling's towel, which gave them an excuse for cuddles and reassuring kisses, and a chance to relive the entire fight, blow by courageous blow. 'I never seen such a fighter,' he admired. 'The way you hit him! No wonder 'e gave in!'

' 'E give in 'cause you was thumpin' the life out of 'im,' she said, blue eyes shining with admiration. 'Four at once you was fighting one time, I 'ope you realize. Four. *An'* you sent 'em packin'.'

It should have worried him that his behaviour had been violent and aggressive and not at all in his father's submissive style. But it didn't. He gloried in it. He was proud of himself for putting up a fight and proud of her for fighting beside him. 'You're like Queen Boadicea,' he told her. 'I can just see you in a chariot, d'you know that, drivin' through the enemy, crackin' heads. Splat! Splat! I'll bet she had blue eyes!'

'We showed 'em,' she crowed. The strong sunlight was

shining straight onto her face and her eyes were as bright as shields.

'Kiss me,' he said. It was right to demand kisses of such a warrior.

She kissed him hard. And again, harder still until they were both gasping. Then because his shirt was a mere two inches away from her eyes she noticed the stains on it again, and saw that there was a smear on his jacket too. 'Come on,' she said. 'Take that lot off. Let's get the worst out.' And this time he obeyed her and stripped to his trousers and the woollen combinations he always wore under his cycling suit.

'You look like a prize fighter,' she said, stroking the dark hairs on his bare forearms.

The delicate caress gave him goose pimples, and when the jacket had been sponged and hung on the back of a chair, and the first stains on the shirt were soaking in salt water, they sat on the bed and returned to kissing. Soon he had unbuttoned the top of her bodice so as to kiss the lovely salty flesh of her neck, and, greatly daring, she was slipping her hands under the warm cloth of his vest to stroke his chest. And that led to the discovery that he had a crop of very colourful bruises blooming below his shoulder blades.

'You really 'ave been bashed about,' she said, touching the bruises tenderly with her fingertips. 'I should'a cleaned you up 'fore I started on yer clothes. Look at the state a' your knuckles.'

'I'm all right,' he said airily, trying not to make a fuss. But she was already out on the landing emptying the jug in the sink and getting fresh water. 'Be a fine thing if I let you turn septic,' she scolded affectionately, 'after the way you cleaned me up so lovely.' So he sat beside the washstand and allowed her to bathe his hands. 'Miss Nightingale attends wounded soldier,' he declaimed, striking a pose to hide his embarrassment.

'Hero of White's Row,' she said, plunging both his hands into the bowl. His knuckles were actually quite badly torn, and bled profusely when she immersed them in the water, and this worried her. 'Ain't hurtin', am I?' she said, forehead wrinkled.

'Hero faints with the pain!' he said, laughing at her, and pretended to collapse, spreadeagled in the chair.

So of course he had to be resuscitated by being kissed until he opened his eyes. Then she discovered a graze on his left cheek which needed attention, and stood between his knees to bathe it with fresh water, and that rapidly became the most loving exercise of all. The kisses grew longer and longer and more and more passionate. And they forgot all about the canary.

'We oughter soak your bloomer suit an' all,' he said looking down at the red blotches trailed across the front of that pretty blue cloth.

'Be a bit of a job,' she hesitated. 'I'd 'ave ter take it off ter get at all a'them.'

'Take it off then,' he said, and was delighted at how easy and natural he'd made it sound.

'I don't know ...' she said, tempted by such a daring idea, but feeling she ought to resist for appearances' sake.

'No one'll see,' he urged. 'Go on! Why not? You'll never get the stains out once they dry.'

'Well ...' she said again. But she was unrolling her cummerbund, thoughtfully, debating the possibilities inside her head. It would be horrid to have her lovely bloomer suit ruined. But on the other hand she knew very well that young women weren't supposed to run around in their underwear in front of young men. But he was in his underwear and that didn't seem to matter. And surely there'd be no harm in *him* seeing her in her chimmy.

'Could yer lock the door?' she asked.

The door was locked, and fresh water poured into a second bowl, and when she'd taken off her boots and set them neatly underneath the bed, the bloomer suit was unbuttoned and removed.

She was wearing combinations too, a pretty one-piece garment made of white lawn, the bodice cut so tight and so low that he could see the entire swell of her breasts, the waist neat and slender, and the drawers open-fronted like harem trousers and ending in lace frills just below the knees. The sight of her so delectably and desirably undressed concentrated such intense pleasure in him that he had to close his eyes for a second.

When he opened them again she was busy dipping the bloodstains in the second bowl, working methodically and neatly, rub-rub-rub, and on to the next spot. And he noticed that she wasn't wearing any corsets.

'You ain't got no stays on,' he said delighted.

'No,' she grinned back at him, pleased, after all, to see how much he admired her. 'I've given 'em up when we go cycling. They pinch.' And her throat flushed with soft colour.

The sight of that flush and the thought of her supple flesh being pinched by whalebone filled him with tenderness. He stood behind her, protectively, and put his hands round the soft lawn at her waist and held her gently. 'If I was your stays, I'd hold you so light an' gentle you wouldn't believe,' he said. 'I wouldn't nip yer.'

She leaned back against his chest and sighed. 'You go on like that, I shan't get me suit clean,' she warned.

'How many more spots you got ter do?'

'Three. Four if you count that little'un.'

He stood behind her, almost cuddling her while she scrubbed the last four marks, squeezed the damp patches in a towel, patted the cloth smooth again, and arranged her pretty suit over the back of the tallest chair to dry.

But then he couldn't resist temptation any longer, and bent his head to kiss the nape of her neck. And the kiss was so pleasurable he let it travel down her throat towards the lacy frill on her chemise and the soft breast swelling just below it. The flush on her throat deepened and now he could see her nipples rising towards his mouth, rising and hardening, showing their pleasure just as his own flesh was doing. And he was aware of the lovely pearl pink texture of her flesh, and recognized that her nipples were exactly the same colour as her lips, a soft muted red, like raspberries.

But then she was purring in her throat, 'Um um, um,' and the sound drove all other thoughts from his mind. He turned her in his arms and found her mouth and kissed it until they were both trembling. It was such a satisfying, enticing kiss and the sensation it produced in them both was so intense that when they finally drew apart their legs wouldn't support them. They sank down onto Aunty Dumpling's nice convenient bed, side by side and panting. And kissed again. Greedily. And their next kiss drew them down into the feather mattress.

'Take that awful belt off,' she said, wincing away from it as he drew her body towards him again. So it was removed at once, with apologies, and as his trousers wouldn't stay up without it and his boots were in the way, they were kicked off too. And now there was nothing to impede them and they could kiss with unrestrained pleasure and the most exciting sense of daring.

By now her breasts had escaped from the soft constraints of her chemise and lay in his hands, full and eager. They lay thigh to thigh, letting instinct and strong sensation lead them on. knowing they ought to resist, but too entranced to make the effort. He kissed her mouth and her neck and her breasts and her eyes, moving from one to the other, on and on and on, taut with desire, in an ecstasy beyond words. And she kissed him back instinctively, rolling against him in a torment of pleasure so sharp it was making her feel dizzy.

'I love you, love you, love you,' he said, sliding his lips up her neck towards her mouth again. And in that one easy movement he was inside her, so quickly and so naturally it was done before either of them realized it.

For a second the shock and the pleasure of it stopped them both in mid-breath, and they stayed still, flushed and panting, knowing what was done and wanting to continue. Then he was moving again. He simply couldn't help it, and she simply couldn't stop him.

'I must,' he groaned, his face paler and his eyes darker than she'd ever seen them.

'Yes, yes,' she said, almost fiercely. 'Go on!' They were all instinct now, and all pleasure, and their pleasure rose and became ecstasy, better and better, sharper and sweeter, stronger and stronger.

And that was how, in the luscious summer of their seventeenth year, and the privacy of Aunty Dumpling's hospitable room, they came together.

And came, miraculously, together.

Afterwards they slept, quiet and contented and sated, their arms about each other. And the canary, having given up all hope of food, slept too.

Chapter Twenty

When they woke, the sun was slanting in through the window at a completely new angle and the canary was singing passionately, the feathers at his throat throbbing and fluttering, his high whistling melody flute-shrill in the sleepy room. In the street below a cart was creaking past, the steady clop clop of its horse's hooves as slow and predictable as the tin clock on the dresser. It was nearly eleven o'clock.

'We been asleep fer hours,' he whispered, still lapped in contentment. 'What a way to go on!'

'Did we oughter get dressed?' she said sleepily. But she made no effort to move away from his side. It was too warm and comfortable beside him.

She looked more beautiful than he'd ever seen her, but softer and vulnerable. 'Are you all right?' he asked.

'Yes,' she said rather fearfully, thinking, please don't say we shouldn't 'ave. I know we shouldn't 'ave. But I done it fer you.

The anxiety in her voice released a flood of protective affection. 'I shall love you fer ever an' ever,' he said. It upset him that she was feeling guilty, especially as guilt was creeping into his mind too.

'I love you so, so much,' she said touching his cheek tenderly. 'It wasn't wrong, was it?'

That was a question he couldn't answer and remain truthful. 'We will get married,' he said. 'Soon as ever we can. I promise.'

She remembered the newspaper cutting. Now, she thought, let him see it now. There'll never be a better time than this. 'I got sommink ter show you,' she said, sitting up, but gently so as not to disturb him. 'Stay here. I shan't be a tick.' And she eased herself out of the bed and padded across the lino to the tall chair where her bloomer suit was drying.

She'd found the cutting yesterday evening when she was getting ready to go and visit her mother. Was it really only yesterday evening? It had been folded away inside the brown paper cover of an old exercise book she was using to keep accounts in. When it fell out onto her counterpane she had no idea what it was. She'd opened it idly and glanced at the picture and read the headline before she realized how useful it could be. Now she took it from her pocket and padded back to the bed with it and spread it out across Aunty Dumpling's patchwork quilt. 'There!' she said, more boldly than she'd intended. 'Whatcher think a' that?'

He read the headline aloud. 'Slum houses make way for Mr Rothschild's new Industrial Dwellings. Demolition teams at work in Flower and Dean Street.' And looked at the picture, piles of rubble, jagged walls and a line of urchins all staring owl-eyed at the camera. 'I remember that,' he said with surprise and delight, 'all them old places comin' down. I was on'y a little'un. I went down ter see it, I remember. With Alfie Miller. Look, there's 'is sister Ruby. An' that's me. An' there's Amy Miller an' Johnny What-ever-'is-name-was. Where d'yer get it, Ellen? And that boy used ter foller Morrie about all the time. I remember him. An' that awful Smelly Ellie, look, on the end a' the line. Trust her ter push herself in where she wasn't wanted. She was awful! Smelly Ellie Murphy. Pinched my cake, she did.'

He was so busy examining the picture he hadn't noticed the distress on her face, but now she caught her breath suddenly as though she had a pain, and he looked up straight into her eyes, and her eyes were anguished. 'Ellen?' he asked.

'It was a good cake,' she whispered. 'Tasted lovely.'

'Ellen?' he said again, scowling at her. She couldn't be Ellie Murphy. No, no, no, it wasn't possible. She was Ellen White, beautiful Ellen White. But then he remembered that awful room in Chicksand Court.

'I never 'ad no breakfast,' she explained and burst into tears.

Then how tenderly she was cuddled and consoled, and how anxiously he regretted his stupid thoughtless words. And she assured him that she was quite, quite changed now she was Ellen White, and he assured her that he knew it, that nobody

263

could ever dream of calling her Smelly Ellie when she was the sweetest girl alive, and just let anyone try, he'd give 'em a right pasting. And her tears were kissed quite away and his battered hands were held tenderly in hers. And now there was no doubt at all that they would marry, and marry soon.

'I tell you, bubeleh,' he said passionately. 'I say thanks to the good Lord every single day a' my life fer lettin' us meet. An' now we're man an' wife – yes, yes, we are. Man an' wife in everything bar the ceremony – I shall be grateful to Him for ever an' ever. It don't matter what you was like as a kid. That's all over an' done with.'

'Oh!' she said, tearful with joy this time, 'I shall love you fer ever an' ever. You'll see.' And she kissed his battered hands. 'Oh your poor hands.'

The sight of his torn knuckles and the knowledge of who she was triggered another memory. 'We 'ad a fight once, you an' me,' he said. 'D'you remember?'

'No we never,' she said, surprised into forgetting her tears. 'Boys don't fight girls.' She'd given plenty of boys a thump in her time, but not David. Never gentle Davey Cheifitz.

'It was down the Lane,' he said. 'We must 'a been about seven. No more. I 'it the wall, I was so wild. Cut all me knuckles. You called me a mug.'

'The ring trick!' she said, remembering. 'They made yer pull the ring trick. Alfie Miller, wasn't it? Alfie Miller and the bloke they called Crusher. Oh Davey! Fancy me callin' you a mug!'

'I was a mug,' he admitted ruefully. 'Caught me good an' proper they did with that ol' ring trick. You knew though, didn'tcher?'

'You learn young if yer live in Dorset Street.'

'You'll never live in Dorset Street again,' he promised.

'I'd 'ave a job,' she grinned at him, 'seein' they've pulled it down.'

'Oh Ellen!' he said laughing at her, 'That's what I love about you. Give us a kiss!'

Three kisses later, and at last, they remembered the poor canary and hastened to fill his seed bowl and clean his cage and provide him with fresh water, allowing themselves to feel safely ashamed of this particular unworthiness.

Then it was time to put on their clothes and tidy the bed and resume the rest of the day. They dressed slowly, partly because they were still languid with lovemaking, and partly because they recognized that every movement they made was taking them back into the ordinary world again, where neither of them wanted to be.

'No point us trying to catch the club up,' he said as he tied his bootlaces. 'They'll be gone much too far by now.'

'We could 'ave a pie somewhere an' go to Hyde Park,' she said pinning up her hair, and watching her daytime face reappearing in the looking glass. They were two separate people again, two individuals, not man an' wife, and the corners of her mouth were drooping at the sadness of it.

'Soon we'll be married, bubeleh,' he said, putting his arms round her. 'I shall speak to my father tonight, the minute I get back.' He hadn't the faintest idea what he would say, but he knew it would be done.

It was past ten o'clock when he got home that night. The air brooding over Whitechapel was still warm and the sky was the dusty mauve of untouched grapes, but for the first time in his life the beauty of it didn't move him at all. He was tense with the certainty of conflict. 'Soldier of the line prepares fer battle,' he told himself, trying to make a joke of it. But he couldn't fool himself. Whatever he said in the next few minutes and however carefully he said it, somebody was bound to be hurt. Oh, if only he could restrict the damage to his own emotions. *Halevai*!

Most of the parlour windows were open to the heavy air, and behind them the gaslights shone like Chinese lanterns. His parents were sitting underneath their particular gaslight, beside their open window, he reading studiously, she sewing buttons on a shirt, and both of them lapped in contentment with each other, the very picture of *sholem bayis*, the ideal of Jewish domesticity.

The sight of them squeezed David's heart with a pang of foreboding and regret. Until this summer he'd loved them so entirely and easily, his thin, stooping, upright father, a *chawchem*, a man worthy of admiration, and his pale,

265

hardworking mother, with her chapped busy hands and the humility of that downcast look, a woman to shield. Now he remembered all the errands he'd run to save her strength and all the odd jobs he'd undertaken to earn her the money for this flat, and all the old protective love for her filled his chest and made his eyes sting with tears.

He hung Aunty Dumpling's key on the nail above the dresser, glad that it was down at the dark end of the room and that he could stand with his back to them for a second and recover the calm he needed.

'So you fed the bird, nu?' his mother said mildly.

'Yes.'

'No troubles?'

'No.'

'So vhy she don't let me feed that bird I can't imagine. After all these years. I should give it the evil eye maybe.'

'Rachel!' Emmanuel demurred, drawing his eyebrows into the downward flicker that was the nearest he ever got to frowning at her.

'Come and sit beside your Mama,' Rachel said, patting the chair beside her. 'You had a good day vid your cycles, nu?' Then as he walked into the gaslight she saw his torn knuckles and let out a little shriek, dropping the shirt and stretching out her hands towards him. 'David, bubeleh, vhat they done to you?'

He'd forgotten all about his injuries. 'Drunks,' he explained waving away scars, concern and explanation. 'Shouting their mouths off. Bit a' punchin'. Nothing, Mama. Nothing really. I got something much more important to tell you.'

'So let me see,' she said taking his right hand firmly and turning it towards the light. 'Ai-yi! Vhat more important than your health, I should like to know. Did you bathe it? Show me the other one. Ai-yi-yi, vhat a state!'

He looked at her face, all loving concern, all innocent loving concern, and he felt like a butcher. 'I want to get married,' he said.

Emmanuel closed his book and set it aside, and David knew he was alert and attentive even though he could only see him out of the corner of his eye. But his mother paid no attention at

266

all. 'You should have come home,' she grumbled affectionately. 'I vould a' bandaged you up good. Vhat a state! Ai-yi!'

'You vant me to make inquiries?' Emmanuel asked.
'Somebody to make a match, nu? *Shadchanim* ve don't have in
Vhitechapel, but there's plenty here know the art.'

'He's too young for matchmaking yet,' Rachel said too
quickly, giving his hands a little shake of exasperation.

'Don't it say in the Shulchan Aruch, "At eighteen a young
man should take a wife"?' David tried, looking his father full
in the eye and wishing he could control his erratic breathing.

'True,' Emmanuel said. 'That is vhat it says in the Shulchan
Aruch. But you should know it is also written there, "Marry an
estimable woman of respectable family". I start to ask for you,
nu?'

'No,' David said, staying calm with a great effort. 'I've
already found a wife, Papa. I know who I want to marry.'

'The idea!' his mother exploded. 'So vhat next? I never
heard nothink so ridiculous. A *meshuganer* we bred, Emmanuel.
Chose your own vife. Ai-yi! Vhat sort of a vorld ve live in?'

'Her name's Ellen White,' he said, speaking quickly before
they could stop him or he could lose his courage. 'She's
eighteen. She works in 'Opkins an' Peggs, where Josh works.
She's very pretty, and I love her.'

'Ellen White?' his mother said. 'So vhat sort a' name's that?
That ain't a Jewish name.'

Tell them quickly, David thought. Now, while it's possible.
'She ain't Jewish, Mama.'

'A *shiksa*!' Rachel wailed, both hands fanned across her
mouth as though she could prevent any further upsetting
speech by their pressure. 'He vants to marry a *shiksa*. Speak to
the boy, Emmanuel. A *shiksa*! Ai-yi-yi-yi-yi!'

'You ain't got no choice, David,' Emmanuel said. 'You must
marry a Jew.'

'No,' David said, stubborn but still reasonable. 'I want to
marry Ellen.'

'Ve marry for life,' Emmanuel warned.

'Yes,' rapturously, 'that's what I want.'

'How vill you keep Shabbas vid a *shiksa* for a vife? You ain't
thought of that, nu?' his mother said. 'Does she cook good? I

267

bet she don't cook kosher.'

'It don't matter how she cooks. We'll manage. We love each other.'

'Love!' his mother snorted. 'Such nonsense. Love!'

His father sighed anxiously. 'You ain't thought of your childer?' he asked.

'No,' David answered honestly. 'What's to think?'

'Vhat's to think?' his mother shrieked. 'Vhat's to think? Ai-yi-yi! She's put the evil eye on him, this *shiksa*. Vhat's to think? So vhat vill they be? Half an' half, neither one thing nor the other, poor childer. Vhat's to think!'

'So maybe they'll be Jewish, Mama. I don't know.'

Emmanuel's long face was pale even in the gaslight, the lines denting his cheeks and forehead deeper and blacker than ever. 'The family is the centre of life,' he said, passing his long hands over his eyes with a terrible weariness. 'The core. There ain't nothink more important. Ai-yi! Is this for vhy I send you to study the Talmud? Vhat you thinking of? Vhere's your modesty? You don't choose your own vife? It ain't modest. You think I chose your mother? Nu, nu!'

'Times change,' David said stubbornly. 'This ain't Poland.'

'You ain't thought of Yom Kippur,' his mother accused, weeping freely. 'And how vill you celebrate the Passover, you tell me?' And she blew her nose as though that was a clinching argument.

'I'm goin' ter marry Ellen,' he said and his spine was rigid with determination. It wouldn't matter what they said now, he had made up his mind by action.

The argument went on and on, round and round, threshing and struggling and making no progress at all, a snake eating its own tail. When the church clock struck twelve, Emmanuel decided to call a truce. 'Tomorrow ve see the Rabbi, nu?' he suggested. 'Ve hear vhat he says, nu? Now ve sleep, odervise ve ain't fit fer nothink in the morning.'

David agreed to see the Rabbi even though he knew it wouldn't make the slightest difference. Rachel wailed into the bedroom and cried herself to sleep, and Emmanuel sighed with distress and guilt, remembering the words of Deuteronomy, 'This our son is stubborn and rebellious, he will not

268

obey our voice.'

And one crowded mile away, among the muttering sleepers in Mr Pegg's second dormitory, Ellen lay wakeful, tossed between ecstasy and worry. Now that she had time to think about what they'd done, she was remembering that it could have awful consequences. What if she had a baby? Plenty of girls did, as she knew only too well from her life in Dorset Street. Perhaps they ought to have waited till they were married. That was the proper way to go on. But oh, the memory was too close and too rapturous to be denied. And they'd be married as soon as ever they could. He'd promised. Married and together for ever and ever, sleeping in the same bed, loving like that whenever they wanted to. Even the thought gave her goose pimples.

But then practical considerations came plodding into her mind. If she got married she would have to leave her job, because Hopkins and Peggs didn't employ married women. And that would mean the loss of at least half a guinea a week. And the more she thought about it, the more stupid it seemed that she should have to forgo her wage simply because she and David had decided to live together. 'I shan't tell 'em,' she decided. 'It's no concern a' theirs what I do with me private life. I'll ask permission to live out. I don't 'ave ter say nothink about getting married.' She could tell them she was living with a relative, which would be true enough. That way she could have the wage and David. And goodness knows they'd need the money. She was still plotting warmly when sleep drifted her away for the second time that day.

David was late for work next morning. He was most upset and apologetic, especially when Mr Quinton assumed he'd got a thick head and made a joke of it.

'We're doin' a piece on the Thames Embankment,' he said. 'Cleopatra's Needle, Hotel Cecil, Savoy, Somerset House. All straight lines. Draw a straight line, can yer?'

'Don't tease the lad, Quin,' Mr Palfreyman said, stepping neatly into the office. 'Good morning, Cheify. Fine weather again. Five minutes at the end of the day to make amends. Is that acceptable? Yes, yes, of course.'

'You got off light, Cheify,' Mr Quinton said as they went striding off towards the Embankment. 'Think yerself lucky an' don't go makin' a habit of it, that's all.'

'No, Mr Quinton,' David assured him. 'I won't.' And he sighed deeply. Telling your parents you were going to marry someone they couldn't approve of wasn't something you'd ever want to repeat. Nu-nu!

Mr Quinton gave him a quizzical look but no further comment. And presently they arrived on the Embankment where the roadway was rattling with cabs and trams and scuttling with pedestrians, and the river was choppy with the wash of boats and barges. 'River scene fer a start,' Mr Quinton said and darted across the road to Somerset House, notebook in hand, leaving David to get on with it.

Work was a blessing that day. It occupied his mind and passed the time and, rather to his surprise, gave him an appetite. But he was preoccupied, despite all his efforts to appear as normal as he could, and the perceptive Mr Quinton noticed, of course.

'There's sommink up wi' young Cheify,' he told Mr Palfreyman, when the two gentlemen met in Craig's Oyster Bar for their usual liquid lunch with shellfish.

'*Cherchez la femme*, dear chap,' Mr Palfreyman said, and, turning to the waiter, 'Could I have a *dry* glass, do you think? Thank you so much. Is it affecting his work, would you say?'

'No.'

'Then it's his affair, not ours. Yes, indeed. He'll sort things out, I daresay. He's a sensible lad. Just keep an eye on him.'

'I'd every intention,' Mr Quinton said. The speed and delicacy of those drawings were too good to be lost. And besides, he liked the kid.

Ellen worked hard that day too, for the store had plenty of custom. But she worked automatically and that gave her plenty of time to daydream. It seemed an age since she'd last seen him and seven o'clock was hours and hours away. She'd have liked to have told Maudie she was going to get married, but she knew that wouldn't be at all wise, because Maudie was such a gossip. On Wednesday she'd tell Ruby and Mrs Miller, and see what they said about it. But in the meantime she'd just got to get through this Monday. Oh what a very long day it was!

And it got longer. For when the goods had finally been covered and the shutters drawn and the doors bolted, and she had gone skimming up the stairs to the dormitory to change her clothes and escape, there was a postcard waiting for her. 'I told my parents. Now I got to see the Rabbi tonight. I will be outside the store at nine o'clock, I promise. I.L.Y. David xxxxx.' Two more hours! It was a lifetime. But if he was seeing the Rabbi that probably meant he was fixing the wedding, so it was time well spent, even if they couldn't see one another till later. When they met again they'd know when they were going to get married. We shall 'ave ter find somewhere to live next, she thought, and decided to occupy the intervening hours reading the advertisements.

It never occurred to her that his parents would actually refuse to accept her. They'd go on making a fuss, for a little while at least, because Jews usually married Jews, but she felt vaguely sure that they'd come round to the idea in the end. She knew they were good caring parents because they'd always fed him well and seen to it that he had warm clothes and that his boots were mended. So they'd hardly refuse him now, over something as important as this. Not when he'd made up his mind. There was an inflexibility about him when he'd made up his mind, a quiet unspoken determination that would be very difficult to oppose. No, it would all come out right in the end. She was certain. Well, very nearly certain.

So it upset her to see how downcast he looked as he came up Shoreditch High Street to meet her just after nine o'clock. He was striding, because his legs were too long for him to walk in any other way, but there was no eagerness in his stride, and his face was taut and hard with unhappiness. 'Oh Davey!' she said, slipping her hand through the crook of his arm to comfort him, and the tone of her voice told him at once how well she understood what he was feeling.

'I can't get them ter see sense,' he sighed. 'They just keep on an' on.'

'Did yer see the Rabbi?'

Oh yes, he'd seen the Rabbi, and a fat lot of good that had

271

done. Sitting blackly in his high carved chair with a brown dusk filling the room around him and three thousand years of tradition heavily behind him. He'd been kind and courteous and quite quite firm. Jews married Jews, honoured their fathers, perpetuated their race. The only possible hope he could offer was the thought that the young lady might care to convert to Judaism.

'She ain't Jewish,' David had said, recognizing how unpleasantly truculent he sounded, but powerless to say anything else.

'You have asked her?'

'No.'

'So, maybe you should, nu?'

And that was how they'd left it, with no decision made, and no hope of making one. Impasse.

'I won't give in,' he told Ellen fiercely as they walked north past the Music Hall towards St Leonard's Church. 'One way or the other we'll get married.'

'I know,' she said, giving his arm a squeeze. 'What say we catch the last house? Cheer ourselves up. My treat.'

So they went to the Music Hall, although he wouldn't allow her to pay for the tickets, and were cheered for an hour. But when he kissed her goodnight in the staff porch his eyes were sombre again.

'It'll work out, you'll see,' she said, with her arms about his neck and her cheek against his chin. 'Just so long as we love each other. P'rhaps your Aunty Dumpling'll bring 'em round.'

But he groaned into her hair. 'Bubeleh, bubeleh.' He was ashamed even to think about Aunty Dumpling after what they'd done in her room. Oh why was something as simple and wonderful as love so terribly complicated?

Had he known it, Dumpling was doing her best for him at that very minute. At the end of the interview he'd stormed out of Rabbi Jaccoby's room and rushed down the stairs two at a time in his anger, and his father had gone sloping back to the flat. And there he'd found both his sisters waiting for him, Rivke eagle-fierce, Raizel all tremulous anxiety.

'Vell?' Rivke said.

He sat wearily in his chair and told them what had been said.

'He ain't move an inch. He says he'll marry her.'

'Ai! Ai!' Rachel wailed. 'Vhat ve gonna do, Dumpling? Like a madman he is.'

'So the boy's in love,' Dumpling said, defending him although she wasn't sure she ought to, knowing what they'd been up to. Her neighbours had been quick to tell her all the scandal the minute she got back.

'I seen your nephew, Sunday, Mrs Esterman,' Mrs Smith said. 'Brought a young lady wiv 'im. Did yer know?'

'Yes, yes,' Dumpling assured her. 'They come to feed the bird.'

'Took 'em hours!' Mrs Smith said. 'Can't think *what* they could a' been doing up there all that time.'

'Cleaning the room, Mrs Smith,' Dumpling said, covering for them at once. 'Left it lovely, they have.'

'Very kind of 'em, I'm sure!' Mrs Smith said, and her expression said, you don't fool me!

Ai! Dumpling thought. So young and so much in love, vhat you expect? It's only human nature.

'A *shiksa*!' Rachel moaned. 'I never hold my head up in the Buildin's ever again. Ai! Ai! Ai!'

'We should'a found him a vife months ago,' Rivke said, lopsided but stern. 'This never vould'a happen, we found him a vife months ago. Nice Jewish girl. Izzie's girl maybe.'

'She's twenty-five already,' Dumpling pointed out reasonably. 'She got a wall eye.'

'So who's perfect?' Rivke said. 'She's a good Jewish girl. Make a good Jewish vife. Ai-yi, dolly! Don't you vish you listen vhen ve tell you?'

But Rachel was too grieved to hear the rebuke. 'Vhat for he do this to his Mama? I never hold my head up again. Maybe ve find him a pretty girl, nu?'

'You could take the prettiest girl in the whole a' Whitechapel, and plate her vid gold, vouldn't make no difference, bubeleh. Still he vould love this girl.'

'It's so unreasonable,' Rachel complained.

'She vants love should be reasonable!' Dumpling said to her brother.

Emmanuel had been sitting quietly in his corner, listening to

273

the storm of his wife's distress. Now he lifted his head and gave his opinion, quietly and sadly. 'Ain't no earthly use ve oppose,' he said. 'Raizel's right. The boy's in love. Ve got to accept.'

'But he'll marry her!' Rachel wailed. 'Ai-yi-yi! It's the end a' the vorld. All my life I say I should only live to see him under the *chuppah*! And now ...' And she dissolved into bitter tears and refused to be comforted. 'Vhat for he do this to his Mama?'

'So you vear him down,' Rivke suggested. 'He's young yet. You vear him down.'

Emmanuel shook his head. 'Von't vork,' he said.

And it didn't.

Chapter Twenty-One

The struggle continued all through the lovely warm June and well into the heat of July. David lived between ecstatic happiness when he and Ellen were alone together and stubborn despair when he had to be at home with his parents. Between them, his family kept up a relentless pressure upon him, all the more difficult to withstand because it was so varied. His mother nagged. Had he thought of the children? The Shabbas? His duty? His religion? His father mourned. How could he marry? No Jew could be married in the synagogue unless he was marrying another Jew. If he married this girl none of his family could attend the wedding. Rivke and her husband simply assumed he would capitulate; Aunty Dumpling kept out of the way, grieved that her darling was so unhappy but powerless to help him. And Rabbi Jaccoby padded about the building on his soft cloth shoes, and waited.

After two weeks, Ellen was woken one morning by the familiar ache low down in her belly, and knew that at least she wasn't going to have a baby. But as she hadn't told him she was worried, she couldn't share the relief with him either. And his distress was becoming more and more plain as the weeks progressed. He was all eyes, she thought, and his pale face looked gaunt.

At the end of June, Aunty Dumpling asked them both to supper with her and Mr Morrison, and made a great fuss of them. But they were careful not to speak of love or weddings and even though the two women kissed most lovingly when they parted, theirs was the affection of the powerless and they both knew it.

In the end it was Mr Palfreyman who found the solution.

He and Mr Quinton were 'pondering' a lengthy operation

that would eventually decide which of three possible articles would be included in their next issue. Mr Quinton's office was curtained with print-outs and sketches, the Shaver had been sent out for fresh coffee, and David, having time on his hands, had found a space in the corner of the print room and started a sketch of his favourite model, wearing her pretty straw hat and her blue bloomer suit and leaning on the handlebars of her bike. He was so absorbed he didn't notice that Mr Palfreyman had come out of the office on the look-out for the Shaver and had been standing behind him for several minutes, watching the progress of the sketch. When David realized he was being watched he was embarrassed into stammering excuses. 'Oh, Mr Palfreyman, sir, I was just – um – I mean – all the other sketches are done, sir – um ...'

Mr Palfreyman brushed his confusion aside with a small benign wave of his white hand. 'A beautiful girl,' he observed, noticing David's blush before the boy ducked his head to hide it. 'Drawn from the life, I daresay.'

'Yes, sir.'

'If I had artistic talents, my dear chap, which I must confess I have not, I would choose just such a model. Yes, yes indeed.'

David looked at Ellen, and sighed, and Mr Palfreyman looked at David, and considered, and Mr Quinton came out of the office, and understood, and the presses clattered all around them for several metallic minutes.

'If I had such a model,' Mr Palfreyman said at last, 'which I must confess likewise I have not, I would want to marry her.'

David looked his master straight in the eye and decided to tell him. 'I'd marry her termorrer, sir. If I could.'

'She is married to another?'

'No, sir, nothink like that. I'm Jewish, she ain't.'

Mr Palfreyman made two immediate decisions. 'We will print the Thames by night and the building of Kingsway, Mr Quinton,' he said, 'and I would be much obliged if you could spare me young Cheify for twenty minutes.'

So they retired to Mr Palfreyman's quiet, dry office, to the prognostication of matchsticks and the consideration of pros and cons.

'Firstly, she returns your affection, I presume,' Mr

276

Palfreyman began, holding the first match between finger and thumb, and when assured that she did, 'Yes, yes, of course. Then this is our first pro. However. Your parents are in oppositon, you say.'

It took a quarter of an hour for all their hopes and disappointments to be enumerated and discussed and laid in line. And at the end of that time there were two identical rows of matchsticks facing each other on the tidy desk. Youth, love, beauty and natural inclination to the right; obedience, religion, duty and parental disapproval to the left. He's a kind man, David thought, looking at the matches sadly, on'y he ain't told me nothing I don't know already. It's a stalemate. Impasse.

However Mr Palfreyman still held a matchstick neatly between thumb and forefinger. 'It is my opinion, David Cheifitz,' he said with immense seriousness but with the beginnings of a smile twinkling behind those gold-rimmed glasses, 'my opinion that we have underrated one of the factors in this case. A factor that should never be underrated. No indeed. I refer of course to your love for the lady and her love for you. Which, in my opinion, is worth two points. At the very least.' And he laid the final matchstick at the head of the pro column, and smiled like sunshine. 'I think you should marry,' he said, 'and the sooner the better.'

It was such a surprise it took David's breath away. Fancy Mr Palfreyman, dry, quiet, contained, careful Mr Palfreyman saying things like that.

'You would have to marry in a registry office, of course, for *you* would not be acceptable in a church, I believe, nor *she* in a synagogue. However, the form of the ceremony would be of very little consequence, I daresay, in the light of your present situation. If I were you, dear chap, I would go to the Town Hall in Commercial Street, and made inquiries. That should be your local office if I am any judge.'

How easy he makes it sound, David thought, watching the man's gentle face with stunned admiration. 'We'd still have ter get our fathers' consent,' he said, 'seein' we're both under age.'

'That is true,' Mr Palfreyman agreed mildly. 'Yes, yes, indeed.' And he gave thought to the problem, his white hands

277

spread neatly before him on the polished mahogany of his desk. 'You must be firm, my dear chap,' he advised, 'firm but polite, of course. Yes, yes indeed. Polite and firm. If I were you I think I should tell my father I intended to marry the lady with or without permission.'

'But that would mean waiting three whole years!' David realized.

'Yes, indeed. An impressive apprenticeship, don't you agree? Now then, my dear chap, you have a good father, you say. And I see every reason to believe you. Every reason. Would he not be impressed by such constancy?'

Put like that, David had to admit it seemed more than likely. 'But ...'

Mr Palfreyman waved him to silence. 'But,' he said, 'I would also point out, politely but firmly, of course, that I would prefer to marry her at once and with my father's consent.'

Excitement and hope ballooned inside David's chest. Yes, yes, yes, this was how it could be done. Mr Palfreyman was right. Although he didn't know it, his face was blazing with smiles. 'Yes,' he said. 'That's what I'll do. Thank you very much, sir. Very very much.'

'Think nothing of it, dear chap,' Mr Palfreyman said, warm with beneficence. 'Just cut off and give Mr Quinton a hand, eh?'

So the next evening David and Ellen took a stroll down Commercial Street, and found that registering their intent to marry was simplicity itself, and seemed to be what the registrar expected. It was merely a matter of calmly filling forms, one to call the banns, which they both signed, and two others which were to be signed by their fathers 'to indicate that they have given their consent'. It all sounded very reasonable and entirely probable.

'Tomorrow is Shabbas,' David said, tucking his form into the top pocket of his jacket as they walked back along Commercial Street. 'I'll ask him on the way back from the synagogue. Then he'll know how serious I am.' And besides, his mother and Aunt Rivke wouldn't hear what they were saying if they talked in the street. They were so quick to bully these days. It didn't give Papa a chance to think.

'What'll you say?'

278

'What Mr Palfreyman said. Dontcher think so?'

'You know 'im, I don't,' she said. 'I tell yer what though, I know a trick worth two a' that fer my ol' man.' But she wouldn't tell him what it was. 'You'll see,' she promised, and she folded her precious form into neat quarters and secreted it in her pocket. 'I bet I get mine signed 'fore yours.'

'You're on!' he said, catching her excitement. 'Daring gamble by the man who broke the bank at Monte Carlo.'

So that evening they went their separate ways, he to the synagogue, she to the pub.

It took her quite a long time to hunt her father down, but eventually she ran him to earth in 'The Bell' on the corner of Goulston Street. He was in a splendidly muzzy state, surrounded by cronies, already lurching and staggering, and bellowing with drunken good humour. She stood just inside the door and waited until she could catch the eye of a passing pot-boy, who struggled through the mass of cheerfully steaming bodies to find out what she wanted.

'I got a message fer me ol' man,' she said. 'Paddy Murphy, 'im over there. Ask the gov'ner if I can come in an' give it to 'im. 'E'll never make it out 'ere.'

That was true enough, as the governor was quick to appreciate, and as she looked a respectable girl in her neat shop clothes, he sent word back that she could come in 'jest fer a tick, if she looked sharp about it'.

Paddy was too far gone to feel surprise that his daughter was standing in the pub beside him and when she asked him, 'How's me darlin' daddy?' in the most blatantly flattering tones, he took the question as evidence of pure affection and threw his arms clumsily and exuberantly about her, calling on his friends to witness how much she loved him. 'Me own darlin' daughter, so she is, me own darlin' daughter.'

Those of his friends who could still focus their eyes were very taken with her, and declared they'd be jiggered, and wanted to know where he'd been hiding her all these years, and how he'd come to raise such a looker, old dog that he was. Those who were too drunk to see more than three inches in front of them pressed their blotchy faces as close to her as they could and offered to take her out the back an' show her a thing or two, leering horribly and belching their stale breath straight into her mouth. This put her father in the most affable humour but it also meant that she had to wait while he received their admiration and drank their tributes. She stood quietly among them, smiling at them and hating them thinking what a mucky-mouthed lot they were. I wouldn't stand 'em fer a second, she thought furiously, if it wasn't fer my Davey.

'Old Johnno's givin' me one of his old looks,' her father said, grinning at the publican. 'Will ye look at that, Barney.'

' 'E don't reckon your gel should be in 'ere, tha's the truth of it,' Barney explained.

'Sure an' can't a man see his own daughter jost once in a while, fer the love of God?' Paddy whined.

' 'Course yer can, Pa,' Ellen said seizing her opportunity quickly. 'An' you can sign a little form for me an' all. Who's ter stop yer?'

'Whashat?' Paddy said, perplexed and squinting. 'Wha' form's dat?'

'Won't let me sign it,' she explained, showing him the fold of paper. 'It's got ter be a man. Got ter be me father, so they said. I can't see why, but that's what they said.'

'Quite right,' he said beaming again. ' 'Tis business so it is, an' no concern of yours. Quite right. Don't you worry your pretty head. Your old father's the man fer business so he is.' And manoeuvring his body until he was almost facing the bar, he called to the landlord in his most peremptory tones, 'I'll trouble ye for pen an' ink, Johnno!'

They made a ceremony of it, bringing two pens and an inkstand and even a blotter. And her father signed as though it was Magna Carta, beaming at his audience afterwards and nodding his head and boasting, 'Paddy Murphy's the man for business.' But his daughter had folded the paper and shadowed out of the circle with it before any of them could notice, and was running north towards Hopkins and Peggs, rosy with triumph. Stupid old fool! she thought. He'd sign his own death warrant if you caught 'im when 'e was sozzled. Wonder how David's gettin' on.

At that very moment David and Emmanuel were emerging

280

from the Machzikei HaDath in Fournier Street a few hundred yards away. Rabbi Jaccoby had been preaching there, speaking most eloquently of the joys and sorrows of family life. 'Better a dinner of herbs where love is, than a stalled ox and hatred therewith.' The value of filial obedience had been stressed, but so had the more subtle rewards of tenderness and understanding, and he had ended with a plea for the exercise of 'that most delicate and difficult of all the arts, the art of compromise'.

So as they walked down Brick Lane towards the Buildings, David striding and his father stooping, what more natural than that they should hope for compromise and speak of marriage and the founding of families.

'The von great vish of your moder's life is to see you under the *chuppah*,' Emmanuel sighed.

'I *will* marry, Father.'

But that only provoked a sigh like a furnace. 'Ai! If only she vere Jewish. Ai-yi! Your heart is set on it, nu?'

'Yes, Father. Matter of fact, we're …'

'I should only live to see him under the *chuppah*,' his father repeated. 'So much it means to a moder.' He didn't look up at his son's eagerness, only inward to his own aching bleakness. 'For vhy *this* voman, David?'

It's a waste a' time trying to tell him, David thought. We've been over all this time an' time again an' he still doesn't understand. He put a hand on his father's arm to gentle him to a halt. 'We called the banns yesterday,' he said, speaking quickly before he lost his courage. 'We're getting married in the Town Hall, soon as we can. A civil wedding. All we need is your consent.'

His father stood quite still, gazing at him, his long face puckered with thought, but not angry. The soot-smeared houses stood on either side of them as flat and impervious as cliffs. Trams buzzed past them along the rails. Brick Lane went about its usual raucous business. The sky didn't fall.

'This is vhat you vant, nu?' Emmanuel said at last, and David noticed that he was only fingering his beard, not tugging it.

'Oh it is! It is, Father. More'n I've ever wanted anythink in all me life.'

Such an open face, Emmanuel thought, and with such beauty.

281

And he remembered the newborn David gazing at him with those same limpid eyes, and how powerfully love had risen in him, even then, at the very start of the child's life. 'Grandsons I vould like,' he admitted.

'Grandsons you shall have. I promise.'

'But a *shiksa*, David.'

David shrugged the word away. 'Never mind *shiksa*, she's the best girl in the world,' he said. 'A beauty. Well you know that. You seen the drawin's. A good daughter. Looks after 'er Ma like nobody's business. Eye fer a bargain. You should see 'er.'

Maybe I should, Emmanuel thought, but he said nothing.

'If you was ter meet 'er, I bet you'd love 'er an' all,' David insisted. 'You would. Honest!'

But still Emmanuel said nothing.

'I shall marry 'er in the end,' David said, offering his warning in the most respectful voice he could manage. 'No matter what. The minute I'm twenty-one I shall marry 'er. I'd rather marry with your blessing, a' course, but I *shall* marry 'er.'

They stood facing each other in the middle of the busy pavement while the synagogue emptied and the Shabbas crowds argued and jostled around them. He is a man now, Emmanuel thought, looking at his son's passionate eyes and the dark moustache, silky in the manner of virgin hair and curled so tenderly round the red curves of his mouth. His neck might still be slender as a girl's but he has the hands of a worker and the face of a man already settled into a world he knows. And it occurred to him that this was a modern face and an English one, the yarmulke unobtrusive on the back of his head, a mere patch of cloth against his springing hair, his prayer shawl tucked under his waistcoat and not left dangling above his trousers for all the world to see. A new kind of Jew we breed in this city, he thought. We ain't the same. I who left the old country behind, he who has no knowledge of it. Jewish he may be, Polish he ain't.

But he was still child enough to plead. 'Please, Papa!'

'I think about it,' Emmanuel promised. 'Ve don't say nothink to your moder, nu? I think about it. I tell you Sunday, nu?'

And oddly enough, although nothing had been decided, David felt satisfied.

The next day, Emmanuel Cheifitz did something he had never done on the Sabbath in the whole of his life. He actually set foot inside a shop. Not to buy anything. Nu-nu, that would have been unthinkable. Nor to observe the goods on offer. He was extremely careful to avert his eyes from any such temptation. But to allow himself the possibility of a glimpse of Ellen White.

He was profoundly uncomfortable in such a setting and knew, from the sudden image of himself that confronted him in one of the long mirrors, that he looked as incongruous as he felt. But it was a necessary penance, a chastening of the spirit before he made his decision. He lurked behind the rolls of fine cloth in his shabby gabardine, plucking his beard and trying to look inconspicuous, while the store's elegant customers raised their elegant eyebrows at him, and signalled wordless amazement to one another that such a creature should have been allowed inside their store.

Fortunately Ellen White was very easy to find. She was serving at the centre counter where Josh had said she'd be, and she was exactly like her pictures. Only prettier. He saw that at once. Much prettier. Even at this distance he could see how slender she was and what startling blue eyes she had, and note too that her hair was pinned into a modest bun at the back of her head, and that the collars and cuffs of her uniform were immaculately white. He watched as she flicked a heavy roll of cloth over and over between her hands, expertly unrolling the required length, and then stood back politely from the counter to give her customer a clear view, and he admired her skill and liked her discretion.

The customer was being difficult. She had already examined four rolls of cloth and from the way she was pouting and puffing it didn't look as though the fifth would satisfy her either. Sure enough, a sixth was called for as he watched, and had to be hauled down from the top shelf. But it was done with a smile, he noticed, even though the weight of it made the poor girl arch her spine, and that was a mark in her favour too. Oy-oy, he could see why David would love her.

The customer had three children with her, two little girls who stood beside her in their dimity dresses stolidly enduring their boredom, and a baby boy, still in petticoats, who clung to her skirt and grizzled for attention. 'Want to go home, Mama. Mama! Mama! Want to go home!' When the seventh roll had been pouted aside and she still ignored him, he began to cry in earnest.

His mother shook her skirt away from his tears and told him not to be a brat, but the girl leaned over the counter and, to Emmanuel's delight, tried to coax him into a better humour. 'Perhaps 'e'd be better behaved if we was to sit him on the counter, ma'am,' she suggested.

'Beastly creature,' his doting parent said. 'You may do as you please with him. It's all one with me. Just so long as he don't yell!'

So the weeping boy was lifted onto the counter and had his face wiped on his pinafore, most expertly, as Emmanuel was quick to notice, and was given a price ticket to play with. And then the two patient little girls were noticed, and two chairs were found for them to stand on so that they could be part of the proceedings too.

A good mother she will make, yet, Emmanuel thought, noticing how tactfully she was handling all three children. If only she were Jewish she would have all the virtues. But then he saw the floor walker moving rather too purposefully in his direction and knew it was time for him to leave.

Whatever it was that had urged him to Hopkins and Peggs that morning, the need to do penance, the wish to act fairly, or simple curiosity, it left him in an even worse state than ever. Now that he'd seen her, his dilemma was as sharp as a razor. How could he deny his son, knowing the quality of the woman he'd chosen? But if he agreed to this marriage, how would he explain to Rachel? The inevitability of the pain he was bound to cause crushed him into anguished sighing as he stooped back home along Commercial Street.

He wrestled with the problem all through Saturday night, quite unable to sleep but lying as still as he could and trying not to sigh too often so as not to disturb his family. By the morning, he was pale with fatigue but his mind was made up.

When David left the flat and wheeled his bicycle out of the balcony and prepared to bump it down the stone stairs, Emmanuel mumbled an excuse to Rachel and followed him.

They walked out of the courtyard together, and once they were safely out of sight of the windows and underneath the archway, he took the paper from beneath his belt and slid it gently into the top pocket of his son's jacket.

David's look was inquiring but hopeful. Ellen had shown him her father's signature the night before and the sight of it had renewed his optimism.

'Yes, my son,' Emmanuel said, speaking calmly as though what they were saying was unimportant. 'I have signed.'

David found that his throat was so full he could hardly utter a word. 'Thanks,' he said huskily.

Emmanuel put his hand on his son's shoulder and patted it. 'So ve don't tell your moder just yet avile,' he suggested. 'Vhen you leave is time enough. Ain't no cause before, nu?'

'No,' David agreed, recognizing with a pang that they were avoiding the moment when they would upset her. But then such happiness swelled and bloomed inside him that he forgot all about his mother. He wanted to run and jump and sing aloud. They had permission! Permission! They could marry. In three weeks they could be man and wife. His face glowing, he pushed the bike into speed and leaped upon it to cycle off down Flower and Dean Street with the reckless abandon of total happiness. Just wait till I tell her!

Watching him go, Emmanuel felt deserted.

It was a marvellous Sunday, with so many plans and so many rapturous kisses to share. They were like birds let out of their cage, full of energy and exuberance and chirruping high spirits. It didn't take them long to choose a date for their wedding. It would be the Saturday before Bank Holiday Monday, which would mean marrying in their dinner hour, but would give them two whole days to themselves afterwards. What could be better? Ellen said there was no point in asking any of her family because they wouldn't come. Her parents wouldn't care, she said, and her brothers and sisters would be too far away and working. They decided to invite Aunty

Dumpling of course, and David said he would tell his father, but apart from that it would be their secret. Theirs and their witnesses. Now it was simply a matter of finding their witnesses.

They left the cycling club to its own tame devices and set off at speed to Hymie Levy's house to ask him, and when he'd recovered from his surprise and agreed and bought them a drink to celebrate, they were off again, this time to Mrs Miller's to ask Ruby.

Mrs Miller said she never did, and kissed them both, and Ruby said she was honoured, and Amy wanted to know if they 'was 'avin' a weddin' breakfast', which was something they hadn't thought about.

'Monday, perhaps,' Ellen said. 'We could 'ave a party Monday. Whatcher think, David?'

'They got ter find 'emselves somewhere ter live first,' Mrs Miller told her youngest. 'You thought where yer goin', 'ave yer?'

Only vaguely, it had to be admitted. They were both too dizzy with happiness to think straight about anything. 'I'll come wiv yer, Wednesday,' she said to Ellen, laughing at them. 'Find yer somewhere nice. You don't want ter get rooked, do yer?'

She was as good as her word, and that Wednesday afternoon, she and Ruby and Ellen went house hunting. 'Somewhere tucked away nice an' private, fer a kick off,' she suggested. 'You goin' on workin', are yer?'

They found two attic rooms at the top of a tenement house in Quaker Street, where there was gas laid on and Mrs Undine the landlady was thin and wary and proclaimed her cleanliness and respectability by the whitest doorstep in the street. True, the nearest tap was down two flights of stairs and the W.C. was shared by three other tenants, but at least they were both indoors and looked clean even if they didn't smell too good.

'It'll do fer a start,' Ellen said. Anything would have done for a start. It was the start that was important.

There was so much to do, curtains to make, a hat to trim, furniture to find, Miss Elphinstone to be persuaded that she would work just as well if she lived out, and finally in the last week when the rooms were theirs and paid for, floors to scrub and windows to clean, and on Friday evening their own little larder to stock. Hymie came to Quaker Street as soon as he'd finished work and fitted their secondhand gas cooker for them, and Ruby and Ellen hung the curtains, and as the dusk gathered outside their high window they kissed one another goodbye, stunned by the speed of their preparations. And David went home for the last Shabbas meal he would eat with his parents. And he still hadn't said anything at all to his mother.

Tomorrow at breakfast, he thought, as she broke the *challah* bread. I can hardly tell her now. But she was so happy at breakfast time, he couldn't tell her then either.

So he departed for his wedding secretly, feeling a little ashamed of his cowardice. But happy. Oh so happy. Happier than he'd ever felt in his life.

*

Chapter Twenty-Two

Aunty Dumpling was ready and waiting on the steps of Stepney Town Hall for a good twenty minutes before the appointed time. She was honoured to be invited to the ceremony and had no intention of missing a second of it. Her bubeleh was getting married so she was going to be there to support him. Naturally. She was wearing her best straw hat for the occasion, and her tightest corsets, and her plump arms were full of equally plump gifts, a bolster dangling before her skirt like a fat sausage, the folded bulk of a patchwork quilt, homemade and stuffed to capacity, one of Mr Monickendam's rich cakes for the groom and an armful of red roses for the bride. What with the tight corsets, the bulky parcels and the heat of the day, she was finding it difficult to breath and was quite pink in the face in consequence. But what of that? It was her Davey's wedding day.

Ten minutes later Mr Morrison arrived from work and came quietly up the steps to join her, bearing an unobtrusive cardboard box, and smiling shyly. The two of them stood together in the sunshine and told one another what a fine day it was, because there were so many other things that couldn't be said. Neither of them knew that Emmanuel was standing on the other side of the road. Not that Dumpling would have changed her behaviour in any way if she had.

He had taken great care to keep well out of sight in the shelter of the pawnbroker's side entrance, for it wouldn't have done to let David see him. There'd be trouble enough when Rachel was told, ai-yi, without that. But he couldn't stay away, not even to please his wife. He wanted to see his son's wedding, to feel he was offering support even if nobody could see it. You need support when you marry, he remembered. So young you are, so little you know. And he grieved again to think that David was marrying alone, except for Raizel, and in secret, when he ought to have been escorted by all the men in his family. Ai yi!

While he was sighing, David arrived, jumping down from a tram, striding across the road, leaping the steps two at a time, young and eager and obviously happy. And there was the bride tripping towards him through the crowds, trim in a new white blouse, her face shining under the brim of an enormous Floradora hat. Such a pretty pair, he sighed, as they caught hands and smiled their love at each other. Then there was a bustle on the steps as Mrs Levy's son arrived and he and David cuffed one another in greeting and they all disappeared into the building.

It was too late for argument. The modern world was rushing them all onwards, regardless of their feelings. Now he could only stand on the edge of the affair and pluck his beard and grieve. He shifted his feet miserably and sighed and prepared himself for a long wait.

But they were very quick. It hardly seemed any time at all before the party emerged into the sunlight again, all talking at once and laughing and making such a noise he could hear them above the traffic. There seemed to be more of them now but as they were all on the move, hugging and darting and dancing about, it was difficult to tell. It wasn't until a photographer arrived and stood them in line enough to get a picture that he saw they'd been joined by a plump girl in a pink blouse and a woman who looked like her mother, and was certainly mothering the bride. Relations maybe? Nu, he grunted with approval, just as well, for she was young too and needed support every bit as much as David. Although at the moment, he had to admit, they looked as though they had been blessed. She was clinging to David's arm and smiling with such obvious happiness, it brought a lump to his throat to see it, and David's face was glowing in the sunshine, his dark hair springing above his forehead as thick as a mane. Their guests were throwing confetti into the air above their heads, and soon his white shirt and her white blouse were dotted with bright colour so that they seemed to be shimmering.

'Happy the bride the sun shines on,' the motherly lady called.

And Emmanuel said, 'Amen.'

And then it was over, and they were all going their separate ways, back to work and the ordinary world. Even the bride and groom were parting, and that gave him a pang of the sharpest regret, for it seemed unnatural and cruel. But it was all too late, the steps were empty and the street was full of strangers. Sighing, he trailed back to his work and the dread of the evening when Rachel would finally have to be told.

It rather surprised him when David came back from work that evening as though nothing had happened. But surprise rapidly changed to pity, for David and his mother, when he saw how clumsily the boy was handling this moment.

'You vill eat now, nu?' Rachel asked timidly. '*Kugel* ve got.'

'No, Mama,' he said and his voice was brusque. 'I ain't stoppin'. You might as well know. I only come home ter pack, then I'm off.'

'Off?' she said, hurt and bewildered. 'Vhat you mean off?'

'I got married terday,' he told her, his voice cold and his expression withdrawn as though she were an enemy. 'I've come home to get me things, then I'm off.'

'*Gottenyu!*' Rachel whispered. Dear God! And she sat down weakly on the edge of his truckle bed as though she'd lost the use of her legs. 'Emmanuel?'

'It is true, bubeleh,' he had to confess. '*Nebbish.*'

David had left a cardboard box out on the balcony. Now he retrieved it and began to fill it with his possessions, his paper and brushes, his paintbox, his folders, his two spare shirts, keeping his eyes firmly focused on his own hands and working with dreadful speed. She watched him silently, too stunned and miserable to speak, her face pale and drawn, and it seemed to Emmanuel that even her eyes were shrinking.

It was over so quickly. The box was packed and tied together with string. The cover on the truckle bed was straightened. One dry brief kiss was dropped on his mother's bowed head. 'I will visit you,' he said, and he was gone. It was as quick and cruel and unnatural as the wedding.

Then the storm broke, and she began to wail, a wordless keening, on and on and on. 'Ai-yi-yi-yi-yi!'

'Don't cry, dolly,' he begged, smoothing her hair. 'Don't cry, my chicken. Sooner or later ve had to let him go. You know that, nu?' But she didn't hear him.

It wasn't long before Rivke arrived. 'I seen your Davey ...' she began, but then she saw Rachel's stricken face. 'Rachel bubeleh, vhat's the matter, dolly?'

Emmanuel explained as well as he could, but the fury gathering on his sister's face chilled the words on his tongue.

'Married?' she shouted. 'Vhat you mean married? He's eighteen yet. He ain't old enough. Permission he'd need. You ain't give permission, Manny. You ain't never give permission. Don't tell me that.'

'If I could tell you different, I'd tell you different,' Emmanuel sighed. 'He'd a' married her anyvay, I tell you.'

Rivke's right eye seemed in imminent danger of sliding off her cheek, her distress was so acute. 'A fine *chawchem* ve got here, Rachel,' she cried. 'He give permission! Oy oy oy! Ve vas vearin' him down. Vearin' him down, good. Another two, three veeks vould a' seen all the difference. For vhy you vant to do this fool thing?'

'All my childer I lose,' Rachel wailed. 'All! All! Only Davey ... For vhy he do this, Rivke?'

'To let him marry vid a *shiksa*!' Rivke said. 'Begin vid strange vomen, end vid strange gods, I tell you. Oy oy!'

'I never see him again, I tell you,' Rachel wept. 'Never ever again.'

Then the rest of the family came trooping into the flat, agog for news, Ben and Becky, Jo and his wife, Josh and Maggie and their children, and the noise of astonishment, disbelief and commiseration was so loud it was impossible to hear what anybody was saying, which Emmanuel thought wryly was just as well. When Dumpling came in through the open door ten minutes later they were all shouting at once and Rachel and Rivke were crying with abandon. She made quite a good job of pretending surprise, but there wasn't any possibility of speech among all that clashing sound. She pushed her way through the howling bodies until she reached her crumpled brother, sitting in the eye of the storm, with his head bent, enduring.

'So I tell you,' she said, stooping so that her mouth was just above his ear, '*you* are the best brother in the whole vide vorld.' And she cuddled his beleaguered head against her bosom, and dropped tears of pity on his poor thin hair. 'Every day I say thanks to the good Lord for such a brother.'

By the time the shop was shut that evening, Mrs Ellen Cheifitz was feeling very tired. She seemed to have been on her feet all day, running from one moment to the next, and now her back ached and her feet were sore, and to make matters worse she was hungry too, having missed her midday meal. She gathered her belongings together and packed them neatly in Mrs Miller's carpet bag, and told Maudie not to cry, and at nine o'clock finally let herself out of the staff entrance into the gaslit street, where to her great relief David was waiting for her.

He took the carpet bag without a word and tucking her hand into the crook of his arm, led her away to the steak house in Norton Folgate.

'It's all very well this gettin' married lark,' he said, 'but it don't 'alf make you hungry.' It was necessary to put a pleasant experience between himself and his cruelty to his mother. 'I'm starvin'.'

'So'm I.'

They had a sixpenny steak and fried onions, a great treat, and then much refreshed and with their energies restored, set off arm in arm to take possession of their kingdom.

It was very quiet in Quaker Street, for most of the inhabitants were home from work and settled, glad to be at ease behind their own closed doors and open windows. The hall was empty, there was no sign of their landlady, and no sound from the rooms below theirs. At the top of the stairs, where their front door blocked off the rest of the house, he put down the carpet bag and took out his key.

'Groom carries bride over threshold,' he said, picking her up in his arms as though she were a baby.

'Daft ha'p'orth,' she laughed at him, holding him tightly round the neck. 'You'll drop me.'

But he didn't. He carried her easily and tenderly, kicking the carpet bag before them, then waiting for her to pull the door shut behind them. And then they were on their own at last in

292

the darkness of their narrow landing with the door to their bedroom invitingly open.

'Welcome home!' he said.

They slept late next morning and didn't get up till nearly eight o'clock, long after the factory sirens had woken them.

'Luxury, nu?' he said, opening the curtains. 'What's for breakfast?'

'After all you ate last night!' she mocked, laughing up at him from the pillows. 'You got hollow legs?'

'Good healthy appetite,' he said, and then the sight of her gazing up at him so lovingly aroused another appetite and he went back to the bed to kiss her hopefully.

'Did we really oughter be goin' on like this?' she asked when they finally settled down to their bread and jam breakfast. There was no anxiety in the question, only gratified pleasure and a passing curiosity.

But he took it quite seriously. 'Oh yes,' he said. 'It says so in the Shulchan Aruch. "A healthy man should perform his duties nightly." '

'What's the Shulchan Aruch when it's at home?'

'It's a book with all the laws in. All the Jewish laws.'

'D'you mean ter say you got laws about … that?' It was an amazing idea. The only thing she could ever remember the priests saying about it was that it was sinful and you shouldn't.

'We got laws about everything,' he said laughing.

'An' the law says every night?' It was making her shiver to think of it.

'If that's what the wife wants. It's up to her.'

That was another extraordinary idea. She bit her bread and jam and thought about it.

'Tell you another thing,' he went on, 'after the first time, we're supposed to say a prayer.'

'Never!'

'Don't laugh. It's a good prayer. You'd like it.'

'Go on then. Tell us.'

He licked his fingers clean of jam and took both her hands in his, very gently. 'Blessed art thou, oh Lord our God,' he quoted, 'King of the universe, who has planted a nut tree in Eden.'

'A nut tree in Eden,' she said, charmed by the image. 'Yes, you're right. It *is* a good prayer. I like it. A nut tree in Eden.'

He kissed her fingers. 'It will grow to the most beautiful tree anyone's ever seen,' he said. 'I promise.'

And so the weeks passed and the tree grew and they were happy in their private Eden and almost forgot about their parents, although David went to the synagogue with his father every Friday. Before they knew it, it was September and the coalmen were hawking their wares in the streets of Shoreditch and the Thames was grey with the chill of autumn.

It was quite cold in their two attic rooms, especially first thing in the morning, when the lino struck chill under bare feet warm from bed.

'I shall make a rag rug,' she decided.

'I'll design it.'

'I'll ask me sister fer rags. They're bound to 'ave lots in that great house.'

'I'll ask Papa, shall I?'

She thought about it, puckering her forehead. "Would 'e mind?'

He was delighted, although he did no more than nod his head in agreement when David asked him. They had taken to walking along Fournier Street when they came out of the synagogue on a Friday evening. It gave them a chance to talk to one another and extended the time they could be together.

For David, going to synagogue was more often painful than rewarding. It was surprising how frequently the Rabbi spoke of the blessings of a good Jewish marriage, or read the story of Ruth and Naomi. 'Thy God shall be my God.' What a marvellous thing for a woman to promise. And to her mother-in-law too!

Oh, if only Ellen could cook like Aunty Dumpling, he would think. What a difference that would make! But she cooked such English things, cottage pie and chops, and he didn't really enjoy them at all. And when he brought a Jewish dish home, she wrinkled her nose and ate it slowly as though she was forcing it down. It was all very difficult. Still, at least she was obviously trying to make a home for them, and that was commendable. Look how his father was commending it.

294

'A sensible woman, nu?' Emmanuel approved as they reached Christ Church and Itchy Park. 'I see vhat I find.'

There was a brown paper parcel full of off-cuts left at the top of the stairs to greet them when they came home from work next day. The note pinned to the topmost piece read, 'I can get more for you. You tell me the colour maybe. Papa.'

From that moment on, the rug became a labour of love for all three of them.

It was certainly very big, large enough to cover the entire space in front of their little fireplace, and when it was finished, they both declared it made the whole room warm and cosy, and Ellen wondered whether they ought to invite David's parents for a meal to show them how fine it was.

'Not just yet,' he said. They had to choose exactly the right moment. His mother was still too angry to speak to him, as he knew because he asked his father about her, anxiously, every Friday. 'Better we just wait a bit longer, bubeleh. We ain't seen your Ma neither, don't ferget.'

'Time enough fer them later on,' Ellen said, patting her work of art. 'Feel how soft that bit a' velvet is.' She had no desire to see either of her parents, then or later.

But as it happened, she saw them both sooner than she intended.

It was Wednesday evening and outside their living room the sky was heavy with purple cloud and rain was rattling the windows. She was feeling specially pleased with herself that evening. She'd cooked fish for supper, inside their little gas oven what's more, and to her surprise it had turned out quite tasty, although she wasn't sure whether David had liked it or not. He never said anything about the food they ate, and she wished he would. Now they were sitting on either side of the fire, working on the next rug, he cutting cloth into strips, she hooking strips into sacking.

And suddenly, without any warning at all, she knew that her mother was in trouble. The knowledge drained all colour from her face. 'Oh dear,' she said. 'Oh dear, oh dear!'

He recognized one of her 'moments' and put his scissors down at once. 'What is it, bubeleh?'

295

'It's Ma,' she said, and her eyes weren't looking at him, but inwards to some vague unfocused centre. 'She's hurt. Not bad, I don't think. I can hear 'er cryin'. It'll be the ol' man, I'll bet any money. Poor Ma.'

'Whatcher want ter do?'

She went on watching her inner world for several seconds, her face perplexed, and her hands fumbling the cloth, and when she finally lifted her head and looked at him he had to repeat his question, because it was plain she hadn't heard him the first time.

'I'll 'ave ter go over,' she said.

'Now?'

'If you don't mind.'

'I'll come with you,' he said at once. And when she looked worried, 'I won't come in. I'll wait round the corner. Be there if you need me, nu?'

'You're a love,' she said, already putting on her coat and hat. 'It's daft really, but I know she's in trouble.'

'You don't have to explain,' he said, putting on his own coat. 'Come on.'

It was a cold journey to Russell Street and they were both shivering by the time they got off the tram at the London Hospital.

'You wait in the porch out the wet,' Ellen said, glancing at the hospital entrance. 'I'll be as quick as I can.'

'You know where I am if you need me.'

The rain was running off the brim of her hat onto her shoulders. 'Course,' she said. 'I can 'andle 'em, you know. I've 'ad years a' practice.'

But he worried about her all the time she was gone, and she seemed to be gone a very long time.

When she came back she was scowling with anger. ' 'E's give 'er a black eye,' she said. 'I dunno why she sticks it.'

'Where is he now?'

'Up the pub, spendin' 'er wages. Come on quick, there's our tram.'

As the tram rattled them back along the Whitechapel Road, past the sodden plane trees and the fine houses she'd admired so much when she first came there to find the flat, she told him the rest of the story. Her mother had refused to hand over her earnings, pleading that some of it, 'on'y some, gel!' should be set aside for food, and after a row he'd lost his temper and beaten her.

'She 'ad a letter from her cousin too. She showed me. Ever such a nice letter. Said to come to Liverpool an' take the kids an' live there with 'er, an' the silly fool writ back an' said no. I ask yer! To 'ave a chance like that an' turn it down. I'd a' gone like a shot out've a gun.' She looked so splendidly fierce, he wanted to kiss her.

'She loves him maybe?'

'She couldn't. 'E's a brute.'

They travelled on in silence for a little, while she scowled and he admired. 'Anyway,' she said. 'I promised ter go an' see 'er again next Wednesday. She's on early shift. Shan't need an escort. 'E'll be at the brewery.'

'Better news then maybe,' he hoped.

It wasn't just better. It was extraordinary.

When Ellen arrived late that afternoon the door to her mother's room was wide open, and the floorboards were damp. Nell was on her knees scrubbing out the last corner. 'Nearly done,' she said. 'Step over the wet, there's a good gel.' The two kids were sitting on the table surrounded by bundles.

'Whatcher doin', Ma?' Surely she wasn't leaving the flat. Not after all the good work she'd done to get it her in the first place.

'Movin' out,' her mother said, and she sounded proud, which was most unlike her. 'Should a' done it years ago. Movin' out.'

The pride started a new idea. 'Leavin' 'im d'yer mean?'

'That's right. We're off ter Liverpool. I got the tickets. Jest a matter a' finishin' up 'ere, that's all. I want ter leave it nice fer Mrs Nym. She's been ever so good to us.'

'Well, good fer you, Ma,' Ellen said. ' 'Ere, give us that bucket. I'll empty it for yer.'

'Ta,' her mother said, lifting herself from her knees, gradually and one foot at a time, as she always did when her back was aching. Poor Ma, Ellen thought, recognizing what the careful movement revealed, she's 'ad a rotten life of it. She

297

carried the heavy pail out onto the landing, wondering how her mother had found the energy to escape after all those awful years. 'What's brought this about, Ma?' she called over her shoulder.

Her mother was hanging up the net curtains. They'd been washed too and as they were still wet, they took a bit of arranging. 'Oh I dunno, gel,' she said. 'One thing an' another. 'E said some beastly things ter Mrs Nym. No call fer it, there wasn't. I've left 'er the curtains. Make amends, sort a' thing.'

' 'E sicked up on them curtains,' Maudie said. 'Two nights runnin'.'

'Well, they're all washed lovely now,' Nell said, giving them a last shake. 'Whatcher think, Ellie?'

'Best thing you've ever done,' her daughter approved, hugging her. 'Should a' done it years ago.' Even though she knew they were saying goodbye, and recognized, in a vague way, that they'd be very unlikely ever to see one another again, she was warm with pleasure at her mother's decision.

'You'll be all right, wontcher, gel?' her mother said. 'You got a good job, aintcher? You can look after yerself?'

She needs reassuring, Ellen thought, looking at her mother's anxious face, and her pleasure increased at the knowledge of how easily it could be done. 'I'll be fine,' she said, superbly casual. 'I got married last month.'

'Oh Ellie!' her mother said, turning away from the curtains to look at her wearily and with immense pity. 'An' you said you'd never. Who is it?'

'David Cheifitz. An' 'fore you start, you might as well know 'e's a Jew.'

'I never said nothink,' Nell protested weakly. 'There's no call ter go jumpin' down me froat like that, gel. Is 'e good to yer?'

'Yes, 'e is. Good as gold.'

'Well, I s'pose that's all right then. There, I've packed all I can. D'yer think young Maudie'll be able ter carry all this lot.'

' 'Course,' Maudie said. And she climbed down from the table and slung her bundle over her shoulder, trying not to buckle under the weight of it. 'There's yours, Johnnie.'

'We're off then,' Nell said. 'Look after yerself, duck.'

'Send me a postcard.'

'Um,' her mother said vaguely. 'You 'old yer brother's 'and, Maudie, there's a good gel.'

They bumped their bundles down Mrs Nym's brown staircase, blinking in the darkness. It was an odd way to be saying goodbye, Ellen thought, and realized that she was growing sadder with every descending step.

'Give you a bit of advice,' Nell said abruptly to her eldest daughter as they stood on the doorstep together for the last time.

'What?' Ellen said, lifted by an equally sudden delight. Her mother loved her after all. Advice! Who'd a' thought it?

'If you 'ave curtains at yer windows, always see they 'ang straight. Nothink looks worse'n twisted curtains. You take my word fer it. Ah well, ta-ta, gel.' And she was gone, drooping under the weight of her bundles with a burdened child on either side of her.

For a second, Ellen didn't know whether to laugh or cry. Then she saw the funny side and began to giggle. She was still laughing when she got back to Quaker Street, and by then her laughter was entire and infectious. David had just come home from work and she told him what had happened between gasps of mirth she couldn't suppress. Soon he was laughing too, and she had tears streaming down her cheeks.

But secretly he knew he was glad that her awful mother and those dirty children had taken themselves out of her life. Now if only his mother would accept her ...

Chapter Twenty-Three

Just before Christmas, when David was busy drawing shop windows full of toys, and boxes of garish crackers and over-burdened Christmas trees, and wondering why he was squandering his art on such trivial nonsense, a letter arrived at the *Essex Magazine*. It had been forwarded by Mr Eswyn Smith and was a request from Mrs Fulmington for a second portrait of her 'dear Fifi.'

'What a bit a' luck!' Ellen said. 'Just think, we could buy ourselves a dresser.' She'd had her heart set on a dresser ever since they got married. It was such a respectable piece of furniture. 'A nice dresser with hooks fer the cups an' everything. I could keep it lovely.' If she could furnish this room really well it wouldn't be quite such an ordeal to invite his parents to tea, which was something she knew he wanted.

'So we trade the fat Fifi for a nice respectable dresser,' he promised.

It was done within the week. Mrs Fulmington greeted him like an old friend and said she'd be more than happy to pay the six guineas he suggested, and Fifi, who had grown fatter than ever, was also a good deal more amenable and sat still long enough for him to catch a likeness on the first afternoon.

The dresser was a triumph. Even though they only had two cups to hang on it. 'I'll get another commission, maybe,' David hoped, 'then we'll buy a tea set, nu?'

He got three, within two days of each other, as his gushing patron spread the word and displayed his talent. 'If this goes on,' he said happily, 'we can have a chest a' drawers an' a new bed an' all.'

The second commission was a Christmas portrait of a

husband and wife, the third was another awkward child, the fourth was Mrs Hiram B. Stellenbosch. 'A friend of my dear husband's,' Mrs Fulmington wrote. 'An American, but a great lady nonetheless, I do assure you.'

She was certainly rich and had a huge house in Tredegar Square to prove it. An ostentatious house, crammed with large expensive furniture and so many *objets d'art* it made his head spin to look at them. The hall contained two full-length gilt mirrors, a gilt table heaped with hothouse plants, three mounted animal heads, a suit of armour, and an aspidistra in a jardinière considerably bigger than he was. And the drawing room was even more impressive.

It was thickly carpeted and full of massive sofas and overstuffed armchairs, upholstered in heavy dark blue velvet to match the curtains which were looped and ruched and draped like bustles. The mantelpiece was green marble and the fireplace, which was surrounded by huge red, blue and green tiles, contained a fire mounded halfway up the chimney. There were lustres everywhere, glittering in the firelight, on the mantelpiece among vases and statuettes and ormolu clocks, on side tables among more hothouse flowers, even on their own gilt stands in front of the two circular wall mirrors. And the walls themselves were hung with the most elaborate wallpaper, all exotic plants and badly drawn peacocks on a dark green ground. It probably cost the earth, David thought. It seemed rather a waste because so little of it was actually on display, since the walls were crowded with sentimental pictures, of winsome little girls with impossibly large eyes, and clean, soulful dogs, and improbably thin ladies draped in blue gauze and looking tragically into the middle distance. I hope she won't want all this in the background, David thought, it'd be ever such a job. Nevertheless such ostentation was more than enough excuse to up the fee. By the time Mrs Stellenbosch gushed into the room on a cloud of potent perfume, it had reached double figures. But his first sight of her very nearly made him forget it.

She was a small fat woman, and she was wearing full evening dress, a white satin gown with a long awkward train, and a very low décolletage which revealed far too much of her far too ample bosom. The front of the gown was decorated with strips of ruched ribbon set with pearls, but it was pulled so tightly over her corsets that all the material above and round her waist was ridged and distorted. Her face was heavily powdered and she was wearing a dusky pink rouge on her cheeks and a similar colouring on her lips. What hair she had was dyed red, but as there was so little of it she had augmented it with artificial curls, which weren't quite the same colour. The whole concoction was drawn up on top of her head in a tortoiseshell mound and topped with a frond of milk-white feathers. She had a triple choker of pearls round her neck and so many rings on her fat fingers he couldn't count them. He had never seen anyone so grotesque.

'Ma dear Mr Cheifitz,' she said, gliding towards him, hands outstretched, 'so good of you. I know *everything* about you. Ma dear friend Chah-lotte gave me the most in-tie-mate description. Pray do sit down.' At close quarters, her perfume was so strong it made his eyes sting.

He backed away from her and sat on the edge of one of her dark blue chairs while she told him how she wanted 'an in-tie-mate portrait for ma dear Hiram. He thinks the world of me, Mr Cheifitz. The whole wi-ide world. So any little thing ah can do for him …'

The flow continued for quite a long time, which was just as well for it gave David a chance to get his breath back and remember his fee. Ten guineas didn't worry the lady at all. 'When ah know I'm buyin' a work of real art, Mr Cheifitz.'

So the work of real art was begun, and two pencil sketches completed which the lady declared 'real charming!' and David escaped into the fresh air of Tredegar Square, where a flurry of snow finally cooled his embarrassment.

'She was awful!' he said to Ellen later that evening when he'd finished describing the lady.

'Never mind,' she comforted, smiling at him. 'Think a' the fee. We can buy all sorts a' things with ten guineas.' It was a fortune, and it had come just at the right time.

He worked on the portrait that night, painting in some of the background detail and getting Ellen to model for the lady's hair so that he could get it to look natural. 'I'm earning this money by tellin' lies,' he said sadly. 'It ain't right, bubeleh.'

'Artistic licence,' she said, smiling. 'That ain't lies. You said so yerself.'

But there was something so false and gushing and horrible about this lady and her portrait, he wasn't at all sure, and made up his mind to paint as much of it at home as he possibly could. By the time he returned for the second sitting, the background was very nearly finished and so was Ellen's hair, and he'd pencilled in the lines of her lovely slender figure inside that dreadful gown.

Mrs Stellenbosch said he made her look perfectly charming. 'You see more in me, mah dear, than even mah own dear Hiram. It takes an artist to see to the soul of a woman, ah've always said so.' And she arranged herself on the blue sofa, leaning forward slightly so that he could see her bosom as well as her soul. 'We have so much in common, don't you think so, Mr Cheifitz?'

What on earth could he say in answer to that? He stood at his easel and painted with the speed of panic, hoping she didn't mean what she seemed to be saying. He was so close to the fire the heat was making him sweat but he didn't dare move, for moving would have taken precious time and, what was worse, might give her an excuse to get up from the sofa. He knew, instinctively, that the one thing he shouldn't do was to allow her to move any closer to him than she already was. All the dire warnings he'd ever heard against evil women rang in his mind, 'For the lips of a strange woman drop as a honeycomb, but her end is bitter as wormwood.' 'A man should never be alone with a strange woman.' 'Avoid the lure of the painted woman.' And his mother's voice, 'So keep your eyes down, my son. Vhat you don't see don't hurt you.'

But how could he paint her without looking at her? He glanced up quickly, to check the line of her nose, and was more alarmed than ever. She *was* giving him the eye, *has vesholem*. It wasn't his imagination. Oy oy! How could he discourage her without making her angry? 'Would you like Mr Stellanbosch to see how it's gettin' on?' he suggested. A chaperone would make everything much easier.

'I'm sure he would just *love* to, Mr Cheifitz, but just at this present mo-ment he is right on the other side of the Atlantic, in little ol' New Orleans. I have this great house all to mahself, mah dear. Now don't you give mah Hiram a *thought*!'

Worse and worse, David thought, painting the nose very badly, and glancing at the ormolu clock to see how much longer he had to endure. The eyes weren't right, but he daren't look at *them*. I'll do the rest of the face, he thought, and finish the eyes when I get home. But even glancing at her face seemed dangerous now. He worked in silence, scowling at the paper, keeping his head down.

'It is a fact, is it not, Mr Cheifitz,' the lady went on, 'that the artist has the most ex-quisite sensibilities, the most ex-quisite.' He mumbled agreement but she didn't seem to be listening. 'Take the Pre-Raphaelite brotherhood, for instance. Mah dear, the things they did! But of course, you would know far more about the Pre-Raphaelite brotherhood than little ol' me. They do say Dante Gabriel Rossetti had a mistress who took poison, but that I don't believe. What do you think, Mr Cheifitz?'

'I couldn't say,' he said, blushing at the indelicacy of the topic. 'You could turn your head to the side just a little maybe. Thank you.' Anything to get her to stop talking like this.

She held the pose for a minute or two, and without talking, so that the room was suddenly and blissfully quiet. I'll do the white feathers next, he was thinking, when she stood up, did her best to smooth down the creases in her gown and strode across to the fireplace to ring the bell.

'Ah have a surprise for you, Mr Cheifitz,' she said. As if she hadn't surprised him enough!

'Should I continue?' he said, brush in hand, hesitating.

'No, no.'

He began to clean his brushes, relieved that his ordeal was so nearly over. And the butler entered, followed by an anxious man in a cook's hat, who was pushing a dinner wagon laden with covered dishes. 'A little supper, Mr Cheifitz. You *will* join me, will you not?'

It was almost impossible to refuse her. The butler opened a bottle of wine with an explosion that made him jump, then the servants retreated and the covers were removed, but by now he was so tense and nervous he had no idea what food was being offered.

'Champagne, mah dear,' the lady said, pouring out a glass full of white bubbles. 'Cold beef, ham, tongue, a little Russian salad? Or would you like me to choose for you?' He took the fizzy liquid and nodded helplessly at her, and at that she patted the sofa and smiled at him archly. 'You must come and sit beside me, you know,' she ordered.

It was like a nightmare, slow-moving but inevitable. He took a sip of the champagne and found that the bubbles were sharp. He set the glass down quickly on a little table beside the sofa. Then because he couldn't think how to avoid it, and she was bullying him with her eyes, he sat down beside her, like a mouse in a trap, and was given a table napkin to cover his knees and received a plate piled with unfamiliar meats and salads, and an unwieldy fork to eat it all with. And his heart was thumping with fear of her.

'Ah have the greatest admiration for the artist,' she told him, forking cold meat into her mouth. 'The *greatest*.'

He ate some potato salad politely and tried to smile.

'Ah really do feel the artist should have our permission to live in total freedom. If a man of talent takes a mistress, well what of that? It is only natural, after all. In America we take a more liberal view of such things, Mr Cheifitz. Have some more of that Waldorf salad, it's very good.'

He helped himself to the salad, and realized that she'd given him a thick slice of ham. But that was the least of his troubles at the moment.

Then, to his horror, she leaned across and patted him on the knee. 'A young man like you, Mr Cheifitz,' she said. 'A young man of talent should have a patron, wouldn't you say so? Or a patroness. A rich American, maybe, with a husband out of the country. Wha'd'you think?'

It was intolerable. He couldn't bear any more. She was ogling him, leaning at him, holding his knee in fingers like claws, so that the flesh all over his body cringed as it contracted away from her. He put his plate on the side table and stood up so abruptly that her clutching fingers were dislodged and trailed down his trouser leg dragging the table napkin with them. He was white in the face and trembling. 'No, Mrs Stellenbosch,' he said. 'No, no, no,' blundering towards the door, stumbling over stools, bumping into chairs, but escaping. He could hear her voice behind him, 'Mr Cheifitz, mah dear!' but nothing mattered now except getting away from her. And getting away as quickly as possible. 'Her end is bitter as wormwood. The strange woman. Jezebel.'

It wasn't until he was on the tram and rocking past the People's Palace that he realized he'd left his paints and brushes behind him. But it didn't matter. Nothing mattered now except getting away. Getting away and going safely home to Ellen, to his own dear, modest, beautiful Ellen who was everything Mrs Stellenbosch was not.

He ran through Mrs Undine's open door and hurtled up the stairs, careless of the noise he was making. His heart was still beating fearfully as he opened his own front door and rushed the last few steps into his own front room. Ellen was sitting beside their modest fire, in her modest white blouse, with her thick dark hair loose down her back and her boots on the rag rug, patiently sewing, the little pieces of white cloth in her hands clearly illuminated by the gaslight above her. The relief he felt was so overpowering he had to sit down. He folded his long legs under him and knelt on the rug at her feet, dropping his head onto her lap, and clasping the rough wool of her skirt with both hands. 'Ellen bubeleh, I *do* love yer.'

She put the sewing down at once and held his head between her hands as though he were a child in need of comfort. 'What is it? What's up? Tell your Ellen.'

The words poured out, unstoppable. He told of insinuations, ham, champagne, being given the eye, rouge, Jezebel, fire-heat, embarrassment, the awful moment when that awful woman grabbed his knee, all jumbled up with no sense or sequence, and she held his head and listened, watching his eyes. It wasn't always possible to understand his words, but his emotions were as clear as daylight. 'My poor Davey,' she said when he finally stopped for breath. 'It's no fun bein' pawed about. Don' I know it! Then what 'appened?'

'I ran. Straight out the house.'

' 'Ere,' she said, noticing he'd returned empty-handed,

'where's yer paints an' things?'

'I left 'em behind,' he admitted sheepishly.

She withdrew her hands and looked at him crossly. 'You never! Whatcher want ter go an' do a thing like that for? All the money you spent.'

'I jest ran,' he said, feeling a bit aggrieved that she didn't understand. 'You wouldn't a' wanted me to stay an' run risks, would yer?'

'Risks!' she said, and her eyes were brightening as though she was going to laugh. Surely she couldn't be going to laugh. 'Oh Davey! You wasn't in any risk. You on'y 'ad ter say "no". After all, she couldn't very well make you do nothink, now could she?'

'I *couldn't* a' stayed!' He was horrified that she should even suggest it. 'She was making advances!'

'If you'd been a shop gel you'd a' been fightin' off advances every day a' yer life,' she said, tartly. 'How d'yer think we managed? That's daft, runnin' off an' leavin' all yer things. Well, you'll jest 'ave ter go back tomorrow an' get 'em.'

The idea filled him with such horror he let go of her skirt and sat back on his heels to get a good look at her. He could hardly believe his ears. He'd run home so fast, aching for her sympathy, and now she was mocking him. 'I ain't goin' back,' he said, and the truculent note of his childhood darkened his voice.

'An' did you get yer fee?'

He'd forgotten all about his fee. 'No.'

'You'll go back fer that then, surely ter goodness.'

'No,' he insisted. 'Don't you understand? I can't go there ever again. Not after this.'

'That's ten guineas you're throwing away. How am I supposed to get this place decent? You want your mother ter come an' see it, dontcher?'

What had his mother got to do with it? 'We ain't poor, Ellen,' he said. 'I earn a good wage. I don't have to go grovelling to a woman like that fer money.'

'If we ain't poor,' she said fiercely, 'it's because I work an' all, don't ferget. S'pose I couldn't go on workin'. We'd be poor enough then. We'd need them ten guineas right enough then.'

'But you *are* workin',' he said, baffled by the turn the conversation had suddenly taken.

'Not fer long,' she said, and now she was glaring at him, almost hatefully. 'That's the point. 'Nother couple a' months I shan't be workin' no more. What then?'

'Why not, Ellen?' he asked, still bewildered but feeling anxious too.

'We got a baby on the way,' she said flatly. 'That's why not. Now can you see why you got ter to go an' get them things?'

It took a little while for the information to percolate through the dullness of misery this first unexpected row had pressed down upon him. But when it did he was filled with exploding happiness. 'A baby! You clever, clever girl! You sure?'

Despite her annoyance, his delight was infectious. 'Yes,' she said laughing at him. 'Oh yes, I'm sure.' She'd missed three times now, and by the evening she felt so queasy there really wasn't any doubt. 'I was tryin' ter find the right time to tell yer.' An' I done that with a vengeance, she thought ruefully. But it was too late now.

He threw his arms round her and cuddled her protectively. A child. It was the best piece of news a man could ever be given. 'When?' he asked.

'Beginnin' a' June.'

'You clever, clever girl.'

For the next half hour they spoke of nothing but the baby, rejoicing with kisses, and happy with hope. But then she asked a question that plummeted them both down into misery again.

'So you'll go back fer the fee?' It was almost a rhetorical question now, she felt so sure the answer would be yes.

'I can't, bubeleh. I would if I could, but I can't.'

All her joy ebbed away. He said he loved her, and he couldn't even do that for her. 'We'd better get ter bed,' she said wearily, removing herself from his arms. 'We shall never get up in the morning else.' Perhaps she'd have more energy to argue in the morning.

For the first time in their married life they slept back to back and miserable. Neither of them felt inclined to cuddle, he because he still felt humiliated and unclean, she because she was hurt by what she saw as pig-headed selfishness. He could make an effort if he wanted to, she thought. It ain't much to ask, specially when you compare it to carryin' a baby fer nine months. We shall be ever so short a' money if 'e goes on like this. *I'll* go back to that woman tomorrer an' get 'is things. She don't scare me. I'll give her such a piece a' my mind. 'E won't get no more commissions anyway. Not after carryin' on like that. Well, there's on'y one thing for it. I shall 'ave ter go on workin' for as long as I can, that's all.

But that was easier thought than done. She went to Tredegar Square the very next afternoon and was told to wait, by a very snooty butler, who presently returned with a brown paper parcel that contained all his things. But there was no fee, and despite all her pleading he wouldn't go and ask for it. It took them more than two weeks before they could recover their balance with one another and begin to forget what had happened. And in the meantime her pregnancy had become just a little more obvious.

Hiding her marriage from the staff of Hopkins and Peggs had been easy enough. She'd simply gone on answering to 'Miss White', and taken off her wedding ring before she left the house in the morning. She'd worn it, of course, but on a ribbon round her neck, hidden away under her blouse. It had upset David the first time he saw what she was doing.

'So now you're ashamed of me, nu?' he'd said, face darkening. 'You want to hide we're married?'

'Davey, Davey,' she cried, running into his arms to bombard him with kisses. 'You ain't never ter think that. Never. Never. Never.'

'So you hide your ring,' he said, holding his body stiffly, unyielding.

'It's fer work,' she said. 'If I tell them I'm married, they'll give me the sack. Jest fer bein' married. That ain't fair.'

He had to agree it wasn't, and after that it was relatively easy to persuade him. 'It ain't deceit,' she said. 'I just don't tell 'em, that's all. You don't want us to be poor, do yer? Not when we're goin' on so well and gettin' everything so lovely.' And she kissed him again, so lovingly that he put his doubts aside and kissed her back.

But hiding a pregnancy was another matter. She could obscure the increasing size of her breasts simply by pouching the bodice of her blouse. It was high fashion to wear a blouse in this way and as half the other girls quickly copied her example, there was nothing remarkable about her appearance. At the start. Besides, Christmas kept them all too busy for gossip, and after Christmas there were the New Year sales.

But soon it was February and trade was slack, and the difficulties of disguise increased with her girth. As her waist grew thicker and her belly swelled, she tried every trick she knew. She let out all the seams of her skirt as far as they would go, she gave up wearing a belt, and finally, when it was no longer possible to fasten the waistband, she made herself a second looser band and wore it over the top, hoping that no one would notice that the two materials didn't match. It was a vain hope, for gossip was already doing its work.

Jimmy Thatcher started it by remarking to his boss one afternoon that Miss Icy White was looking mighty plump these days. 'Wouldn't surprise me if she wasn't in the pudden club.'

'Nah!' his boss said. 'Not our Miss White.'

'Be a fine thing if the customers was ter find out,' Mr Thatcher insinuated. 'Dontcher think you oughter say sommink?'

Three days later Ellen was summoned upstairs to 'see Miss Elphinstone'.

'It has been brought to my attention, Miss White,' that formidable lady said, looking through her pince-nez at the top of Ellen's skirt, 'that you are in "a condition". Is this so?' The girl's original application form lay on the table between them, with its damning query 'Illegitimate?' She looked at the skirt again. Oh yes, history was repeating itself. What a shame. 'Well?'

Panic fluttered in Ellen's chest. 'It ain't what you think, ma'am.'

'You are not in "a condition"?'

She couldn't avoid the truth. 'Well, yes. But I'm a married woman, Miss Elphinstone. See!' And she hooked her wedding ring out of her blouse and removed it from its ribbon and put it on her finger.

'Dear me,' Miss Elphinstone said, 'and how long has this been going on, pray?'

'Since August, ma'am.'

'Ah!' Miss Elphinstone said, consulting the file again. So that was why she would live out. 'I see. Well, my dear, you realize you can't go on working in this store.'

'No, ma'am.'

'You should have left us in August by rights, of course, but I shan't say anything about that, considering what excellent service you've given us until now. We will give you a week's pay in lieu of notice. Leave by the back stairs if you please. It wouldn't do to have you walking through the shop.'

And that was that. It was so sudden and implacable, she was in the street and walking home before she'd taken it in. Then the tears welled into her eyes in an equally sudden rush, obscuring her vision like a waterfall. She was crying so much she didn't even see Aunty Dumpling waddling towards her. But Dumpling saw her and bundled her into a cushiony embrace, vociferously sympathetic. 'Vhy you veepin', dolly? Vhat they done to my liddle chicken? You ain't sick, bubeleh? It ain't the baby, nu?' her fat face creased with concern.

'They give me the sack,' Ellen sobbed.

'Vhat a lot a' shysters!' Dumpling said indignantly. 'They vant their heads examine. You come home vid your old Aunty Dumpling, dolly. Ve don't take no notice a' them.'

And home they went, to lemon tea and muffins, and an extraordinary sense that she had suddenly become one of the family.

'Ve don't take no notice of that Miss Elphinstone,' Dumpling said, nodding so hard all three of her chins were wobbling. 'Ve feed you up good, nu? Look after the liddle one. You got a cradle, nu?'

'I *do* like your Aunty Dumpling,' she said to David when he got home that night. 'She made such a fuss a' me.'

'Well 'course,' he said. 'You're one a' the family.'

And so it seemed to be. That Friday Dumpling invited them both to the Shabbas meal, which was the first Ellen had ever attended, and which she found curiously moving, although she

311

didn't like the food much. And on Sunday Emmanuel arrived with a little wooden crib, and the bedding to go with it.

Within a week she'd almost forgotten Hopkins and Peggs. Within a month it was as if she'd never done anything else except stay at home and keep house. Somehow or other they seemed to be managing on his wage. They went to Aunty Dumpling's nearly every Friday and now and then they walked down to the Rothschild Building and paid a call on Emmanuel, who welcomed them lovingly, and Rachel, who was distant but at least asked them in.

'It's a great step forward,' David said, as they walked home arm in arm. 'She wasn't going to see me ever again. I think you've done wonders, you an' the baby.' Ellen didn't feel she'd done anything at all, but pregnancy was making her too lethargic to want to argue with anyone, and especially not with David. The baby was making itself felt now, kicking and squirming and very much alive, and that was absorbing and miraculous and far more important than petty family squabbles. As Aunty Dumpling said, 'Vhat joy they bring, these liddle ones!'

Unfortunately, this little one brought a problem.

One afternoon in May, David came home rather later than she expected and announced that he and his father had 'been to see the *mohel* to arrange the brit for the baby'.

It was a hot afternoon and there was very little air up in their attic rooms. She had let the top half of the kitchen window right down in a vain attempt to disperse the heat from the stove. But all that had done was to suck in the sour fumes from the breweries.

'Well I 'ope it's cool whatever it is,' she said, wiping the sweat from her forehead.

He laughed at her lack of knowledge. 'You are lovely!' he said, kissing the top of her head as he passed her on his way to the bowl of water she'd set ready for him. He hung up his jacket, rolled up his shirt sleeves, and plunged his arms into the water. 'Oy! That's better. You're a good wife, bubeleh.'

'So what's this brit when it's at home?' she asked, pleased by his praise.

'It's for our son, when he's ten days old,' he said, throwing water onto his face with both hands. 'Circumcision, you'd call it.' And he groped behind him for the towel.

Usually she would be standing behind him at this point with the towel ready and outstretched. Now she was so surprised and shocked she forgot to offer it. 'Cuttin' him about, do yer mean?' she said.

He blinked his eyes open and took the towel as though she had offered it. 'It's all right, Ellen,' he said, 'It's over in a minute. He'll hardly feel a thing. An' anyway you don't have to be there. It's only the men and the *mohel*. The mother waits in another room with all the other women. Dumpling'll look after you.' His face was dry now. He hung the towel over the rail and smiled at her. 'It's a good job done,' he said, trying to encourage her because she was looking at him so strangely.

She folded her hands protectively over her belly and prepared to give battle. 'If you think you're going ter cut bits off my baby, David Cheifitz,' she said, 'you got another think coming.'

'He's my baby too,' he said, but mildly because he couldn't see why there should be any argument.

'You ain't carried him nine months, nor give birth to 'im neither.'

'Oh come on, Ellen. He's a Jewish baby. All Jewish babies are circumcized. It's the custom.'

She was glaring at him, her blue eyes furious. 'Not fer my baby, it ain't. I won't allow it, an' that's flat. An' if you bring your rotten mogul feller into this house, I'll cut a lump off him, so help me God.'

I've made an awful mistake, David thought. I should have prepared her for it gradually. She's not used to the idea, that's what it is. 'Well,' he said, 'we won't discuss it now, nu? We got plenty a' time.'

'There's nothink to discuss,' she said, and her determination was massive. 'The answer's "no". You can ask from here ter doomsday, it'll be "no" all the way. My baby ain't Jewish.'

And no matter how often he tried to return to the topic, she was adamant. Nobody was going to mutilate her child, and that was the end of it.

He was more distressed about this than he'd been about any

313

other matter since they married. It had never occurred to him that she might refuse, and now that she had, he couldn't think of any way to persuade her. But he couldn't leave his own son outside the Jewish community.

'So what do we do?' he asked his father as they walked along Fournier Street after synagogue.

'Ve leave it vid the Lord, maybe?'

But David worried on. It was unthinkable to have an uncircumcized son. 'There must be something I could say to make her change her mind. If I could only think of it. How can I persuade her, Papa? She refuses no matter what.' Oy oy! What a situation! It was insoluble.

In the event, the baby solved the problem for him by being born a girl, a peacemaker from the first day of her life.

Chapter Twenty-Four

Early the next morning after the child was born, Dumpling arrived with a blue paper bag full of groats for Ellen and a set of long petticoats for the baby. 'I come the minute I see your card, bubeleh,' she said to David. 'Oy oy vhat a beauty! Such eyes, I tell you,' and she quoted from the Talmud, ' "The birth of a daughter is a blessing from the lord." So vhat you call her?'

'Grace,' David told her. 'Whatcher think?'

'Tuesday's child,' Ellen explained, fondling her daughter's dark head. 'Tuesday's child is full a' grace.'

'Very nice,' Dumpling approved. To have named her after her grandmother would have been more diplomatic, but it was a pretty name. It suited her.

'I'm off to work then,' David said, kissing Ellen goodbye, 'You got everything you need, nu?'

'Me she got,' Dumpling said happily, escorting him to the door. 'Vhat more she vant?'

She was certainly a very good nurse and most attentive. When the midwife came for her morning visit she busied herself in the kitchen, and when the baby woke to be fed she cooked the groats for Ellen, 'best thing in the vorld for making milk, bubeleh', and at midday she scrambled eggs, 'Liddle an' tasty, ve build up your strength', and when they'd eaten every mouthful she insisted that they should both take a 'liddle nap'.

'I shan't sleep in the middle a' the day,' Ellen protested, but she put her head on the pillow just to satisfy Aunty Dumpling, who was nodding and smiling most persuasively. And woke two hours later, to find her sitting on the bed with the baby cradled in her capacious lap, silently crying tears of joy onto the little girl's dark head.

'Such a beauty, don't I tell you,' she said when she saw Ellen was awake. 'So vhat your moder think of such a beauty? The proudest voman alive I bet, nu?'

'Well ...' Ellen said, musing. Until that moment she'd always been very careful to avoid any mention of her family when she was with Aunty Dumpling. Now she decided to risk it. 'To tell the truth, she don't know yet. We've sent a card, same time as yours. On'y she's gone ter live in Liverpool, you see.'

'Oy oy oy!' Aunty Dumpling said, taking Ellen's hand at once and giving it a squeeze. 'Such a sadness! All that vay avay! Never mind, bubeleh, she come down to see the baby, nu?'

'I shouldn't think so.'

'She don't travel good?'

'Ain't got the money.'

Dumpling gave the hand another squeeze. 'Never mind, bubeleh,' she said, her face puckered with earnestness. 'Ve make it up to you. You got Davey and me and Davey's father. Plenty of family now, nu?'

'Not Davey's mother though,' Ellen said greatly daring. 'She don't think much 'a me an' that's a fact.'

'Give her time, bubeleh,' Dumpling advised. 'Vait till she see this liddle precious.'

But this little precious had had enough of conversation and decided to give tongue for food. And it took a long time to satisfy her because she suddenly seemed to have acquired an appetite. And then her nappie had to be changed, so Dumpling was able to admire her dear little plump legs, and kiss her toes, and stroke her soft skin, before she was wrapped and bundled again.

'The greatest sadness of my life I don't have children,' she confided, beaming at her new grandniece.

'You should a' married again,' Ellen said, cuddling the baby into her neck.

'Should, vould. It ain't so easy. Good husband's a rarity, I tell you. They don't grow on trees, nu-nu.'

'What about Mr Morrison?' Ellen asked, surprised at how bold motherhood had made her.

'It don't enter his head, *nebbish*.'

316

'P'rhaps it will,' Ellen said smiling at her.

'Pigs might fly,' Dumpling said, but she sounded cheerful. 'I just rinse this liddle nappie out, nu?'

That evening while Ellen was recounting all the day's events and her daring conversation, Emmanuel and Rachel arrived to see their first grandchild. Emmanuel was delighted with her and said she was the prettiest baby he'd ever seen, even prettier than David, and he'd never thought such a thing was possible. But Rachel was quiet and watchful, saying very little and taking everything in, and she brought no welcoming gift, as Ellen was sensitively quick to notice.

When they'd gone she burst into tears and wept unconsolably for far too long. 'She hates me,' she cried. 'The way she was lookin' at us! An' she never said nothink nice about our Gracie, d'yer notice? An' I seen 'er at all the wrong time too. Stuck 'ere in bed an' the place all any old how.'

'It wasn't any old how,' he tried to comfort. 'Dumpling had it all lovely.'

But she was beyond reason. 'She hates me,' she sobbed. 'She'll always hate me, Davey. She's made up 'er mind to it, you can see. She was lookin' me over all the time, lookin' fer things ter criticize.'

'She ain't like that, bubeleh,' he argued. 'She's a good woman. She'll come round in time. You'll see. She was just being quiet, that's all. She's a bit shy.'

He was wrong. Ellen had assessed her mother-in-law's state of mind with almost total accuracy.

'A pretty baby,' Emmanuel tried, as they walked home together in the balmy evening. 'There is truth in the saying, nu? A man should look on the birth of a daughter as a blessing from the Lord.' He spoke in Yiddish, because he had a vague feeling that he would be more persuasive in that language.

'The birth of a Jewish daughter, maybe,' Rachel said. 'But this is neither one thing nor the other, poor child. Half and half. An outcast, Emmanuel.'

'Only if we make her an outcast, bubeleh.'

'She *is* an outcast, Emmanuel. An outcast by birth, neither one thing nor the other.' Her face was stiff with rejection and obduracy.

'She is our David's daughter,' Emmanuel tried.

'She is that woman's daughter. That woman's! Ai-yi! What a terrible waste!'

Fortunately little Grace Cheifitz couldn't speak English or Yiddish yet, so she didn't know what a terrible waste she was. She only knew, deep down in the most instinctive part of her nature, that she was a blessing and that she was loved. So she thrived. In six weeks she had lost the first fragility of the newborn and had grown prettily rounded and learned to smile. By six months she was a fine fat baby, with her mother's dark curly hair and her father's soft brown eyes, sitting in the high chair her grandfather had made for her, playing with the bricks her grandfather had made for her, and endlessly repeating her own happy songs. And Ellen was making plans for their very first Christmas together.

'It ain't religious,' she explained when David scowled his doubt. 'It's a celebration, that's all. A nice meal, chicken an' things like that, an' candles, like you 'ave at Shabbas, an' givin' presents. We put 'em in a stocking at the foot of the bed an' say it's Santa Claus.' She'd never had a stocking at the foot of the bed in the whole of her supposedly Christian life, so that was all the more reason for her daughter to be given one.

'Well ...' he said. 'I suppose it's all right, seein' it's for our Gracie.' There were times when he felt he was slipping inexorably further and further away from the ways of his parents and their relations, and then he was torn, part of him wanting to welcome new ways, part of him clinging with a nostalgic desperation to the old.

This time he needn't have worried, for Gracie's little stocking was an enormous success, with its sugar mouse, and the woollen ball Ellen had made, and the monkey-on-a-stick he'd carved so carefully, and the dolly mixtures wrapped in silver paper, and the orange stuffed so neatly into its toe. They sat, still snuggled into the comfortable warmth of their double bed, and watched while their daughter discovered one present after the other, crowing with pleasure, and then they gave presents to one another and were delighted because they were so similar, a hairbrush for her and a shaving brush for him. And Christmas was everything she had always dreamed it could be. Even if the chicken did take a terribly long time to cook.

Dumpling was charmed when she heard how happy they been, but Rivke and Rachel took it as evidence of the mos dangerous backsliding. 'So vhat I tell you?' Rivke demanded. 'Begin vid strange vomen, end vid strange gods.'

'Oy-oy! A present ain't gods!' Dumpling said.

But they only snorted.

It grieved Emmanuel that his wife was so unbending. As the months passed and Gracie learned to stand and toddle about he grew more and more fond of her, and wished with all his heart that Rachel would love her too. 'She's such a good little girl,' he would urge, 'and so loving.' But he was wasting his breath. Her answer was always the same.

'Good she may be, Jewish she ain't.'

When June came round again and it was her first birthday he scraped and saved and connived until he had enough money to buy her a doll. Dumpling made it a full set of clothes, all beautifully embroidered, and the two of them delivered it together and were kissed and hugged and thanked until they were all quite breathless.

'I vish my Rachel could've seen it,' he mourned as he and Dumpling travelled home together.

'A hard heart to melt,' Dumpling agreed. 'And that dear little soul so pretty and loving. Ai yi!'

The hard heart still hadn't melted when the child's second birthday came round.

'I don't reckon we'll ever please your ma,' Ellen sighed, as she tucked the covers round their sleeping daughter at the end of her special day.

'Never mind,' David said, putting his arms round her and turning her towards him. 'You please me. You both please me.' And his eyes were saying, especially you, and especially now. She was looking quite delectably pretty, with her cheeks so rounded and her eyes shining and that full mouth ever so slightly parted, and love stirring so magically in both of them. 'Beautiful Ellen.'

She kissed him lingeringly. Their eyes were so close there was no room for secrets. 'Guess what,' she said.

'Um,' he said when they'd kissed again. 'I thought yer might be.' Her breasts were so full and welcoming.

319

'December,' she told him, holding him about the waist and drawing him closer and closer towards her. And then words were superfluous.

They decided to keep their precious secret for as long as they could. 'Time enough when I begin ter show,' Ellen said. And this time they avoided the subject of the brit altogether. Time enough for that when the baby was born. They were far more mature now, David thought, three years married and with a daughter to care for. They'd find an answer. At the right time. He was sure.

So they went on hugging their secret and enjoying their daughter, living at their own rate in their little kingdom above the goods yard. Now that Gracie was beginning to babble into speech there was so much to say. 'Choo-choo, Mummy,' she would call, and the two of them would stand by the window and watch the great engines juddering past. 'Balk?' she would ask, looking hopefully at her bonnet hanging on the door, and then they would go out into the sunshine to the sour smell of the breweries and ammoniac horse buses and the oily reek of the new motor cars, and walk down to Spitalfields Market to buy themselves some fruit or, even better take a tram to the Embankment or the fine green parks of the West End. It was a gentle life and a private one and it suited them all so well they almost forgot about friends and relations.

So it came as quite a surprise when Hymie arrived one evening, blushing with embarrassment, to tell them that he was going to be married and to invite them to the wedding.

'*Mazel tov!*' David said, thumping his old friend on the back and dragging him into the kitchen. 'So what's she like? Where d'you find her?'

At that Hymie blushed more furiously. 'The mothers arranged it,' he confessed. 'She ain't a looker an' that's a fact. She's ... well ... she's *haimish*, ter tell the truth.'

'What's *haimish*?' Ellen laughed.

'Well ...' Hymie hesitated again. 'Hideous really.'

'Oh she ain't,' Ellen teased.

'*Haimish* is homely, not much ter look at, nice enough,' David translated.

And at that she laughed again. 'How d'yer meet her?'

'I told yer,' Hymie confessed uncomfortably. 'It's arranged. I ain't met her yet, ter tell the truth. I seen her picture.'

They were horrified. 'Oy oy, Hymie!' David said. 'You can't marry a woman you don't even know. That's downright primitive.'

'I don't mind,' Hymie said sheepishly. 'I don't reckon I'd ever get a wife on me own, not with my looks. We shall do well enough fer each other I daresay. She cooks good, keeps house good, all that sort a' thing.'

Ellen looked at him with open-mouthed wonder. But you got to go to bed together, she was thinking. How could you do that with someone you didn't even know? The idea was obscene.

'Say no,' David urged. 'Wait till you find someone to love. It's much the best way, honest. You might take a lot a' stick ter start with but it sorts itself out in the end. Ain't that right, Ellen?'

It wasn't quite right but she said yes, for Hymie's benefit.

'We shall get ter love each other after the weddin',' Hymie hoped. 'Anyway I can't say no now. It's all arranged. I've brought yer invite. End of October, see.'

'I shall be a fair ol' size be then,' Ellen said, looking at the date. So of course Hymie had to be told their news, and it was his turn to offer congratulations. And be sworn to temporary secrecy.

'You'll come to me weddin' though, wontcher?' he said, and his ugly face was anxious.

He needs support, David thought. Poor old Hymie. He's putting on a brave show, but he's nervous and he's worried. 'We'll be there,' he promised. And Ellen propped the invitation on the mantelpiece and gave him a kiss. 'I shall wear me best hat,' she said, ' 'cos nothink else'll fit.'

'I'd never a' thought it of old Hymie,' David said when his friend had gone striding off to deliver the rest of his invitations. 'I always thought he'd be modern like me.'

'It gives me the willies,' Ellen said. 'Fancy goin' ter bed with someone you don't even know. It's horrible.'

'It's Jewish.'

'Well, I don't think much of it.'

321

'Neither do I.'

'Was that what they was goin' ter do ter you?'

'I expect so.'

'Aintcher glad they never?'

'Don't ask soppy questions,' he said joyfully, prepared to answer her with action.

'I never been to a Jewish wedding,' she said, unbuttoning his shirt. 'What's it like?'

A sudden chill of sadness checked his ardour for a few seconds. Oh, if only she could have been to their own Jewish wedding, accepted from the word go! What a difference that would have made! But then she was cuddling against his chest and his body was aware of her again, and silencing his mind. 'It's a weddin',' he said. 'Same as all the others. Why are we still in the kitchen?'

But it wasn't a wedding the same as all the others. For Ellen it was a ceremony unlike anything she'd ever seen before.

For a start she was very put out to discover that she and Gracie were relegated to the balcony with all the other women, and that it was only the men and the bride who were allowed down into the body of the synagogue. 'I shan't know *nobody* up 'ere,' she whispered furiously, mindful of the sharp ears all around her. 'I wouldn't a' come if I'd known.'

'I'll look up an' wave,' he promised. 'It's all watchin' anyway, wherever you are. You got a good view up 'ere.'

'Hum!' she said crossly. 'I don't think much of it, an' that's a fact.' But she gave him a smile as he left her, because she didn't like to see him looking upset.

'Daddy gorn,' Gracie said, catching their emotion and bewildered by it.

'No 'e ain't,' she said, as calmly as she could. 'There 'e is. See? Down there under that cover with yer Uncle Hymie.'

It was a splendid canopy, all red and gold embroidery and fringed with heavy gold tassels. Hymie looked uglier than usual standing underneath such opulence, especially as they'd made him wear a long white shirt instead of a coat. It's more like a shroud than a garment, she thought. They're a funny lot these Jews. Fancy getting married in a shroud.

But then the bride was making her entrance and she forgot

322

about the vagaries of the Jewish race and leaned forward to catch her first glimpse of Hymie's intended. She was certainly very fat, even if you allowed for the yards of material in her white dress, but her face was covered with such a thick veil that only the bump of her nose could be seen through the cloth. Everybody in the synagogue was singing some Jewish song very loudly, and the Rabbi had joined all the young men under the canopy, resplendent in a long black coat and a huge hat trimmed with brown fur. She watched as he unfurled the scroll of parchment he carried and the service began.

It was all in Yiddish. What a sell! She couldn't understand a word of it. But she recognized the moment when Hymie put the ring on his wife's finger and then at last the veil was lifted and they could all see the bride's face. And she *was* hideous. Poor Hymie. She had a broad squashed face, like a pug, with a stubby nose, and small eyes and a mouth that was downturned with discontent, even at this moment when it ought to have been looking happy. Poor old Hymie!

While she was still feeling sorry for him, one of his friends put a wine glass on the floor at his feet and he smashed it to bits with the heel of his shoe, and they all yelled '*Mazel tov!*' as though he'd done something clever. They really are the most peculiar lot, she thought, as the Rabbi started another chant. Oh 'e's off again. Wonder what David's thinking about. He looks very soulful.

David was listening to the words and envying his friend. For they had reached the moment of the seven benedictions, when the words brought all their hopes of happiness into passionate focus. 'Blessed art thou, O Lord our God, King of the Universe, who hast created joy and gladness, bridegroom and bride, mirth and exultation, pleasure and delight ...' And he felt the surge of support for Hymie all around them, the full loving power of their tight-knit tribe, and he regretted his own exclusion from it. This was what he should have been given on his own wedding day, love and support and approval. And he knew, as he stood beside his friend, enriched by the emotion of this most Jewish of all Jewish occasions, that if his second child was a boy he ought to have his brit. I'll bring him to the synagogue when he's ten days old, he thought, and he can be circumcized and entered into the Covenant of Abraham along with all his relations. Nothing less would do.

Jack Cheifitz was born on 15 December. He was a fine fat baby, every bit as pretty as his sister had been, with the same dark blue eyes and the same thick hair. But undeniably male.

Now, David thought, looking into his son's trusting eyes for the very first time, now we shall have to decide. But there were still ten days for them to make up their minds and arrange the ceremony. Nothing need be said just yet.

Aunty Dumpling appointed herself nurse again, and Gracie was her helper in her own nurse's cap and a miniature white apron specially made for the occasion. 'You go ter work, Pa,' she said, 'an' me an' Aunty Dump'in'll look after Ma, nu?' And that little, expressive, overworked Yiddish word caught at his heart and made him more determined than ever that both his children should be accepted by his tribe.

But he said nothing until a week had passed and he was quite sure Ellen was recovering and the new baby was settled. This was a delicate subject and had to be approached with care.

It wasn't until late on Friday evening, when Aunty Dumpling had gone home for Shabbas and Gracie was curled up in her little cot fast asleep and the baby was dozing in Ellen's arms after his late-night feed, that a moment presented itself.

'Mrs Mullins says I shall be up an' about in nice time fer Christmas,' Ellen said. 'Whatcher think a' that?' It had been one of her major concerns that she might still be lying-in when Christmas Day arrived.

'That's good,' he said, stroking the baby's head with his forefinger. 'We got another special day to look forward to an' all.'

'What's that?' she said, but apprehension was already tightening her throat as she spoke.

'The brit,' he said, not looking up at her yet. But hoping.

She could feel her heart sinking through her chest into her belly. 'Oh not that again, Davey, please!' she said. 'We been through all that. We decided.'

'No,' he said, quiet but determined. 'We deferred, bubeleh.

324

Tha's all we done. We deferred.'

He looked so handsome and she loved him so much, with their two pretty babies sleeping beside them. It was going to be very difficult to deny him but it had to be done. 'It's all superstitious nonsense,' she said. 'Out a' date. Like poor old Hymie's marriage. You said so yerself.'

'No,' he argued calmly. 'It ain't the same. This is the way all Jewish boys are accepted. They enter the Covenant of Abraham. They belong. Dontcher want our Jack ter belong?'

' 'E belongs to us,' she said stoutly as she settled the sleeping infant into his crib. 'That's enough fer me.'

'But he's Jewish.'

'Half Jewish.' And she tried a joke to lessen the tension that was building up between them. 'You can 'ave the top half.'

He sighed profoundly, upset by a joke at such a time. 'We can't leave him out in the cold,' he said. 'You wouldn't want that, surely ter goodness?'

' 'E's here, in the warm, with me,' she said, still trying to laugh him out of it. 'You do talk tripe. Out in the cold!'

'It's got ter be done, Ellen.'

'No it ain't,' she said, turning from the crib to face him, suddenly fierce. 'I told yer before. Nobody ain't choppin' bits off a' my baby.'

He stood up and went to stand beside the window, parting the curtains with both hands and looking down into the snowy garden beneath them. 'It's fixed,' he said. 'I've fixed it, Ellen. I've seen the *mohel*. It's got ter be done.' His spine was rigid with determination, his jaw implacable.

She was out of the bed and across the room and standing beside him before he realized she'd moved. It surprised them both, for she wasn't supposed to get out of bed until her lying-in was over, and the speed of her movement drained all the colour from her face and made her feel frighteningly dizzy. She hung onto the curtains to steady herself, then the blood returned to her cheeks and her face blazed with protective fury.

'I love you more'n anything in the world,' she said, 'except my babies. Nobody ain't doin' nothing to my babies. I don't care who it is or what it's for. Not even you. Nobody.'

'They're my babies too,' he said stiffly, feeling the angry

colour flooding his own cheeks. He knew she was running risks getting out of bed and into the cold air, but the brit was so important it even blotted out his concern. He had to make a stand now, or his son would be ostracized. Why couldn't she see it?

'You never carried 'em, an' you never birthed 'em,' she said. 'That's what counts when it comes to 'aving bits cut off of 'em.' The determined fury on her face was so daunting he had to drop his eyes. 'I won't allow it, an' that's all there is to it. If that mogul comes anywhere near my little Jack, I shall take his stinkin' scissors and carve a great lump out 'a him, so help me God. An' then I'll pack me bag an' take me babies an' go off somewhere you'll never see me again.' She was panting with anger and exhaustion.

'You don't mean that,' he said aghast. 'You wouldn't leave me. That's just talk.' But it frightened him and his eyes showed it. 'Where would yer go?'

'Anywhere,' she said wildly. 'Liverpool with me Ma.'

Anger made him scathing. 'An' where would yer get the fare?' It was a cruel thing to say, and when she winced he felt ashamed. But only momentarily.

'I'd walk,' she said. 'I'd walk every inch a' the way. You ain't touchin' my baby.' She knew she was losing blood. She could feel it trickling down her leg. But although the knowledge frightened her so much it made her shake, she went on fighting. They stood within inches of each other, red-faced and panting.

'I'll never give in,' she said, glaring at him.

'It's got ter be done,' he answered.

'Just try! That's all! I've warned yer!'

The tremor in her legs was making her nightgown flutter, and the movement flicked a splinter of anxiety into his mind and he knew he was afraid for her. 'Come back to bed,' he said. 'You'll make yourself ill.'

She clung to the curtains like a lifeline. 'Not till you agree 'e ain't to be cut.'

'We'll talk about it tomorrer.'

'No, now!' We got ter decide it now, she thought. I couldn't fight like this again. She gathered all that was left of her

326

trembling strength. 'You'd better make yer mind up,' she said. 'Either you say 'e's to 'ave this brit or 'e ain't. If you insist 'e's to 'ave it, I'll leave yer, an' I'll take 'em both with me. I mean it. So, what's more important to you, 'avin' the brit or stayin' with me?' Her eyes were challenging him, and although she was trembling, there was no weakness about her anywhere.

She'll do it, he thought. She really will. And it seemed to him that this wild-eyed woman standing beside him in their familiar room was a sudden stranger to him, the weight of her determination equalling his. There was no way he could persuade her. She *would* leave him. And even with anger blocking off every other emotion he knew he couldn't bear that.

'Well?' she said.

He knew the answer but it was several seconds before he could bring himself to give it. 'Stayin' with you,' he admitted, and he looked away from her, sighing miserably, because he knew he was defeated.

She gave a little sobbing sigh and he could feel her drooping away from him, her body folding towards the floor, and he turned quickly and caught her as she fell. Her face was pale as paper and there were mauve shadows under her closed eyes. 'Ellen!' he said. 'Ellen bubeleh!' his chest torn with remorse. What had he done to her? Why had he fought her, now, so soon after the baby?

To his great relief she was struggling back to consciousness as he set her down in the bed and wrapped her in the blankets and cuddled her cold body close against his warm one. And she clung to him and shivered and cried, and told him over and over again how sorry she was but how she *had* to do it. And he smoothed her hair and told her over and over again that he loved her more than anything in the world, and he wouldn't have hurt her for anything, only the brit was so important.

And finally when they had cried their way back together, she tried to find some words to comfort him. 'It's who 'e is what counts,' she said, 'not what they done to 'im.'

And he tried to agree with her. But what should have been done to this child was so important. If only she could understand it. *Halevai!*

327

So the brit was cancelled, 'for the time being', and Jack was allowed to grow uncircumcized. And they both pretended that the topic was forgotten.

But from time to time in the months that followed it returned to plague them. He would try to explain the religious significance, stressing how quickly and easily the thing could be done, providing the child was young enough. Or he would talk vaguely about everybody's need to belong, and touch on the special needs of Jews who were strangers wherever they lived. And she would ignore him, or change the subject, or argue it out all over again, in the same words and with the same demoralizing conclusion. It was a thorn of discord that neither could dislodge, and as winter gradually gave way to a reluctant spring, the pain it caused intensified.

But by the end of May, something happened that stopped all argument. Infant cholera came to Whitechapel.

Chapter Twenty-Five

However trenchantly Aunt Rivke might disapprove of things, like mixed marriages in general and Ellen and David's in particular, when it came to protecting small children from epidemics, her action was immediate and liberal. The minute she heard there were two babies in the Buildings struggling for their lives with violent sickness, she put on her wig and her second best hat and stomped off to warn her relations. She did a round tour, starting next door with Josh and Maggie, who had already heard and were frantic with worry, then on to Joe in the Wentworth Buildings, and finally to Quaker Street and Ellen.

She came to the point without preamble, even though she could see that the girl was alarmed by her precipitate arrival. 'Ve got cholera in the Buildings, dolly,' she warned. 'Boil all the vater. Don't drink nothink vhat ain't boiled. You take my advice, keep your pretty chickens indoors. Ve don't vant they should catch it. A terrible disease, don't I tell you. You got kettles, nu?'

The pretty chickens were sitting on Ellen's latest rag rug directly underneath the open window, now protectively barred by their doting grandfather. They were both in their petticoats because of the heat and to Ellen's considerable relief they looked healthy as well as angelic.

'Thanks ever so much er telling me,' she said to Aunt Rivke.

And Rivke was warmed by her gratitude and clicked her teeth and told her to 'think nothing of it'.

Ellen was so shocked that it wasn't until Rivke had adjusted her wig and crashed off down the stairs again that the full impact of the news she'd just heard caught her heart in a vice.

Cholera! Dear God! Kids died like flies of the cholera! She looked at Gracie's pretty round face and little Jack's thin arms and her mind spun with panic. Outside, the frowsy air of Shoreditch was lethal with lurking germs. She could almost see them circling among the motes in the column of sunlight slanting visibly into her room. We must move, she thought. I can't stay here and let them catch the cholera. And she made up her mind at once.

'We'll go an' find another place,' she said to her children. 'Out in the country, in the fresh air. You'd like that, wouldn'tcher?' And little Gracie seemed to agree for she smiled and said 'In a' tuntry' most amiably, even though her brother was far more interested in his toes. 'No time like the present,' their mother said. 'Come an' get yer clothes on, there's good kids.'

She wrote a note to David, in case he got back before they did, 'They got cholera in the Buildings. Your Aunt Rivke has been. I have gone to look for a place somewhere else, Love E.' Then she fed the baby and slung him onto her back inside a shawl and she and Gracie set off to look for the country. And naturally enough they started their search in the Mile End Road, where Ellen had taken her escaping mother all those eventful years ago.

When they left Quaker Street she really had very little idea what she was looking for. It had to be a step up from two rooms in a tenement, and she wanted a tap in the kitchen, because lugging water up and down two flights of stairs every day was no joke, but apart from that the necessities she sought were nebulous things like fresh air and good health, and safety from infection. Her children were in danger and her children had to be protected. Somehow or other they had to escape.

The corner shop advertisements were all for rooms and they all turned out to be in teeming tenements that she rejected at sight. Gracie grew tired of trudging from house to house in the heat, and trailed behind her mother, tearful and weary. It was a long way for a three-year-old to walk, and she was too young to understand that it was all for her own good. 'We'll find somewhere soon, lovey, you'll see,' Ellen comforted, as the child wept and dragged her feet.

330

Finally, and in some desperation, she took her problem to an estate agent.

'Well now,' that gentleman said when he'd seated her in his office and she'd taken a weary child on each knee. 'It all depends on what you are prepared to pay.' He'd been impressed by the information that her husband worked for the *Essex Magazine*. 'Good accommodation is usually pretty pricey. I've got a very nice house in Mile End Place, clean, immediate vacant possession, twelve and six a week. Would that suit?'

A house, she thought, all to ourselves. We could get right away from the cholera in a house. So although she was rather afraid of the price, she said she'd see it.

'It's just along the road,' the estate agent said. 'No distance at all, and so handy for the trams.'

It was almost as near as he claimed, but at first sight it wasn't at all promising, for the entrance was through a narrow brick archway beside the Tyne Main Coal Company, and the brickwork was dank and blackened and forbidding. It'll be another tenement, she thought, as sure as God made little apples.

Nevertheless she followed him through the archway. And found herself in the country. Two rows of neat white cottages faced each other across a cobbled street, each with its own front garden full of flowers, and beyond them, forming the fourth side of the square, was a low brick wall and an open skyline, fringed with thick trees. It was so totally unlike anything she'd ever seen before that for a few seconds she simply stood where she was and enjoyed it. There's so much sky here, she thought, and the air smells quite different, with all them lilacs and wallflowers. You wouldn't catch any rotten old diseases in a place like this. It reminded her of Kent and the freedom of the hop fields. She tucked the baby more firmly onto her shoulders and took little Grace by the hand. 'Yes,' she said. 'This might do.'

It was a lovely house, with its own neat front garden, like all the others, and a fine front door inset behind its own porch, and three white-framed windows, two upstairs and one down. 'It's a country cottage,' she said to her daughter, as the agent eased the key into the lock. 'Whatcher think a' that?'

331

'Gracie like a tunty cottage,' the child lisped, and followed her mother happily through the front door.

It was even better inside. The front room was light and airy, looking out over the front garden the way it did, and it had a lovely fireplace, with a mantelpiece and an overmantel and everything. We could get really snug in 'ere of a winter's evening, she thought.

Between the front room and the back there was a flight of steep stairs leading to the upper floor. They toiled up to inspect the main bedroom which stretched across the front of the house and the back bedroom which had its own window overlooking, wonder of wonders, a real back garden. 'Look at that, Gracie. Wouldn'tcher like ter play out there? Oh, we shan't know ourselves in a place like this.'

She already knew that the house was the refuge she wanted, but she decided to look at the kitchen anyway. 'Might as well, eh Gracie?' And the kitchen was perfect, a fine modern room, painted a nice brown, and so clean! The wooden table that took pride of place in the centre of the room was scrubbed almost white. She went into the walk-in larder, and admired the Welsh Dresser, and the coal hole and the iron range, which was the most up-to-date model she'd ever seen, with an oven and four hobs. Plenty of room for kettles and irons, she thought. How much easier washday would be in a place like this. Leading out of the kitchen was a narrow scullery with a quarry-tiled floor and its own yellow sink with its own tap, and boxed into a little closet in the corner its own W.C. What luxury! No more emptying chamber pots of a morning or lugging heavy pails of water up and down stairs all day long. I can have all the water I want and boil it up lovely. It'll be like living in a palace, and even at twelve and six a week, well worth it.

'Keep it for us!' she told the agent imperiously. 'Mr Cheifitz'll be round first thing in the morning to pay the rent. We could move in termorrer, couldn't we?'

So it was agreed.

'Won't your Pa be surprised!' she said to Gracie as the tram rattled them back to Shoreditch High Street and the smell of the breweries.

But he wasn't. He was relieved.

When he came home to an empty flat and her terrifying note, he'd been seized by a panic every bit as strong as hers had been, and had instantly come to the same conclusion. They must put a distance between their children and the infection, and the sooner the better. If she hadn't found a suitable place, he'd go out himself as soon as the kids were settled for the night, and between them they'd keep on looking till they found somewhere. He kept an anxious vigil beside the bedroom window, worrying and scheming, working out how much rent they could afford, which he estimated would be somewhere between ten and eleven shillings, and trying to remember the sort of places where they could live in safety for such a sum.

It seemed a very long time before he saw his dusty family trailing along the road. He rushed down the stairs two at a time, to carry little Gracie the rest of the way and hear their news. And when Ellen told him about the country cottage, he agreed to it at once, taking twelve and six in his long stride as though it were no more than the weight of his drowsy toddler.

'The rent's a bit steep,' Ellen said, feeling she ought to criticize, as he hadn't.

'We'll manage,' he said, as they climbed the stairs. 'I might get a rise. You never know. I'll ask Mr Palfreyman. No harm in asking, nu? Or we could take lodgers, maybe.'

'Not till there's no more cholera, though,' she said, her eyes fearful again.

'Nu-nu, bubeleh,' he reassured. 'We'll stay in our own house all by ourselves till there ain't a trace a' ... that.' It was too terrible to name.

'I done the right thing, ain't I, Davey?' she asked as they closed their front door behind them and were alone at last in the privacy of their flat. Fatigue had brought a sudden uncertainty with it.

'I'd a' done the same if it'ud been me,' he said. 'I think you're a giddy marvel the way you look after us, an' that's a fact. I've never known anyone so quick off the mark.'

It was the same fiery protective instinct that had made her oppose the brit so passionately. But that was forgotten. For this time he agreed with her.

Which was more than all his relations did. Dumpling was

impressed, of course, especially by how quick she'd been, and Emmanuel said she was a woman of sense, and he wasn't a bit surprised, and he'd be round on Sunday to fix up a little gate across the stairs and to see if the windows needed bars. But Rivke and Rachel were annoyed.

'Rushing off vidout a vord!' Rivke snorted. 'Davey, he don't tell even.'

'He should a' married a nice Jewish vife,' Rachel said. 'A nice Jewish vife vould a' know'd better. For vhy she got to go rushing off all that long vay? Vhen ve was young ve stayed vhere ve vas. Spending good money, rushing off!'

'She got money to vaste, maybe?' Rivke said. 'Vonce a *shiksa*, alvays a *shiksa*!'

'A house!' Rachel said. 'Ay-yi! She get above herself that *shiksa*. So vhat's wrong vid rooms, I ask you!'

'A house!' her sister-in-law agreed. 'They should be so lucky!'

David and Ellen knew very well how lucky they were. Even if they did have to pay twelve and six a week for their good fortune. As May blazed into June and infant cholera continued to rage in the tenements they'd left behind, Jack and Gracie bloomed. Soon their cheeks were as pink as the roses in their front garden and Ellen was relieved to notice that the baby's legs were growing fatter by the minute. Even David's initial disquiet over the rent was eased, for Mr Palfreyman gave him a rise, at the first time of asking and without consulting a single matchstick. The terrible apprehension that had precipitated them into their new life gradually eased a little.

They made friends with their next door neighbours, a family called Streete on one side and a nice quiet lady called Mrs Brunewald who lived with her bachelor son on the other. And they were pleased to think that they weren't 'all living on top of each other' and that their landlord was somewhere on the other side of London and wouldn't be watching them every minute of the day the way Mrs Undine had been just a little too fond of doing. But the most rewarding privacy of all was a separate bedroom for the kids.

Dumpling came to see them two or three times every week, to check that they were all still healthy and to play with her

334

'chickens' while Ellen nipped down to the shops. They would have their dinner out in the garden under the shade of a sprawling bush laden with sweet-scented white flowers. Mrs Streete, who was knowledgeable about such things, told them it was called a syringa, and offered to show them how to prune it when the time came, and Mr Streete, who 'took the air' in his own back garden every evening, told them they'd got a nice little plot of earth down the end there and gave David a box full of seedlings to grow in it.

'Ol' farmer Giles at work in his vegetable garden,' David said happily striking a pose, trowel in hand. It was the first time he'd clowned about like that since Rivke brought her awful news. Things *were* getting back to normal.

'What are they?' Ellen asked, looking at the little green shoots.

'I dunno,' he had to admit. 'I didn't like to ask. Never mind. If they're edible we'll eat 'em.'

'An' if they ain't?'

'We'll stick 'em in a vase and put 'em on the table.'

'We ain't got a vase.'

'A jam jar then.'

'Oh Davey!' she said, throwing her arms round his neck. 'Aintcher glad we come 'ere?'

They were so happy they almost forgot about the cholera, and the brit, and the fact that she wasn't Jewish, and that he didn't like English food and she couldn't cook kosher, and that his mother didn't approve of them.

335

Chapter Twenty-Six

Emmanuel Cheifitz was always anxious these days.

'You vorry too much, dolly,' Dumpling rebuked him lovingly. 'So you get old before your time, I tell you.'

But he only smiled his tolerant smile and patted her plump shoulder and went on worrying. 'I *am* old, Raizel,' he said, 'and life ain't easy.'

There were so many reasons for anxiety. The dread of cholera was a perpetual heaviness dragging his mind, even though the number of cases were said to be dropping, and Gracie and the baby seemed safe enough for the time being. And then there was Rachel who was making herself so unhappy because she wouldn't accept David's marriage; to say nothing of the usual alarming fluctuations in the rag trade. Nu-nu, life was not easy and it got more difficult year by year.

He went stooping off towards Mr Goldman's workshop in Wentworth Street, his spine bowed, plucking at his tatty grey beard, muttering to himself, 'If only she would visit a bit more, see the childer, say something good about the house. Ai-yi! Who would have thought my Rachel could be so stubborn. A mule, *has vesholem.*'

Commercial Street was so crowded that summer it was impossible to move more than five yards at a time without halting to make way for somebody else. Only the trams made unimpeded progress and that was by dint of such a clangour of bells that even the donkeys stepped clear of them. Even though he was accustomed to the grinding noise and the incessant pressure of too many people in too little space, by the time Friday evening arrived Emmanuel felt enfeebled by it all. The pavements were so hot they were making his feet ache and what little air was left in the chasm between the tenements was frantic with flies and bluebottles. They flicked against his face as he walked along, and everywhere he looked they were crawling and buzzing, on fresh meat and rotting fruit, horse dung and vegetables, or gathered in obscene black clusters round the eyes of the horses waiting patiently beside the stalls, so that the poor creatures stamped and snorted and tossed their heads in a useless, repetitive effort to shake themselves free of torment.

We live like flies in this place, Emmanuel thought. We breed, we swarm, we die. Only the Lord God is dependable. Stable and eternal and incorruptible. And the thought cheered him a little, as it always did. 'The Lord reigneth: the Lord hath reigned: the Lord shall reign for ever and ever.'

Just ahead of him a furious row had begun with a roar of exasperation, 'You take me for a *schlemiel*!' The arguers stood toe to toe, red in the face and glaring with anger at each other, their arms flailing like windmills.

When life is hard, we should try to tolerate each other, maybe, Emmanuel thought, and he stepped into the road to avoid their anger.

The noise behind him suddenly grew louder, with an alerting hysterical edge to it; screams, raucous shouts, 'Be'ind yer! Mind yer backs! Clear out the way!' and above it all the unmistakable pounding of hooves. He turned to see the crowd parting in panic, reeling away to right and left, and charging through the gap a huge chestnut horse, galloping at full tilt, foam-flecked and white of eye, its tilted cart ricketing behind it, two wheels in the air and two stuck in the tramlines. A bolting horse! *Gottenyu*! he thought, paralyzed at the sight and sound of it.

He knew he ought to run, but everything was happening too quickly and anyway it was all too late. The horse was directly above him, up on its hind legs, forelegs flailing, with the carter's grey face shifting and mouthing behind it. And then the hooves chopped down towards his chest and foam flecked his upturned cheeks and he was down in the road, with the breath knocked out of his body and a suffocating weight on his chest. Horse flesh swelled against his eyes, and the acrid smell of its sweat blocked his nostrils, and somewhere a long way away there was a stinging pain in his right hand.

Time and reality detached themselves from him. Nothing was really happening. It was all confusion. And his mind slid away from it into a rocking unconsciousness, and he let it go, placidly.

The horse was being dragged to its feet. He could feel its flanks quivering as it rose and hear its pathetic snorting. 'Don't be angry vid the poor creature,' he begged, but his voice wasn't working properly and the words stuck in his throat. I must get to work, he thought. It *is* the morning, nu? I shall lose pay if I stay here and there's the rent to pay on Friday. And he struggled to his feet, surprised and a little annoyed to find that his legs wouldn't support him properly.

'Where d'yer think you're goin'?' a rough face said, and the voice and the expression were so kind and concerned he wanted to weep.

He staggered on down the road, pushing at his own weakness. 'To vork,' he managed. 'Got to get to vork.' And then his knees buckled and he fell for the second time.

A wall of dark legs obscured his view, dirty moleskins, tailors' black trousers, thick skirts with dusty hems. He had his head in somebody's lap and somebody else was asking questions. 'Where d'yer live, mate?'

He tried to tell them, but the words became groans and he was ashamed to be groaning and tried to stop himself. There was a dull ache in his chest and an odd roaring in his ears like the sea. He wondered where the horse was. He wondered how long he would go on lying in the road. Voices buzzed around him like flies. He drifted.

As his mind swam back to consciousness for the second time, he heard a voice he recognized. 'Mr Levy!' he said, and the words were quite clear.

'Ve get you home, nu?' Mr Levy said, bending down so that their eyes were inches apart. 'Ve bring a door for you.'

'So?' he said, not understanding. And something snapped in his chest like a piece of elastic. And he was struggling for air, and every breath a pain like the stabbing of knives.

Rough gentle hands were lifting him. ' 'Old on, mate!

You're all right now! We got yer.'

'Ve don't say nothink to Rachel,' he begged.

Ellen and Gracie were down at the end of the garden watering their mysterious seedlings. Jack had been fed and settled for the night, and now they were enjoying the one time of the day when they could talk without interruption.

And Mrs Brunewald put her head over the fence and interrupted them.

'Pardon me for bothering you,' she said apologetically, seeing Gracie's frown, 'but there's someone at your door. I thought you ought to know.'

It was Aunty Dumpling, ashen-faced, breathless but entirely dry-eyed. 'Oh Ellen, bubeleh,' she panted. 'The vorst news. The vorst. Is our Davey home yet?'

Her lack of tears was more alarming than any amount of weeping would have been.

'What is it?' Ellen said, opening the door to let her in.

'My poor Manny?' Dumpling gasped as she followed Ellen into the kitchen. 'Ai-yi-yi! My poor Manny! Home on a door they bring him. Ai-yi! Knocked down by a horse he vas, his poor chest black and blue, and such pain you vouldn't believe. And he von't have the doctor. Ai-yi! Vhat ve gonna do, dolly? He could be hurt bad, *has vesholem.*'

It ain't possible, Ellen thought, stupid with fright. He was here only Sunday, helping us lay the lino in the front room. He was all right then. Grey, a bit slower than usual, tired probably, but not hurt bad. 'David'll get the doctor,' she said as she filled the kettle. ' 'E'll be all right, you'll see.'

But Dumpling only sighed.

'Don't c'y Aunty Dump'in',' Gracie said, cuddling the old lady's ample knee. 'Ma kiss it better, nu?'

'I would if I could, lovey,' Ellen said. But the sight of Dumpling's terrible dry-eyed distress was making her more afraid by the minute.

When David came home and heard the news he reacted quickly, a tightly controlled expression on his face.

'We'll go straight back,' he said to Dumpling, putting on his hat again. 'Don't wait supper for me, Ellen.' And they were gone.

The nightmare had returned, with a different terror, but as merciless as ever. 'Dear God,' she thought, 'don't let it be too bad. 'E's a nice old man an' 'e's been ever so good to us. 'E didn't oughter be hurt bad.' And all sorts of vague impressions crystallized into knowledge inside her busy brain. She knew that she was praying, and praying directly to God, even though she'd never given Him a thought until that moment. In fact, she hadn't even considered whether she believed in Him or not. And she recognized that she had grown very fond of old Papa Cheifitz, and that David was very much like him, especially now when he was taking responsibility and worried sick and determined not to show it.

And she had to take Gracie upstairs at once and wash her face and hands and get her ready for bed, or she would have been weeping.

When David and Dumpling got back to the Buildings they found the flat crowded with family, Rivke and Ben and all their children and all their grandchildren huddled in a dark anxious group round the table, muttering and whispering together. Nobody had thought to light the gas and the far end of the room was already diminished by shadow, but a faint steel-blue haze was reflected through the half-open window. It burnished the planes of their faces with an eerie grey-blue sheen, and when David arrived and they all turned suddenly to look at him, their eyes glimmered like blue night-lights. And he thought of unearthly lamps, edging the dark road to death, and the thought made him shudder.

'Vhat ve gonna do, David?' Rivke said, from her seat in the midst of her family. 'Vhat you think?'

'You are the son,' Ben said hovering beside her. 'You must decide.'

They're putting me in charge, David thought. The son. In charge. And even in the middle of his anxiety and his eerie sense of unreality, the thought pleased him. 'I see him first, nu? Then I decide,' he said. And for the first time in his life he walked out of the room where he'd lived and slept and dreamed, and into the private world of his parents' bedroom.

His father was slumped in the bed, propped up by a mound of pillows, but half asleep and making a subdued groaning noise as he breathed. His face was blotched with mauve bruises, and his chest was concave under its thin nightshirt. Even at first glance and by gentle gaslight, David could see how ill he was. Rachel sat beside him, holding his hand, her shoulders drooping with fatigue and anxiety.

'Davey bubeleh,' she moaned. 'Your poor fader!'

The sound of her recalled Emmanuel from his half-sleep. 'Davey!' he said, but even that one word was an effort.

'I think you should see the doctor, Papa,' David said. 'Just to be on the safe side, nu?'

'Is he bad, Davey?' Rachel asked. She seemed listless, unable to decide anything for herself, and her face was drawn and more deeply lined than he'd ever seen it, as if she'd aged since yesterday.

But she must know how bad he is, David thought, pitying her. 'You agree, Papa, nu?' he asked.

Emmanuel had closed his eyes and seemed to be drifting again. It was too serious to wait for his agreement. 'I'll be back as soon as I can,' he promised his mother and tiptoed from the room.

Dr Turiansky lived in Osborn Street at the other end of Brick Lane, and when David arrived outside his premises he was sitting in his consulting room reading by the globed light of an amber table lamp. He listened patiently while David described his father's symptoms, then he set his book aside and rang for his servant.

'Pony and trap, if you please,' he said when the man answered the bell. When the servant had gone he took his familiar high hat from the hat stand and brushed the rim thoughtfully with his fingertips. 'I shall be there before you,' he said.

And he was. But his visit brought little real comfort to any of them. He stitched the gashes on Emmanuel's fingers, and shone light into his eyes and examined his chest and his spine, and required him to sit up and lie flat and turn on his side until Emmanuel was panting with suppressed pain and exhaustion.

Dr Turiansky's eventual diagnosis was cheerful, but it didn't seem to have any relevance to the hunched man suffering so stoically in the bed below him. 'No bones broken,' he said. 'No concussion. Extensive bruising, of course. Some laceration. You have cracked a rib or two, but there's not a lot I can do for that. Your stomach is tender which is why you feel sick. Light diet, Mrs Cheifitz. I shall return on Monday if you need me. If he hasn't improved by then, I will bind him up. Otherwise send him down to the surgery in a fortnight to have those stitches out.'

When David paid his half-crown fee, and escorted him politely from the premises, he felt demoralized with disappointment. He knew instinctively and unreasonably that his father was far more seriously ill than this kindly medical man was telling them.

His mother felt it too and so did Dumpling, and even though Aunt Rivke said, 'Not so bad, nu?' her expression belied her hopeful words. And when Emmanuel struggled to eat a little noodle soup, and then vomited it up again almost immediately and very painfully, they were torn with anxiety all over again.

That weekend was an unnatural limbo, a mixture of anxious labour for Emmanuel's three self-appointed nurses, and long periods of enforced waiting for the rest of the family. David visited him night and morning and was more upset by every visit. But Ellen and the children stayed at home. And that distressed them all, for Emmanuel asked after their health continually, and was so obviously missing the sight of his 'little chickens' that by Sunday evening David was tempted to bring them to the flat and at least let him see them from a distance.

'They could stand in the bedroom door maybe?' he said to Dumpling.

But she wouldn't hear of it. 'The very idea!' she said. 'Nu-nu. You let them stay at home vid Ellen. You think your fader vant them to catch the sickness? Nu-nu! Don't you vorry, bubeleh. Ve look after him good.'

The three women took it in turns to sit beside Emmanuel's bed in a room that steadily became more claustrophobic and sour-smelling. His breathing grew more laboured and eating was impossible. From time to time they tried to coax him to take a little sustenance. But it wasn't any good. They tried *kugel*, and chicken soup with barley, they even tried egg beaten up with a precious spoonful of brandy, but he couldn't keep anything down, no matter how mild or how lovingly prepared. It was a terrible trial to him brought up to be long-suffering and considerate and never to give offence to anybody, and soon he was reduced to tears by the treachery of a body he couldn't control. The smell of his vomit distressed him even more than the terrible retching that accompanied it. After a bout of sickness he would feebly turn his head away from the mess he'd made and try to apologize. 'I am so sorry, Rachel bubeleh. Such vork I make for you.'

And she, dabbing his burning forehead with the utmost gentleness, would croon at him as though he were a baby. 'Hush bubeleh! Don't you fret yourself, dolly. It don't matter. You can't help it, bubeleh.'

He slept fitfully, tossing and moaning, but when he was awake and fully conscious he used all his energy to control himself, keeping his lips tight together and making no noise even though his eyes were shaken with the pain that racked him with every breath. The family were torn by his suffering and on Monday they sent for the doctor again.

This time he agreed with them that his patient was rather more ill than he had thought at first. "He should have been improving by now,' he said. 'His breathing is rather too irregular. The result of those cracked ribs, I daresay. We will give him till Friday, Mrs Cheifitz. If he is no better by then I'm afraid he may have to go to hospital.' He gave them aspirin for the pain and left them to struggle on for a little longer, knowing how desperately they all wanted to avoid the hospital if they could.

On Wednesday Emmanuel seemed to be rallying. He ate a little soup and managed to keep it down. But on Thursday he was worse again, struggling for breath and obviously in pain. And when David came to see him on his way to work on Friday, he was shocked to tears by how ill and frail his father looked. His hands were transparent, like bony fishes, and his skin was wrinkled and yellow like parchment. Because he'd lost

343

what little flesh he had, his chin and nose seemed enormous in his shrunken face, and his grey hair stuck out from his skull like a wig that didn't belong to him. But his expression was calm and he was making a great effort to speak clearly, for what he had to say to his son, now, was important.

'You get Rabbi Jaccoby, nu?'

'Now, Papa?'

'Now.' There was a peaceful finality about the word.

He's giving in, David thought, looking at the oddly composed expression on his father's raddled face. He's going to die and we both know it. And he was surprised that he felt no sorrow and no alarm.

He still felt no emotion as he strode through the Buildings to fetch the Rabbi. It was as if he was an actor in some strange play.

'You will send one of the family to your workplace to make your excuses,' Rabbi Jaccoby said. 'We shall stay with him now. You and I and his wife. It is the time.' But even those ominous words provoked no reaction. David waited beside the bed, silently holding his mother's cold hand, as his father slept with his mouth fallen wide open and his bruised chest visibly pulling in air in a series of high-pitched screaming snores. Nobody spoke, for what could any of them say?

Around midday Emmanuel stirred from sleep and put out a hand feebly towards the chair where David was sitting. Every breath was raspingly audible, the air dragging into his lungs slowly and painfully, but he struggled to form words. 'Hear O Israel ...'

David caught at the hand and held it and Rachel knelt by the bed and gathered his other hand and lifted it against her face, and Rabbi Jaccoby began to pray. 'I acknowledge unto thee, O Lord my God and God of my fathers, that both my cure and my death are in thy hands ...'

This must be death, David thought, but he was still calm, noticing the play of sunlight dappling the bedhead, and the white glint of his father's eyes before those papery lids creased down to cover them. 'O may my death be an atonement for all the sins, iniquities and transgressions of which I have been guilty against thee ...' A slight breeze was curling the edge of

344

the curtain, whorling it back on itself in a fat curved shape like a snail shell. 'Bestow upon me the abounding happiness that is stored up for the righteous. Make known unto me the path of life: in thy presence is fullness of joy ...' The glint of eyes again, his mother's grey hair silver in the sunlight. And that awful screaming snore as the slack mouth shuddered soundlessly towards the last words of the prayer. Then they were all speaking the words together. 'Hear O Israel: The Lord is our God, the Lord is one.'

And in the total silence that followed when the prayer was finished he knew that his father was dead.

Nevertheless Rabbi Jaccoby felt for his father's pulse, standing for an endless time beside the bed, head bowed. And David and Rachel stood too, fearful and resigned.

'Cover the mirrors, my daughter,' Rabbi Jaccoby said tenderly. 'They should not witness our misfortune.' And the words released their sorrow, so that she began to wail and he to sob aloud. But she went off to fetch the cloths from the dresser, obedient as a child, and David closed his father's eyes and straightened his poor thin arms and shut his mouth very very gently, because that was the last duty of a son towards his father.

He carried out all his other duties too, telling the family, consoling his aunts, coaxing his mother to eat, and finally arranging the funeral. But he was numb, and although he wept, his tears brought no relief.

It wasn't until the day was over and he was back in Mile End Place with Ellen and the children that the full force of his sorrow drenched down upon him. Then he wept and raged, 'He can't be dead, Ellen. I can't bear it. He's always been there, all my life, always. A *chawchem*, Ellen, a righteous man, everybody said so. Why should he die?' There was no one left to turn to now this good man was dead. Who would advise him and talk to him and joke with him and stand beside him in the synagogue? There was no one. His mind battered itself against the empty space this death had left. 'Oh, why did it have ter be him? The street was full of people, hundreds of 'em. Why him? I can't bear it, Ellen.'

And she held him and stroked his hair and wept with him. And they were both bleak with loss.

The next day he went to work unshaven and with his hair

uncombed, and that upset her even more than his grief had
done, even though old Mrs Brunewald assured that that was
the way Jews always went on. 'They call it the shiva,' she said.
'Seven days of mourning, the shiva. They don't shave or do
their hair or nothing like that. Some of 'em don't even wash.
They'll have the funeral ever so quick too. You see if they
don't. It's their way you see, dear.'

Chapter Twenty-Seven

The funeral was on Monday and, rather to her relief, Ellen discovered that another Jewish custom was to restrict attendance to the men in the family. 'I shall watch it from the archway,' she promised. The route to the Jewish Cemetery was straight up the Mile End Road, so the cortege would pass the end of their street. 'That'ud be all right, wouldn't it? I could sort a' pay me respects that way.'

He agreed, but vaguely, his assent being more of a grunt than a word, and his eyes looking elsewhere. It was as though his senses had been disconnected, she thought, watching him with aching sympathy. He was so clumsy all of a sudden, walking into chairs, breaking pencils, spilling his tea. Yesterday he'd burnt his hand on the stove and he hadn't even noticed. Poor old love, she thought, as he walked bleakly out of the house, we shall 'ave to be ever so gentle with him when 'e comes back.

In the meantime there was the funeral to be got through. She washed her two children very thoroughly and dressed them in their best clothes, and took them down to the archway into the Mile End Road to see their grandfather's passing. And just before the procession arrived she was joined by Hymie's fat wife, Miriam.

'You don't mind if I watch with you, do yer?' she asked. 'Mrs Levy's gone ter keep old Mrs Cheifitz company, so I'm all on me own.'

Ellen said she didn't mind. But there wouldn't have been time for her to object anyway, for the black hearse was in sight. They watched as it passed, and Ellen was surprised and pleased by the size of the crowd that followed it, relations, of course,

347

she'd expected them, but there were neighbours from the Buildings too, and another group that Miriam said were his workmates from Mr Goldman's. It was very impressive.

'That's the way of funerals, dolly,' Miriam said. 'Make a feast, make an enemy; make a funeral, make friends.'

'You goin' to the Buildin's now?' Ellen asked hopefully. She was finding this huge woman's presence rather overpowering in the enclosed heat under the archway, and Jack was really quite heavy to hold for any length of time.

'Nu-nu,' Miriam said. 'Hymie wouldn't allow it. Wouldn't hear of it. In case of "the baby".'

What an odd way to talk of it, Ellen thought, noticing the curious inflection. 'In the family way, are yer?' she asked.

'Well ...' Miriam said, looking archly at her new friend. 'You can never be quite sure, can yer?'

Ellen agreed with her politely, even though she'd always been quite sure when she was expecting, and almost from the first day. The long line of men was still walking past them, and Jack was half asleep.

'I've never enjoyed good health in that respect,' Miriam went on. 'So if your Hymie wants me to give him sons he'll just have to wrap me in cotton wool for nine months, that's all.'

The thought of this huge fat woman wrapped in cotton wool gave Ellen a sudden attack of the giggles. She had to turn her head aside and busy herself unnecessarily with little Jack's bonnet. How dreadful to be wanting to laugh at a time like this! But the next thing Miriam said froze her back to gravity at once.

'I suppose Mrs Cheifitz'll move in with you when shiva's over.' It wasn't even a question, she was so sure of the answer.

'Why would she do that?' Ellen asked, glad that her voice sounded casual despite her alarm.

'Well now, dolly, she couldn't live alone, could she?' Miriam said. 'Jewish women never live alone. It ain't proper.'

'She wouldn't be alone,' Ellen said. 'Not in the Buildin's. There's hundreds a' Jews in the Buildin's.'

'You got the room though, aintcher?' Miriam said, dabbing her forehead with a handkerchief.

They had, Ellen thought. They'd got a darn sight too much

room. They could hardly say no to the woman if she made an issue of it. And in that instant she had an overpowering sense of what it would be like to be forced to live with her mother-in-law. And she knew she couldn't bear it. It was bad enough being disliked from a distance, but to have to see it day in and day out, and without old Papa Cheifitz to temper the unpleasantness. No, no! Something would have to be done to forestall her. And done quickly. She turned away from the tail end of the procession and looked Miriam Levy straight in the small dark eye.

'We was thinkin' a' taking a lodger,' she said. 'Matter a' fact, it's almost fixed.' She was fixing it in her mind as she spoke, so she wasn't really telling a lie.

'Oh!' Miriam said. 'You ain't!' And her fat face crumpled like a balloon deflating. 'I wish you'd said. We'd 'a loved it.' And she burst into tears.

It was surprising and embarrassing, but even while she was feeling both those emotions fairly keenly, Ellen's brain was busily testing a possible solution to her immediate problem.

'Come into the 'ouse,' she invited. 'Tell me all about it.'

So they went back into Ellen's nice brown kitchen and the baby was put in his cot to sleep and Gracie was given two wooden spoons to play with. And Ellen poured tea and Miriam poured out her troubles.

'We ain't 'ad a minute's peace since we got married,' she sobbed. 'It's no joke 'avin' ter share with yer in-laws, I can tell yer. She treats me like a skivvy. It's do this, do that, every minute a' the day. She won't let me get the water of a mornin' 'till Mr Levy's gone down to the shop. I call that cruel ...' The catalogue of grievances went on and on, the most recent washday being detailed splash by quarrelsome splash, and Ellen made murmuring noises of encouragement and appeared to listen. But really she was plotting.

After the second cup of tea and the umpteenth complaint, Miriam paused for breath. 'What's ter become of us?' she implored.

'Tell yer what,' Ellen said. 'This lodger I was tellin' you about 'asn't made 'is mind up yet. You could come 'ere if yer liked. On'y you'd 'ave ter look sharp about it.'

'Dolly!' Miriam shrieked. 'We could move in terday.'

'Come round ternight, when David's 'ome,' Ellen said quickly. 'See what 'e says about it, eh?' She could hardly have them installed before he knew.

'Oh we will, we will,' Miriam promised, effusively grateful. 'You jest can't begin ter know what this means ter me!'

Gracie hurled her spoons into the corner. 'G'acie firsty,' she said.

After her new friend had gone puffing off home, Ellen had second thoughts about her offer. It was underhand and she knew it. She ought to have talked it over with David first. But if she'd done that he'd've told his mother to come and live with them, and then where would they have been? No, she decided, it was a dreadful thing to have done, but she didn't have much choice. 'You got ter be cruel to be kind sometimes, aintcher, my lovey,' she said to her sleeping baby. And Gracie lifted her head out of her mug of water and said, 'Yes.'

Her doubts returned in most uncomfortable strength when David finally got home that evening, for he was grey with fatigue, and almost incapable of speech. But she fed him, and made him tea with lemon, and set a chair in the garden for him, and was ashamed to realize that she was doing these things as much to assuage her conscience as to care for him. But it would all be for the best in the long run, she consoled herself. And it had to be done. She didn't say anything about Hymie and Miriam until they knocked at the door. Then she went out into the garden to explain quickly. 'That'll be Hymie. 'E's got sommink 'e wants to ask yer. I said you wouldn't mind 'im comin'.'

'Nu-nu,' David said vaguely, but as though he agreed. He was too overwhelmed with grief to argue about anything. If Hymie wanted to visit, then let him. Very little mattered now after the misery of the last few days.

They sat in the garden as the sky clouded red and orange and the long day cooled. The two men talked gently about the funeral, and Papa Cheifitz, and how movingly Rabbi Jaccoby had spoken about him. And Miriam sat silent, watching their faces.

And at last Hymie got around to the subject that had brought them to the house. 'Um – Ellen says you was thinkin' a' takin' lodgers,' he said, head bowed, scowling a little, anxious not to give offence to his friend but eager to please his wife.

'Ellen?' David said, still vague.

'When we first moved. You remember,' she prompted. 'We was thinkin' a' lettin' the big bedroom.'

'Yes, yes. I suppose we was.'

'You wouldn't like to take us on, would yer?' Hymie asked. 'We're desperate fer a place of our own. Miriam don't get on with Ma.'

And at that Miriam broke into wailing. 'We're having the most terrible time,' she cried. 'Oy oy! You'd never believe ... We can't stand it another day, I tell you.' And she was off into her complaints again, shaking her head from side to side and crying with abandon.

The sound of her weeping was more than David could bear. He'd heard so many sounds of grief that day that he was lacerated with sorrow. 'Don't cry,' he begged. 'Hymie, make her stop. You can come 'ere if you like.' Anything, only just make her stop that noise.

It was accomplished so easily, Ellen felt weak with relief. She'd been preparing herself for arguments or even a downright refusal. But one glance at her husband showed her that there was no fight left in him at all. And that made her feel ashamed of herself all over again. 'I shouldn't've done it, she thought. Not now, when 'e's 'ad more than 'e can stand. I'll make it up to 'im after, I swear ter God.

'Oy! D'yer mean it?' Miriam said, and she stopped crying at once and flung her arms round Ellen's neck and kissed her moistly. 'Oy, you're so good to us. We ain't never 'ad such friends.'

'We didn't ought to 'ave come,' Hymie said, because his friend looked more ghastly than he'd done all day. ' 'Specially terday. I'm that grateful you can't think, Davey. We'll talk about it termorrer, nu?'

'You can 'ave the one room,' Ellen told him, feeling she ought to be businesslike about it. 'Water when yer want. Tuesday washday. You can come up an' see it now if yer like.' And give

351

poor Davey a bit 'a 'peace and quiet.

So they saw the big bedroom and told her privately how much they appreciated it and how kind she was. And Hymie fitted a gas ring in the grate the next morning and they moved in at the end of the afternoon. And even Ellen felt it had all happened too quickly.

But David didn't complain. Not even when they went to bed in their new small bedroom downstairs and could hear their new lodgers clumping about above their heads. Not even when Gracie woke in the middle of the night and she had to go upstairs to attend to her. It was as though none of it was happening to him. He slept fitfully and ate what he could, and spoke when he was spoken too, his eyes gaunt and his face dirty with stubble. One day was much the same as the next. He drew the pictures required of him, knowing them worthless, and spent the evening at his mother's because it was the duty of a son to comfort his mother during the shiva. And the terrible ache of his loss took a very long time to fade.

On Thursday, when the seven days were nearly over Rivke and Dumpling walked him off to Brick Lane to 'make a decision'.

Rivke came straight to the point, brusque as ever, even in mourning. 'So,' she said. 'You moder vill live vid you now, nu?'

He supposed so. He had always known that was how it would be. 'I'll tell Ellen,' he said.

'Sunday she should move,' Rivke said. 'The next rent's due Monday.'

It came as a profound shock to him when he got back home that night and Ellen said it wasn't possible. 'We got six people in the 'ouse already,' she said. 'Where'd we put 'er?'

'Hymie'll 'ave to go, then.' That was simple.

But she scowled and looked uncomfortable. 'You can't do that, Davey,' she said. 'That ain't fair. We've give 'em our word. Can't yer Ma find somewhere else?'

'Somewhere else?' he echoed stupidly. 'She's my mother, Ellen. She's my responsibility.'

'Not no more, she ain't!' she insisted. 'I'm your responsibility now. Me and the kids.'

'We got duties to the older generation too.'

'Oh come on!' she mocked. 'What's she ever done fer us?'

'She brought me up, Ellen.' Surely she wasn't expecting him to deny that.

'Well, she never brought me up.' Her face was set and stubborn. 'She don't like me, Davey. She don't like me and she don't like the kids. She'd be miserable being with us.'

That might be true. The thought made him falter. 'I dunno,' he said wearily. If only his father were still alive. He'd have known what they ought to do.

'Well, she can't come here!' Ellen said, massively stubborn now. 'We got a house full.'

And you filled it, he thought miserably, but he didn't have the energy to fight over it.

'I dunno,' he said again, and he remembered the only person who could help him. 'I'll ask Dumpling.'

'You ain't!' Dumpling shrieked when he confessed he'd got lodgers. 'Oy oy, Davey bubeleh, vhat you thinkin' of, vid your moder the vay she is?'

'They was in a state,' he explained. 'Miriam said she couldn't go on. I dunno. It seemed the only thing ter do at the time. I dunno, Aunty Dumpling, I don't seem to be able ter think straight these days.' He looked so woebegone, she kissed him at once.

'Never you mind, bubeleh,' she said. 'You're an *edel* boy. Ve couldn't vish for a better. You done all you could. You leave this to your Aunty Dumpling, nu?'

'Are you sure?' he said anxiously.

She gave him a little shake. 'Don't I tell you?'

It was as if she'd taken a great burden from his back. He felt an overpowering need to lie down and sleep. But first he had to show her how grateful he was. 'A woman of valour, who can find?' he said. 'For her price is far above rubies.'

The woman of valour was even more valiant than he knew. On Sunday she relinquished her dream that Fred Morrison would marry her, and decided to take her widowed sister-in-law into her home.

For once she and Fred Morrison stayed indoors and spent the evening talking things over. They both found it very distressing.

'So it's the vay ve are,' Dumpling tried to explain, having fed

353

him with prune cake and lemon tea as the very least she could do to soften the blow. 'A vidow voman ve don't leave alone. The same vid me. Vhen Mr Esterman died, my dear Rivke she takes me in the self same day. Such a good voman! I stay vid them years, till she marry.'

'Of course,' Mr Morrison agreed, stroking his narrow moustache anxiously. 'It has to be done. I quite understand. Only … I hope I may come to visit you now and again, after …'

'Nu nu, Mr Morrison, von't make no difference,' Dumpling promised. 'Sunday ve go out, same as alvays.'

He was comforted, but only marginally. 'I wouldn't want to butt in or nothing. Not being Jewish, if you see what I mean.' He was so upset, he couldn't raise his eyes to look at her.

'So you're a good man, Fred Morrison,' she said trenchantly. 'Jew or no Jew, a good man, don't I tell you. You visit vhenever you vant.'

But of course he didn't, even though their Sunday outings continued. How could he? It would have been intruding.

Rachel was unhappy about the arrangement too. 'I should a' gone vid Davey,' she complained. 'If it hadn't a' been for that shiksa, may she be forgiven, I'd a' gone vid my Davey.'

'Nu,' Dumpling agreed sympathetically. 'So you better here vid me, maybe.'

'I should have gone vid Davey. We could've settled in good. I could've help her vid the children.'

'But you don't like her!' Dumpling said surprised.

'Nu nu, I like her vell enough.'

Dumpling decided it would be prudent to ignore this. 'We get along good,' she tried to encourage. 'Two old vidow vomen, ve got a lot in common, don't I tell you.'

But Rachel wept and wouldn't be comforted for a very long time. A month went by and she was still aggrieved, even when she was sitting in Dumpling's comfortable chairs eating Dumpling's delicious cooking. 'It ain't right, Dumpling,' she said over and over again. 'I should a' gone vid Davey.'

'Your Davey got enough to cope vid vid that Miriam,' Dumpling said one evening, giving her the conspiratorial smile of the gossip. 'You should hear vhat I hear about that one this

354

morning. The vorst voman in the vorld, so Mrs Levy says. A monkey ain't such trouble.'

'Oy, oy!' Rachel said, interested out of her grievance at last. 'So tell me, Dumpling?'

Miriam Levy certainly was a very disagreeable young woman, as Ellen and David were discovering to their considerable discomfort. It was almost impossible to please her, for she seemed to have made up her mind that everyone in the world was out to make her unhappy. She was always complaining about something. Even the weather was deliberately against her. 'It ain't fair giving me Tuesday washday,' she grumbled to Ellen. 'It always rains of a Tuesday. You get the best a' the weather every time.'

'It rains on Mondays too,' Ellen said reasonably. 'Six a' one, 'alf a dozen a' the other.'

But reason was something Miriam was congenitally unable to recognize. 'It was a lovely day this Monday,' she wailed. 'You got all your washing lovely an' dry. Me, I still got it drippin' on me 'ead terday. It ain't fair!'

Hymie couldn't do anything right either. If he came home late for his supper, she said he'd gone out of his way to ruin it; if he was early it was because he was spying on her. And as she decreed that the difference between early and late was a matter of a mere five minutes or so, he had a very hard time of it. As the months passed and her complaints grew shriller and more persistent he spent less and less of his time in the house, preferring the company of his gambling friends, who smoked a lot but spoke very little.

David was upset at the change in his old friend. 'All the life's gone out of him,' he said to Ellen.

'Can yer wonder?' she said. 'She don't give 'im a chance, poor beggar.' The longer they all lived together the more she regretted her decision. But she couldn't admit it. Not even to David. Not when she'd manoeuvred it the way she had. It's a punishment, she told herself, an' serve yer right.

But at last, after nearly a year, nature provided her with an excuse to get rid of her uncomfortable tenant.

'We got another baby on the way,' she told David, when two months had passed and she was quite sure. 'They'll 'ave ter go,

355

won't they? We shall need the room.'

He was doubly pleased by her news this time. 'I'll tell old Hymie ternight,' he said.

But Hymie had news of his own. 'Oy oy!' he crowed. 'We got a baby coming an' all. Whatcher think a' that? Beginnin' a' January she reckons.'

She also reckoned there was no possibility of moving until long after the birth. 'You vant I should lose the baby?' she asked shrilly. 'You know I don't 'ave good health in that respect.' Which was true enough, for she'd had two miscarriages already. 'Ai-yi-yi! Vhat's the rush? Ve got plenty room. It ain't no vay to treat a voman in my condition, I tell you.'

So they had to let her stay, and very difficult and unpleasant it was for all of them.

Chapter Twenty-Eight

David and Ellen were eating their breakfast early one January morning when Mr Quinton came knocking at their door.

'Hello, Quin. Come in quick,' David told him, shutting the door on the chill air in Mile End Place. 'Whatcher doin' down this way?'

'Just had a telephone call from old Palfrey,' Quin said. He was proud of his ownership of one of these new devices and especially now that it had earned its keep. 'Apparently we're workin' down this way today. Sidney Street. D'yer know it?'

'Just across the road,' David said, finishing his bread quickly. 'What's up?'

'Bunch of anarchists,' Quin said laconically. 'Been shootin' policemen, by all accounts. Anyway, they've barricaded 'emselves inside some house in Sidney Street, an' old Palfrey reckons we ought ter go an' have a look-see.'

Ellen was sitting on her heels in front of the hearth, trying to coax the fire to light properly. She was very near the end of her pregnancy now and she and the baby were very uncomfortable. David kissed the top of her head. 'Mind how you go,' he said. 'I shan't be late back.'

'This coal don't catch like the last lot,' she said, and she addressed the fire sternly. 'Come on! Burn will yer!'

It was a grey morning and the Mile End Road was swirling with mist that obscured their feet and trailed dampness into their lungs. 'Oy! It's perishing,' David said, blowing on his fingers to warm them. 'Let's go down the Underground and draw the trains.' They'd done a lovely piece on the Metropolitan District Railway just before Christmas. He'd been as warm as toast for three blissful days.

'Never boil your cabbages twice, my son,' Quint advised as they turned up their coat collars and prepared to face the chill.

'I hope this'll be a nice quick job, that's all,' David said.

But it was a rotten long one.

It was just five past seven and still dark when they reached Sidney Street, which was a poorly lit, insignificant place lined with flat three-storey tenements and baroque pubs, dirty, overcrowded and poverty-stricken, exactly the same as all the other alleys in the East End. Front doors stood ajar, as they always did in tenement houses, dim gaslights cast a yellow mist through some of the dirty curtains, early risers were shuffling off to work. There was nothing remarkable about the place at all.

As his eyes grew accustomed to the lack of light, David saw that there were several policemen standing about beside the 'Rising Sun', looking self-conscious and pretending not to be there, and that over on the other side of the road, gathered at the corner of Sidney Street and the Mile End Road, were three equally obvious newsmen, hunched in their overcoats, smoking and gossiping.

'There's old Tin Ribs,' Quin said, lighting a fag as he took stock of the situation. 'From the *Express*. 'E'll know what's what, if anyone does. Got a good nose fer news has old Tin Ribs.'

It was certainly a very red one, David thought, as they crossed the road towards the young man, almost the same colour as his muffler. But he was a friendly young man and greeted them affably, introducing his colleagues from the *Mail* and the *Graphic*.

'Whatcher got?' Quin asked.

'Murderers, so they reckon,' Tin Ribs said. 'Gang that shot them coppers down Houndsditch way. You remember. Two, three weeks ago. Done a jewellers.'

'Peter the Painter an' his mob,' the man from the *Mail* told them lugubriously. 'Terrible villain, Peter the Painter. Won't take him without a fight.'

'They're in No. 100, opposite the 'Rising Sun',' Tin Ribs said. 'Police sergeant says there'll be a shoot-out.' He was licking his lips happily at the thought.

358

'Just in time, eh Cheify?' Quin said.

'Looks like it,' Tin Ribs agreed, rubbing his red nose on a grey handkerchief. 'Hope they look sharp. It's brass monkey weather.'

A black shadow approached them ponderously and became a police sergeant, bulky in his thick cape. 'Don't suppose none a' you gents could speak Yiddish by any chance, could yer?' he said.

David admitted to the talent, wondering why he asked.

'What a bit a' luck,' the sergeant said. 'Do a little job fer us, would yer?' He began to walk back down the road again, indicating by the tilt of his body that David should follow.

'What sort a' job?' David asked, falling into step beside him.

'Nip in to one 'undred,' the sergeant said, 'an' tell all the others to make 'emselves scarce. They got six families in there beside the mob, you see, sir. Super wants 'em out of it before the sparks fly. Mob's on the top floor. Don't go beyond the first flight a' stairs, an' you should be safe enough. Not much sign a' life so far. Most of 'em are asleep.'

It was better than standing around in the cold doing nothing. So he agreed.

No. 100 was a squalid, decrepit house, smelling of damp coal and burning bones and stale piss and shit. He'd spent such a long time now in Ellen's well-scrubbed home he'd forgotten what it was like to live in dirt. The hall was full of cardboard boxes and smeared paper and bits of ancient rag, and the banisters were so badly broken he thought it prudent not to touch them as he made his way cautiously up the stairs. He could hear voices on the floor above him and when he reached the landing a bearded man wearing long side ringlets and a Polish peaked cap eased his head out of the nearest door and looked at him anxiously.

'Shalom!' David said. 'I am David Cheifitz, a Jew like yourself.'

'Ai yi!' the man said. 'Come in, my friend. You tell me what is happening, nu? Is it true the police surround the house?'

David stayed where he was on the landing. There was no time for visiting. 'You must leave this house at once,' he said. 'The police may use guns.'

'*Gevalt!*'

'Do you have relations you could go to?'

'In Poland.'

'Friends?'

'In this room, as you see.' It was crowded with young men, sleeping on the floor, under sacking.

'Then you must go to neighbours. Anywhere. Wake up!' he said to the sleepers. 'You are in danger. You must leave this house.'

By this time the sound of urgent Yiddish had alerted the occupants of the other two rooms on the floor and the landing was full of people, all talking at once, and in a state of frantic agitation. 'Hush! Hush!' he said. 'There are men on the floor above we must not wake.'

'Yes, yes,' a fat woman said. 'The Russians. We tell them too, nu?'

'They are the ones the police have come for,' David tried to explain above the hubbub. 'Peter the Painter and some others, nu? You must leave them where they are.'

'Peter the Painter?' the woman said. 'No. No one of that name, I assure you. Two young Russians, nice quiet young men. Anarchists. Wanted by the police in Russia they are, for opposing the Tsar-murderer, may the good Lord bless them. So to England they came for safety.'

But then another woman took over, wailing, 'I cannot leave my work. All these skins to finish. How shall I live if I leave the skins?'

'Gather them. Take them with you,' David urged. The noise they were making and their total lack of comprehension was making him feel panicky. 'You have ten minutes,' he said to them all. 'That is all. I must tell the people downstairs.' And he left them milling about on the landing, blundering in and out of their doors, weeping and arguing.

As he turned to go down the broken stairs again he could hear furniture being dragged about on the floor above his head. They've woken the Russians, he thought, and was suddenly afraid, and wished he hadn't volunteered for this impossible job. What if they really *are* murderers with guns? They could come out on the landing and blow us all to pieces.

360

'Hurry!' he yelled as he leaped down the stairs.

The hall was full of people too, women in shawls, with small children clinging to the ragged edges of their skirts and men in peaked caps and fur hats, with bundles clutched to their chests. Pale hands reached up to grab at him as he reached the bottom of the stairs. 'You must tell us, young man. Is it true they've come to arrest us? We have done nothing, you understand. We work well. We make no trouble. You must tell them.'

'They do not come for you,' he said, over and over again. 'They come for the Russians who live at the top of the house. You must leave for the time being because it is dangerous for you to be here.' He couldn't understand why they were arguing. 'You must leave.'

'Tell them we have done nothing.'

'Ai!' he roared at them, raising his arms in exasperation. 'Such fools you are. Stay and be killed, then. I can do no more than warn you. I have tried. If you are shot it will be your own foolishness.'

'You are a good man,' one of the women said, patting his shoulder. 'We do as you say, nu?'

But even with her help it was far more than ten minutes before the last of the tenants finally agreed to leave. David was on tenterhooks all the time in case the Russians appeared with their guns, but he couldn't leave until they were all out, no matter how foolishy they were behaving.

'That the lot?' the sergeant said, when he walked back to the corner of the street where the police were gathered.

'There's two Russians on the top floor,' David said. 'That's all. No one's heard of Peter the Painter. They didn't know what I was talking about.'

But the policeman had other things on his mind now that the house was clear. 'If I can just trouble you gentlemen to get right back,' he said, urging them to retreat with sweeping movements of his outstretched hands. 'Right down the end a' the street, if you don't mind.'

'Now what?' Tin Ribs said, when they'd gathered at the corner of the Mile End Road and David had told them all his story.

'Watch and wait,' Quin said. 'That's about the size of it.

361

Watch and wait.'

So they watched and waited, and David made a few quick sketches of his extraordinary evacuees, and the sky gradually lightened above the sooty brickwork of the tenements, smearing itself with dirty grey rags of cloud. When he looked up from his last sketch, he was surprised to see how much lighter it had become and how thoroughly the police had cleared the street.

'I could use some breakfast,' Tin Ribs was saying, when a huge pantechnicon, drawn by two horses, came rumbling round the corner. They watched as it was pulled to a halt in the middle of the empty road outside No. 100. Then there was a long pause, and David drew a sketch of the vehicle. A small crowd gathered at the end of the street, and four pigeons flew down into the road and strutted about beside the horses' hooves hopefully.

Then the back of the pantechnicon opened and a police sergeant dropped out, picked up a handful of pebbles, walked round to the front of the van and began to lob them at the windows. The street was so quiet they could hear them clattering against the glass. 'Police!' he called. 'Come quietly! You're surrounded.'

The answer was immediate and brutal. The window at the top of the house was raised, the black barrel of a gun protruded, there was a spurt of red flame and the sergeant fell backwards clutching his chest.

'Good God!' Quin said. 'They've shot him!'

The horror of it made David's legs shake. Then so many things happened so quickly, he didn't have time to feel anything.

Six or seven policemen tumbled out of the van and ran to their injured colleague. They improvised a stretcher with two cloaks and slung him inside it before any of the newsmen saw what they were doing. Then they were carrying him off, running across the road with their bundled burden swinging danger-ously between them, straight through the open door of the house opposite. The pantechnicon drove off at great speed and then the landlord of the 'Rising Sun' was standing beside Mr Quinton offering them a ringside seat on the roof of his pub, 'at a quid a time'.

'You're on!' Quin said. 'Come on, Cheify!'

They had to run back along Sidney Street towards that gun,

362

and the patch of dark blood on the cobbles. But no guns fired and soon they were safely inside the pub and climbing the stairs towards the roof. 'We got a good stout parapet,' the landlord said. 'You'll be as safe as 'ouses up there.'

It *was* a solid parapet, to David's considerable relief, but it was also extremely cold. 'Was 'e dead?' he asked, as they sat themselves down on the chilly lead sheeting.

'No,' Tin Ribs said. ' 'E was still groanin', poor beggar.'

'They'll bring the troops out now, sure as fate,' Quin said. But even he wasn't prepared for the number of troops they brought. The first batch arrived within half an hour. Scots Guards, armed with rifles, who took up positions against the walls to right and left of the house. By ten o'clock in the morning no more shots had been fired but the street was swarming with troops and policemen. Over a thousand, according to the knowledgeable estimate of the man from the *Mail*. And Tin Ribs returned from a foray downstairs with the news that the injured policeman was called Sergeant Leeson. He'd been taken to the London Hospital and operated on, and although he was in 'a serious condition' he was expected to live.

I shall certainly 'ave something to tell Ellen when I get home tonight, David thought. I wonder if she's heard what's going on?

But over in Mile End Place, Ellen wasn't the least bit interested in guns and gunmen. She had problems enough of her own.

Half an hour after David left, when the fire was just beginning to draw and the chill was lifting from the room, she had her first labour pain. It was surprisingly strong. And so was the second, which came twenty minutes later. Well, that's a mercy, she thought. Perhaps this one'll be quick. Jack had been ever so slow.

As there was still warm water in the kettle she washed the breakfast things before she sat down and wrote a note to the midwife and a postcard to Aunty Dumpling. 'It is today. Hope to see you later on. Love, Ellen.' Then she rattled the back of the hearth with the poker to call Mrs Streete, who had promised to look after Gracie and Jack when the time came.

And Hymie put his head round the kitchen door. 'Could yer come up to the missus?' he said, squinting at her in his anxiety. 'She's ever so poorly.'

Now what? Ellen thought. She'd had just about enough of Miriam and her illnesses. There'd hardly been a day in the last nine months when she hadn't complained about something or other, indigestion, aching feet, constipation, piles, swollen ankles, and all suffered with the maximum noise and drama.

'I've just give Mrs Streete a knock,' she said. 'Will it wait?'

'She's ever so bad,' Hymie said, drooping in the doorway. 'We been up most a' the night.'

'Oh all right,' Ellen said wearily. 'You stay here an' let her in.' And she toiled up the stairs to attend to her troublesome tenant.

Miriam was mounded in the bed, huge-bellied as a whale. 'Oy-oy-oy!' she groaned as Ellen entered the room. 'Such pains you wouldn't believe!' Her face was shiny with sweat despite the cold in the room.

Not her an' all, Ellen thought. That'ud be too much. 'Whereabouts?' she asked.

'Vhereabouts vhat?'

'The pain.' Stupid woman!

'All over,' Miriam said, rolling her eyes. 'All down me back, me legs, down there. All over, I tell you. Oy-oy-oy! D'yer think it's the baby, Ellen? Oy-oy! It ain't the baby, *has vesholem*. Such pains you wouldn't believe, dolly.'

Ellen had a pain of her own to contend with just at that moment, so she sat down on the edge of the bed and closed her eyes and let it ride. She could hear Hymie opening the door to Mrs Streete and was relieved to think that her signal had been heard.

'Get up! Get up!' Miriam shrieked, rolling her bulk away from the tilt of the mattress. 'Cantcher see I'm in agony?'

'No you ain't,' Ellen said, when her pain had faded, 'you're in labour.'

'Ai-yi-yi-yi!' Miriam yelled. 'So get the midwife. Vhat you vaiting for?'

'She's on 'er way,' Ellen said. 'I've started an' all.'

'You can't have!' Miriam said, opening her eyes wide in

disbelief. 'Oy! You're selfish! You never think of me! Who'll look after me now?'

'You'll 'ave ter look after yerself fer once,' Ellen said sharply. 'Do yer good!'

Miriam threw the covers over her head and howled like a baby.

'An' if you're gonna make that noise, I'm off,' Ellen said. 'I got a lot ter do, if you ain't.'

'You're heartless!' Miriam said. 'That's vhat. You ain't got a sympathetic bone in the whole a' your body!'

It was bitterly cold on the roof of the 'Rising Sun', but the newsmen were equal to it. As the lull continued, they took it in turns to retreat to the pub for hot pies, hotter spirits and any gossip that was going. Soon there was quite a party atmosphere up on the lead sheeting, for there was plenty to see and plenty to talk about. The curtains were still drawn across the attic window opposite, but the Scots Guards had been deployed at every vantage point. Guns bristled from the windows facing the beleaguered house and the doorways were thick with uniforms.

The firing began without any warning. It was so loud and so sudden it made them all jump. 'Get yer 'eads down!' Quin warned, ducking behind the parapet, for bullets were hitting the walls of No. 100 and hissing off at every angle. But David was determined to see what was going on, so although he crouched down he managed to keep watch through one of the decorative gaps in the parapet. It was a very long bombardment and it came from every side. There was even a detachment of Scots Guards lying on newspaper placards at the end of the road, firing from their bellies in true military style and providing him with an excellent picture. But it was the attic window that tugged most powerfully at his imagination.

When Sergeant Leeson had been shot, he'd been horrified and afraid, viewing the nozzle of that black gun as utterly evil and threatening. Now, as the two Russians fought back against the barrage, their guns spitting red defiance at the hundreds below them he realized he was seeing them in quite a different way. His first sketch of the fighting showed a volley of smoke and flame all spurting in the same direction. His second was a quick line-drawing of those two isolated guns, and as his pencil hissed across the paper, he knew he was feeling a sneaking sympathy for them.

After half an hour there was a halt in the barrage and a police inspector with a megaphone, keeping at a safe distance from the house, called on its occupants to surrender.

'Fat lot a' good that is,' David said, 'seein' they don't speak English.'

'Ours not to reason why, old son,' Quin said. ' 'Ave a gasper.'

'They know they gotta surrender, don't you worry,' the man from the *Mail* remarked. 'Bleedin' anarchists! We should never a' let 'em in the country in the first place.'

'Didn'tcher say they was Russians, Cheify?' Tin Ribs asked.

'Well, there you are then!' the *Mail* said contemptuously. 'We all know what Russians are like.'

'Nice quiet young men,' David said, quoting the fat woman on the landing.

'They're the worst,' the *Mail* said.

But worst or best, they didn't surrender and presently the barrage started up again.

'I'm off fer a spot a' dinner,' Quin said. 'You coming, Cheify? This could go on fer hours.'

And he was right. It did. For two, three, four hours until the street stank of cordite and the cobbles were littered with spent cartridge cases. And still the Russians wouldn't surrender.

Just after one o'clock an important personage arrived, flanked by high-ranking officers bright with brass. They took shelter behind the dividing wall at the end of the terrace and watched events with great interest and obvious enjoyment.

'Home Secretary, that is,' Quin said. 'Mr Winston Churchill. Bit of a card by all accounts. Wonder what he's told them ter do. We'll 'ave a sketch of him, Cheify.'

So David sketched the Home Secretary, and the firing continued, and Tin Ribs said he wouldn't be a bit surprised if they didn't carry on all night.

The end, when it came, was as sudden and dramatic as the start had been. A haze of grey smoke clouded out of the attic window, 'Hello!' Tin Ribs said. 'Burning their papers, I'll bet. Any sign of 'em coming out?'

They craned over the parapet at the dark doorway, but it remained empty, even though the volume of firing had certainly decreased.

'Must 'ave a lot a' papers,' the *Mail* said. 'They're kicking up a proper stink.' So much smoke was billowing from the window it had already risen above the chimneys. And then there were yellow sparks spurting out of the chimneys and flames glowing red behind the curtains.

'It's on fire!' David yelled. 'That ain't papers! That's the room!' And he remembered the furniture being dragged across the floor in that room, and wondered how the Russians would get out.

They had very little time to do anything, for within ten minutes the top floor of the house was ablaze.

Aunty Dumpling saw the smoke as she got off the tram at Mile End Place. Someone's on fire, she thought, but she forgot about it as soon as she let herself into the house, for she could hear Ellen panting and groaning in the front bedroom, and the midwife urging her on. 'Push, dearie! Push!'

'You vant any help?' she said, peering round the door.

'Wore herself out running up an' down stairs to that one,' the midwife said, nodding towards the ceiling. 'Now she ain't got the strength.'

'Miriam, is it?' Dumpling said, listening to the high-pitched, continuous wailing above them.

'Wants *all* my attention *all* the time,' the midwife said. 'She's got a good long way to go yet. Not like Mrs Cheifitz. 'Nother one, dearie? Let's see if we can use it, shall we?'

'Aunt,' Ellen gasped, as the pain began to grip. 'Make 'er – stop 'er – row – fer Gawd's sake … Can't – do nothink …'

'So don't you vorry, bubeleh,' Dumpling said fiercely. 'I see to her good.' And she went lumbering up the stairs at once to put paid to the aggravation.

Miriam was sitting on the floor with the blankets round her shoulders. She'd cried so much her face was covered with red blotches, but when she saw Dumpling she sniffed to a halt.

'Ai-yi! Vhat you doing down there?' Dumpling demanded. 'You catch your death a' cold.' And she put out a plump hand to haul Miriam to her feet.

It took a lot of doing, for the pregnant Mrs Levy weighed considerably more than Dumpling did, and reluctance increased her weight even further. 'Leave me be!' Miriam wailed. 'I might as well die on the floor as anywhere.'

'So first you look after your health,' Dumpling said sternly, lugging at her arms. 'You can alvays die later.'

And that made Miriam grimace, and lifted her spirits and her bulk for a few valuable seconds, so that Dumpling was able to lower her into the cane chair by the fire. 'Cup of tea ve make,' she said. 'You ate today, nu?'

'Ellen bought me sommink up dinner time.'

I bet she did, Dumpling thought. You take advantage of my bubeleh. 'I vonder your moder ain't here,' she said rather tetchily. 'You need a moder, a time like this.'

To her dismay Miriam's face crumpled into tears again. But she didn't howl. She cried quietly, letting her tears fall as though she didn't notice them. 'She don't love me, Aunty Dumpling,' she said.

'Oy! Such a thing to say! 'Course she love you. A moder!'

'She don't. Nobody loves me. She an' Pa went off ter Salford the minute they'd married me off. That's why they done it. First me big sister, then me little sister, then me. An' off they went, them an' me brother Izzie. Pleased ter see the back a' me they was. They never loved me.' She sighed and mopped her eyes with the cuff of her nightdress. 'They don't even write, an' I send 'em a letter every week, reg'lar as clockwork. Nobody loves me. Hymie thinks I'm hideous. 'E said so. An' 'is Ma can't bear me. She said I was ter get out the 'ouse.'

Despite herself, Dumpling felt sorry for her, so fat and ugly with no one to love her. 'So ve get this baby born,' she comforted, patting Miriam's vast belly. 'Then they love you, don't I tell you.'

Talk of the baby reminded Miriam of her pains. 'Oy!' she said with surprise. 'I ain't had a single pain since you come in.' Then the knowledge worried her. 'That ain't right, surely ter goodness.'

'Oy! Such a voman,' Dumpling laughed. 'Pains she vants! Listen, dolly, I fill the kettle, nu? Ve all have a nice cup of tea. Vhat you say? You get your pains soon enough, I tell you.'

'Oy! Tea!' Miriam sighed. 'I'd love it.'

'Get the cups,' Dumpling commanded. 'Ve keep ourselves busy ve don't notice pains, nu?'

So they made the bed, and lit the gas, and stoked the fire, and tidied the room, while the kettle boiled on the hob. And Miriam didn't moan once, although she had two pains that were really quite strong. And then while they were sipping their tea in front of the fire, they heard the first reedy cry of Ellen's newborn baby.

Dumpling went puffing off down the stairs at once to see what it was. She was alarmed to see that Ellen looked completely exhausted, lying on the pillows with her eyes shut and her face deathly pale in the gaslight. But the baby was a fine specimen. She watched, controlling her impatience, as the midwife bundled it into a napkin and suspended it from her hand scales, its pink limbs threshing and kicking. 'A boy,' she told its proud aunt. 'Seven pounds.' And she wrapped the protesting infant in a shawl and handed it back to Ellen for comfort. And Ellen opened her eyes and kissed her baby, and to Dumpling's relief the colour eased back into her cheeks again.

'A dolly!' Dumpling said, weeping freely. 'Great is our God and greatly to be praised for His loving kindness. So pretty! So look at that liddle head, vhy don't you. Such thick hair, nu. You ever see such eyes? A dolly.'

'Nip next door an' bring the kids back,' Ellen begged. 'They been in there hours.' It had worried her to be parted from them for such a long time, and now the sooner they were all together again the better.

So Dumpling went off to collect them as quickly as her fat legs would allow, and they crept into their mother's room, overawed by the strangeness of the occasion and the stern eye of the midwife, and were introduced to their new brother. And Gracie said she thought he was quite nice. But Jack wanted to know when it was teatime.

Miriam was disgruntled by the news 'A boy!' she said enviously. 'Oy oy! She should be so lucky! Mine'll be a girl, sure as eggs is eggs.'

And so, four hours later, while Hymie was biting his nails in Ellen's kitchen, she was.

Chapter Twenty-Nine

When David came back to Mile End Place that evening he was
so drained by the emotions of his extraordinary day that all he
wanted to do was eat and sleep.

He and Quin and Tin Ribs had stayed in Sidney Street until
the fire had finally been extinguished and two pathetically
charred corpses had been carried out of the wreckage. The
troops marched away as soon as the blaze was well established,
there being no possibility of anybody being left alive in the
house for them to shoot at, and the police followed them soon
afterwards as a sooty dusk descended to blot out what little
light was left under the pall of smoke and the steam from the
firemen's hoses.

It was a melancholy darkness and the three men standing
about in its chill watched the last ghoulish act of the tragedy
with a growing sense that justice had not been done.

'I reckon they fired that house deliberate,' Tin Ribs said.

'Who?' David asked. 'The Russians?' Surely they hadn't
committed suicide. Not after putting up such a fight.

'Nah!' Tin Ribs scoffed at his naivety. 'The rozzers!'

'Wouldn't be surprised,' Quin said. 'Makes yer wonder why
they done it, though, don't it?'

David was remembering the fat woman and the way she'd
spoken about the Russians. Nice, quiet young men. 'What if
they got the wrong ones?' he wondered. 'What if it weren't
them stole the jewellery?'

'Never know now, will we?' Quin said. 'That's the beauty of
a fire. Burns all the evidence, one way or the other.'

It was an uncomfortable idea and it worried him all the way
home. So much so, that when Aunty Dumpling came to the

door to greet him, bubbling with the news that he had another son, his first reaction was a flicker of annoyance.

Then he remembered himself and went into the bedroom to see his newest child. But he was leaden-footed with weariness.

At first sight and in the soft light from the gas lamp he thought the bed was full of children, for there were so many little hands and so many wide-eyed faces and such a tumble of dark hair above the white linen of their nightgowns. But then he realized that one of the little faces belonged to Ellen, and that she was lying propped against the pillows like a doll, her hands listless and her blue eyes shadowed with fatigue. Jack was cuddled against her side, sucking his thumb, his long face sombre, but his sister sat in the middle of the bed with the new baby weightily across her knees, watching with fascination as he grasped her forefinger with his tiny hand and gazed at her with all his newborn intensity.

'Look what we got, Pa,' she said. 'Ain't 'e a duck?'

But he was too far gone to respond. 'You oughter be in bed!' he told her irritably.

'We sittin' up,' Jack said solemnly. 'Aunty Dump'in' said.'

'Till yer Pa come in,' Ellen said, trying to smooth the moment. 'You was ter sit up till yer Pa come in. Now 'e's in. So you ought ter go ter bed, didn'tcher?'

'Liddle boys vhat come ter bed good get dolly mixtures,' Aunty Dumpling promised from the doorway.

'And little girls?' Gracie said, smiling because she already knew the answer.

So to the great relief of their parents they allowed themselves to be led upstairs, where Miriam's baby was mewing like a kitten and Miriam was scolding her husband.

David took off his boots and hung up his jacket and removed his tie. Then he stretched himself out on the coverlet beside his drowsy wife, and they talked in the desultory shorthand of the long-married.

'Was it bad, nu?' he asked.

'I was tired. Miriam's been a pest.'

'A pretty baby.'

'What'll we call him?'

There was only one name possible after such a day.

371

'Benjamin,' he said. Child of sorrows.

'Um, I like that,' she approved, sleepily. 'Benny.' She was too tired even to wonder whether he'd ask about the brit. 'D'you 'ave a good day?'

'Terrible,' he said, but he was too tired even to begin the story. 'Tell yer termorrer.'

When Aunty Dumpling crept back into the room half an hour later, all three were sound asleep, her dear Davey so dark-skinned and red-lipped and handsome, her dear Ellen so pale and exhausted with her lovely hair trailing across the pillow, and that dear little baby tucked under the coverlet between them.

She wrote them a brief note, 'Stew simmering in sorcepan. See you 8.30. Fondest love, R', and left them to rest.

Benjamin Cheifitz woke them up at five o'clock the next morning, when they still needed a lot more sleep. While Ellen was feeding him and changing his nappie, she told his father what a hard time she'd had while he was being born, and impressed upon him that Miriam had *got* to be told to leave. 'You'll 'ave ter get rid of her,' she said. 'I can't stand no more. Not after that.'

David was too tired to open his eyes but he groaned a promise.

'It's easy enough,' she said, volubly practical now that she was awake. 'We want the room back. See if you can get 'em to go 'fore I'm up an' about. It'll be merry hell trying ter share the copper now she's got nappies ter wash. She'll be on and on at me, you see if she ain't.'

She spent so much time talking about Miriam he didn't get a chance to tell her about the siege, and that irritated him because he knew it was a great deal more important than a quarrel between two women. But when he got home in the evening, he didn't need to, because she'd seen it in the papers.

'Is that where you was?' she said, when the kids had been settled for the night. 'Dangerous anarchists, it says 'ere. Sounds awful.'

David was very upset by the reports in the daily papers, and the story in the '*Daily Mail*' annoyed him most of all. ' "Three policemen killed, three severely wounded," ' he read

372

mockingly. ' "One of the men identified as Peter the Painter." ' What rubbish! I don't know how he could write such lies. He was there with me. He *saw* what was going on. *One* policeman they shot. Chap called Sergeant Leeson, an' the last we heard of *him* he was still alive. It's a disgrace, printin' stuff like this. That's what it is. A disgrace. Peter the Painter, my eye! Two men! That's all. Two Russians. Nobody knew their names. Nobody. They could've been innocent.'

'Wouldn't do 'em much good if they was,' Ellen said pragmatically. 'Either way they're dead now, poor beggars.'

'That's the whole *point*!' David said. 'If they was innocent then they didn't oughter *be* dead. They should a' been took without all that carry-on. One thousand men they called out. Troops an' police all blasting away as if it was a war. No sense in it. They should've talked to 'em.'

'Oh come on, Davey,' she said, 'you can't talk to a man wiv a gun in 'is 'and.'

He didn't know how to answer that because it sounded reasonable and his emotions wanted it to be wrong. So he returned to his original grievance, scowling. 'I don't care what anyone says,' he growled. 'Newspapers have got a bounden duty to tell the truth. They shouldn't print lies. Lies are an abomination at any time, but it's ten times worse when they're in print.'

He looks so handsome when he's holding forth, Ellen thought, but the things he was saying were making her cringe. 'You got ter lie sometimes,' she tried. 'White lies. To keep the peace. Or not tellin' the whole truth in case you upset people. That ain't a bad thing.'

'Lies are always bad things,' he argued passionately. 'Always wrong, believe me. Ain't no such thing as a white lie. Truth is the greatest good, bubeleh. You should never ever lie.'

She was remembering the way she'd manoeuvred Miriam into renting that room, and her heart contracted with fear at the thought of what he'd say if he ever found out. I been punished for it though, she thought. Ain't had a day's peace since she moved in. 'I've suffered enough from Miriam Levy,' she said, apparently inconsequentially. 'You will get 'em ter go, wontcher?'

373

Despite his high ideals, it took David a long time to pluck up enough courage to tell Hymie he had to move. The fortnight's grace of the lying-in period was long over and both women were up and about and ready to quarrel before he could find the words and the moment.

But he needn't have worried, for Hymie almost forestalled him. ' 'Course you will,' he agreed affably, when David ventured that he'd need another bedroom soon. 'I seen that coming, Cheify, don't you worry.'

'You don't have to rush,' David said, shamed by the humility of his friend's compliance.

'Matter a' fact,' Hymie said, 'there's a place going in the Buildings, if we can get it. Be about a fortnight.' He gave a rueful glance. 'We been a sore trial to your Ellen.'

Such a direct admission embarrassed David even further. 'Nu-nu,' he mumbled, avoiding Hymie's eye.

'Yes we 'ave,' Hymie persisted. 'Me an' my missus. Your Ellen don't understand 'er, to tell the truth.'

'Do you?' David asked intrigued.

'Yes,' Hymie said. 'Leastways, I think I do. She 'ad a pretty rough time of it when she was a kid. Makes her prickly, yer see. Quick to take offence. She don't mean it, 'alf the time. She's got a good heart. She'll make a good mother once she gets the 'ang of it.'

David sighed. 'Good mothers spend all their time thinking about babies, don't I tell you,' he said. Sometimes he wondered where his lovely Ellen had gone.

'Be better when you got the place ter yerselves,' Hymie commiserated, misunderstanding his gloom.

They left Mile End Place three weeks later, and the minute the front door closed on the last of their belongings. Ellen rolled up her sleeves and set to work to eliminate all trace of them. By the time David got home that evening she had restored the house to its original condition.

'We shall get a proper night's sleep now,' she promised. Miriam's baby had been very fretful, crying for hours and hours, day and night. 'Peaceful, innit?'

And it was. Peaceful enough. But underneath their apparent contentment, unanswered questions were gathering uncomfortably like boils. She was afraid he would comment on the way she'd treated his mother. While for him, attendance at the synagogue was a weekly reminder of his cowardice. He knew very well how vital honesty was, particularly between husband and wife, and yet he went on avoiding difficult topics. Nowadays, he and Ellen were only truly close on those rather too rare occasions when they had the time and the opportunity to make love. And even then, cuddled against her warm familiar flesh afterwards, his contentment would be whittled away by regrets.

Spring came early that year with a sudden balm that tugged the daffodils into flower and made the blackbirds sing with abandon. Benny put on weight and learned to smile, and by the time summer arrived he was sitting up in his high chair as much a part of the family as either of the others. He was a sociable baby and very fond of company, so, small as he was, they took him on outings, to Epping Forest and the Hackney Marshes, to feed the ducks on the Serpentine and the pigeons in Trafalgar Square, for a boat trip on the Thames and a bus ride to Madame Tussauds, where he slept contentedly on Ellen's shoulder while his brother and sister squealed at the waxworks.

Now that she had three children of her own, Ellen would have liked more contact with her mother. She wrote to her regularly every week, but the letters back were infrequent and very uninformative, for Mrs Murphy either claimed to be 'going on alright' or 'in the pink' and she rarely said anything about Maudie or Johnnie beyond the fact that they were 'getting on alright at work'. But she comforted herself that the lack of a mother who had been so distant for so long was a minor sadness. At least she had a good home and enough to eat and a husband to love her even when they were angry with one another.

Aunty Dumpling came to visit them at least twice a week, and once a month they went to visit her and Mama Cheifitz, and were welcomed and fed, and with mutual caution managed to make an apparent success of nearly every occasion. But it was Wednesday afternoons that Ellen enjoyed without reservation, because that was when she took the kids back to Whitechapel to see Mrs Miller and Ruby. Ruby was still in service and hating every minute of it even though Amy had joined her now and they were both working in the same kitchen.

'You ain't 'alf lucky, Ellie,' she would say, looking enviously at Ellen's growing brood.

And Ellen would say, 'Your turn'll come.' And wonder whether she ought to disenchant her, and decided against it because it wouldn't have been fair.

Later that spring she was glad she'd held her tongue, for she arrived in Mrs Miller's kitchen one Wednesday afternoon to find Ruby scrubbed and clean and in her Sunday best, glowing with the news that she was walking out.

' 'E's ever such a nice feller,' she confided. 'Name a' Sid. He's a roundsman. Delivers the bread where I work. We been passing the time a' day fer weeks and weeks. Didn't 'alf make cook wild. I never thought he'd ask me out. How do I look?'

'A treat!' Ellen said. ' 'E's a lucky feller.'

He arrived ten minutes later, a thickset burly young man with a timid red face and huge red hands covered with callouses. When they were introduced and he shook hands, he apologized for his rough touch. 'It's on account a' pulling the van, yer see,' he said. 'A full load takes a bit a' doing.'

Ellen could imagine him between the shafts, pulling the van, like so many of the roundsmen she'd seen, working like a horse, with the same strength and patience, and she liked him at once, for his gentleness and his diffidence and because he was courting Ruby. 'You're gonna be very happy tergether,' she told Ruby, thinking 'despite the odds'. Life would be hard for them because they were poor, but at least they didn't have religion between them. And that was a lot to be thankful for.

At the end of June, just after Gracie's fifth birthday, David walked them all down to the People's Palace to introduce them to Mr Eswyn Smith, who was as dishevelled and welcoming as ever and had his left arm in a sling.

'A slight contretemps with a stair rail, dear chap,' he

explained when David commiserated. 'Nothing at all.' And he changed the subject quickly. 'I see you're doing well with Mr Palfreyman. We take the magazine every week, just to keep an eye on you.'

Yes, David admitted, pink with pleasure, he was doing well. And he introduced his family, equally proudly.

'So now you have four beautiful models, eh?' Mr Smith said, beaming at them.

' 'E don't draw us!' Ellen laughed. 'I only wish 'e would. 'E's too busy wiv bridges an' markets an' such like. First nights at the theatre. Very a la!'

'A wasted opportunity, ma'am!' the Art master said. 'If you don't mind me saying so. At last year's exhibition we sold every single child study on show. They're all the rage.'

'There y'are!' Ellen said to David, delighted with the information. 'I been on an' on at 'im ter draw the kids.'

'A collection,' Mr Smith suggested. 'Ready for this year's show. Sell like hot cakes, I promise you. You've got five weeks. See what you can do, eh?'

So Ellen turned the empty front room into a studio, with an easel in front of the window, and a shelf for his paints, and all his brushes neatly arranged in one empty marmalade jar and all his pencils in another, and watched with great pride while he produced three portraits, one of each child.

They sold for ten guineas apiece. It was wealth unheard of. They all had brand new coats for the winter and David determined to exhibit a collection every year from then on.

In the meantime, it was September and time for little Gracie to go to school. The child took it all in her sure-footed stride, but it worried her father so much that he arranged to be allowed to arrive late to work for the first week of term so that he could escort her safely to the gates. The memory of his own miserable first day was still too vivid and too painful.

But Gracie liked school and came home after her first day full of enthusiasm. 'Isn't he a funny old Pa to worry so?' she said to her mother.

'It's because 'e loves yer,' Ellen said and they were both pleased with the answer.

*

The seasons came and went, and one year followed another, and very little happened that was of any consequence. Ruby Miller married her affable Sid and gave up work to keep house for him in two rooms above a corner shop in Commercial Street, and a year later had a daughter of her own to pet. David sold more of his paintings and learned how to prune the roses, Gracie learned to read and write, and Ellen fed her family and learned to recognize the birds that sang in her garden and felt quite a countrywoman. And although they weren't so happy as they'd hoped they would be, at least they'd achieved a balance. But sometimes, brooding quietly on his way home from the synagogue, David would yearn for honesty and remember the ease of their courtship when there was no need to dissemble. And Ellen, standing beside the sink up to her elbows in soapsuds, would remember how happy they'd been in the old days and how very much they'd loved each other when there were no bills or chores or anxieties to subdue their pleasure.

And soon it was 1914, and Ruby had another baby, a boy called Tom who was the 'spit an' image' of her Sid, and Jack Cheifitz was five years old and had to follow his sister to school. He didn't think much of the idea. 'Ain't going!' he said, his long face determined. 'I'm stayin' 'ome.'

'You got to,' Gracie told him with the splendid superiority of her seven and a half years. 'If you stay 'ome, the School Board man'll come an' get yer.'

'Don't care!' he said with tearful bravado.

She knew the answer to that too. 'Don't care was made ter care, Don't care was 'ung, Don't care was put in a pot, An' boiled till 'e was done.'

'Leave yer brother be,' Ellen said. ' 'E's only little. Now dry yer eyes like a good boy an' don't make a fuss. Yer Pa'll come with yer.'

But this time Pa was too busy, because there was going to be a war and he'd gone down to a place called Chatham to draw a battleship.

Chapter Thirty

Bank Holiday Monday was always the best day of the year. The Cheifitz family planned for it and looked forward to it for months. It was a day set apart, a day for enjoyment, when work and worries and taboo subjects could be completely forgotten. And this year it was going to be the best Bank Holiday ever, everybody said so.

They'd already had eight weeks of perfect weather, for the summer that year had begun in May and was one of the longest that any of them could remember. The sun shone day after day with such predictability that soon they were leaving chairs out in the garden overnight, and the kids were rarely in the house. Fruit and flowers all blossomed early. The rose bushes were heavy with scented blooms and the syringa flowered in such profusion that it dropped its yellow pollen as thick as snowflakes on anyone who brushed beneath it. The cherries in Mrs Brunewald's garden ripened fat and early too and their little strawberry patch began to crop in June. It was a beneficent season and it did them all good.

It also gave David an idea. It was so hot in London, he said, too hot for comfort, especially at night. What they all needed was to be beside cool water somewhere. 'What say we spend this Bank Holiday at the seaside?' he suggested. 'That'ud be nice, nu?'

Jack's long face lit up at the very idea. 'See the sea!' he said rapturously. None of them had ever seen the sea, although they all knew what it looked like from the pictures in the papers.

'I'll buy you all buckets an' spades,' David promised. 'Be some fun!'

And it was. They chose Brighton because everybody said Brighton was one of the best places, and they set out early to make the most of the day. As Gracie said rapturously afterwards, it was a day and a half.

By the time they emerged from under the high vaulting of the railway station, all three children were in a high state of excitement.

'Quick, quick,' Gracie urged. 'Which way's the sea?'

The answer was obvious, for they walked out of the station into a road that was absolutely crowded with holidaymakers, all walking in the same direction and all very excited, waving Union Jacks and singing 'Rule Britannia' with raucous enthusiasm. It was a fine road, lined with rich-looking hotels and pubs hung with red, white and blue bunting. It led straight downhill towards a clock tower, and beyond that the glimpse of a green lake that must be the sea. There was a sharp sea breeze blowing and the air tasted of salt. 'Come on!' Jack said. 'Slow-coaches!' So off they went with the crowd, marching along together and singing at the tops of their voices.

The whole town seemed to be on the move and quivering with excitement. In no time at all they were down on the sea front, where bunting flicked and swirled above both the piers, and the shop blinds cracked like whips. Ribbons tangled, petticoats frothed and straw bonnets were lifted into the air despite the stoutest hat pins, so that their owners were forced to shriek and giggle and had to be held steady by the eager arms of their excited escorts. The balloon sellers were having a hard time of it too, as their leaping wares bounced into the air, their strings tangled and knotted, emitting rubbery squeaks as they bobbed against each other. Above them the sky was busy with clouds, curved like rosy cauliflowers and sailing with the speed and recklessness of great clippers, while the greeny-blue sea galloped towards the shore with such eagerness that there was no time for the first wave to recede before the second engulfed it, hurling spun foam and a triangular wedge of sandy water straight up into the air.

'Cor! What a place,' Ellen said. 'Jest look at all that sea!' It was enormous, going on for ever and ever. You couldn't see the other side.

'There's donkeys,' Gracie noticed. 'Can we 'ave a go on the donkeys, Ma?'

So they had a go on the donkeys, and then they all went skipping on wooden planks laid out on the sand beneath a skipping rope so long that it had to be turned by two men. And after that they needed sustenance.

There was an Italian ice-cream vendor down by the pier. They remembered him because he'd draped his stall with two Union Jacks, and people were flocking to buy. 'Rule-a Britannia, eh?' he said as he handed over their nice fat cornets, and that gave Ellen and Gracie an attack of the giggles. They sat on the pebbles and ate their ice cream while the band on the pier played 'Land of Hope and Glory'. And after that they took off their shoes and socks, David and the boys rolled their trousers up to the knee and Ellen and Gracie tucked their skirts into their knickers and they all went paddling in the nice cool water and got marvellously wet. Then they discovered they'd worked up an appetite for dinner, and they had fish and chips, sitting down, in a café, and Ellen said it was the sweetest fish she'd ever tasted in her life.

As they walked back to the beach again, David noticed that the more sedate people sitting in their striped deck chairs all along the promenade were all busily reading newspapers. It seemed rather an odd way to be passing the time when they were down beside the sea with so many other things to do, but then he noticed the headlines on the newspaper placards, 'War imminent', 'General mobilization', 'Ultimatum sent to Germany', and he realized why the crowds had been singing patriotic songs.

'D'you know what, Ellen,' he said. 'I do believe they're going ter start this war after all.' He'd been drawing soldiers and sailors and guns for months now, and in July the magazine had sent him to Spithead to draw the Naval Review, which had been the biggest gathering of warships the world had ever seen, but he'd never thought they'd actually get around to declaring war.

'Fancy,' Ellen said, without much interest. ' 'Ere, what say we 'ave a ride on one a' them ships?'

So they went down to the beach beside the aquarium, where

they found a splendid sea captain in a black glazed straw hat and a jersey that looked as if it had been knitted with tar. And when he shouted, 'Any more for the *Skylark?*' they trooped aboard. It was the biggest treat of the day. A boat trip! Just like real sailors!

It was magical out on that sparkling sea as the *Skylark* hissed and creaked through the green water and the spray showered their faces and prickled down on their bare arms like rain. In the sharper breeze offshore, Ellen's hairpins were soon blown out of her hair which fell about her face and streamed behind her in long tangled curls. She and David had taken their places on the long bench with their children sitting between them. Now, as he looked at her. tousled and rosy in the sunshine, her forehead wrinkled in the anxious expression she wore so often these days, he remembered the Lady of Shalott in her magical boat and thought how very much alike they were. Except that the painted Lady had been caught in perpetual youth and he and Ellen were visibly growing older. We're twenty-eight, he thought, and he remembered how passionately he'd loved her ten years ago, and wished he could put the clock back and have just one of those rapturous days all over again. And the thought made him feel guilty.

'I love you,' he mouthed to her, vaguely trying to make amends.

She smiled back at him, trailing her fingers in the water.

'I don't 'alf feel sick,' Jack said.

'Don't you go sickin' up on me,' Gracie said. 'You do it in the water.'

The sky was rose pink with sunset before they decided they really ought to go home. The walk back uphill to the station took a very long time, because Benny was tired and had to be carried, and Jack and Gracie had to stop every few hundred yards to ' 'ave a little rest'. So they missed the fast train and there wasn't another for nearly half an hour.

'Never mind,' Ellen said. 'The slow one'll do. They'll sleep on the way 'ome any'ow.'

But as it turned out none of them slept at all, because the journey home was exciting too.

There were soldiers on the train.

At first there were only two of them, their khaki caps protruding from the window in the next coach, but Jack saw them at the very first stop. And ten miles further on there were five, he counted them on his fingers, and at Three Bridges they were joined by three more, which Gracie said made eight. They got off at Caterham, and the platform there was crowded with soldiers. 'Hundreds and hundreds!' Jack said with awestruck admiration, standing at the window to get a really good view.

Scores, certainly, David thought, amused by his sons's exaggeration, and a tough-looking bunch, regular Army without a doubt, their crushed caps worn at a jaunty angle, their faces lined and tanned, their moustaches trim, their eyes watchful. In their heavy khaki uniforms they looked bigger and more solid than the holidaymakers around them, a dark heroic note among all those striped blazers and flowered bonnets and white blouses. Good material for a sketch.

'Grand lads!' the man in the corner seat said proudly. 'Off to show the 'Un what's what!'

'Are they goin' ter fight a war?' Gracie asked, much impressed.

'Off to France, they are, to fight fer King and Country,' the man said, nodding with great satisfaction.

And the woman beside him nodded too. 'Makes yer glad to be alive,' she said, 'with fine lads like that showin' the flag.'

'I shall be a soldier when I grow up,' Jack announced.

'So shall I,' Gracie said.

'You can't, n'yer!'

'Why not?'

' 'Cos you're a gel. *I* shall be a soldier an' fight in the war.'

'Not in this one you won't,' Ellen corrected, because Gracie was looking so downcast she had to find some way of putting him in his place.

Now it was his turn to ask, 'Why not?'

'Because it'll all be over in six months,' David told him. 'Everybody says so.'

'It's been coming long enough, in all conscience,' the man in the corner said. 'It's a real relief now it's started.'

'Have we declared war, then?' Ellen asked.

383

'Be termorrer they reckon,' the man said. 'We sent an ultimatum.'

Now that the adults had taken over the conversation and reduced it to boring nonsense, the children leaned out of the window to admire their new heroes who were still standing together on the darkening platform looking brave and handsome and dashing, just like all the soldiers they'd seen in their picture books. They watched as the men lit fresh cigarettes for one another, cupping their hands to protect the flame and nipping out their spent matches between finger and thumb, their movements practised, and guarded, and foreign. It was marvellously exciting.

'I hope this war goes on an' on an' on,' Jack said.

Chapter Thirty-One

By Christmas it looked as though Jack was going to get his wish, for the confident predictions of the politicians had been proved wrong. The war certainly wasn't over, in fact it looked set to go on for quite a long time. Not that David and Ellen paid very much attention to it. They read the newspaper accounts of the battles, of course, and were duly horrified when the Germans overran plucky little Belgium and brought their big guns to within shelling distance of Paris, but it was all a long way away and nothing to do with them.

Mama Cheifitz and Dumpling and Rivke, on the other hand, actually got some benefit from the outbreak of hostilities. Government orders for khaki uniforms were immediate and enormous, and although the material was heavy and hard to work, at least it gave them the chance to earn higher wages, and as the war continued the demand for it grew. Rivke tossed the greatcoats across her kitchen table like slaughtered oxen and stitched them dourly with the face of one to whom all work was a trial, but Dumpling said the new orders had come just in the nick of time. Her eyesight had deteriorated so rapidly over the last five years that fine work was really beyond her. Now she rejoiced, settling her spectacles on her little snub nose, 'I see this vork good!'

Gracie was impressed by the solid uniforms the three women were producing and spent most of her Sunday mornings with her grandmother, winding bobbins and threading needles, to the delight of her father and the puzzled acceptance of her mother.

'You don't 'ave ter go ter Brick Lane every Sunday,' she said. 'Not if you don't want to.' If the old lady was putting pressure on the kid then the sooner it was stopped, the better.

'I don't mind,' Gracie said openly. 'I like it. I'm useful. 'Sides, I like Mama Cheifitz.'

Even though she'd often sensed the child's affection for her grandmother in a vague instinctive sort of way, it was a surprise to hear it spoken. 'Do you?' she said. 'Why?'

Gracie thought about it, but only for a second. ' 'Cause she loves Pa,' she said, 'Ever so much. Like I do.'

Serve me right fer asking, Ellen thought. I might a' known that. But it hurt her that her mother-in-law had inspired affection when she'd been so unwelcoming. And she knew that jealousy was a mean emotion, too. Sometimes, she said to herself, you can carry this honesty business just a bit too far, and I don't care what he says!

Gracie grew more fond of Bubbe Cheifitz with every visit. It was peaceful sitting in Aunty Dumpling's crowded room away from the clamour of her two brothers. Boys were all very well, but they didn't know how to talk. And it was talk that fascinated Gracie. She would sit up at the table between her aunt and her grandmother and listen with both ears while they gossiped and told stories and remembered the past. She heard how clever her father had been, 'even as a very liddle boy, don't I tell you', and how he'd bitten the teacher, 'Oy, oy!' and found himself a job in the Lane when he was only seven years old. And their tender pride was a source of great pleasure to her.

'A *chawchem*, your fader,' Bubbe said one afternoon after a particularly affectionate story. 'Like his fader before him, a *chawchem*.'

'What's a corkum?' Gracie asked, looking up from the needle she was threading.

'A good man, dolly,' Bubbe explained. 'The best. A man ter depend on, nu-nu.'

'I shall be a corkum when I grow up,' Gracie decided.

The two women beamed their love at her for such an ambition. 'A *chawchem* is a man, bubeleh,' Bubbe explained, patting the girl's hand lovingly. 'Alvays a man. A good Jewish man.'

'So what's a good Jewish woman?'

They didn't know the answer to that. 'A moder maybe,' Bubbe suggested.

'All right then,' Gracie said. 'I'll be a good Jewish mother.'

'Ai-yi!' Dumpling wailed, throwing her apron over her head. 'She vould! She vould!'

'You ain't Jewish, bubeleh,' Bubbe said, but so gently and with such a tender expression on her face.

'I'm half Jewish,' Gracie said. 'Pa's Jewish ain't 'e, an' so are you, an' so's Aunty Dumpling.' Howling agreement from under the apron. 'All right then, I shall be Jewish an' all.' It seemed such an obvious thing to say, she was surprised when her grandmother burst into tears and took her into her arms, to kiss her over and over again.

'Oy oy!' Dumpling wept, wiping her eyes with the corner of that useful apron. 'Vhat a girl! Oy oy oy! Great is our God and greatly to be praised for His loving kindness.'

Just after Christmas, Ruby's Sid joined the Army, and was soon drafted into the Army Service Corps and sent to France to look after the horses. His family missed him terribly, but they were all very proud of him. 'All got ter do our bit, when all's said an' done,' Ruby would say, gazing fondly at his photograph in the place of honour above the fireplace.

In April Alfie Miller followed his brother-in-law into the war, and came back to Petticoat Lane peacock-proud of his new status and his glamorous uniform, his tomcat face all grins under a perky cap, his hair cut short and his ginger moustache waxed to black points as sharp as needles. Mrs Miller and Ruby now had two soldier heroes, and kept their postcards on the mantelpiece for everyone to see. The censor had blacked out all the place-names but they knew where their menfolk were, for the name of the place was printed below the view on the front of several of the cards, YPRES.

'Could a' saved hisself the bother a' blackin' that lot out, silly beggar,' Ruby said. 'I can't even pronounce it, leave alone know where it is. Ippers! I ask yer. What sort a' place is that?' But Sid seemed very cheerful in his new life as a soldier and always wrote that he was 'in the pink', and 'A1' and advised them all to 'keep smiling', and that was a great comfort to her.

Alfie's occasional laconic note gave no indication that he was in any danger, although as his mother was quick to point out, 'Not that he'd tell us if 'e was.'

Alfie and Sid were the only soldiers David and Ellen knew, for none of their other friends had volunteered. The recruiting sergeants never came to Whitechapel, knowing what sort of reception they'd get, for as David and his friends told one another on their way home from the synagogue, this was a British war and they were Jewish.

From time to time, when Miriam's nagging made him more wretched than usual, Hymie would sigh that he 'had half a mind to go fer a soldier'. But as the war went on and increasing numbers of men left their jobs at the Gas Board to enlist, there was more and more work to be done by those who were left behind. So he was kept comfortably busy by day and spent his extra wages gambling the evenings away, and managed to avoid his wife that way instead.

In the second autumn of the war, food shortages began and sugar was rationed. But a shortage that struck terror into middle-class bellies had very little effect in Whitechapel. They were used to being short of food there.

Ellen was more concerned about the health of her children. Just after the New Year, when Benny was due to start school, they all went down with chicken pox. And after chicken pox, they all caught the mumps, and after the mumps it was measles.

This time Ellen was frightened, remembering her brother Seamus, but David took it deliberately calmly to reassure her. 'They won't die, bubeleh,' he said, 'because we'll look after 'em properly. We won't leave 'em for a minute. We'll give 'em the best of everything. They're strong. You'll see.'

So they took it in turns to sit up at nights with their delirious young and Aunty Dumpling came in every day to help with the chores and tempt them to eat, and although the disease ran its course in its usual frightening way, none of them had any complications and eventually they began to recover, although by the time they were up and about again, they all seemed to have grown several inches, and their legs were as thin and shapeless as broom handles.

388

When August came and the war was two years old, David and Ellen were so exhausted by the strain of so many illnesses they spent the Bank Holiday sitting in their garden.

'It makes you wonder what you're in for next,' Ellen said, when the kids had been coaxed into bed at the end of the day. 'It's just been one thing after another this year.'

'So maybe now we're in the clear,' he said hopefully. 'All our troubles behind us, nu?'

But the next thing that happened was trouble of a very different order and it walked into their house on the stout flat feet of Miriam Levy.

Miriam Levy came to visit them whenever Ellen wasn't quick enough to think up an excuse to prevent her. On this occasion she didn't even try, for she had to admit that the poor woman had had more than her share of trouble recently too, and deserved a chance to grumble some of it away. In June, after a dramatic pregnancy, loudly suffered, she'd given birth to a stillborn boy.

'We'll 'ave ter let 'em come, poor things,' she said when the postcard arrived. 'Whatcher think, Davey?'

David said he supposed so. But his youngest was aggrieved. 'They ain't bringing that Baby, are they?' he demanded.

Miriam's daughter had been named Zillah five and a half years ago but nobody called her anything other than Baby. She was an unprepossessing child, overweight like her mother and with her father's bushy hair and close-set eyes, and Miriam treated her as though she were still in the cradle, pandering to her every grizzling whim and demanding special treatment for her 'because she's only little!' So all three Cheifitzes loathed her.

' 'Course she's coming!' Ellen said. 'They could hardly leave 'er be'ind, now could they? 'Ave some sense!'

'Ain't fair,' Benny said, and he began to gather up his toys, tucking his favourite, a model engine he'd been given for Christmas, safely under his arm.

David watched him and scowled at the unpalatable thought that was entering his mind. 'Where you going with that lot, son?'

'Upstairs,' Benny said with determination. 'I'm gonna hide

'em under the bed where *she* can't get 'em.'

'You'll do no such thing!' David told him sternly. 'Ellen, d'you allow this?'

Ellen had always allowed it. It seemed common sense to her to put precious things out of harm's way. 'Yes,' she said. 'What's wrong wiv it?'

'I'll tell you what's wrong with it,' he said, angry and disappointed that she hadn't seen it for herself. 'It's selfish an' dishonest an' no way to teach a kid to behave. You'll put all them things back in the box,' he told his son, 'an' learn to share.'

'But Pa,' Benny protested, 'she'll smash 'em ter bits.'

But David was firm. 'You'll learn to do the right thing,' he said. 'And that goes for you too,' looking at Jack and Gracie.

So all playthings remained where they were till Sunday afternoon, and when Baby arrived on her much dreaded visit, she had first pick of the playbox which had been put out in the garden in the middle of the grass so that the kids could play while the grown-ups had tea. And, of course, the first thing she seized upon was Benny's engine.

'You can 'ave a go of my doll if yer like,' Gracie offered in a vain attempt to divert her.

But no! Nothing but the engine would do.

'So let her have it,' Miriam called from the kitchen. 'She's only little. You don't vant it, do yer, Benny?'

'Yes,' Benny growled. 'I do too. So there!' But none of his guests took any notice of him, so he tried a new tack and suggested a game. 'You push it ter me an' then I'll push it back.'

'Shan't!' Baby said truculently, and she took the wooden toy to the end of the garden and tried to roll it along the top of the fence, scraping the undercarriage most cruelly.

'It'll fall off!' Benny warned. 'You'll break it.' He looked back anxiously for his brother and sister, but Gracie was skipping at the other end of the garden and Jack was busy building bricks.

'See if I care!' Baby said, and as she glanced away from the fence to sneer at him, the train fell onto the path.

He made a dive for it and grabbed it before she could. One

390

of the wheels was a bit squiffy. 'Look what you done!' he said,
so angrily that Jack looked up from his bricks.

'Give it back!' she said imperiously. 'Ma says I'm to 'ave it.'

'You bent my wheel!'

'Let's 'ave a look-see,' Jack said, stepping in to support his
brother.

Baby planted her plump feet solidly on the path. 'If you
don't give it back ter me this minute,' she threatened, 'I'll
scream.' And she took a deep breath, ready.

'Shut yer face!' Jack said, but pleasantly enough. It was the
sort of warning he often gave to his friends.

But it didn't work this time. Baby grabbed the train violently
with both hands and began to yell, a loud, high-pitched,
wailing squeal that had all the grown-ups running out of the
house in no time. As soon as she saw her mother she threw
herself face downwards on the grass and screamed louder than
ever. ' 'E pinched me, Ma! Oy-oy-oy!'

Miriam scooped her pathetic infant into her arms and
carried her into the house, contriving to glare at Benny and
Jack and murmur soothing endearments at the same time.
'Don't you cry, my precious. That naughty Benny von't pinch
you no more vid your mother around.' And Baby's tears dried
miraculously, and leaning on the protective bulk of her
mother's heaving bosom she flung the engine into the air as far
and as hard as she could. 'N'yer!' she said. 'You can 'ave yer
rotten old engine. See if I care!'

The toy fell heavily, skidding along the path with an audible
scraping of paint. Two wheels spun off into the strawberry
patch and disappeared under the leaves, and the funnel was
horribly bent. Benny dropped to his knees on the path and
burst into tears.

His father was beside him at once, controlling him into
better behaviour. 'Stop that row, d'you hear. Get up, and
don't be such a baby.'

'Pick up the pieces, lovey,' Ellen said kindly. 'It'll mend.
You'll see.'

So he struggled to master his rage and find all the pieces,
neither of which was easy, especially with Aunt Miriam going
on and on inside the house.

'You oughter control that kid a' yours,' she was saying to Ma. 'Could a' done my poor baby a mischief. Don't you cry, bubeleh. Mama got you.'

'No bones broken,' Hymie said, trying to placate her into a better humour.

'She broke Benny's engine,' Gracie said, and even though Pa said, 'Shush!' and Ma made a warning grimace at her, she went on boldly, 'She done it deliberate.'

'Oy! Vhat a spiteful thing ter say!' Miriam yelled, rounding on the child. 'You dropped it, didn'tcher, Baby.'

'No she never,' Gracie persisted. 'She threw it. Deliberate. I seen her.'

'Are you going to sit there an' let that child insult my Baby?' Miriam said. 'Really, some people got no control over their kids at all!'

'Apologize to yer aunt, Gracie,' David said sternly, and he continued to be stern even though the child's face was crumpling with distress.

Oh no, Ellen thought, I can't 'ave that. Fair's fair! 'Gracie's right,' she said. 'There's no call fer apologies. She *did* throw it. I seen 'er mesself.'

'Oh that's right!' Miriam yelled. 'Take 'er side! I should! You ain't got the slightest concern fer me. Never 'ave 'ad.'

'Fair's fair, Miriam,' Ellen said, trying to stay calm. 'She done it deliberate.'

'So my child's destructive. Is that vhat you're saying, nu?'

'If you want the truth of it, yes.'

'Truth! Truth!' Miriam shrieked. 'The truth ain't in you, Ellen Cheifitz. You vouldn't know the truth if it come up an' bit yer! Truth! I lived in your rotten 'ouse eighteen months all on account a' your rotten lies. Don't talk ter me a' truth. All that cock an' bull story about some lodger, an' ve vas ter be quick. I should never a' come 'ere if it hadn't been fer that.'

Ellen paled visibly. Hymie was so nervous his cup and saucer were rattling like castanets. But it was David who answered her, speaking quietly and with such control that Ellen grew more afraid by the second.

'What lie was that, Miriam?'

'Told me you 'ad a lodger waitin' ter take our room. That's

vhat she done. Mrs Brunevald never heard nothink about it. She told me after. But me, I believe her. So ve rush. Ve take it, *nebbish*. And vhat's the result a' that? I tell you vhat it vas. Misery. Unhappiness. The vorst time any voman ever 'ad vhen my poor baby vas born. The vorst time. Hymie, vill you stop making that silly row! If you can't hold a cup proper, put it down!'

'No you never!' Ellen argued, glad of a chance to refute something else, and turn their attention to another topic. 'You 'ad the same midwife as me. There was nothink the matter with the way you was treated, so don't you say so, 'cause I won't 'ave it.'

'Nothink the matter! Nothink the matter! Ai-yi-yi! So I'm left on my own for hours an' hours in absolute agony, I tell you. Not so much as a cup a' tea ...'

'I was up an' down them stairs every minute a' the day,' Ellen roared back, glad to be able to release her fear and her temper in safety. 'You 'ad tea an' dinner an' God knows what ...'

Both women were on their feet, shouting without listening, red-faced and wild-eyed, with their children sitting around them, avid with half-terrified curiosity. None of them noticed that David had gone quietly to the door to get the hats. He put them on the table among the tea things, still unnoticed as the row continued, and walked delicately through the group of listening children to Hymie. 'Take your wife and child,' he said in Yiddish, 'and go home. This is not good for any of us. We must stop it.'

And to everybody's surprise, Hymie stood up and put on his hat, solemnly as though it were a judge's wig, and actually ordered Miriam to come home!

'Vhat?' she said, halted in mid roar.

'You 'eard what I said, Miriam. Enough's enough. You too, Zillah. Put yer 'at on. We're off!'

'Vell!' Miriam puffed. 'So I ain't ter speak me mind, is that it?'

'Trouble with your mind,' her loving husband told her, 'it's too darn loud. Come on, Zillah. Sorry about all this, Ellen.' And he took hold of Baby's hand and walked her out of the kitchen towards the front door.

'So vait fer me, vhy don't you,' Miriam said, and she seized her hat from the table so violently that it knocked over the milk jug which bounced on to the floor. There was a trampling and banging in the hall, and they were gone.

It was suddenly so quiet in the kitchen that they could hear a bluebottle buzzing against the window.

'Clear the tea things,' David told his children, sternly. 'Gracie, you get a cloth an' mop up that milk. Then you can wash up and the boys can wipe. Then you're to put yer toys away. I want that garden tidy. Yer Ma an' me've got things to talk about.'

They obeyed in silence, for their father wasn't a man to argue with when he was in a mood and they all recognized that this mood was one of the worst and quietest they'd ever seen. Miriam *had* upset him.

When the tea things were cleared he shut the scullery door on his children and turned his awful attention to Ellen. 'So now you tell me,' he said, and his nostrils were pinched with rage.

This was the moment she'd been dreading ever since she told that silly lie to Miriam. But she stood her ground, even though her throat was constricting with fear at the thought of what might be said next. 'I done it fer you,' she said, swallowing nervously.

He saw the movement in her throat but his anger was too extreme for pity. 'You lied!' he said. 'You lied, Ellen! After all we've said about telling the truth, you told a lie. A deliberate lie.'

'I had too. Honest!' His face was so dark and threatening. Such a hard face. Flesh turned to stone. 'Davey, please, I had to.' She knew she was yearning for his gentleness to return, but she couldn't think what to say to change him. Because she had lied. He was right. Oh, how she wished she hadn't.

'You told that lie to keep my mother out the house,' he said. 'Don't think I don't know that. Hymie an' Miriam all settled in nice an' quick before I could tell her to come 'ere, where she ought to 'ave been. How could you?'

'She'd a' made us all unhappy,' Ellen said. 'I done it for the

394

best. Honest ter God!'

'She wouldn't, she's a good woman. Look how she loves our Gracie.'

'She don't like me, Davey.' But that sounded petty.

'She'd 'ave come round if you'd a' give 'er a chance. It's because you ain't Jewish.'

'That ain't my fault!'

'I thought we was building this marriage on truth,' he said. The anger he was still holding in check was a tight knot of pain in his chest. 'Truth's more important to me than anything else in the world. You know that, dontcher? I give up my religion fer you, my family, my friends, a whole way a' life. Even my sons. Oy-oy! Even my sons.' The pain was welling into his throat. 'I got two sons an' they ain't even Jewish. All for you, Ellen. Nobody else. Just you. An' this is how you repay me. With a rotten, ugly, disgusting lie.' It was no good. His control was breaking. Anger was taking him over. 'I loved you an' you lied. Oy, how could you?'

'I've give up things too!' Ellen said, terrified by the power of his emotion. Quick, quick, think of some. But she couldn't. Her mind wasn't functioning properly.

'What are you talking about?'

'Things we've give up.' Weren't they?

'We're talking about lies. Lies!'

'It was only one, Davey.'

The old ridiculous argument. 'There ain't no such thing as *one* lie,' he said passionately. 'Either you lie or you don't. There's truth an' there's lies. And you lie. Dear God. All these years wasted!' The room was flaming with terrible red light. He could barely see her face. 'Wasted! Twelve years living a half-life. Never a shabbas in my own house in all that time. Never one single Shabbas.'

'We could've 'ad Shabbas. You never said ...'

'If you'd a' been Jewish I wouldn't've had ter say. Can't yer see? All these years ... Eatin' food I couldn't stand. Married in a register office. Ai-yi-yi!'

'It's been 'ard fer me too.'

'I gave up my religion fer you. My religion. Ai! They were right. We should never a' married. It was a mistake from the first day ...'

'No, no!' Neither of them noticed their children at the scullery door.

'We've lived on a lie. Don't you understand? I thought we had a good marriage ...'

'We did. We did! We do! We still do!'

'It was all a lie. I thought we was building on firm foundations. There ain't nothing there, Ellen. Nothing.'

'There is!' How inadequate that sounded. But what else could she say? 'We got a good home.' But he didn't respond. He seemed to be brooding, gathering his strength. 'I'm sorry I lied, Davey. Truly, truly sorry. If I could call it all back an' do it all different, I would. You know that, dontcher?'

'It's too late fer that now,' he said. 'The damage is done.' He wasn't even sure what the damage was, but he felt it most keenly.

'What'll you do?' she asked fearfully. Her voice was almost a whisper, because she was so afraid.

'There's nothing else I can do,' he said knowing what it was as he spoke. 'Our marriage is a fraud. We must break it up. Destroy it. That's all.'

He couldn't! Please God, he couldn't. 'It ain't a marriage you're breakin', Davey, it's me.'

But the need to destroy was overpowering. 'I can't stop here another minute,' he said. 'I can't bear it. To think you would lie. You of all people! I shall 'ave to go, Ellen. I can't stay 'ere. I can't bear it!' And he had his hat in his hand and was out of the door before she had a chance to think of any answer at all.

Mile End Place was full of the luscious, innocent scent of roses. But that only increased his pain. To have come so far and with such hopes and all for this! Angry images jostled in his mind; Hymie under the *chuppah*, and his own intolerable sense of being an outsider; his father's bewildered face when he first told him about Ellen; the Lady of Shalott, drifting towards death because she'd broken her solemn promise; Miriam's fat mouth, 'that cock an' bull story about some lodger'; his realization that the lie had been told to keep his mother out of the house. And the pain was more excruciating than he could

396

bear, so that he groaned aloud, walking down the Mile End Road in the warm, mocking sunshine. It must all be destroyed, wiped out, annihilated. That was the only clean way.

He had reached the corner of Tredegar Street, where the bathhouse was, and as a crowd of young men were barring his progress along the main road, and he was too angry to ask them to make way, he turned down the side street, still walking furiously. And found himself standing in front of the Army recruiting office. There was a poster in the window declaring 'Your country needs you'. And although he'd never given the war or the Army a thought until that moment, he knew with a passionate upsurge of fury that this was the answer. He would join up. Get right away. Make a new clean start.

Still trembling with anger he marched in through the door.

It was cool in the office, and the uniformed man behind the counter was pale and calm and controlled and gentlemanly, as though anger and war and pain and death simply didn't exist in his well-ordered world. He took David's furious entry with a flattering air of approval, and within ten minutes was pressing the King's shilling into his hand and requiring him to sign on the dotted line. When David stepped out into the sunshine again, clutching his copy of Army Form B2505A, Short Service, he was a soldier.

It was a terrible anti-climax, for although his anger had diminshed it was still bubbling, and although he'd taken action he was still in exactly the same place. For a few minutes he stood on the pavement, looking across at the baths and completely at a loss to know what to do next. He could hardly go home, after all that. Nor to his mother's. Nor to Hymie. So as he couldn't think of anything else to do, he took a bath. But the warm water only cleaned his body. His mind was still in turmoil.

There was nothing for it but to walk about. Down the Mile End Road, past Sidney Street and the London Hospital, along Whitechapel Road, up Commercial Street, through the Lane. He came to the Aldgate pump and took a drink of water from the tin cup, clinking the chain against the basin as he drank. Then on again, aimlessly, striding and thinking, into the empty City, through the narrow cavern of Fenchurch Street stifling in the heat, and down Gracechurch Street to the muddle of roads at the Bank. And there was the Thames, shining in the sunshine, and the straight road over London Bridge.

Apart from a carter and one lone hackney cab, he had the bridge to himself. He walked to the middle and stood, leaning on the parapet, gazing down at the blue water. He had walked all his anger away and now he was weary and demoralized. There was nothing left for his mind to consider. He'd been angry. He'd taken action. It was over.

But now, and quite unbidden, memories of Ellen and the children took easy possession of the void his passion had left behind. Ellen sponging the blood stains from her blue suit, laughing at him on the steps of the Town Hall as confetti danced in the air before their eyes, holding up their newborn daughter for his approval, kissing him and kissing him, his own beautiful Ellen, looking at him with loving eyes, and the children playing in the garden, sitting round the table, cruising down this very river in the pleasure steamer last summer. Was it only last summer? So much happiness and so much good. And he put his head in his hands and groaned to think of what he'd lost. 'What have I done?' he said aloud.

Chapter Thirty-Two

In the silence that followed the reverberating bang of that front door, the children crept into the kitchen and Benny and Jack began to cry.

'Don't start that!' Ellen said irritably, because she wanted to cry herself. The terror of their row was still whirling about her in that quiet brown room. She could still see his face, distorted and withdrawn, and, what was worse, she could still feel the awful destructive force of his anger. She'd seen it before, on rare occasions and always briefly, when he tore a newly finished drawing and threw it away in angry dissatisfaction, but never directed at her, and never like that. Never in such terrifying, unstoppable fury. Her heart was still beating painfully, even now, and she knew she would cry if she didn't keep tight hold of herself. But she mustn't break down. Not in front of the kids.

' 'E said 'e was gonna break something,' Jack wailed. 'What 'e gonna break, Ma?'

'I want my Pa!' Benny howled.

' 'E said 'e was going,' Gracie told them, 'that's what 'e meant. 'E's walked out on us, ain't 'e, Ma?' She was shocked to think that her father could have done such a thing, but shock made her calm.

' 'E ain't, 'as 'e?' Jack said crying more than ever.

'No!' Ellen said stoutly. ' 'Course not! 'E don't meant it. Dry yer eyes! That's all silly talk. Grown-ups do talk silly sometimes. 'E don't mean it. What say we make a jam roly-poly fer supper?'

'It's too hot,' Gracie said. And her eyes were saying, he meant it. You don't fool me.

'Red currant pie then. There's still some on the bush. Get us a jug, Jack, there's a good boy.'

So she and the boys went out into the garden to scavenge what was left of the currants. But Gracie stayed thoughtfully indoors.

They made the pie and boiled some potatoes, and somehow or other Ellen managed to keep them all cheerful and occupied, although Gracie was a good deal quieter than she would have liked. But when the meal was cooked and their father still hadn't reappeared, they were anxious again.

'Ain't 'e coming back, Ma?' Jack wanted to know, his long face puzzled, mouth drooping.

'I expect he's working somewhere,' Ellen said, trying to sound convincing. 'You know 'ow 'e does.' And there was some truth in the suggestion, for he often went out in the evenings to draw a first night or the posh people going to the opera or something like that. 'We'll 'ave ours, shall we? We can hot his up for 'im when he comes in.'

So they had their supper and washed the dishes, and the heat began to drain out of the day. And he still hadn't come back. What if he's done something dreadful, Ellen thought, smashed something up and been arrested, or got in a fight and been beaten up. It wasn't like her gentle Davey, but the man who'd stormed out of the house was a stranger to her, a dark-faced, destructive stranger and capable of anything. She remembered how violently he'd fought Jimmy Thatcher and his gang, and was more worried than ever.

'I'll just pop down the end a' the road, an' see if I can see any sign of 'im,' she said. But that filled them all with apprehension.

'You won't go far, will yer?' Gracie asked. And Jack began to weep again. One parent suddenly disappearing was bad enough, but if Ma went there'd be no one left at all.

She understood his fear, and fidgety though she was, changed her plans at once. 'I shan't go nowhere an' leave you,' she promised. 'Tell yer what, we'll ask old Aunty Dumpling to come down an' look after you, while I nip out. How would that be? You'd be all right then, wouldn'tcher?'

That was different. They'd be all right with Aunty Dumpling. So it was agreed and Gracie was despatched to Brick Lane with a note and two pennies for the tram fare.

400

'Now then,' Ellen said to her anxious boys. 'We'll 'ave them dirty faces washed an' you can get ter bed. If you look sharp I'll read you a story.'

'Each?' Benny asked. This was better. This was more like a normal Sunday.

'Each,' she promised, kissing him.

But while she was reading the first story, which was Benny's choice and interminable, she suddenly had the clearest impression of David standing beside an expanse of water. It was a very strong impression and very alarming, but it receded at once under the rhythm of the story.

'Hold on a tick,' she said to the two boys. 'Must just nip out the back fer a second. Keep yer finger in the place, Benny. Shan't be a minute.' She had to have a few minutes on her own, and going to the W.C. was the only excuse she could think of.

They let her go, grudgingly, although Jack informed her solemnly that he would 'listen fer the chain', and she went downstairs slowly, willing the vision to return. It came back when she got into the kitchen, where the brown walls were still echoing with angry words and the trailing stain of that spilt milk still darkened the tablecloth. He was standing on a bridge. She was sure of that. Leaning over the parapet, looking down at blue water, and she could feel his misery, oh so strongly. Oh God, she thought, 'e ain't thinking a' jumpin' in or anythink silly like that? And the very idea made her shake, remembering his terrible driving urge to destroy something or somebody. Hurry up back, Gracie, she willed her daughter. I've got ter get down there an' find him.

She was reading the second story, which was Jack's choice, when she heard the key in the door at last. 'There you are,' she said with relief. 'That'll either be yer Pa, or old Aunty Dumpling come back with Gracie. You be good boys while I go down an' see.'

It wasn't either of them. It was Gracie, with a belligerent expression on her face, and behind her Mama Cheifitz, looking oddly sheepish, her head bowed.

'Dumpling's out,' she said placatingly. 'Sunday is her night out. Alvays. I come instead. Your Gracie showed me the note. I hope you don't mind. So vould I do?'

It was asked so humbly that Ellen felt quite moved, but then she realized that her mother-in-law must know about the row, and that made her blush with shame. 'We 'ad a bit of a barney,' she admitted. 'Nothink much on'y 'e's gone rushing off somewhere. Come in.'

'Alvays the vay, vid our Davey,' Rachel said, taking it with amazing calm. 'Such a temper you never saw, don't I tell you. First day at school he bites the teacher.' She took off her hat and gave it to Gracie to hang it on the hook behind the door. 'Gracie an' me, ve look after the childer,' she said. 'Don't you vorry.'

'It's ever so good of yer,' Ellen said. And they both knew she meant it. 'I got an idea where 'e's gone, you see. If I could just nip out fer a minute, I'm sure I could find him.'

'Nu-nu,' Rachel said, 'so you go quick, you find him.' She'd never been a suitable wife for David, this *shiksa*, but she was showing a lot of spirit now. And besides, she was Gracie's mother, and Jack's and little Benny's even if they weren't Jewish.

'Bubbe, is that you?' Benny's voice called down.

'Yes, yes, my liddle chicken,' she called back. 'So you go to sleep, I come up an' see you maybe.'

Ellen had already put her hat and coat on. 'I'll be as quick as I can,' she promised. 'Help yer grandma, Gracie, there's a good girl.' And she set off on her search.

She started with Tower Bridge, which was the nearest, but he wasn't there, although the sense of water and bridges was stronger than ever. Never mind, she told herself, I'll just move up-river and try every single one. And she caught the next bus to the foot of London Bridge.

She saw him as soon as she began to walk across, leaning on the parapet, looking down at the water, his outline unmistakable even in the half-light of a gathering dusk. Then she ran, eager to be with him and help him, even though she hadn't the faintest idea what she was going to say, But it didn't matter, for neither of them needed to say anything. He heard the rush of her approach and looked up, his face anguished, and then they were in each other's arms and he was kissing her face and telling her how sorry he was, and she was holding him round the neck and telling him she'd never lie again, never, never, never, and they were together again, despite everything, and the sense of loss was fading.

'Come 'ome,' she suggested, when they'd recovered a little. 'Our Jack's been ever so worried.'

Now he remembered the children. 'Who's lookin' after 'em?' he asked. 'Our Gracie?'

'No,' she said, delighted by the answer she was going to give him. 'Your Ma.'

He looked momentarily pleased. Then he scowled. 'Did you tell 'er?'

'On'y that we 'ad a bit of a barney, that's all.' Then as he went on scowling. 'It's all right now, ain't it?'

'No,' he said slowly, 'it ain't.'

'Ain't yer forgive me?'

'Yes.' With a kiss to prove it. Now he couldn't think why he'd been so very angry with her, when he loved her so much.

'Well then?'

'I joined the Army.'

'You never.' She was still smiling at him, not taking it seriously.

'I 'ave.'

'Well,' she said comfortably, 'you'll just 'ave ter go back tomorrer an' tell 'em you've changed yer mind.'

'I can't do that, Ellen,' he said, touched by her naivety. 'I've took the King's shilling.' And he pulled the short service form from his pocket and showed it to her.

'D'you mean you're goin' ter France?' she asked, understanding at last.

'Yes.' It made him miserable even to admit it.

'How *could* you?'

He shrugged and sighed. There was nothing he could say. Now that his temper was over, it all seemed ridiculous, like a bad dream. And yet she *had* lied. He'd been right to make a stand. If only he hadn't made it in this way.

'We'd better go 'ome,' she said. 'The kids won't sleep till you're back.' If he really had done this stupid thing, she would have to accept it, but she couldn't even think about it now.

So they went home and told his mother, who thought it was

'vhat you vould expect', and didn't seem displeased, and the children, who were still awake and thought it was thrilling.

'Fancy you goin' fer a soldier, Pa,' Jack said, his eyes shining. 'Will you go ter France?'

' 'Course 'e will, silly,' Gracie said. 'They all go ter France, don't they, Pa? That's where the war is.'

And Ellen wondered whether she was the only one who had seen any wounded soldiers or looked at those awful casualty lists. He could be killed, she was thinking. He could go to France and be killed and we'd never see him again. But they were all being so cheerful and encouraging, she kept her thought to herself. It was enough that the row was over and they were still together.

He took his mother all the way home, feeling that was the least he could do to make amends. And she was easy and loving with him as though he hadn't done anything unusual. 'So I see you Sunday, nu?' she said as they kissed goodbye. It was a little unreal.

By the time he got back to Mile End Place again, all three children were in bed and asleep and Ellen was sitting in the chair by their bedroom window watching out for him. When he tiptoed into the room, she turned towards him at once to greet him. She was in her nightgown, with her long hair brushed free and her white feet bare, and her face was tremulous with love.

'Oh Ellen!' he said, weak with desire for her. 'How could I have walked out on you like that? I must've been out a' my mind. I love you so much.'

Her answer was a kiss so welcoming and so passionate that words were superfluous. He gathered her body towards him, with the gentlest pressure in the small of her back, and kissed her throat and her mouth over and over again, and fondled her breasts, until she was moaning with pleasure. They fell into bed together almost without noticing what they were doing, their desire for one another stronger and more powerful than it had been for years, and were rewarded with a pleasure so exquisite that it had to be experienced again. And again.

Afterwards, in the clear air of their reconciliation, they talked.

'Why didn'tcher tell me you didn't like my food?' she asked.

'Didn't want to upset you. Anyway, I like some of it.'

'You'll tell me now, wontcher?'

' 'Course,' he said, tracing the outline of her mouth with his forefinger.

'About the boys bein' Jewish ...' she said.

'We let them chose when they're older, nu?' Why hadn't he seen that possibility sooner?

'And Shabbas?'

'We'll talk about Shabbas tomorrow,' he said drowsily. Contentment was washing him into sleep. 'Oy! I *do* love yer!'

Thank God! Ellen thought, as she watched his eyes close. 'Dear Davey!' she murmured. And then she was asleep too.

It upset David that he was regarded as a hero, especially when his friends on the *Essex Magazine* treated him to a slap-up meal at Craig's Oyster Bar, and Mr Palfreyman made a speech about him and said he was one of the finest young men who'd ever worked on the magazine. 'A credit to us all, dear chap,' he said, the pale dome of his bald head shining with sweat and excitement. 'All the best and bravest young men of your generation have answered the call, so naturally you would wish to join them. Yes, yes of course.'

Fortunately, Quin's cheerful cynicism was a healthy antidote to too much adulation. 'Keep yer 'ead down, young Cheify. That's my advice. Dead heroes are all very well, but I never knew a cause worth dying for yet. When yer going?'

'I don't know,' David confessed. 'When they send for me, I suppose.'

'It will be a day or two before you hear,' Mr Palfreyman surmised. 'Bound to be. Yes indeed.'

And David thought privately that they could take as long as they liked.

'Months if they like,' Ellen said, agreeing with him. 'I wish you 'adn't done it, Davey.'

The days went by and became weeks and still he hadn't heard. She began to feel quite hopeful again. 'Perhaps they've forgotten yer,' she said.

But in the first week of September, just after the kids went back to school, an official envelope arrived. It contained a travel warrant from Liverpool Street Station to Chelmsford, and instructions that he was to report to the Rail Transport Officer at Chelmsford Station at 12.00 hours on Monday, 11 September 1916.

Ellen burst into tears at the sight of it, but there was no possibility of argument or disobedience. To Chelmsford he was ordered, so to Chelmsford he went.

The day was miserable, damp and overcast, the sky sultry with cloud, but the new recruits climbing aboard the Ipswich train in their hundreds were determinedly cheerful. 'You an' all!' they greeted one another. 'Attested, was yer?' And they exchanged names and cigarettes, and showed off photographs of their families, so that by the time they arrived outside the R.T.O.'s office they already felt they belonged. But whether to the Army or to one another they weren't quite sure.

At Chelmsford they were loaded into trucks and driven south under rain clouds as dark as bruises through a flat, sodden countryside.

'What a place!' David said to the man beside him, as they passed yet another track full of churned-up mud. 'Don't much fancy marchin' about in that lot.'

'That,' his companion said lugubriously, 'is the whole h'object a' the h'exercise. H'up to our h'ears in mud we shall be. You mark my words.'

'Oh no! We got a right one 'ere!' another man said. 'Proper ol' growser, aintcher?' He was a cheerful young man with a very pale skin and lank brown hair, and as far as David could remember his name was Evans.

'Keep yer pecker up, that's what I say,' another recruit said.

So they all smiled to show him he wasn't the only cheerful one. But David was thinking of Ellen.

Their camp was as muddy as a pigsty. They were splashed to the knees with the stuff the minute they jumped down from the trucks.

'What did I tell yer?' Lugubrious complained.

Evans wasn't deterred. 'Good fer the skin,' he said, grinning.

'You're welcome to it,' Lugubrious told him. 'My old woman 'ud die if she could see the state a' my bum-bags.'

But then the Army descended upon them in the person of an enormous sergeant major with beefy arms bulging under his uniform and a voice so loud it made their eardrums ring. They were stood in line and roared at, and given uniforms and roared at, and given regulation haircuts and roared at, and shown where they were to store their kit and wash and eat and sleep, and roared at, and marched up and down and roared at. Finally they were all stood in line again and each man was given a pay book, an identity disc and a number, and told to commit the number to memory and never ever forget it.

'Wherever you present yourselves,' the sergeant major said, 'anywhere in the world, for any purpose whatsoever, you give your name and your number. And don't let me catch any of you ever forgetting it. Because I tell you, you 'orrible little men, without your number you do not exist in the Army, and if you do not exist in the Army, your life is not worth living.'

When they fell into their tents at the end of the day, they were footsore and exhausted. Even the discomfort of a straw palliasse laid on bare earth was no bar to sleep. Evans said he could have slept standing up, and David, who was glad they were in the same tent, said he'd been asleep on his feet for the last two hours, and decided that when he got a bit of spare time he would draw a sketch of his new friend and send it to Ellen.

The bit of spare time couldn't be found until they'd been in camp for nearly a week, and by then David and Joe Evans had found another friend.

He was a skinny eighteen-year-old, raw and uncouth, with long awkward limbs and the hang-dog look of the chronically underfed, the sort of boy who could easily become the butt of the entire squad. 'Soldierin'! That's nothink!' he said, brash with anxiety, his loose lips quivering.

'All in it together, nu?' David said to reassure him. There was something about the boy's long face and the anxious alertness of those overbold eyes that reminded him of Jack.

'One fer all an' all fer one, eh!' Evans said.

But that bewildered him. 'What's 'e on about?' he asked David.

'It's from a book, old son,' Evans explained. '*Three Musketeers*. Cantcher read?'

'Yeh! 'Course!' the boy said scornfully. 'Not big words though.'

'What's yer name?' David asked.

'Clifford.'

'Caw, dearie me! What a monicker!' Evans said. 'Well, you stick by us, Clifford. We'll look after yer.'

Which they did from then on, doggedly.

'It is a strange life,' David wrote to Ellen, when he sent her the sketches of his two new friends. 'No logic in anything. We have to clean our boots till you can see your face in them and then we go out and march about in filth all day. Then when we come back we have to clean them all over again. I can just imagine what Jack is saying about that. The food is rotten. The weather is rotten. The Sergeant Major is indescribable. I will draw him for you next time, if I can bear to. I miss you. I.L.Y. I.L.Y. David. PS Keep the sketches. I might use them when this is all over.'

It rained every single day, monotonously, rain, rain, and more rain until the camp site was slimy with slush and mud.

'We should 'a been issued wiv boats not boots,' Evans said, knocking the caked mud from the heel of his boot.

'Don't 'alf make yer feet ache,' Clifford complained. 'Them boots are a ton weight wivout the mud.'

'You'll get used to it, son,' their corporal told him. 'Rub the inside a' yer socks wiv soft soap.' He was full of useful tips, having been regular Army since he was sixteen. 'Soak yer feet in salt water. That's the thing. Toughen 'em up. Don't take boots too small fer yer. Feet swell up sommink rotten on a route march. You'll get used to it.'

David didn't think he ever would. The marching and drilling seemed interminable and unnecessary, the food tasteless and unappetizing, and the daily ritual of kit inspection more ridiculous and demoralizing than anything he'd ever experienced. To see twelve grown men line up beside their beds in a crowded bell tent, stiff-necked with apprehension because the sergeant major was coming to inspect their kit and roar at them, was only bearable when he could draw sketches of it afterwards or when Evans turned it into a joke.

408

The best joke of all was when the tormentor asked to be shown the 'housewife', a small canvas bag containing needles and cotton for running repairs. He would insist on calling it 'arse-wife', and the request became steadily and more irresistibly funny every time they heard it. 'Show me your arse-wife.'

'Arse-wife, I ask you!' David whispered to Evans when one inspection was nearly over.

'I could do wiv one a' them,' Evans whispered back ruefully. 'Six weeks I been away from my old girl.'

'Me an'all,' David said, suddenly missing Ellen with a constricting emptiness that made him feel totally bleak.

'Carry on, Corporal!' the sergeant major said.

'Right lads, stow yer kit,' the corporal ordered.

That evening, when he was writing his daily letter to Ellen, David wondered whether he could tell her the joke about the arse-wife and decided it was too coarse. So many things about this new life were too coarse, the words of their marching song, for example, eleven verses of 'Mary had a little lamb', and only one of them respectable. It was a rough, rude, male world and he found it exhilarating despite all the hardships. But he couldn't share it with a woman and especially not with his own tender Ellen.

At that moment his own tender Ellen was having a furious row with a man in the Tyne Main Coal office. 'Whatcher mean, no coal?' she was shouting.

'There's a war on,' the man explained patiently. 'Ain't my fault, missus. There's a shortage.'

'Shortage my eye,' she said. 'There's plenty a' coal down the depot. I seen it.'

'Then you'd better go down the depot.'

'Don't you worry! I will,' she told him fiercely. 'Come on Gracie. You an' me'll go down termorrer wiv a pram. I don't see no reason why we got ter freeze, war or no war. My 'usband's a soldier, I'll 'ave you know.'

'I don't doubt it,' the man said wearily. ' 'Im an' all the others.'

It made her so angry that he was in the Army. She missed him so much, especially at night in that great empty bed.

'Surely they ought ter give 'im some leave soon,' she said to Aunty Dumpling when November began. 'I ain't seen 'im fer two whole months. Benny'll ferget what 'e looks like.'

He came home a fortnight later, on four days' embarkation leave.

'Oy!' Rachel said when she heard what a short leave it was. 'Only four days! Vhy so liddle? It ain't right!' She and Dumpling had come down to Mile End Road to welcome him, because Ellen had sent them a postcard the minute she heard he was coming home. A good voman, Ellen Cheifitz, even though she vas a *shiksa*.

'So we don't waste a minute of it,' he told her. 'What say we all go to the theatre?'

'Us an' all?' Jack asked, delighted at the idea.

' 'Course!'

'When?' Gracie wanted to know.

'Ternight!' He was expansively happy. To be home in the warm and the dry with Ellen hanging onto his arm and his family all around him was nothing short of blissful. 'Returning hero takes family on special outing!' he said striking an heroic pose, one foot on a chair.

They went out every evening, to the Standard and the Britannia and the Pavilion and the London Music Hall, in a large, happy, family party, Ellen and the children, his mother, Aunty Dumpling, and even on one occasion Fred Morrison, who was extremely shy but said he was honoured. And they sang 'Keep the Home Fires Burning' with tears in their eyes, and 'Sister Susie's sewing shirts for soldiers', nodding their heads in time to the music, and they laughed at all the comics, whether or not they were really funny, and they were warm and happy together in the plushy stalls. Nobody mentioned the war or the Army and he and Ellen were careful not to remember their row. It was bad enough being in the Army; having to relive the reason for it would have been intolerable.

But better than all the other pleasures added together was the fact that at night he was sleeping in his own welcoming bed with his own welcoming Ellen. They had both been starved of love for such a very long time neither of them could get enough of it. They spent most of their afternoons in bed too, usually remembering to make themselves respectable just in time before the kids came home from school. It was a rapturous leave, and of course it ended much too soon.

'Keep smiling,' he said to her on that last morning.

'You keep out a' trouble,' she said earnestly. 'Don't you go getting shot or nothink.'

'I'll write every day.'

'Me an' all,' she said, very near tears. 'Oh Davey, I wish you wasn't going.'

'Don't cry,' he begged, 'I couldn't bear it. Give us a smile, nu?'

So she smiled at him, mistily, but as well as she could. And they kissed for the last lingering time, while the rain spattered in upon them through the open door.

'I'll be back,' he promised. 'Stay inside. You'll get wet if you come to the gate.'

But she walked to the gate and waved goodbye to him until he'd disappeared through the archway and she couldn't see him anymore.

Then she cried.

Chapter Thirty-Three

It was a miserable crossing, for the sea was rough and the troop ship overcrowded. Within half an hour of leaving Folkestone, most of the new recruits were feeling seasick, David amongst them, and by the time they'd rocked into Boulogne and bumped to rest alongside their first foreign street, they were too sore and weary to pay much attention to it.

David had a vague impression that there was a row of higgledy-piggledy houses fronting the quay, each one honeycombed by rows of tall windows but all different colours and different heights. Behind them the ground rose sharply, crowded with other sea-viewing houses and surmounted by a grey church with an inelegant squat tower. But he didn't have the slightest urge to record any of it.

As he stumbled down the gangplank he saw that there was a hospital ship alongside, marked with bold red crosses, and that wounded men were being embarked. There was a long queue of ambulances on the quay unloading the stretcher cases. The sight of them gave David a profound shock, for these were not the tidy wounded he'd seen on the streets of London in their neat blue uniforms and clean bandages. These were men straight from the battlefield, caked in mud and filth from head to foot, their bandages bloodstained and their flesh grey-green in the winter light. Several of the stretcher cases looked dead. Their faces were as pallid as wax and their arms flopped from the stretchers to trail limp-handed just above the cobbles. They're broken, David thought. Hundreds and hundreds of broken men. And he looked up at the line of walking wounded, instinctively seeking a more hopeful sight.

But the walking wounded were just as bad. They were

shuffling along in such an odd halting way, each with his right hand on the shoulder of the man in front. It wasn't until he'd watched them for some time that he realized, with a *frisson* of horror, that they were all blind. Patient and uncomplaining and quite unable to see. And his heart sank at the thought that this was what wars did to the men who fought them, and that unless he was very careful, or very lucky, or both, he would end up in the same state.

'Are you downhearted?' a voice boomed down to the new arrivals from the deck of the hospital ship.

Their answer was immediate and automatic. It was a familiar question now, and they knew how to respond. 'No ... o ... o!'

'You bloody soon will be!' the voice called mockingly.

'Don't much like the sound a' that,' Clifford said as they formed fours ready to march away.

'They're only kidding,' David said, hoping they were.

'Where we going, Corp?' Joe Evans said.

'Eat-Apples,' the corporal told them.

'I hope we got transport,' Clifford said, shifting his pack into a more comfortable position between his shoulder blades.

'Fer you,' the corporal said, 'the Orient Express.'

As the column trudged off, past another fleet of ambulances, a horde of small boys appeared, ragged, dirt-smeared and buzzingly cheerful, scampering along beside them and calling, ' 'Allo Tommy!' 'You got ciggies?' 'Choc-late?' 'You like my seester. Good jig-a-jig. Five francs.'

And David looked at them with pity and loathing, thinking that this was what wars did to children. And their sisters.

Later that evening when they were settled into their uncomfortable bell tents at a place which turned out to be called Etaples, he drew his first sketches of the war, the unconscious boy on the stretcher, one arm trailing; the meek line of the blind; and three leaping urchins. He wrote a postcard to Ellen to tell her that he'd arrived safely and was in training camp and that he loved her and missed her. But that was all, for everything else was either too disturbing or wouldn't get past the censor. And anyway they were already in two different worlds.

The next day, after being issued with a cap badge, a rifle, an oil bottle and pull through, and a gas helmet, in short what the quartermaster sergeant called 'all the necessities of modern warfare', he was introduced to the rigours of the bull ring.

It was a vast, cold, wind-scoured plain between the railway station and the sand dunes, where nature had collaborated with the Army to ensure that everybody would be as miserable and uncomfortable as it was possible to be. The earth there was always trodden hard and on this particular morning it was coated with an ice-sharp frost. But it was the size of it that struck them all most forcibly. There were literally thousands of men being drilled there, some stripped to their shirts and trousers, others running at the double in full kit, but all of them bullied and cowed by their sergeants and instructors who seemed to have been chosen for their ugliness and their loud voices and their inhumanity. They were called the Canaries because of the yellow sashes they wore, and they were universally hated.

At the end of their first gruelling day, David released *his* hatred by drawing a vitriolic cartoon of the man who'd been screaming abuse at his squad. His fellow sufferers were thrilled with it and pinned it on the walls of the overcrowded tent so that they could spit at it the minute they got back every evening.

'You're a credit to the Army,' Evans said admiringly. 'Dunno what we'd do without yer.'

Back in Mile End, Ellen was finding it very difficult to do anything without him. His absence filled every corner of the house, from the painfully empty studio in the front room to the vacant chair that cast a sadness over every meal. At night she found it hard to sleep in the emptiness of a bed now more than ever unnecessarily large, and she was glad when one of the kids was wakeful too and came creeping in for a cuddle. But by day, once they'd all gone to school, there were far too many hours available to worry in.

'This'll never do,' she said to Aunty Dumpling as they were sorting out the washing one Monday morning. 'We could be years an' years like this. I don't see no sign of 'em ever endin' this war, do you?'

'Var! Var!' Dumpling sighed. 'Vhat's the use of var? I put a

414

darn in this liddle jersey, nu?'

'I've 'alf a mind ter get mesself a job,' Ellen said. 'Whatcher think? Take me mind off things. Earn a bit a' cash.'

'You ain't short, bubeleh?' Dumpling asked, with quick concern. 'I got plenty money just now. You ain't ter go short.'

'No,' Ellen said, touched by her generosity and thinking how typical of her it was. 'We manage. It ain't that. It's just ... I need ter keep mesself occupied, that's all. Gracie's a good age now. She could look after the boys if I wasn't here.'

'So vhat sort of job?' Dumpling said, squinting a length of wool through the eye of the largest darning needle.

'I don't rightly know,' Ellen said, easing the sheets into the copper. 'There must be something. I'll 'ave a look round.'

But in the event it was her sister Tess who found work for her.

She arrived one wet Tuesday morning when Ellen had three irons on the go, the clothes horse was draped with steamy washing, and the kitchen walls were running with moisture. She was transformed. The last time Ellen had seen her she'd been swathed to the ankle in a faded blue apron covered with brown grease; now she wore a smart blue uniform of a very different kind, a peaked cap, an impressively military jacket with brass buttons all down the front, black boots, leather gaiters, and a skirt so short it barely covered her knees. Her hair was all tucked inside her cap and without it her face looked clean and exposed and confident. 'I changed me job,' she said.

'So I see,' her sister said. 'Done you a power a' good an' all.'

'Guard on the Metropolitan Railway,' Tess said proudly. 'Whatcher think a' that? Beats bein' a skivvy any day a' the week. I didn't 'alf give that old girl a piece a' my mind when I give in me notice.' The memory of it made her chuckle.

'You've put on weight,' Ellen approved.

'Hard work gives you appetite,' Tess said. 'I 'ave pie and mash every evening now. The pay's ever so good.'

'I was thinking a' taking a job mesself,' Ellen said, holding the next iron close to her cheek to test its heat.

'Go down the London General Bus office,' Tess advised. 'It's right near 'ere, just up the Mile End Road, corner a' Lawton Road. They're on the look-out fer women conductors. My driver was tellin' me on'y yesterday. His niece is going along.'

'I'd 'ave ter write ter David,' Ellen said, starting on the first petticoat. 'See what 'e says.'

'D'you write every day?'

'Every day as ever is.'

'Poor old Ellie. I bet yer miss 'im. I'm walkin' out. Did I tell yer?'

No, she hadn't. What a piece of good news! 'Tell us!' Ellen said eagerly.

' 'Is name's Bill. 'E's in the Artillery. Ever so 'andsome. I got a photograph. D'you want ter see it?'

'Is 'e in France?' Ellen asked putting down the iron at once to admire the portrait.

'Went last Thursday. That's one a' the reasons I come ter see yer, ter tell the truth.'

'Both in the same boat eh?' Ellen said.

'You an' me an' 'alf the world,' Tess said, sighing.

David's next postcard gave a rather absent-minded consent. 'Cannot tell you where we are now. Near a famous battlefield. Very dull country. Miles and miles absolutely flat, criss-crossed by canals. I will send you a parcel of sketches soon. My love to the kids. Keep smiling. I.L.Y. David. P.S. You will make a beautiful conductor.'

Although he couldn't tell her so, he'd been moved to Hoograaf, just went of Ypres, to join the 17th London Rifles, and the war was only a few miles away.

The parcel of sketches arrived on the day Ellen started work. She'd got the job so easily she could hardly believe her luck.

'Five questions that superintendent asked,' she told Aunty Dumpling afterwards. 'Just five an' I was on the pay-roll.' And only one of them was really important. She'd known that the minute he'd asked it.

'You can get some pretty rough types on the buses these days,' he'd said, trying to assess the strength in those slender wrists. 'Could yer cope with drunks, d'yer think?'

She'd drawn herself up to her full five foot six. 'I can handle 'em,' she'd said. 'I was born in the Nichol.'

'Was yer?' the superintendent said, much impressed. 'Oh well then.'

'Never thought it'ud stand me in good stead ter be born in that dump,' she said to Aunty Dumpling.

'God moves in a mysterious vay his vonders to perform,' that lady told her, nodding happily. 'So vhat's in the parcel?'

They examined the sketches together, but rather perfunctorily, because Dumpling had come without her glasses and couldn't really see them, and Ellen was preoccupied with the arrangement of her blue cocked hat. But they agreed that they were 'ever so good' even if they were all drawings of soldiers, and Ellen said that the very first thing she would buy when she got her wages was a good chest of drawers to keep them in. 'All laid flat with tissue paper in between,' she said, buttoning her jacket. 'I could keep 'em lovely for when 'e comes 'ome. How do I look?'

'Smart as sixpence,' Dumpling said. And so she did.

They put her on route 14, and once she'd got used to it she thoroughly enjoyed it. It ran from Putney Bridge in the south-west right across London to the edge of Epping Forest, and there were so many places on the route to remind her of David and happier times: Hyde Park and Trafalgar Square, the Strand and Essex Street and the magazine, Ludgate Circus where she'd watched the old Queen's Jubilee, the Aldgate pump where she and David had stopped to drink, and Whitechapel High Street and the long familiar width of the Mile End Road.

Before long she felt really at home on the route and had learned to deal with drunks and jolly the munition workers along and ease wounded soldiers into their seats without appearing to help them. True to her vow, she bought a chest of drawers with her first pay, and she and Gracie put all David's sketches safely and reverently away. It was very satisfying to be earning extra cash. 'We shall eat well this winter an' no mistake,' she told the children. But more rewarding than anything else was the sense that she was doing an important job and being valued for it. Even being drenched to the skin in heavy rain was worthwhile now, and when the first flurries of snow began to swirl about the traffic, she simply wore an extra jersey under her uniform and went on with the job, red-nosed and feeling valiant.

417

'So you can see some good has come out of this war, after all,' she wrote to David. 'I feel I am somebody, not just old mother Cheifitz, but Mrs Cheifitz the bus conductor. I can see why men work. It is very cold here. Looks like more snow. We are well. Hope you are same.'

It was very cold in Hoograaf too, and the first snow was falling on David as he read her card. The flat fields were already dusted with delicate white powder, and Clifford had discovered two more chilblains on his swollen toes.

'We could do with a spot of action,' he complained. 'Least it'ud warm us all up.'

His wish was granted almost at once and with such noise and brutality it stopped them all breathing.

The white air was full of diabolical noises, screams and howls and high-pitched whines, and they could feel the pressure of a terrible wind rushing and battering just above their heads, and reed-thin in the uproar a voice was shouting, 'Take cover! Take cover!' But there was no cover to take, David thought, stupid with fright. Where were the dug-outs? Then bodies were hurling to the ground, and he fell with them, automatically, his hands scrabbling in ice-sharp grass, his mind not functioning at all. Then the first explosion roared behind him, and he could hear the patter of earth or shrapnel, followed at once by a series of explosions so close together that they produced one long continuous roar. There was a pain in his ears and he could feel the sweat running down his back and dripping from his armpits, his heart was thudding against the hard earth and he knew he was praying, but wordlessly, almost without thought.

A sergeant came crawling over the grass towards them, waving his right arm to indicate that they should follow him, which they did, copying his every move, flattening themselves whenever he did, and scrambling to their feet to run the last few yards towards the cover of the barn, crouched low and moving so fast they had no breath left at all when they finally flung themselves down behind the wall.

'Bli! That was close,' Evans shouted to David.

'They ain't finished with us yet,' the sergeant shouted back. And as if to prove him right the shelling doubled in intensity,

418

with an outburst of explosions that were uncomfortably close. The noise above them continued, paining their eardrums and making their stomachs shake, but now there was another kind of screaming mingled with it, a wailing noise, like an animal in a trap.

'Some poor bugger's copped it,' the sergeant shouted, peering round the edge of the barn. 'Stretcher party's on the other side. You, you an' you, foller me!'

One of the men he'd pointed to was Joe Evans. The third was David.

Afterwards it occurred to him that he hadn't felt any fear when he was obeying that order, even though he knew he was running straight back into the line of fire. He simply jammed his tin hat firmly on his head and ran, following the sergeant. There were three men lying on the ground little more than a hundred yards in front of them, and he could see that one of them had had his leg blown right off at the knee. Shreds of flesh were trailing from the stump, but he was sitting up and grinning, as if he was enjoying some private joke. It wasn't until they were right on top of him that David saw that the man was dead. The sergeant wasted no time on a corpse. The two other men were obviously alive, writhing and groaning, one with a gaping flesh wound on his thigh, the other clutching his chest. He and Evans lifted the man with the flesh wound, supporting his weight between them in the way they'd been taught, and urging him to 'hop lively' as they ran back again, their only thought now to get behind the safety of the wall.

'Thanks, mate,' the wounded man said as they joggled him over the rough ground. 'Thanks, mate.' Over and over again. And when they were all back behind the wall and he started to shake violently, he was still trying to thank them. 'Th – th – th – thanks.'

'Save yer breath, mate,' David told him, putting his head close to the man's face so that he could hear, and applying the first aid pack as quickly as he could because he was losing blood at an alarming rate. 'Somebody give 'im a fag.'

And then the sergeant returned with his casualty and took over. 'Well done, lads. That's the style. Billings.'

'Sah!'

'Cut across to the farm. Tell 'em two casualties.'

While Billings was running, there was a loud crump followed by a clatter, and peering out they could see that a shell had crashed through the side of the other barn. The air was pink with swirling brick dust and there were two legs hanging limply out of the hole. Clifford began to moan.

'Put a sock in it!' the sergeant told him brusquely. 'We don't want none a' that.'

But he went on moaning, 'Ma! Ma! Ma!' over and over again until the barrage died down. Then he crawled into a corner and was sick.

It all seemed to have lasted for a very long time, but the sergeant looked at his watch and told them it was 'quite a short one. Half an hour, that's all, lads. You can think yerselves lucky.' And while they were still blinking the brick dust out of their eyes he organized them into rescue parties and digging parties, and set about restoring order. 'Now you can all write 'ome an' say you've been under fire,' he told them. 'You're one a' the lads.'

David was quite shocked by the speed with which their seven corpses were gathered up and bundled out of sight. It didn't seem respectful to be treating them so casually. War, he thought. No time for ceremony or kindness. One minute you're alive, next minute you're dead. Quick and cruel and inevitable. But even while he was feeling critical and disapproving, he knew he was going to draw this attack in as much detail as he could remember, and he had a sneaking feeling that that was disrespectful too.

His squad spent the rest of the morning clearing the rubble, the barrage didn't start again, and by mid afternoon they were all back to normal.

'Overshot the mark, that's what,' the corporal told them. 'Wasn't meant fer us, that lot. Somebody got the range wrong.'

And for that, David thought, seven men died. There was no sense in this war at all.

During the next four days he spent every spare moment he could scrounge making rapid sketches, of those dead legs suspended from the hole in the wall, of the dead man grinning, and the man with the thigh wound smoking, and Clifford

420

being sick, and Billings running bent double with chunks of earth and shrapnel falling all around him. They were fierce angry drawings, the lines heavy and black, and when they were finished his new friends found them rather shocking.

'You won't show that to my Ma, will yer?' Clifford asked, looking at his portrait anxiously. 'I wouldn't like 'er ter see me like that.'

' 'E don't know yer Ma, you daft ha'p'orth,' the corporal said.

'Upset 'er, that would,' Clifford persisted. 'I wouldn't want to upset 'er.'

'Whatcher going ter do with 'em?' Evans wanted to know.

'Send 'em home.'

'Never get past the censor.'

'Why not?'

'Oh do me a favour. You got a corpse in that lot. They ain't supposed ter see corpses back 'ome.'

He was probably right, David thought. '*I* won't send 'em then,' he said. 'I'll find someone down the village ter do it for me. Make up a parcel, pay 'em the postage, little tip. You'll see.' In a passionate unreasonable way he felt it was necessary to tell the truth about this war and to send it back to England.

He found his first postman the next afternoon when they went down to the village bath-house for their weekly dip. Despite the fact that he couldn't speak any English the keeper of the local inn managed to understand what was required of him. '*Bien, je comprende,*' he said, nodding his head vigorously. '*Je mettrai le pacquet á la poste. Oui. Bien entendu.*' And he was more than pleased with his *pourboire*.

So David returned to camp that evening relatively clean and extremely pleased with himself for outwitting the authorities.

'More ways a' killin' the cat, eh?' Evans said. 'What's your old lady gonna say when she gets that lot?'

'Nothink much,' David said. 'She'll understand why I drew 'em. She'll keep 'em for me.'

But when the sketches arrived in Mile End Place a week later, Ellen was very upset by them. They were so very different from anything he'd ever drawn before. Even the style of the drawing was different, with those thick heavy lines instead of the short delicate ones she was used to. He's changing, she thought, and the thought upset her. But the subject matter was more frightening than the style.

'What terrible pictures,' she wrote back. 'You have drawn them ever so good. I don't mean terrible like that. I mean that poor feller with his leg. I never thought war was like that. It's awful.'

'I got to tell the truth about this war,' he answered. 'Now I'm here, it's the least I can do. I'm beginning to think that was why I was given my talent. For a true record. To let people know how it really is. I had no idea, either, before I came here. I didn't intend to join. That was my own stupidity, which I now regret. But now I'm here, I must draw what I see, as truthfully as I can. There is another parcel on its way. We are going somewhere else in a couple of days, so I might not be able to write for a day or two, but don't worry. My love to the kids. I.L.Y. David. P.S. I am going to buy a watch. Sometimes it is necessary to know the time out here.'

He sent her drawings of a concert party just after Christmas, and they cheered her, because they were funny and everybody in them was healthy and alive. But as a wet spring gave way to an even wetter summer, the sketches he sent grew steadily more sombre. Dejected men trailing waterproof capes, exhausted men squatting on their haunches eating food from a battered tin, men on the march looking miserable. And all drawn in the new style, the black lines quick and angry.

He's growing away from me, she thought sadly, and wrote him the most loving letter she could, to try and remind him of the life he'd left behind. But the things she really wanted to say would have been embarrassing on paper, and the letter was dull and ordinary.

Then late in May she got the postcard she'd been dreading.

'We are going up the line in a day or two. I will write as soon as I can. I.L.Y. David.'

Chapter Thirty-Four

They trudged into the Ypres salient by night, moving steadily nearer and nearer to the noise of the guns. The preliminary bombardment had already begun and the distant sky was punctured by continual red flashes and shaded by the prolonged pink glow of flares. It was a long march and they were carrying the full weight of a sixty pound pack, so although they began with songs they ended in weary speechlessness, with only the appalling thunder of the guns and the rhythmic suction of their own boots for accompaniment. Not that they could have heard a song even if they'd had the energy to sing it, for the noise of the bombardment was so intense it was like a physical presence, pressing down on their heads. The air was full of solid sound, high-pitched, nerve-wracking screams, an endless howling and groaning, and so many explosions they formed one continuous pulsing roar that beat in their ears like blood. After an hour they were all shaking under the intolerable pressure of it.

David was trying to remember the Psalms, 'The Lord is our refuge and strength, a very present help in trouble. Therefore we will not fear though the earth be removed, and though the mountains be carried into the midst of the sea.' But the words brought no comfort. He *did* fear, and the nearer he got to the front the stronger and more constricting the fear became. As he stumbled along the duckboards, with that awkward pack rubbing a sore between his shoulder blades, and his sense of hearing swollen to a physical pain in his ears, his other senses were being saturated too. The stench of decaying flesh rose sickeningly on either side of him out of the darkness, and he wondered how it would be to have his own flesh torn by hot steel, and what the pain would be like, and how he would behave when the time came. We're marching towards agony, he thought, and all we do is sing and grumble and make a joke of it.

They passed a line of dead mules, bloated and decomposing. It was impossible to see how many, but the smell of them was overpowering. Then the column was snaking down into the communication trenches and David realized that they were nearly there. They already knew what lay ahead of them: two days in the reserve trenches while the attack on the Messine Ridge began, and then it was their turn. Why do we do it? he thought, as he slithered into the trench. What is it for, all this pain and effort and destruction? But he knew these were questions he had to keep to himself.

They marched blindly through the communication trenches, each man following the one in front, zig-zagging towards the line. The noise reverberated between the sandbags and the smell here was so dreadful that many of them were gagging as they marched. It was a combination of all the worst smells they had ever experienced, shit and piss and the sickly sharpness of the chloride of lime that was supposed to disguise it, mildew and slime and rotting vegetation and the appalling putrescence of decomposing bodies, a noisome mephitic stench almost as tangible as the noise of the bombardment. 'The Lord is our refuge.'

'I shall be glad of a spot a' shut-eye,' Evans shouted, when they finally arrived and were allowed to drop their kit.

Thank God for Evans, David thought. He was always so phlegmatically normal.

But sleep was a luxury at the front, as they were soon to discover. No sooner had they found a nice hole for their kit than David and the phlegmatic Evans were sent on sentry-go.

'Oy! This is the life!' David shouted to his mate above the tempest, taking his own peculiar refuge in sarcastic resignation. 'Never a dull moment!' But the sight he saw when he stood on the fire-step and looked over the parapet for the first time shocked him so much his sarcasm seemed very petty.

For this was a ghostly, unearthly landscape they'd come to, a terrible combination of sinister darkness, unnatural silhouettes

424

and an intermittent glow of lurid, artificial light. Above his head, star shells drew parabolas of searing brightness, and as he watched, two Very lights went up and the ground beneath was mottled with coiling shadows as their bright green signals slowly descended. Observation balloons tugged at their cables, drifting and shifting like long silver clouds. Despite himself, he could see a beauty in this fantastic sky and the artist in him knew it would be worth painting.

But the earth beneath it was sheer horror, a picture of devastation far beyond anything even the most fevered artist could ever have imagined. Miles and miles of pitted earth stretched before him and every foot of it was marked by war. There was no grass at all, only a vast shell-pocked expanse of churned-up mud, and no living trees, only their pathetically broken remains, mere stumps, leafless and lifeless, winter trees in the middle of summer. It looked like an enormous rubbish dump littered with debris, coils of barbed wire silhouetted in the bright light from the flares, discarded guns, broken wagons, shell cases and he dared not imagine what else. Miles and miles and miles of wreckage. He was overawed and afraid and sickened. So much so, he was almost glad when a shell burst in front of the trench, because the shower of earth it threw into the air blotted out the vision. And as the earth pattered down, he remembered words from another Psalm, 'Yea, though I walk through the valley of the shadow of death', and vowed that he would draw this place as soon as the attack allowed him the time to do it.

The night and the bombardment continued endlessly. They snatched what little sleep they could huddled in funk holes in the side of the trench, and when morning came their backs ached, they were shattered by noise, crawling with lice and weary to the bone.

It was a lovely summer's day, warm and gentle, and the sky, where they could see it through the drifting pall of smoke, was the clear innocent blue of forget-me-nots. Now, the dreadful landscape of war was all too clearly revealed, and he saw that the misshapen lumps he'd glimpsed in the darkness were discarded greatcoats and helmets and respirators, and that some of the shell holes were so big they could have held a

425

London bus. He thought of the men who had once worn those greatcoats and stood on the bare earth when the great shells exploded. And terrible images filled his mind, until his heart juddered with the terror of them, and he was glad when the corporal roared at him to join the digging party for repairs, because it recalled him to the trench and the ordinary normal faces of Evans and young Clifford. The full horror of what man had done to nature was too painful to contemplate.

Breakfast, which consisted of cold porridge and a muddy liquid that was probably tea, was accompanied by the rumour that the attack on the Messine Ridge was due to start at dawn the next day.

'We shall see it all from 'ere,' Clifford said, quite cheered by the thought of such vicarious excitment.

'We should be so lucky!' David said. But Clifford couldn't understand him.

'They got the ridge mined,' their corporal told them. 'Seventeen mines, so they say, all goin' up the same time.'

'Cor!' Clifford said. 'That'll be worth seeing. Sommink ter write home about, eh?'

But then the lull was over and the bombardment began again and talk was impossible.

That day they were kept on the run from the moment they opened their eyes until long after they needed to close them again, bringing up endless ammunition, repairing trenches, digging latrines, collecting stores. The night was divided into watches, and the bombardment continued.

But at three o'clock in the morning there was an abrupt, terrifying silence. Suddenly they could hear the rats squealing out in no-man's land and people coughing and talking and shuffling their feet. David and Joe Evans were bringing up trench mortars, which were like great metal footballs on a stalk and had to be carried over the shoulder, so they were stooped under the weight and couldn't see anything except the yard of ridged mud immediately under their feet. But by common consent the entire squad stopped moving and put their burdens down and looked up. And what they saw then was so extraordinary they couldn't believe their eyes.

Below them, to the south, huge sections of the hillside were rising slowly into the air, projected upwards by glowing red columns of fire and expanding like black sponges to blot out the skyline.

Uncannily, the mines had exploded before they heard them, and when the detonations came, they were so enormous they were like something out of a nightmare.

'Cripes!' Evans said, his eyes bolting.

'*Gevalt!*' David echoed. We will not fear, though the earth be removed and though the mountains be carried into the midst of the sea.

And then there were men rising out of the trenches below them, helmet rims and bayonet edges reflecting the red light. Small black vulnerable figures crawling up the distant hillside under the thick rain of that falling earth. And some fell, arms flung upwards, and some dropped suddenly like stones. And David shuddered with the terrible knowledge that he was watching men die. But then the sergeant was chivvying them into action again. 'Come on, lads. Look lively. We ain't got all night.' And their labours took them away.

The attack continued all through the day, but they were kept too busy to be able to see any more of it, and by now the enemy shells were falling uncomfortably close to their own trenches, and they'd had several casualties. But at nightfall the message came down the line that the attack had been a success and that three miles of the ridge had been captured.

'Our turn next, lads,' the corporal said cheerfully. 'Make the most a' that stew. Could be yer last 'ot meal fer quite a while.'

The following evening they were issued with extra trenching tools, sacks for bagging, rolls of barbed wire, boxes of ammunition, grenades and mortars, and the regulation six tins of cigarettes to keep them going during their six-day stint on the new front line. They toiled away from the support trench, staggering under a load nearly equal to their own weight.

'Beasts a' burden, that's all we are,' Evans said, shifting his cigarette into the corner of his mouth.

'Give us any more ter carry an' we shall be breakin' into a trot,' David said, his sarcasm as heavy as his pack, for he was mortally afraid of what he would see and hear once they reached the front.

427

The first mile they covered was a morass of shell holes and mud-spattered debris. Then they began to pass the corpses, huddled and distorted and grotesque, some already swelling and decomposing in the heat, or streaked with congealed blood or thickly speckled with a crawling mass of flies and bluebottles, buzzing obscenely. They were so hideous that it was hard to realize they had once been men, and so terrifying that David wondered whether it would be within his competence to draw them truthfully. But he knew they must be drawn, for this truth had to be told in its entirety. It was no good looking away.

The sergeant urged them past at speed, because there was a lot of sniping and they were far too exposed out in the open even at night. 'Look lively,' he said, and David wondered whether he was the only one who could see how inappropriate the words were. Or perhaps they all did, and none of them had the breath or the energy to say so. Then, quite precipitately, they arrived at a German strongpoint.

It was a deep square dug-out, with thick concrete walls and a wide entrance which was now facing in quite the wrong direction for their purpose, straight at the new enemy lines above them. The occupants were all gone, but they'd left their bunks behind and most of their equipment, which was littered in the doorway and blocked the passage trench.

'Right, you lot,' the corporal said, 'this 'as all gotta be clear by daybreak.'

'Where's Jerry, Corp?' Clifford asked.

'Don't ask me,' the corporal said. 'In them woods up there, I 'spect. Leastways that's where I'd be if I was a Jerry.'

The woods were a dark shadow about six hundred yards away. *Gevalt*! David thought. So close! He lit a cigarette to steady his nerves, wishing they could dig another opening to their new quarters. But there was no digging through four feet of concrete. So they set to and cleared the rubbish.

The British guns were still pounding away behind them and as they were plainly aiming at the wood it looked as though the corporal was right. They were horribly exposed in their isolated gun emplacement and facing the wrong way, wide open to counter-attack. But the counter-attack didn't begin

428

that night, although the firing was continuous. When morning came the barrage died down and, odd though it seemed, the ridge was relatively calm. A very young man in an officer's uniform and splendid thigh boots strolled into the strongpoint just after dawn and informed them that they were to lie low by day and keep very very quiet, and when it was dark they were to get the Lewis gun out into the passage trench and up into the next communication trench along the line, where, so he said, 'you should have a jolly good field of fire'.

So they took it in turns to cat-nap all through the next jittery day, waking to listen out or stand guard. The latrine was already very well used and extremely foul, there was no food and precious little water, for supplies couldn't be brought up until dusk, so they were horribly uncomfortable, cramped together in their concrete cell. But at least the shells fell short of them, and they had no casualties and a certain amount of cover. When darkness fell and they emerged to haul the Lewis gun into position, they felt they were making progress. Now if the counter-attack began they would be ready for it.

But the counter-attack didn't come. Supplies trickled through, there was a heavy barrage, and towards midnight a sinister line of flickering lights went snaking down the ridge towards the old front line, but there was no attack. They smoked incessantly, in a state of continuous, nerve-wracking alert, shifting about in the communication trenches, cramped and tense. But when daylight brought the possibility of sleep they were too fatigued to take advantage of it.

'How long we been 'ere?' Clifford wanted to know, easing himself down from the middle bunk as the sun went down for the fourth or was it the fifth time. ''Bout time we was sent back ter base.'

'Six days, old son,' the corporal said. 'Anyone got a fag?'

'I reckon they've fergot us,' Clifford grumbled. 'Stuck out 'ere in the middle a' nowhere. We shall be 'ere months.'

But at last the order came. They were being sent to Westoutre for rest and retraining. It was 13 June and they'd been in the trenches for ten days. It felt like a lifetime.

Oh, the relief to be trudging away from that awful place, leaving the smell of death behind, heading towards green grass and dry tents and the chance of a wash and the possibility of some food that would at least be hot. Their heavy packs grew lighter with every mile.

Skylarks were carolling into the air as they settled into their tents, and the fields were greening in the early morning light. They removed their mud-caked boots and puttees, took off their tin hats, fell onto their palliasses, and slept like drunkards.

Two hours later they were all woken up again to be de-loused and given a hot bath, which David thought was just as well, because they were all crawling. It seemed unreal to be marching along such an ordinary village street, between ordinary whitewashed houses with windows framed by ordinary wooden shutters over roads smeared with nothing more dreadful than ordinary pungent horse dung. They sang as they marched, because the sun was shining and nobody was shooting at them. 'What do we want with eggs and ham, when we got plum and apple jam? Form fours, right turn, how shall we spend the money we earn? O, O, O, it's a lovely war!'

The bath-house was a converted brewery which had been cleared of everything except twelve huge tubs full of hot water and six foot troughs. They stripped in the outhouse, leaving their filthy clothes in a mud-stained pile below the number they'd been given, and then ran into the brewery, free and giggling, their mud-smeared bodies as naked as white grubs. The contrast between their brown hands and faces and the innocent pallor of their bodies was so extreme it quite startled David. Dirt darkened the lines around their eyes and mouths, increasing their look of anxiety and exhaustion, and their fingers were black-rimmed workers' fingers, broken-nailed, calloused and scarred, yet, in between, their flesh was pale and vulnerable and soft as the newborn.

'Oh my fuckin' life! Jest look at you lot!' a voice jeered cheerfully. 'Bollock-naked the lot a' yer. Where's yer towels? Towels on the 'ooks first if yer don't mind.'

It was a private in the R.A.M.C. come to collect their dirty uniforms.

'Shut yer cake-'ole,' they shouted back. 'Bring on the dancing girls. Show you a thing or two then!'

430

David was already standing in one of the troughs, lathering himself very thoroughly with a huge bar of soft soap. The luxury of feeling he would soon be clean was absorbing him almost to the exclusion of their ridiculous jokes. But he glanced up idly at the private, ready to join in, and found himself looking at the tomcat face of Alfie Miller. 'Well, I'll be darned!' he said. 'What you doin' in the Medical Corps?'

'Who wants ter know?' Alfie said, squinting at him.

'Cheifitz. We was at school tergether.'

'Well, I'll go ter Jericho! Whatcher doing in the Army?'

'De-lousing.'

'There y'are!' Alfie said, producing a thick clean towel from the pile hanging across his arm. 'Jest fer you. Seein' 'as 'ow you're a friend a' mine.'

They swapped news as David wallowed in the second tub, enjoying the clean smell of soap and disinfectant. It didn't surprise him to learn that his artful friend had found a way to keep out of trouble.

'Got mesself a nice cushy number 'ere,' Alfie said. 'Copped a Blighty one early on, you see. Leg wound. Jest enough, as you might say. You oughter see me limp when I come up before the Tribunal. Would a' brought tears to yer eyes. So now I got a cushy billet, little mademoiselle, plenty a grub, one or two odd jobs on the side. You take my tip, Davey Cheifitz, get yerself a Blighty one. It's a mug's game out there.'

When he was clean and clothed again, David sat on the low wall beside the brewery and drew a quick sketch of his old friend, soft cap rakishly askew, cigarette in the corner of his mouth, thick hair tumbling over his forehead, a handsome, well-fed, prosperous soldier of fortune.

'Yerse,' Alfie said, approving of it, when it was done. 'That's me.'

For the rest of his stay at Westoutre, David spent every spare moment he could scrounge scratching his remembered images onto paper, quickly and blackly before they faded. There wasn't much time left over after the marches and the endless drill and all the other exhausting occupations the War Office had so kindly designed for soldiers returning from the front, but he worked at speed, feverishly, sitting up at night long after

431

his friends had fallen asleep, to draw by candlelight in the corner of the hut.

'There is so much I want to say about this war,' he wrote to Ellen. 'Keep my sketches, no matter how messy they are. I will work on them when I come home. There is a picture of Alfie Miller in this batch. Tell Mrs Miller he is alive and well and nowhere near the front. My love to the kids. Keep smiling. Maybe we shall get some home leave for Christmas! I.L.Y. David.'

Chapter Thirty-Five

Fred Morrison was in a dilemma. One minute he was feeling really quite proud of himself, and amazed and gratified at his good fortune, and the next he was twitching with nervousness and wondering how on earth he would ever find the words to express his emotions or make his intentions clear. And it was so important that his intentions should be quite quite clear. For he was going to ask his dear Dumpling to marry him.

The *East London Weekly Pictorial*, now seriously short of experienced workmen, had offered him promotion. Suddenly and without any warning he was in charge of the print shop, with a salary so princely he could afford to rent an entire flat all for himself. If that was what he wanted. And of course, it was what he wanted, if he could persuade his dear ... Mrs Esterman to share it with him.

Now, dressing himself most carefully in his new grey worsted, his boots polished until they gleamed, his watch chain hanging neatly across his waistcoat, and a clean pocket handkerchief in the breast pocket of his jacket, he was rehearsing the words he would say and making himself blush at the very sound of them. Oh dear, oh dear, what if she said 'no'? Or worse, what if she laughed at him? But no, his dear Dum ... Mrs Esterman wasn't the sort of woman who would laugh at a man in such a predicament. Oh, if only he'd known a few weeks ago, he could have told her on Bank Holiday Monday, in amongst all the crowds, where he wouldn't have felt so conspicuous. Sighing with an exquisite blend of hope, excitement and apprehension, he carried his bowler hat across to the kettle and began to give it a good steaming.

Dumpling was looking forward to her Sunday evening with

mixed feelings too. It had been a long week and not an easy one, and now her back was aching and her feet were sore.

'Oy my back!' she said to Rachel as she hobbled in through the door with half a pail of water.

'So stay in tonight, vhy don't you,' Rachel suggested. She was going to visit Ellen and the children. 'You got the place to yourselves. Vhy go traipsing all over London, nu?'

'I ask him maybe,' Dumpling said, sinking heavily into her chair. 'If he got tickets for somethink I make the effort, nu.'

'Pot of tea, peace an' quiet, liddle rest,' Rachel insisted. 'Vhat more vould any man vant?'

'This man, maybe you're right. Ai! You tempt me, dolly. Vicked temptation.'

'I come back half past ten,' Rachel said, sliding a stool under Dumpling's battered shoes. 'You rest good, dolly. You earned it, nu.'

It was true, Dumpling thought, adjusting the angle of her legs and easing her back against the chair. So maybe I'll have forty winks. Then we'll see.

She was still snoozing when Fred came tapping at the door and his knock was so gentle it didn't rouse her. He knocked twice, three times, inclining his head towards the wooden panels in case she was calling to him to come in. But it was all alarmingly quiet. 'Are you there, Mrs Esterman?' he said. But she still didn't answer. Was she out, perhaps? Or ill? Oh dear me! He couldn't bear to think of her being ill. And on her own too. Perhaps he ought just to peep in and see.

Greatly daring he opened the door and tiptoed in. And just at that moment Dumpling woke up with a visible start.

It would have been difficult to judge which of them was the most embarrassed, Fred because he'd been caught entering her room uninvited, Dumpling because she was still in her apron and had been caught fast asleep. They both began to babble excuses. 'Vhat you must think ... to be sleeping ... oy oy vhat a vay to go on!' 'My dear Mrs Esterman, I'm so sorry ... I had no idea ... bargin' in ... ain't got no manners, no manners at all. I'm so sorry.'

Then Dumpling began to giggle. 'Oy, Fred Morrison,' she said. 'You oughter see your face.'

'You all right?' he asked anxiously. 'You're not ill or nothink, are yer?'

'Nu-nu,' she assured him. 'Just tired, that's all. So ve all get tired, nu?'

'Stay where you are,' he said at once, 'an' I'll make a nice pot a' tea.' He knew exactly where everything was. Hadn't he made tea for them on many many occasions?

'You're a good man,' she said gratefully. Jew or no Jew, a good man.

'We could stay in tonight, if you'd rather,' he suggested.

'Ve could,' she said, settling her feet on the stool.

So far so good, he thought, and busied himself with the cups and saucers, because he was feeling embarrassed all over again. His hands were trembling so much he was making the china rattle.

Dumpling was too discreet to comment, but as he handed her the tea, at last, she put one hand down over his cold fingers and patted them. 'A bad week, nu?' she asked sympathetically.

'No,' he said, and managed a smile. 'It was a good'un. Best ever, matter a' fact.'

'So?' she asked, sipping her tea.

He took his own cup and sat in the chair opposite her. There was enough darkness now to mask his apprehension. 'Yes,' he said. 'Matter a' fact, I been offered a rise.'

She put down her cup at once. 'Dolly!' she shrieked, eyes bright with delight. 'Vhat news!'

'Yes,' he said. This was it. This was the moment. He cleared his throat nervously. 'Matter a' fact, it's enough fer me ter take on them rooms I was tellin' you about. The ones in Underwood Street.'

She remembered. 'Vid a kitchen an' scullery, on the ground floor. No stairs, think a' that. Nu-nu, no stairs!'

He coughed again. 'Matter a' fact,' he said, 'it was stairs I was thinkin' about really. Seein' how bad your legs are.' But that sounded so dreadful he could feel himself blushing. 'What I mean ter say is ... Stairs ain't the easiest things. Not when you got a bad back, I mean. Or bad feet.'

'You ain't got bad feet, 'ave yer, Fred?' she said, her eyes beaming at him over the rim of her teacup.

435

'Oh no,' he said, blushing again. 'They ain't so dusty. It was your feet I was thinkin' of. On them stairs. It don't seem right fer you ter be up an' down them stairs all day an' every day. I mean ter say ... Not when ... Not now I ...'

She put the cup down and folded her hands in her vast lap and waited, almost as if she knew what he was going to say next.

'Two can live as cheaply as one,' he struggled. 'What I mean ter say is ... Well, not cheaply, no. I got a rise when all's said an' done. An' I'd look after yer. You wouldn't 'ave ter worry. What I mean ter say ...'

At that she threw her apron over her head and began to howl. 'Oy oy oy oy!' over and over, rocking backwards and forwards on her chair. He was horribly alarmed.

'Dumpling, my dear, what's the matter? What've I said?'

She lowered the apron like a yashmak and peered at him over the top of it, her eyes gleaming with tears. 'You askin' me to marry you or ain't yer?'

His confidence ebbed away. 'No, no,' he said. 'Not if you don't want me to.'

She seized his face between her hands and kissed him moistly first on one cheek and then on the other. 'A *meshuganer*!' she wailed. 'He don't ask! So yes, yes, I tell you! Vhy you don't ask, nu?'

Relief made him weak at the knees. 'Because I love yer,' he confessed. 'I couldn't've borne it if you'd said no.'

When Rachel came home they were still planning their new future together. Dumpling had been so happy all evening, she'd quite forgotten about the others members of her family. Now she just had time to warn him not to say anything. 'Not yet, bubeleh. Leave it to me, nu?'

'See you termorrer?' he said. They'd already agreed that they would go and look at the flat, but he needed reassurance now that the outside world was walking up the stairs towards them on Rachel's shuffling feet.

'You van' it in writing?' she teased.

That night she lay awake, sorting things out in her mind. It was going to be very difficult telling Rachel and Rivke. They wouldn't approve, either of them. Better maybe to work up to it gradually. Wouldn't do to shock 'em. Nu-nu!

So the next morning while she and Rachel were eating breakfast, she started to reminisce, singing Rivke's praises and rememembering how kind she'd been when Mr Esterman died. 'A good voman, don't I tell you, to take me in the vay she done. I stay vid her years an' years, right up to the day she married.'

But Rachel misunderstood her intentions. 'So now you take me in,' she said. 'You're a good voman too, Dumpling, praise be to God. Don't think I ain't grateful.'

Oy oy, so how do I talk my way out of that? Dumpling wondered.

Fortunately they were both rescued by the noisy arrival of Goldman's van which had come to pick up the finished overcoats and deliver the next batch. And by the time the delivery boy had clumped into their room and dropped two greatcoats on his way downstairs, and left mud on the rag rug, the topic was more or less forgotten.

That afternoon, she tried a different approach. 'Oy, them stairs give me gyp!' she said after her regular trip to the tap. 'Vhat a blessing it vould be to live on a ground floor somevheres.'

'Cost the earth,' Rachel pointed out. 'Ground floor! Ve should be so lucky! Oy oy! Vhere ve get the money for the ground floor?'

Rent, Dumpling thought, realizing the implications of this conversation too. When I marry Fred she'll be left behind vid this room to pay for all on her own, and it's been hard enough to make ends meet with both our wages put together. I should ask her to live vid us, maybe? But her flesh quailed at the thought. This was going to be even more difficult than she'd imagined.

On Tuesday evening, when the work was done for the day and supper was over, she spoke about loneliness, hoping to evoke a little sympathy for her intended. 'Poor Mr Morrison, living alone all these years. It ain't good, nu-nu.'

'He got a good job, dolly,' Rachel pointed out. 'Ve don't get all ve vant in this vorld, nu nu.'

'Vhat you think?' Dumpling said, seizing the opportunity. 'This week he got promoted. Better job, better pay, better flat maybe.'

Rachel went on drying the cups and didn't comment.

'But on his own you see, dolly. It ain't natural. Poor Mr Morrison.'

'So ve all need company,' Rachel agreed easily, but she didn't pursue the topic. She seemed to be paying more attention to the washing up. 'I take the dirty vater down now, nu?'

By Thursday morning her good news was still a secret and more impossible to deliver than ever. And the canary was dead. As she drew the blinds she saw its little yellow body lying stiffly at the bottom of the cage, twig legs in the air, claws curled. 'Oy oy oy!' she mourned, holding the fragile corpse in the palm of her hand. 'Poor liddle thing! Vill you look at that, Rachel. Gone in the night. Poor liddle thing!'

'He vas a good age, dolly,' Rachel pointed out, sympathetically. 'They don't live for ever, these liddle birds. Ve get a new one, nu? Club Row, Sunday. Vhat you think?'

But Dumpling didn't want a new bird. Not now. Not in this room. A new bird could wait until she'd settled in with Fred. 'No,' she said, more firmly than she realized. 'Not Sunday. Sunday is too soon. Ve vait.'

Rachel let this pass. 'So vhat ve do this afternoon?' she asked. They always took a little time off from their sewing on Thursday afternoons.

'I vas thinkin' a' going shopping,' Dumpling said, but she looked oddly shamefaced about it. 'Fred, he vants to choose new curtains ... Hopkins and Peggs maybe.'

Hopkins and Peggs reminded Rachel of Ellen. 'I shall go an' see liddle Gracie,' she decided. 'He don't need me to choose his curtains, nu nu.' She'd had a lovely letter from David the day before, with a column of tiny sketches in the margin, and she always took his drawings to Mile End Place to show young Gracie.

Ellen had had a letter from David too, and a particularly long one. 'We shall be going up the line again soon,' he wrote. 'This is the last chance I shall get to write for some time. This

438

war goes on and on. There is no end in sight that any of us can see. It is an endless nightmare. I will say this for it though. It puts things into perspective. Before I come here I thought I knew what was important to me, like the brit and celebrating Shabbas, and being born a Jew. Now all these things are trivial, not important at all. There is no God in the trenches, I can tell you. We are forsaken, all of us, Jew, Christian, atheist. We all die the same way. What is important is surviving, coming home to our wives and children. That is what we dream about and keep alive for. One day I will explain all this to you. Sorry this is not so cheerful. I don't mean to depress you. Better next time maybe. I.L.Y. David.'

Oddly, for all its sombre theme, the letter didn't depress her. Rather the reverse. She felt comforted by it.

'Whatcher think a' that?' she asked Ruby when she and the children came to visit that afternoon.

'Serious stuff,' Ruby said, grimacing. 'I don't like all that about we all die the same way. 'Nough ter give yer the creeps. Tommy, don't eat mud, lovey.'

Ellen could see she hadn't understood the letter at all so she changed the conversation. 'You 'eard from Sid?'

'Sat'day,' Ruby said happily. 'Goin' on all right, 'e sezs. They're learnin' 'im ter drive a motor car. Whatcher think a' that? 'E reckons 'e'll get a job drivin' a van when 'e comes 'ome. Good job an' all. Didn't do 'im no good at all luggin' that great bread van round the streets. Back-breakin' that was. 'E'll be a sight better in a van.'

'We seen some changes on account a' this old war,' Ellen said. 'And not all of 'em bad neither.'

'Amy's got a job in munitions,' Ruby said. 'It makes yer skin go all yeller, but it's ever such good pay.'

'We're starvin'!' Jack informed them, coming into the scullery from the garden where they'd all been playing.

'We'll 'ave tea,' Ellen said.

'Tommy won't need much,' Ruby said. 'All the mud 'e's ate.'

Tea was an unappetizing meal these days, with sugar so scarce it was almost unobtainable, and the national loaf grey and gritty, and jam more swede than fruit. But it was pleasant to eat it in the sunshine, no matter how bad it was.

'If it keeps fine we'll 'ave tea in the garden when Bubbe comes,' she said to Gracie when Ruby had kissed them all goodbye and gone. Being on early turn was tiring because it meant getting up so early in the morning, but at least it gave her a chance to see her friends in the afternoons. And although neither of them had admitted it yet, even to themselves, she and Mama Cheifitz were more friendly towards one another than they'd ever been. They greeted one another kindly, if not affectionately, and there was always plenty to talk about these days, what with the war and the children's schooling and David at the front. But this Thursday, the conversation began in quite an unexpected way.

'I come to ask advice,' Rachel said when she'd kissed the children and was following Ellen into the house. She knew exactly what she wanted to say, and she said it at once before she could lose her courage. 'Mr Morrison got promotion, bubeleh. I think he vant to marry Aunty Dumpling.'

''Bout time too,' Ellen said, turning to look at her as they walked into the kitchen. She was thrilled by the news. 'Oh I know 'e ain't Jewish, but 'e's a good bloke, Bubbe. 'E'll be ever so good to her.'

'Nu-nu, I know it,' Rachel agreed, putting her shopping bag on the kitchen table. 'It ain't that. Vonce it mattered. Vonce, I tell you. Now, vell now, I ain't so sure. So many good men dead. A Jew, a goy, vhat's the odds?'

'Sit down,' Ellen said, plumping a cushion to put behind her mother-in-law's back. 'I got sommink ter show yer. Your Davey's been saying just the same thing.' And she gave Rachel the letter.

She read it quietly, sitting in her son's chair, while the kettle fizzed on the stove and the children chirruped like birds in the garden, and when she'd absorbed every word she set it aside on the table and nodded her head. 'Jew, goy,' she said again. 'Vhat's the odds?'

'So when's the wedding?' Ellen asked, warming the teapot.

'Ellen, bubeleh, that's vhat I come to say. Tomorrow they'd marry, you ask me. Only they don't ask me. And for vhy? Because your Aunty Dumpling got a kind heart. That's for vhy. Oy oy!' And she began to cry, her face forlorn, and the tears

440

oozing from the corners of her eyes.

Ellen put down the teapot and came and sat at her mother-in-law's feet. 'So tell me,' she said.

'The canary died,' Rachel said through her tears. 'She don't buy a new one. He gets promotion. She says he's lonely. He got a new flat, ground floor, I tell you. She don't manage stairs so good. Ai yi, they vould marry tomorrow. Vhat's to stop them? I am, bubeleh. I stop them. An old gooseberry, that's vhat I am. An old gooseberry. Ai-yi-yi!'

Despite her garbled explanation Ellen understood her completely. 'It's the rent, ain't it?'

'Ten an' six a veek I ask you. Seven bob maybe I could manage. So vhere you get a room for seven bob?'

The solution was so obvious and so easy, it was spoken before either of them realized what an enormous thing it was they were contemplating. 'You can come 'ere an' live with us,' Ellen said. 'We got plenty a' room.'

'So I'm a burden maybe?' Rachel said, her face wrinkling with distress, in case they were making a mistake, after all these years.

'No you ain't, Bubbe. You're a grandma.'

'You sure, dolly?'

'We'll ask the kids. Gracie, come in 'ere a minute will yer?'

Rachel dried her eyes and blew her nose for it wouldn't have done to let the child see she'd been crying.

'How'd yer like yer grandma ter come an' live with us?'

The delight on the child's face was a joy to both of them. 'Now, d'yer mean?'

'In a week or two maybe,' Rachel said.

'Yes,' Gracie said. ''Course. You can 'ave my bed if yer like. I could sleep with you, couldn't I, Ma? It's a nice bed, Bubbe. I could make it up lovely for yer. An' we could 'ave stories of an evening, when Ma was on the trams.'

'An' chicken soup,' Jack said. 'An' borscht.'

'An' *hamantash*,' Benny said, licking his lips. He was very fond of Bubbe's prune cake.

And so it was settled to the satisfaction of everybody except Rivke, who snorted her disapproval through every single day until the wedding, and then surprised the family by turning up

441

at the registry office in a new blue coat and her old black wig to kiss the bride and wish her well.

And after the ceremony Rachel packed her meagre belongings in a carpet bag and caught a tram to the Mile End Road to start her new life with her grandchildren and Ellen, who was a good woman, Jew or no Jew.

And that night, after her enlarged family were all safely in bed and asleep, Ellen sat down and wrote a long letter to David to tell him about it. 'I been praying to God for another chance,' she wrote, 'and he give me one. I will look after her, David, I promise. She is a good woman.'

The letter arrived at Battalion Headquarters two days before the 17th London Rifles were due to leave the front line.

Chapter Thirty-Six

'If the sun rises in the east it's a sure sign there'll be stew fer supper,' Joe Evans remarked as the dixies were carried into the dug-out.

'Least it's 'ot,' David said, speaking as loudly as he could over the noise of the distant barrage. The dixie might contain the inevitable stew but for once it was actually steaming. 'Be thankful fer small mercies.' The night before they'd had cold Maconochie's soup which had been horribly unappetizing and had lain heavily on their stomachs for hours afterwards.

It was a noisy night because the troops to the south were preparing for an attack on the Menin Road and the preliminary barrage had started up at six o'clock that morning. But they were old campaigners now and took it all with ostentatious calm. They'd been in and out of the trenches for the past three months and had learned to ignore any barrage that wasn't aimed their way. Their section of the front was relatively quiet, except for the occasional sniper, so they were making the most of it, squatting round the dixie on piles of shell cases or sitting awkwardly on the edge of the funk holes in mud-stained companionship, a candle on an upturned box to provide them with light. Even Clifford was grinning as he came lolloping in from the other end of the trench.

'What we got?' he said hopefully.

'Roast beef an' Yorkshire pud,' Evans told him.

Clifford's face lit up. 'No!' he said delightedly, and they all roared with laughter at him.

'Believe anything, this kid will,' David said. 'Whatcher think it is, you daft ha'p'orth?'

'Ah well,' Clifford said, resigned to the stew, 'least it's 'ot.

An' anyway we shall all be out of 'ere by tomorrer.'

'Where d'yer hear that?' David wanted to know.

'Officer told me,' Clifford said, bright with importance. 'Movin' out midnight.'

'Where to?'

'Down south, 'e said. They got Aussies comin' in 'ere.'

'Well, good luck to 'em,' Evans said.

'If that's the case,' David said, 'I'd better write to old Charlot an' tell him to send the sketches.' Old Charlot kept an *estaminet* in Wizernes where they were now sent for rest and retraining, and was the most recent of his private postmen. He had quite a collection of sketches waiting to be posted on.

'An' that ain't all,' Clifford said, spooning stew into his face and chomping happily. 'We're gonna get some 'ome leave.'

There was a chorus of voices now. 'When? D'he tell yer when?'

'Two, three days. 'E wasn't quite sure. Two, three days.'

Now that *was* news. Going home! It was too good to be true. Out of this hellhole and back with Ellen and the kids.

'Better write to the old woman,' Evans said, rapturously. 'Wouldn't like ter catch 'er on the 'op.'

Soon the dug-out was full of earnest composition and much licking of pencils.

'Dearest Ellen,' David wrote. 'Have just heard we are due for a spot of home leave. I should be with you in a very little while, about a week maybe. I will write again and let you know exactly. I.L.Y. so much. I can't wait to be with you again. I have so much to tell you. We shall be so happy.'

He was signing his name when the sergeant arrived. 'Night patrol,' he said. 'Rifleman Evans, Rifleman Cheifitz, Corporal Todd, party of six.'

David and Joe Evans growled their disapproval with one voice, 'Not again!' They hated night patrols.

'Last one, you lucky lads,' the sergeant said cheerfully. 'You're on yer way fer a spot a' Blighty termorrer.'

They gave their letters to Clifford for safe keeping before they handed over their pay books and identity discs to the sergeant. 'Keep yer eyes open an' yer 'eads down,' he instructed. 'We're handin' over to Aussies at twenty-four hundred hours, so let's give 'em a good account. They'll want ter know what the old 'Un is up to. Could be movin' south ternight, some of 'em. Wire's cut for yer.'

The one good thing about a night patrol was that they travelled light, taking a rifle, a water bottle and a first aid pack, but very little else, and leaving behind all the rest of their kit and anything that could identify them or their regiment, just in case they were captured. Even so, it was a nerve-wracking assignment, crawling through the wire into the eerie wastes of no-man's land, and David hated it more every time he had to do it.

'Right lads,' Corporal Todd said. 'Sooner we're out, the sooner we're back.' And he led his team out of the dug-out, up onto the fire-step and over the sandbags. They followed him as quietly as they could, saying nothing, and were soon easing themselves through the hole in their own barbed wire and crawling into the mist and murk.

It was a moonless night and very dark, so it took a little while for David's eyes to grow accustomed to the lack of light. The ugly moonscape of no-man's land was swathed in white smoke from the bombardment, a slow-swirling ghostly drift that quickly obscured the advancing bodies of his friends. Only Evans was still visible, inching darkly along at his side, his eyes gleaming as he turned his head from side to side. For all they knew, David thought uncomfortably, they could be entirely alone out there, with only corpses and abandoned equipment for company, but on the other hand the place could be swarming with Germans and one of them could step out of that fog and be right in front of him, bayonet at the ready, before he even knew he was there. Or behind him. *Gevalt!* And he strained his ears for the sound of approaching feet or the slither of an approaching body. But all he could hear under the bombardment were occasional muted voices from the trenches behind him. Or was it in front? Sometimes you could find yourself right up at the edge of the German trenches and hear them coughing and talking to one another quite clearly.

The ground was covered with rusting debris, rifles, bayonets, respirators, helmets, shovels, the remains of barbed wire entanglements, and pitted with shell holes, some of them enormous and filled with water like filthy lakes, so it was necessary to watch where he was going to avoid injury. But this constant reminder of the waste and ugliness of war brought new and more terrifying images into his mind.

The dead could still be lying under those discarded greatcoats. Or the ghosts of the dead, wandering endlessly, their cold fingers outstretched. It was easy to see dead fingers reaching out towards him through that awful fog, dead grey-white fingers, like so many he'd seen curled into the mud. And it seemed to him that the night was full of ghosts, screaming and moaning in the air above the Menin Road, or creeping along the uneven ground, too badly wounded to stand, their faces striped with dark blood. He crawled forward in a trance, frozen with fear, his nerves stretched so taut he could feel their tension making the hair rise all over his scalp.

He heard the shell whining towards him seconds before he flung himself face downwards on the ground, and the explosion was so close the earth rose beneath him. He put his hands across the back of his neck and waited for the pain to begin, he was so sure he must have been hit. Something was falling on him, drumming on his helmet and punching his back with small sharp blows. Earth or shrapnel? But there was no pain, and although he could hear shells screaming over his head and a series of explosions somewhere to his left, he began to look around him.

Not far away there was a mound of earth and rubbish that looked as though it might be an abandoned gun emplacement. There were tattered sandbags heaped around the entrance, and broken boards sticking up in the air. They looked very black so it was probably waterlogged, but it could provide cover, and his one thought now was to get below ground. He felt far too exposed out in the open. He stood up cautiously, legs shaking, and was just about to make a run for it when he saw a body lying on the ground a few hundred yards to his right. He knew it hadn't been there before the shell burst, and he remembered Evans.

He ran to it quickly, crouching low and trying to remember what he'd been taught about first aid. But he couldn't see

446

anything properly until he was kneeling right beside it. And it was Evans. Or what was left of him. The shell must have exploded just below him. His chest was completely caved in, an ugly mess of congealing blood and the embedded spikes of shrapnel. But worse than that was the horror that had been his face. The lower jaw was gone but blood was still pumping up into the gap where his mouth should have been and streaming down from his nose. Surely he couldn't still be alive, David thought. God forbid. His eyes were tightly shut, so it was impossible to tell. But as he watched he caught a glimpse of some pale movement just out range of his eyes, and turning his head he saw that his friend's hands were moving, the fingers clawing the air. He was transfixed with horror. Clawing the air! Dear God, he can't be alive! He can't! Then the hands fell back, dark against the black earth, and he knew he ought to find one of them and feel for a pulse, because that was what he'd been taught to do. But it was so dark and he was so clumsy with fear that it took a very long time, and even when his fumbling fingers touched an arm and found a wrist and felt nothing, not the faintest throb or tremor, he couldn't be sure. And then his gorge rose in his throat and he turned and ran for shelter, weeping aloud with terror and pity. Shells were still screaming overhead but he didn't hear them. To be alive, like that. Dead like that. Dying like that. It was obscene!

It was a gun emplacement. Not that it mattered now. There weren't any corpses, and only an inch or two of water. Not that that mattered either. Evans was dead, or dying, and he'd run away like the worst kind of coward. No one could go any lower than that. He sank to his knees in the mud, weeping and choking, and it seemed to him that it was a very long time before he recovered his senses. But eventually his sobbing subsided and he tried to be sensible, telling himself that Evans must have been dead, and that he was certainly insensible, and that even if he'd stayed there with him, he couldn't have done anything. In the meantime, there were other things to be decided. He couldn't stay in this hole for ever. He hadn't the faintest idea where the rest of the patrol had got to, nor what time it was. He glanced at his watch, and was surprised to see that it was still ticking, miraculously, and that the whole incident could only have taken ten minutes or so.

I'll stay here till I've got my breath back, he decided, then I'll go back. They were dropping flares, the eerie light making the sandbags glitter, so he would stay where he was until they'd died down, because there was no point in providing the Huns with a target. He was feeling much calmer now, but it was an unnatural calm, as if he'd been anaesthetized. Yes, that's what I'll do.

And he looked up idly at the dark entrance to the pit, and there was a figure standing on the sandbags. A figure that froze the blood to a shudder in his veins. A figure with a spiked helmet, horribly silhouetted against the flare-reddened sky. *Gevalt!* A German! He fumbled for his rifle, heart pounding with terror, and the soldier suddenly switched on a torch and swung it blindingly towards him. 'Don't shoot!' he said, in English. 'I'm not a Jerry.' Then the light went out, and they were both in total blackness again.

'I come from Manchester,' the voice said. 'Honest! Don't shoot!' The accent was unmistakable.

'Whatcher doing in them clothes, then?' David said. The total void was clearing and he could just about make out the outline of the man, crouching on the other side of the trench.

'That's a long story. You're a Londoner, intcher?'

'Yes.' Surely it was all right to admit that, even if he was a German.

'Born in 'Amburg, I was. That's 'ow they got me in this lot. Me ol' man was a sailor. I come to Manchester when I were two. We 'ad two rooms over a shop, Jacob Schwartz, the bakers. 'E were my uncle.'

'Were you a baker an' all?'

'No. Cobbler I were. Boots an' shoes. I were a dab 'and at boots.' He paused for a moment and drew a packet of cigarettes out of his pocket. 'Fag?' he offered.

'We deep enough, d'yer think?'

'Under the ledge,' the German suggested. So they crawled under the ledge and lit up. 'What about you?'

'What?' David asked inhaling smoke gratefully.

'What were you?'

'Oh, an artist. I drew pictures fer a magazine.' What a long time ago it all was.

'Honest?'

'Straight up!'

'You ought to draw pictures of this lot. Show 'em all what it's like. High time they knew back 'ome, you ask me.'

'I 'ave. I been drawin' ever since I first got 'ere.'

'Good for you, Tommy. You show 'em, eh? They'd stop it if they knew what it were like.' Their cigarettes made little red circles in the darkness.

'D'yer think they ought ter stop it?'

' 'Course they should fuckin' stop it.'

'You're the German Army though, aintcher?'

'German, French, British, what's the odds? It's the same for all of us.'

'How d'you end up with the Germans?'

'Went back with me old woman, when me dad died. Married a fraulein. Daft, innit?'

It was more than daft, David thought, it was bizarre. Two grown men who were supposed to be enemies sitting in a pool of mud in the middle of the war talking like old friends. And Evans lying out in the darkness …

'Tell you what,' the German said, 'if anyone else were to come down 'ere, we'd better 'ave a plan of campaign. If it's a Jerry, you're my prisoner, if it's a Tommy, I'm yours. What d'you think?'

It seemed eminently sensible. A lie, of course, but a useful one, to keep them both alive.

'I come over 'ere on night patrol two or three times a week,' the German said. 'I feel sort of free out in the open. Me own man, sort a' thing. Can't stand it in them bleedin' trenches.'

'I can't be doin' with night patrol,' David confessed. 'I'd rather be in a dug-out.'

'Takes all sorts.'

He was such an ordinary looking young man, David thought, with a wide formless face and a much broken nose. It was ridiculous to think of killing him, even though he was the enemy. 'This is daft,' he said. 'You an' me sittin' here like this. We're supposed ter be at war.'

'You ask me,' the German said, 'we'd be much better off if we all packed up an' went home. Leave them fucking generals to fight it out between 'em. All by themselves. There'd soon be an end to it then, don't you worry.'

David grinned. 'I reckon that's the best idea I've heard since I come 'ere,' he said.

It was growing darker and the barrage was dying down. They could hear the rats squealing. 'Better be gettin' back,' the German said. 'Take my tip an' nick yourself a German 'elmet for camouflage. Next Jerry you meet, it mightn't be me.'

'We'll go out together, shall we?' David said, peering over the top of the sandbags. It was very dark, but it seemed all clear.

'Run like buggery!' the German whispered. 'Good luck, Tommy!' And he crouched down and crawled rapidly into the mist.

'Good luck!' David whispered back, but the man was already too far away to hear him, and anyway there was a shell approaching.

Then the world exploded with an all-enveloping roar and there was red light all around him and he could feel himself flying backwards through the air in a most peculiar slow motion. 'Ellen!' he called. The redness pulsed like blood, slowly, slowly, and he was struggling to breathe, his hands in slime, and the roaring went on and on and on, in a reverberating echo, pulling him backwards and downwards.

Then nothing.

Chapter Thirty-Seven

Ellen was buttoning up her gaiters when the telegram came, wielding the button hook deftly, with a neat rolling movement of her wrist. The children were at school, the kitchen was swept and tidied, Mama Cheifitz had gone off to Underwood Street to spend the day with Dumpling, and she just had nice time to get ready for work. The knock on her door was a surprise, so early in the morning, but not an alarm.

'Yes,' she said, looking down at her messenger, who was a little girl not much older than Gracie. Then she saw the yellow envelope, and her heart contracted so painfully she had to hold on the doorpost to prevent herself from falling.

'I'm ever so sorry, mum,' the child said.

'It ain't your fault,' she said. 'Stay there a tick.' And she went off automatically into the kitchen to find a penny, because you always paid for the telegram.

Then the child was gone and she was on her own in the middle of the kitchen with the dreadful envelope in her hands, too frightened to open it. There wasn't a woman in England now who didn't know what a yellow envelope meant. She was suspended in misery, because he was dead and the telegram would tell her so and she couldn't bear to read the words and let them crush what little hope she had left. But it had to be done. She couldn't stand there all day. There was a bus to be taken out and a job to do.

She opened the envelope with a knife, slitting it neatly, as if it mattered to keep everything well ordered. Then she put it neatly on the table and read the telegram slowly, even though it wasn't possible to take in all the words, because her hands were shaking so much. 'Deeply regret ...' Yes, there it was.

'Rifleman David Cheifitz ...' Yes, it was him. 'Missing in action on September 20th 1917.' *Missing*. The word roared relief up at her. He wasn't dead. Thank God. Only missing. That was different. Thank God. Thank God. Thank God.

I'll call in at Underwood Street an' tell Mama Cheifitz and Aunty Dumpling on my way back from work, she decided. I can break it to them gently, so they don't get a shock. And she realized that she was still suffering from shock herself, because her heart was beating in such an odd juddering way, and she was tempted to make herself a cup of tea to steady her nerves. But then she glanced at the tin clock on the mantelpiece and knew she'd be late if she didn't leave the house at once, so that was that. She had to forgo the tea and get on with the day.

Rachel and Dumpling were finishing their work when she arrived at Underwood Street and the kitchen was full of steam from the irons, and the strong smell of the fish Dumpling was preparing for supper.

'Vill you look who's here,' she said when she'd opened the door to Ellen. 'Here's our Ellen come to take you home, dolly.'

But Rachel took one look at her face and knew something was terribly wrong. 'Vhat is it, bubeleh?' she said.

Ellen suddenly found she was too near tears to speak. She handed the telegram to Aunty Dumpling without a word and the two women read it together holding on to one another for support.

'Ai-yi!' Rachel mourned. 'My Davey!' She sat weakly in the nearest chair, the tears rolling out of her eyes. But Dumpling didn't cry. Not yet. She was watching Ellen, her eyes strained with tears and control.

' 'E ain't dead,' Ellen said, her face stubborn with grief.

' 'Course not, bubeleh,' Dumpling said, patting her arm. 'It ain't the same. Missing.'

' 'E'll turn up,' Ellen said. 'You'll see.'

'He vill, he vill.'

'I just thought you'd better know, that's all.'

'So you're a good girl, bubeleh.'

'As long as that's understood.'

'Ve understand.' Oh, how well she understood!

'I'd better get 'ome then.'

'I get my hat on, bubeleh,' Rachel said. 'I come vid you, nu.'

'We won't tell the kids yet awhile,' Ellen said. 'No point upsetting 'em for nothing.'

After they'd gone, Dumpling gave herself over to grief and wept until Fred came home. Davey was dead, there was no disguising it. Missing men very rarely turned up. It just meant they hadn't found their bodies. And if they hadn't found Davey's body he must have been blown to pieces. Oy-oy-oy, how could she bear it?

When Ellen and Rachel got home they found a surprise awaiting them. The fire was lit and burning brightly, the table was set, Jack and Benny had had their faces scrubbed and she could smell a cottage pie cooking in the oven.

'Oh Gracie!' Ellen said. 'You *are* a good girl!'

'You got a letter,' Gracie told her. 'You sit down an' read it, an' I'll get the pie.'

It was a letter from David, dated 20th September. 'Well, there you are,' she said when she'd read it, 'that just shows what a lot of ol' nonsense them telegrams are.'

'What telegram, Ma?' Gracie asked, fearful at once.

'I 'ad a silly telegram this morning,' Ellen admitted. 'Yer Pa was supposed to 'ave gone missing on 20th September, an' that's the very day he writ this letter.'

'What's missing?' Benny asked, his face solemn.

'Means they don't know where 'e is,' Ellen explained. ' 'E'll turn up, you'll see. Now, who's fer cottage pie?'

' 'E ain't dead, is 'e, Bubbe?' Jack said.

'Nu nu,' Rachel comforted. 'Missing ain't dead, missing ain't dead, dolly.'

'No 'e ain't,' Ellen said furiously. 'You ain't even ter think it. 'E ain't.'

So Benny and Jack didn't even think it, and Rachel was careful not to let any of them know what she was thinking, and Gracie only thought it privately. But she noticed that her mother was afraid every time the post came, and that she went into the front room and looked at Pa's drawings every single day.

The news quickly spread to the Buildings. Two days later,

Rivke and Ben came to Underwood Street, to see if their support was needed.

'Ve should sit vid Rachel and Ellen maybe,' Rivke asked.

'Nu-nu,' Dumpling said. 'Ellen don't accept yet. She vants he ain't dead.'

'Poor voman!' Rivke said.

'She loves him,' Dumpling said.

'Ve all love him,' Rivke said.

'It's a bad business,' Fred said. 'Poor girl.'

A week later, in the middle of a misty afternoon, when Rachel was out shopping, another packet of drawings arrived. But this time they came by special messenger, a shy skinny soldier with a long ugly face and anxious grey eyes.

'Mrs Cheifitz?' he asked when she opened the door to him. 'I brought some drawin's. From yer 'usband. My name's Clifford. We was tergether at the Messine Ridge.'

'Oh come in, come in do,' she said opening the door wide to him. Now she would know the truth. 'How is 'e?' she said, looking back at the soldier as she led the way into the kitchen.

He was shuffling his feet with embarrassment. 'Well ...' he said, not meeting her eye, 'I mean ... Aintcher got ... um ...'

'They sent me some daft telegram,' she said briskly. 'Supposed ter be missing.'

He scratched the back of his neck thoughtfully for some considerable time. Then he told her about the patrol, and how Evans had been killed and Cheifitz hadn't come back. 'That's all I know, ma'am,' he said when he'd finished. ' 'E was a good bloke, your 'usband. Ever so good ter me. Stuck ter me through thick an' thin, you might say.' He hadn't realized that bringing the drawings would be so awful.

' 'E ain't dead,' she said. And this time she was comforting him too.

'No,' he agreed, glad of the escape she'd offered. ' 'Course not.' Poor woman.

'Don't look as though yer Pa'll be back fer Christmas,' she told the children later that day.

'What'll we do with 'is presents,' Gracie asked delicately. 'If

454

'e's missing, I mean.' She'd been knitting him a balaclava helmet.

'We'll put 'em in the bottom drawer an' save 'em, till we know where 'e is,' Ellen said. 'But we'll just 'ave to 'ave Christmas without him. Same as we did last year.'

It wasn't a bit the same as last year, although they all did their best to pretend it was, and Bubbe joined in the festivities and never said a word about it not being Jewish. But at least, Ellen thought, as she raked out the ashes on Boxing day, we ain't 'ad the other letter. And that was really all that mattered.

The other letter arrived three days later, a neat typed form sent from the records office at Preston. 'It is my painful duty to inform you that no further news having been received relative to David Cheifitz, 17th London Rifles, the Army Council have been regretfully constrained to conclude that he is dead, and that his death took place on September 20th 1917.' Whatever she might or might not believe, she was now a war widow.

She showed Rachel the letter, and the children, but dismissed it. 'It don't make a bit a' difference,' she said. 'It's just what they think, that's all. We know 'e ain't dead, don't we?'

But in fact it made a lot of difference, for a widow's pension was considerably less than a soldier's pay, and within a couple of weeks it was plain that the Cheifitz family were not going to be able to manage on the money they had coming in, not even with Rachel's contribution.

'It's the rent, you see,' Ellen explained to Dumpling. 'Takes such a chunk out me wages.'

'You should move to a smaller place, maybe?' Dumpling suggested practically.

But the idea was rejected with furious tears. 'How could I? We got ter keep it all fer Davey, cantcher see? Just as it was. We *can't* leave.'

'Nu-nu, bubeleh,' Dumpling comforted. 'So you don't leave. Ve find some other vay, nu?' But after two days thinking about it, she was still baffled, and it took Fred's quiet good sense to think of the solution.

When Dumpling came to visit the next Wednesday afternoon, she asked to see David's drawings. 'I could borrow some of them, maybe,' she said. 'Someone I know vould like to see them. I take great care.'

They picked out ten of the very best and folded them lovingly in tissue paper and put the whole bundle inside his folder and the folder inside a waterproof bag.

It's Fred, I'll bet, Ellen thought, and was touched by his interest. But it wasn't just interest. He'd advised Dumpling to sell them.

Essex Street was awash that morning, the brickwork black with moisture, the cobbles steaming and two heady torrents snaking downhill beside the pavements. Dumpling's umbrella dripped so much water before her eyes that she could hardly see where she was going, and when she arrived on the doorstep of the *Essex Magazine* and shook the dratted thing, it had to be done with such vigour it sounded like a whip cracking. She stomped into the office, damp, steaming and determined.

'Mrs Morrison,' she announced. 'Come to see the boss of Mr David Cheifitz.'

The office boy, who was young and thin and apologetic, was thoroughly alarmed by her enormous presence. 'First floor, missus,' he squeaked, lifting startled eyebrows to the ceiling.

'So lead the vay, vhy don't you,' she said, prodding in his direction with the furled umbrella.

She puffed after him up the narrow stairs, her wet skirts and sodden umbrella smearing a damp trail behind her all along the yellow anaglypta.

'You'd better leave that 'ere,' the office boy suggested, looking at the umbrella and pointing to an umbrella stand on the landing. ' 'E don't like the wet. Don't like it at all. Most particular about wet, 'e is.'

So Dumpling deposited the umbrella and hung up her hat and coat, dried her face on her handkerchief and followed the office boy towards her mission.

She liked Mr Palfreyman the minute she saw him, sitting so quietly behind his fine desk, with a grand fire in the grate and leatherbound books on the shelves behind him. A gentleman, she thought, admiring his polished fingernails, and his gold tie pin and the gold rims of his spectacles. A gentleman, talking

456

into that telephone in his nice quiet gentleman's voice.

He waved a hand towards a chair and, covering the mouthpiece, urged her, 'Pray do sit down, dear lady. I shan't be a moment.'

Be as long as you like, Dumpling thought, beaming at him, just so long as you give my Davey vhat I vant.

'Now, dear lady,' Mr Palfreyman said, when he'd finished his call, 'what can I do for you?'

'I come on behalf of Mr David Cheifitz. I am his aunt, Mrs Morrison.'

'I am very pleased to make your acquaintance,' Mr Palfreyman said, shaking her by the hand. 'Yes, yes indeed. How is he?'

'Missing, sir.'

'Oh dear,' he said, his round face changing shape under the impact of such bad news. 'What a pity! What a very great pity! He had a wife too I believe, and children.'

'So that's vhy I come,' Dumpling said, leaning forward eagerly. And she told him all about Ellen and how brave she was being, and what a good mother she was, and how she refused to accept his death, and how determined she was to keep the house going the same as always.

And Mr Palfreyman folded his white hands together in his lap and listened. 'What can I do to help, Mrs Morrison?' he asked when she finally stopped speaking because she was breathless with passion and exertion.

'Vell,' she puffed. 'I bring you some of his drawings, vhat he sent from the var. You could buy them maybe?'

He took the waterproof bag and dried it most thoroughly on one of his dusters, and then he removed the folder and opened it to look at the pictures. He studied them for such a long time that Dumpling began to grow disheartened. They were no good maybe. They looked good to her, but then how could she tell? Nevertheless she decided to keep quiet and say nothing, because the gentleman was so obviously thinking.

'My dear Mrs Morrison,' he said at last, looking up at her with the most peculiar expression on his face. 'But these are magnificent! Magnificent! Of course we will buy them. Yes, yes, indeed.'

457

'Oy-oy!' Dumpling said, clapping her hands with relief and delight. 'So how much?'

The fee he offered took her breath away. 'Shall we say a guinea each for the first six? Would that suit? Then we will see. How many more have you got?'

'Hundreds,' Dumpling said, hoping it wouldn't put him off.

But he was delighted. 'Such treasure,' he said. 'Such riches! My dear lady I can't thank you enough for bringing them here.'

'Strictly speaking they ain't mine ter sell,' she confessed. 'They belong to Ellen by rights.'

'Ask her to come and see me,' he beamed.

'You treat her gentle, nu?' she said.

'My dear Mrs Morrison, of course. I do know something of their history. They were very fond of one another. She must be feeling his loss most cruelly.'

'Such a love you vouldn't believe!' Aunty Dumpling sighed.

'Oh yes,' he assured her, 'I would. Yes, yes, indeed. There were times, you know, dear lady, when I quite envied your nephew his capacity for passion. He was so happy when they married, so full of life and vitality. We all noticed it. Now there is pain in equal measure, of course, but I often think, taken all in all, that his way of living would be preferable to mine. In fact, dear lady, if I had my life over again, I do believe I would try to live it his way.'

'Von life ve get, von life ve got,' Dumpling said, smiling at him. 'So ve do good vhen ve can, nu?'

The drawings were published two weeks later. And they caused a sensation. Letters started to arrive at Essex Street the very next day, within three days sales of the magazine had doubled, and within two weeks they had quadrupled. David Cheifitz, war artist, 'One of our heroes, missing on the Western Front', had arrived.

Ellen was stunned by the speed of his fame. At the end of February, Mr Palfreyman wrote to tell her that the fee he could now offer was five guineas per picture, and wondered whether she would like to visit him at Essex Street to 'talk things over'.

'You are earning quite a lot of money these days, my dear,' he said. 'Perhaps it would be advisable for us to open a bank account. Unless you wish to purchase a house, of course, or to use the money for some other similar expenditure.'

No, she said, she had no intention of buying a house. 'We got ter stay where we are for when 'e comes 'ome, you see, sir,' she explained.

'Yes, yes, of course,' Mr Palfreyman said tenderly. 'Then we will open an account for him. It will have to be in your name, I'm afraid, because officialdom, in its infinite folly, has decreed that you are a widow. You will pardon the word.'

And she did pardon the word, from such a very kind man. ' 'E ain't dead,' she said, but she spoke gently.

'No. No. Of course,' he said.

March began and new leaves put out their hesitant buds.

'It's been six months,' Rachel said to Dumpling, 'an' she don't give in yet.'

'Ai!' Dumpling sighed. 'Poor Ellen!'

But Ellen was living in abeyance, taking one day at a time, and refusing to look into the future. The money meant nothing to her, beyond the fact that she could now afford the rent. David's sudden fame meant nothing to her, beyond the fact that it would please him when he came home. She was waiting.

And then one day, early in the month, when a blustery wind was propelling her down the road towards the garage, she suddenly had the most vivid waking dream. David was standing in a ward full of injured soldiers, looking out of a tall window. For a few seconds she could see him quite clearly with all the blue uniforms milling about behind him and the white light from the window all around his head, then a gust of wind blew her violently forward and the vision was gone. But she'd seen him. Alive and well. Somewhere. She was so happy she ran the rest of the way to the garage.

The next dream began as she was washing her face early next morning. She stood quite still beside the washbasin, with the soap drying on her cheeks, listening to it with all her senses, willing it not to fade. He was walking among green trees towards a white wall of some kind, smiling. She could see the wall quite clearly, a white wall, tall with long windows. Then there were wounded soldiers again. She could sense their pain, but she knew it wasn't his. He seemed to be walking into a ward, but the edges of the dream were blurring, she was losing it, it was going.

She realized, as she sponged the soap from her face, that she was panting as though she'd been running. But what did that matter? Now there was no doubt. She knew he was alive. Alive and in some hospital somewhere. A hospital with white walls. She folded the towel neatly and hung it over the rail. I'll find him now, she thought. There can't be all that many hospitals with white walls. Most of the ones around here are brick red or grey, and that one was very definitely white. I'll start looking right away. The place was full of wounded soldiers. One of them was bound to know. I'll ask every single one, she told herself as she carried the pail of dirty water downstairs. Every single one until I find him.

The wounded soldiers on her bus were all as helpful as they could be, but none of them that day could remember a hospital with white walls. 'Grey?' they offered. They knew plenty of grey ones. But not white.

'Never mind,' she said. 'Someone'll know.' She was abundantly cheerful. It was simply a matter of time.

Her 'dreaming moments' came with comforting regularity, and the walls were always as white as snow. Once she was part of the dream, standing beside a fireplace, with her arm pressed against the cool marble, then walking towards him, with two huge windows on her left and sunshine streaming through them in a square column full of swirling motes. And once they were walking together across a floor made of beautifully patterned tiles, blue and green and buff and white, and she felt sure she knew where she was, but when the dream faded she was torn by frustration because she simply couldn't remember, no matter how hard she tried. But the walls of her dream house were always the same and always white, and that was a comfort and a hope.

After a week she had simplified her question to her wounded passengers, merely asking them if they'd ever been treated in a hospital with white walls. None of them had, and some of them thought the question rather peculiar, but she was determined not to be disappointed.

460

She was sure enough of her dream now to confide in Rachel.

'I *know* 'e's alive now,' she said when she'd told her mother-in-law all about it.

Rachel had seen the suppressed excitement on her face for some time and wondered what it was. Oy! Poor Ellen! she thought. Vhat now? But she listened kindly while Ellen told her all about the dreams and tried to sound as though she believed them. Poor Ellen!

The next week Ellen was on the Epping Forest run, taking her number 14 bus as far as Leytonstone. 'Be some different soldiers down that way,' she said hopefully. 'You never know, eh?'

But there was only one, waiting at the last stop along the line, and he was a grizzled old man who didn't look at all approachable. Never mind, she told herself. Don't do no 'arm askin'. Nothink venture, nothink gain.

'Hospital with white walls, eh?' the old soldier said. 'That'll be White Lodge, down behind the Riggs Retreat at High Beach.'

But of course, she thought, limp with relief and sudden understanding. There'd been something familiar about those white walls every time she'd seen them. White Lodge. The white house in the woods. The place they'd found that day, where she'd had that awful dream about the soldiers. She remembered it in every single detail. Now she knew, without any doubt. I'll go there tomorrow, she promised herself, the minute I finish my shift. I'll get Aunty Dumpling and Mama Cheifitz to do their work at my house and stay with the kids in case it takes a long time, and I'll go there tomorrow.

461

Chapter Thirty-Eight

The Riggs Retreat at High Beach was exactly as she remembered it, with the great sign still balanced on its roof, and the veranda crowded with potted plants and cane chairs and tables swathed in white linen. But the customers were all wounded soldiers, bandaged and scarred, bulky in their coarse blue uniforms, and the familiar planks beneath their boots were littered with fag ends and empty cigarette packets.

They were all more than happy to tell her how to get to White Lodge. 'Follow the road for a hundred yards, ma'am. You'll see the turning. First left. It's all marked. Straight down the 'ill.' And when she left them they cheered her out of sight.

It was a new, wide road curving through the beech trees where she and David had gone exploring all those years ago. As she cycled down, she was remembering the house, standing so quietly in its mossy clearing, empty and delapidated and echoing. The sight of it now gave her quite a shock.

It was full of people, and their presence made it look smaller than she remembered and oddly unfamiliar. And then it was so smart and clean, the stucco brilliantly whitewashed and all that rusty ironwork repaired and painted blue. Soldiers sat in wheelchairs all along the balcony and pale faces gazed vacantly from the upstairs windows, peering out between new dark blue curtains. In front of the house the grass was gone, and in its place was a gravel drive, full of staff cars and Red Cross ambulances and a bustle of coming and going. It was a well-organized, purposeful place, not a bit like the gentle palace of her dreams.

Nevertheless, it was the place she'd come to search, and the dream still occupied a corner of her mind with its unshakable insistence. She got off the bike and stood holding the handlebars while she decided where to begin. There were two neatly painted signposts on either side of the drive, pointing the way to places such as 'Outpatients', 'Wheelchairs', 'Epping Ward', and as one of them directed 'Bicycles to Stables', that was where she went. And having settled her machine among all the others, she found another sign labelled 'Visitors' which led her to a new wooden porch and a side door she didn't remember.

She didn't recognize the first room she entered either, but that might have been because it was full of desks and filing cabinets and movable screens. However there was a kindly lady sitting behind the second desk who asked her who she'd come to visit and said she didn't think there was anyone of that name at White Lodge. 'Is this where you were notified?' she asked, scanning her list of names.

How can I tell her? Ellen thought. She'll think I'm off me head.

The lady was smiling encouragement at her. 'They get things wrong sometimes, you know,' she said sadly. 'There are so many casualties.'

' 'E went missin',' Ellen said, 'Seven months ago. September the 20th. Someone said they seen 'im here.'

'I'm afraid they were mistaken, my dear,' the lady said more sadly than ever. 'If he were here, we would know. We have a record of every single name, you see.'

Strong emotions boiled in Ellen's brain, frustration, rage, anguish and terror. She'd been holding them in check all through those seven terrible months, and now they erupted and overwhelmed her. 'He's here!' she yelled. 'Don't you understand! He's here! I know he's here. I've been askin' an' askin' fer weeks an' weeks an' weeks. He ain't missin'! He's here! You got ter let me see him. Please, please, please!' Her eyes were full of hot tears and her face was distorted. 'Dear God, please let me find him!'

She was aware that the lady had left the room. She heard the swish of her skirt and the sharp tap-tap of her heels, but she didn't care. She was out of control, crying with a total and terrible abandon, choking with sobs, and soon she wasn't even able to stand, but sank to the floor with her head in her hands and the tears oozing between her fingers. 'Dear God, please let me find him.'

Two people were talking in hushed voices at the other side of the room and she knew they were talking about her, but it was all meaningless and the words she heard made no sense to her now. ' … missing … convinced … poor girl.' But presently someone came and stood beside her and she realized that a warm mug was being eased into her hand, and she tried to stop crying long enough to do as she was told and drink.

'Mrs Cheifitz,' a voice said close to her ear, 'if you will come with me, we will look for your husband.'

She opened her eyes and looked up at the speaker with gratitude and a flickering renewal of hope. 'Drink your tea,' he advised. 'You must try to recover a little before we begin.' He was an elderly man, tall and skinny, with thin grey hair and a weary face. He reminded her of someone, but in her present state of emotional exhaustion she couldn't remember who it was. 'We *will* look for him, my dear,' he said.

So she drank her tea and dried her eyes and followed him out of the office and along a corridor, keeping her head down because she'd recovered enough to be self-conscious about the way she must look. And suddenly there were the familiar tiles under her feet, blue, green, buff and white in geometrical patterns. And she looked up and saw that they were in the hall, with its high carved ceiling and the wide staircase leading up to that Venetian window and the lovely, panelled doors still painted with birds and blossom. And the sight of it restored her strength so that she lifted her head and straightened her spine. *Now* she would find him.

'We will begin upstairs,' the elderly gentleman said, 'and I will show you all our injured soldiers, with the possible exception of a few who might be up at the Riggs Retreat.'

'I seen them,' she said. ' 'E ain't there.' And as the words sounded bare and ungracious, she added, 'Thanks all the same.'

'This way,' he said, smiling at her rough honesty, and although she knew that David was behind that painted door in the great room where the fireplace was, she followed her guide without argument, for he was a kind man and trying to help her, and she could hardly expect him to know what she knew.

So they walked from room to room and bed to bed, and in the next half-hour she saw more suffering than she could ever have imagined, for this was where the worst cases were, men without limbs, or mute with shell shock, men riddled with shrapnel or deep in groaning nightmare. She was torn with pity for them, especially when they looked up at her as she passed, but of course David wasn't among them. Not upstairs. She'd known all along he wouldn't be upstairs.

'You're sure?' the gentleman asked. And when she nodded. 'Well, that's a relief at any rate. Now I can show you our walking wounded.' There was a great deal more hope for them.

'We have four wards downstairs,' he said, leading the way again. 'Epping, Bury, Knighton and Great Monk. All named after parts of the forest. We thought it appropriate.'

Who cares? she thought, wishing he'd walk a bit quicker. He did everything so slowly, and the measured tones that had comforted her such a short time ago seemed turgid now, a weight holding her back from where she wanted to be. Oh buck up, do! she urged him, inside her head. Take me to the big room. That's where we oughter be.

But he didn't. They searched the three small wards first and they were so crowded it was another quarter of an hour before she finally walked through the painted door into the room of her dreams. And there were the long windows on all three walls, and the moulded ceiling, still picked out in blue and white, and the marble fireplace and everything, just as she'd seen it in her dream. Her blood was racing with excitement now. She could feel her cheeks glowing with it, and the soles of her feet springing from the floor with every step because she ought to have been running. Now, now, now, her thoughts were crowing. Now I shall find him.

The room was full of soldiers, sitting on their beds or shuffling about on their crutches, and there was a ward orderly moving quietly about among them, swabbing the linoleum with a mop and a bucket of disinfectant. For a brief anguished second she realized that if she *did* find him he could be wounded like all the others she'd seen that afternoon, but her excitement rushed the thought away. Find him first, she told herself. She could think about everything else after.

The men in this room were restored to enough health to take an interest in her. 'Who yer lookin' for, missus?' they asked, as she rushed from bed to bed peering at faces.

'My husband,' she told them. 'Rifleman Cheifitz, Seventeenth London Rifles.'

'We got quite a few a' them,' one man told her. ' 'Ackney an' Poplar. Never 'eard a' no Rifleman Cheifitz though. 'E ain't 'ere, missus.'

'Yes!' she insisted, warm with urgency. ' 'E *is*! 'E's here somewhere.' She saw the pitying looks that passed from one pair of eyes to the next, but she wasn't deterred. And even when she'd searched from one end of the room to the other and looked at every single soldier, including the ones on the balcony, and *still* hadn't found him, she wouldn't admit defeat. 'I must a' left someone out, that's all,' she said. ' 'E's in this room somewhere. I know 'e is. I'll just 'ave ter start again.'

There were two armchairs set beside the empty fireplace and neither was occupied. The elderly gentleman took her by the elbow and led her across to them, for what he had to say to her now was painful and would be better received sitting down.

But she remained obdurately on her feet, leaning against the mantelpiece, frowning.

'It is very hard to accept that a person one loves might be dead,' he began gently.

' 'E ain't dead,' she said stubbornly. ' 'Ow many more times I got ter tell yer? 'E ain't dead.' And then the dream began to wash in and out of her mind in a sudden capricious tide, one moment clear and strong, the next receding and fading. 'Oh hush up, do!' she begged, leaning on the mantelpiece, her forearm pressed against the chilly marble, yearning after those tantalizing images. And he hushed, watching her quizzically.

She was standing here. Right here with her arm on the marble. Yes, yes, that's how it was. And turning. So. Walking forward towards the window. Sunlight dropping square columns through the two at the end. Full a' motes, all swimming about. And walking forward. Uniforms everywhere.

Blue cloth, red ties. Yes, yes, that's how it was. Walking forward and the middle window open to the balcony. And David ...

The ward orderly was standing right in her way, stooped over his bucket. 'Shift!' she ordered impatiently. 'Look sharp about it!' Stupid man! If he didn't move, the dream would fade away altogether.

And he straightened his spine and stood up and looked at her. And he was David. A very thin David, with his moustache shaved off and all his lovely thick hair cut back to a wretched stubble, but undeniably David. Warm and breathing and alive.

For a second she was so full of emotion she couldn't move or speak, joy, triumph, relief and love in exquisite abundance. She'd found him! He was alive! Praise be to God! 'Oh Davey, Davey, Davey!' she said stretching out both hands towards him expecting him to catch her in his arms and hold her close and kiss her and tell her they'd never be apart again.

But he didn't. He didn't put his arms round her. He didn't even hold her outstretched hands. He simply stood where he was, clutching his mop as though it were supporting him. And his eyes were the eyes of a dead man, totally blank, without a flicker of light or expression, two terrible voids in his dear familiar face.

The shock struck chill into the centre of her body. 'Davey?' she said, and she withdrew her hands to cover her mouth because it was trembling. 'Davey! What is it?'

The elderly gentleman was standing beside her. 'Is this your husband?' he said.

She nodded. It wasn't possible to speak to anyone except David.

'You are sure?'

Another nod. Her dear, dear David was still looking at her with those awful eyes. 'Davey. It's me. Don't yer remember?'

'That's old Ikey,' a soldier called to her. ' 'Is name ain't Cheifitz.' And the news was passed along the ward. 'She sez Ikey's 'er old man! Never! Fancy old Ikey!'

'Perhaps he just looks like your husband,' the elderly gentleman was saying.

She tossed her head with exasperation. This was too awful

and too ridiculous. 'I'll show yer!' she said looking at all the faces around her. 'Put that damn mop down!' she said to David, and when he obeyed, oh, far too meekly, she seized him by the hand and led him to the fireplace. He's got no will of his own, she thought. I'm leading him about as if he was young Benny. 'Now,' she said, 'I got sommink ter show yer.' And she stooped and crawled into the hearth, pulling him in after her.

The drawing was still there, a bit faded and smudged at the edges, but still there and still recognizable. 'Look!' she instructed, touching it with her fingers.

He looked at it blankly but at least it provoked speech and his voice was unmistakable. 'A good drawing,' he said.

'You done it.'

'Did I?' But his voice was flat, as though he didn't care.

'It's me. See?'

He turned his lifeless eyes from the drawing to its model, but there wasn't the faintest flicker of recognition for either of them.

'You signed it an' all. Look, there's yer initials D.C. David Cheifitz.'

'Yes,' he said but the word was as lifeless as his eyes, a flat dull pebble of a word.

She appealed to the gentleman. 'What's the matter with 'im?'

'Shell shock, probably,' he said. 'This looks like loss of memory to me, and loss of memory is a very common occurrence among shell shock cases, I'm afraid. I had no idea Mr Ike – um – your husband was a victim. Not that he's ever been particularly communicative. He came to us from Bexhill, you see …'

She wasn't listening to him. 'Don't 'e really know who I am?'

'I'm afraid not.'

She crawled out of the hearth, her brain working furiously. 'There's got ter be a way!' she said. 'We come here before, to this house. Years ago. 'E can't've forgot *that*!'

David had followed her out of the hearth and now he stood before her, humbly, as though he was waiting for orders. The sight of his subservience annoyed her. 'Come on!' she said and she was upset that her voice sounded sharp. But it couldn't be helped. His inability to remember or recognize anything was like an invisible wall between them. She'd have to be sharp if she was going to break through that. 'Come on, Davey!' She was going to remind him.

He glanced at the gentleman to see if he was supposed to obey her, and the gentleman said, 'Carry on!' in his kindly voice and she led him to the door and out into the hall.

'We come in through the back door, an' all through the kitchens,' she said feeling she had to explain everything to him. 'An' we found a flight a' stairs, an' up we come, through this door,' leading him there and opening it. 'Green baize. Remember?' But she could see he didn't. 'Then we went up the stairs,' leading him up, 'an' you said you'd like ter do a drawing a' that winder. Lovers in the winder, or some such. Remember?' But he was still blank. 'We stood at the top a' the stairs on that little landin'.' And you kissed me, she remembered. Surely you ain't fergot that.

There was a nightmare quality about this one-sided conversation. It wasn't natural to be talking to David and getting no response at all. It wasn't natural to be standing so close to one another and not be touching. They'd reached the little landing now and were side by side in front of the triple window. Perhaps it's a dream, she thought. Perhaps it ain't happening after all, and she put out her hands, very tentatively this time, and took him by the shoulders and turned him so that they were facing one another.

And his flesh was warm under her fingers, and as he moved towards her the familiar salty smell of his skin lifted into her nostrils and her senses began to prickle as though they were stirring from a long sleep. She gave a little moan and dropped forwards against his chest, and holding his poor shaven head between her hands kissed him instinctively and passionately full on the mouth.

The blank eyes, a fraction above her own, were reflecting light, the pupils dilating, gathering in upon themselves, the brown irises softening and shifting. And she knew that he was looking at her at last. And then he was kissing her, his mouth urgent, and his hands caressing the small of her back, just as

469

she remembered so well, oh so very well. 'Ellen, Ellen bubeleh,' he said, lifting his head. 'Oy, I never thought I'd live to see you again.' And then his face crumpled into anguished weeping, and his entire body began to shake and he sank to his knees, clinging to her skirt, frantically, as though he were drowning. And she sank with him, cradling his head in her arms, crooning maternal comfort without being aware of what she was saying. 'Hush, my lovey, it's all right now. Hush. Hush. You're with me.'

He wept for a very long time, terrible gulping sobs, on and on and on, clinging to her skirt with both hands and with his head burrowing into her lap. And the soldiers on their way up and down the stairs walked delicately round them, touching their heads in unspoken sympathy with their rough gentle hands.

Afterwards there was a doctor to see them both and questions to be answered and forms that were filled in by somebody or other, but it was all a hazy business and a long way away. They had found one another again, and that was all that mattered. When the questions were over they were allowed to walk in the grounds among the beech trees, where they talked disjointed nonsense and laughed a great deal and kissed one another in every clearing. And when the bell sounded for supper they kissed goodbye almost cheerfully and she promised to come back next day and bring the kids. And he said he remembered the kids although privately he wasn't quite sure.

'They'll let you 'ome on leave soon,' she told him as they walked back towards the new porch. 'Bound to. Wouldn'tcher think?'

But after she'd left him and as she was walking through the hall towards the fine front door, which was now labelled 'Exit', she was waylaid by the elderly gentleman, who explained that he'd been on the telephone to Bexhill and Bexhill thought it advisable for Rifleman Cheifitz to return to them for further treatment.

Her face fell visibly. 'How long for?' she said. 'We thought 'e'd get a bit a' leave. 'E's earned it, surely ter goodness.'

'Two or three days,' the gentleman said. 'A week maybe. He

470

will need careful treatment as his memory returns you see, my dear. I'm sure you appreciate that. Bexhill is an excellent place.'

She stood before him, her eyes very blue in the spring sunshine. ' 'E ought to 'ave leave,' she said stubbornly.

'As soon as I can arrange it,' he promised. 'I give you my word. We shall send him down by ambulance tomorrow morning.' And as her face fell again, he hastened to reassure, 'The sooner he goes, the sooner he will come back.'

And at that she cheered up. Just wait till I tell the kids, she thought, an' Mama Cheifitz and dear old Aunty Dumpling.

They were waiting at the gate as she came through the archway into Mile End Place, Aunty Dumpling looking anxious, with little Ben holding on to her skirt, Mama Cheifitz stooped and grey, holding her solemn Jack by the hand, and Gracie standing between them in her blue pinafore, her dark hair just like David's.

She ran towards them shouting her news, so that they wouldn't waste another second thinking him dead. 'He's alive! I found 'im. He's coming 'ome!'

All the way down to Bexhill David was remembering things. Not in any discernible sequence, but at least without effort. For the first time since the explosion his brain was functioning again, throwing images onto his inner eye, and feeding his memory with smells and shapes and textures and colours. Ellen's dark hair, bristling under his fingers, and her lovely breasts lifting with pleasure and those long legs threshing under the coverlet. Why had they spent such a long time away from each other? The war, was it? He had a vague sense that he was slipping in deep mud somewhere, but then Aunty Dumpling's plump hands filled his mind, sewing ruffles, and he could taste her prune cake. And there was his daughter sitting on his knee, lisping her first words, and giving him goose pimples by stroking his moustache. And it surprised him to remember that he'd had a moustache. He must grow it again. Then a series of paintings and drawings, all enjoyable but making little sense; a child's painting of a procession; a tenement at night, dark blue and with golden candles in all the windows; a beautiful anguished girl drifting downstream in a boat hung with tapestries; sunlight dappling a girl in a blue cycling suit. And then he was standing on the steps of a town hall somewhere as confetti tossed in the air before his eyes and he gave himself over to the sheer happiness of knowing that he had married his Ellen and that soon, in a few short days, they would be together again. Anything was possible now that he knew that.

As the ambulance drew in at the hospital gate he had a moment of apprehension and bewilderment, fearing that he wouldn't know where he was. But the grey walls were familiar, and so was the ward where a young nurse led him. He'd sat in that chair by the window and cried for hours when the doctor asked him who he was and he couldn't remember. He could feel the hot tears on his cheeks even now, and hear the doctor's voice. A tall man, with a long saturnine face. Now what was his name?

And there he was, standing in the doorway, walking towards him, holding out his hand in greeting, his long face smiling.

'Norris!' David said, remembering at once.

'Well, that's a good start!' the doctor said.

The next few days were full of questions, probing, encouraging and, too often, still baffling. But the first one was a pleasant surprise.

'What do you think of that?' Dr Norris said as they sat on either side of his desk in the dark consulting room that David remembered quite well. And he picked up a magazine from the desk and handed it across to his patient.

The *Essex Magazine*! How that cover brought memories! Old Quin in the litter of his office, the presses rolling, Mr Palfreyman consulting his matchsticks. 'I used ter work there,' he said. 'I was a graphic artist.'

'You still are,' the doctor told him. 'Look at page nine. You're quite a celebrity these days.'

He couldn't remember the drawings at all, but he knew they were his. 'I must've sent them,' he said. And he read the captions, hoping they would enlighten him. 'Four more portraits of the war from Rifleman Cheifitz, our own absent hero. By popular demand.'

472

'Well!' he said, bashful with pleasure.

And the doctor told him about his fame and encouraged him to remember his work.

On the second day the questions were domestic. 'You remembered your wife, I'm told.'

'Oh yes!'

'Tell me about her.'

'We was at school together. She pinched my cake ...'

On the third day Dr Norris turned to military matters. 'Can you remember the war at all?' he asked, very casually.

'Not much. I can remember the mud. An' the noise. Nothink particular.' But even as he spoke a very particular image came into sharp focus in his mind.

A headland stretched before him, a wind-buffeted expanse of springy turf, bracken and brambles and squat spiky bushes, and he was afraid. He'd been walking for days, and all on his own. The Jerries could be anywhere, with all them trees fer cover. Terrible stunted trees, survivors, armoured and belligerent, tough hollies with leather leaves curled into spiteful claws, hawthorns, grey and threatening and bristling with spikes, brambles trailing barbed wire, blackthorns like bayonets. And a dark figure running towards him.

'Sounds like the place where you were found,' the doctor told him. 'A farmer brought you in apparently. No marks of identification, barely any clothes, and no idea who you were. You've been quite a problem to the authorities.'

'Why was I on me own?' he asked.

'Oh, we'll get to that by degrees,' Dr Norris said. Horrors had to be absorbed slowly. 'Now we've started, it'll get easier. You have my word for it.'

They returned to the topic next day, and this time it did seem easier. He remembered the dixies and Maconochie's dreadful soup. And the rats squealing when the barrage died down.

'You can remember being under fire?' the doctor asked.

He didn't want to. But he could. 'Evans always used to say ...' he began. And Evans' mangled face roared soundlessly before him, filling his vision, and those terrifying, living hands were still clawing the air. Fear closed his throat and the blood

473

was beating in his ears. He grabbed at the desk as he passed out.

'Do you feel able to talk about it?' Dr Norris said calmly when they'd brought him round. 'It would be better for you if you could.'

It was a long painful confession and by the end of it he was drained and drawn and defeated. 'I left my mate ter die in the mud,' he said. 'He could a' been alive an' I run off an' left 'im.'

'He would have been dead,' Dr Norris said. 'Nobody could have survived injuries like that.'

'Honest?'

'You have my word for it. There's no need for you to feel guilty about it. You did all that anybody humanly could.'

There was a long pause while David digested the information and the doctor wrote up his notes. Then he put down his pen and gave David a smile.

'I think we've progressed about as far as we can for the moment,' he said. 'What would you say to a spot of home leave?'

'When?'

'Well, today's Thursday. Would tomorrow suit? Start with a weekend.'

He sent Ellen a postcard as soon as he got back to the ward. 'Coming home tomorrow evening. Will be on the 6.15, London Bridge.' And with great joy he remembered the way he always used to sign his postcards to her. 'I.L.Y. David.'

The train back to London Bridge was late and travelled slowly. But what did that matter when his mind was full of memories and the tracks were singing. 'On the way *home*! On the way *home*!'

Chapter Thirty-Nine

He was bewildered by the crowds on London Bridge that evening. He hadn't expected to see quite so many people, nor that they would all be walking towards him quite so quickly. Had London always been so crowded and so busy? They reminded him of the 17th Battalion going 'over the bags', all tramping along like that, and with such grim, set faces. And suddenly he remembered the sensations of going over the bags, the sweat running from his armpits, and his mouth dust-dry and the all pervasive smell of fear and shit and cordite and decaying flesh. The memory was so dreadful it suspended all action. He couldn't walk, he could barely breathe and he couldn't think of anything else.

The home-going workers on the bridge jostled around him, heedlessly, another wounded soldier getting in the way, and gradually the tussle of their passage pushed him back against the parapet. His hands touched the cool stone, and he turned, looking away from them, seeking some other, natural sight to comfort him away from nightmare.

And there was the Thames, rippling easily beneath him, its olive green water reflecting the darkening blue of the evening sky, the eternal, peaceful, dependable Thames. As he watched, two coal barges sailed effortlessly under the bridge and the long wash they left ribboning behind them glinted with red and gold. He glanced into the sky, idly seeking the source of the colour, and saw that the sunset was just beginning. A spring sunset in London, just like so many others he'd seen before the war. A peaceful sunset.

Below him cranes cast their stiff patterns against the cliff side of familiar warehouses, and empty barges lay at anchor side by side, nudging each other in the gentle tide. On the north bank an elegant green building gleamed in the sunlight, and he knew it was Billingsgate fish market, and there, straight in front of him, was Tower Bridge, standing firmly on its two supporting pillars, its bright blue risers swelling up towards those familiar white minarets. And he remembered walking towards that bridge with Ellen, and knew that there was a gold crown on top of each of the towers and that fantastic red griffins supported the City arms, and he was pleased to think he could recall such details, useless though they might be.

But then his mind pushed another remembered moment to the fore, and this one worried him. He knew he'd stood on London Bridge before, leaning on the parapet, just as he was doing now, feeling lost and unable to focus his thoughts, but he couldn't remember when it had been, or what he'd lost. Something to do with Ellen, he knew that, but the more he pushed himself to remember, the more the memory flickered and faded. A quarrel? Yes, he was sure of that, for he remembered the sense of hurtful things said, and the knowledge that irreparable harm had been done. But what was it all about?

He was still struggling when Ellen walked across the bridge to meet him. She'd come straight from work and was still in uniform, her boots and gaiters gleamingly polished, and her cocked hat topping newly-washed hair. She'd been in a fever of impatience ever since the postcard arrived, but now she was trotting towards him at last, half walking, half running, because her bus had been late and she was afraid she might have missed him. But no, there he was, leaning on the parapet, in almost exactly the same place as he'd been that dreadful night, and looking so worried. Oh, you needn't worry ever again, my dear, dear darling. I couldn't bear to lie to you, ever again. Not now, after all this.

She was beside him, slipping her hand into the crook of his arm before he was aware of her. He turned towards her, still anguished, and the expression on his face reminded her of the lady in that painting he was so fond of, drifting downriver to die because she'd broken some silly mirror.

'It's all right,' she said. 'I'm 'ere. Did yer think you'd missed me?'

476

'We quarrelled,' he said. It wasn't quite a question but she could tell he wasn't sure about it.

'Yes, we did. But don't you go botherin' yer 'ead about all that. It's over an' done with.'

'It was serious, nu.' That wasn't quite a question either.

'We thought it was then, lovey. It ain't now. Come on, let's go 'ome.'

They caught a number 14 bus, where he was surprised and gratified to see that the driver and the conductress both knew her well and were obviously fond of her. This working life of hers was going to take a bit of getting used to. But it suited her, there was no denying that. She looked so fit and pretty in that uniform, with her eyes so blue and her cheeks pink and her dark hair bushing from underneath the constraints of that jaunty cap.

They remembered landmarks all the way home, 'That's Cannon Street down that way, an' St Paul's. D'you remember St Paul's?' Yes, he thought he did. And there was the Aldgate pump, and Petticoat Lane, where they both worked when they were young, and Commercial Street where they got married, and Brick Lane where Mama Cheifitz and Aunty Dumpling live (I'll tell him about Dumpling later) and Whitechapel Road, and the London Hospital and Sidney Street (oh, he remembered Sidney Street), and finally they were in the Mile End Road where the stall holders were packing up their wares in a muddle of boxes and paper wrappings as the twilight gradually descended.

'Nearly home,' she said squeezing his arm. 'Ta-ta, Poppy!' And the conductress gave them a grin and they stepped down onto the pavement, almost opposite the narrow entrance to Mile End Place. He remembered it so clearly, sights and sounds and smells.

'Wallflowers in the garden,' he said. 'An' roses.'

'Daffs,' she told him. 'It ain't time fer roses yet. They'll bloom later.'

They walked through the archway, past the Tyne Main Coal Company, and into their own little close. And there were the white cottages facing one another across their neat front gardens, and the trees down the end, fringing open sky, and

Aunty Dumpling blundering through the gate, throwing her apron over her head in the most beautifully familiar way, and crying with happy abandon, 'Davey! Davey! Bubeleh!'

He dropped his kitbag and ran to seize her in his arms and be kissed moistly over and over again and have his cheeks patted with those dear rough fingers. And there was his mother behind the gate with his two boys standing very close behind her and a grown-up Gracie holding her hand. How stooped she was, he thought, and very grey, looking up at him shyly, the way she always used to, and crying without a sound, and he kissed her most tenderly and wiped away her tears and told her not to cry and cried himself. And then he had one arm round Gracie, and the other round little Jack, and Benny was hanging about his knees, and he was so happy he felt as though he was going to burst. 'My family!' he said. '*All* my family!'

'We kept yer studio just as you left it,' Ellen said, and she signalled to Dumpling with her eyes, such a quick flickering signal that David missed it altogether. And Dumpling grinned hugely and disentangled little Benny from his father's knees and led them all into the house.

The studio was just as he'd left it. He remembered every brush. And there was his easel standing in the window with a paper on it already stretched and ready, and the marmalade jar full of pencils, all neatly sharpened. 'Oh Ellen!' he said.

But it was his mother who answered. 'Good, nu?' she said. 'You got a good vife in our Ellen, bubeleh.'

He was surprised that she was the only one to have followed him into the front room. Where were the others? Where was Ellen? But then another surprising memory edged into his mind to puzzle him. Surely, he struggled to remember, his mother hadn't always been fond of Ellen. When they got married, she hadn't liked her at all. Because she wasn't Jewish. He could remember that quite clearly. Yet here she was, quite at home, smiling and nodding, 'A good vife!'

'Yes,' he said. 'She is Mama, a wife in a million.'

'So you coming to supper?' Dumpling asked appearing in the doorway. 'A liddle chicken ve got.'

The taste of it was already in his mouth as he followed the two women through into the kitchen, with its remembered

478

smells of baking and warm bread and pleasant spices.

The room was shadowy with twilight and they hadn't lit the gas. But as he stepped inside and took his place at the head of the table, Ellen struck a match, and the little rasping sound made him look up at her and he saw that she was lighting candles, and he recognized his mother's candlestick from the old days in the Buildings.

The candles bloomed one after the other, as yellow as roses, until they were a glowing bunch and he could feel their warmth on his face. He looked up at Ellen again, sitting at the other end of the table, to tell her how much he liked them, and he saw that she was wearing his mother's shawl, the fine red shawl she always used to wear on Friday evenings at the Shabbas meal. And he looked from her to Jack, and the boy was wearing a yarmulke, and so was his brother, the round black caps settled on the crown of their heads in exactly the same way as he used to wear his. And all round the table the faces of his family glowed in the candlelight, eyes gleaming, smiling at him happily as though they were expecting something special to happen. And Ellen picked up the bread and broke it, and dipped one piece in the salt, in the old familiar way, and passed it across the table to him, her eyes shining. And he realized that this was a Shabbas meal, and knew in an instant how very much she was giving him as he took the bread from her hands. Ellen, who wasn't Jewish, presiding over the most Jewish of meals.

And the words of the Proverbs came effortlessly into his mind and he spoke them lovingly, to all his family. But to Ellen above all.

'Her children rise up and call her blessed, her husband also and he praiseth her: Many daughters have done virtuously but thou excellest them all.'